I0760990

STORIES FROM THE GRAVE

BOOK ONE

B.E. Russell

Printed in the United States of America.

For more information, or to book an event, contact:
press@blairedwardrussell.com
www.BlairEdwardRussell.com

ISBN - Hardcover 978-1-966245-14-8

First Hardcover Edition: October 30, 2024

TABLE OF CONTENTS

1 THE PUB DOWN THE BLOCK 1
2 HOME IS WHERE THE HEART IS 19
3 OCTAMO LAKE 37
4 DAYLIGHT 61
5 THE BAG LADY 85
6 THE FACE MELTERS 115
7 PUMPKIN HILL 147
8 THE GARBAGE MAN 165
9 THE MIDNIGHT FEAST 199
10 THE SKELETON PEOPLE 235
11 THE HOUSE ON MAPLE STREET 255
12 THE SKIN WALKERS 279
13 THE STRAY'S 315
14 NIGHT LIGHTS 333
15 THE HEAD HUNTERS 353
16 DARKNESS 377
17 THE WRECK 397
18 THE SEA WHISPERER 419
19 FOOTSTEPS 437
20 THE TROPHY HUNTER 455
21 THE WITCHING HOUR 473
22 THE DOLL 495
23 JACK OF ALL TRADES 517
24 STONE COLD 555
25 VILLAGE OF THE DAMNED 579

26 THE GRAVE ROBBERS 603
27 SURVEILLANCE 621
28 THE SEWER PEOPLE 645
29 THE ARTIST 669
30 SLAP SHOT 689
ABOUT THE AUTHOR 711
ACKNOWLEDGEMENTS 713
FURTHER READING 715

1

THE PUB DOWN THE BLOCK

Alderwood was the kind of town that faded into the landscape, a quiet little place just on the edge of the big city, full of narrow streets lined with dimly lit bars and diners that looked like they hadn't changed in decades. But there was one place that stood out among the rest, a place everyone knew by reputation alone: *The Pub.*

It had no proper name, just a sign that read "The Pub" in crooked red neon letters, the "P" flickering every so often. It sat at the end of Alderwood's main street, its dark windows reflecting the occasional streetlight, its heavy wooden door standing like an ominous invitation. The locals knew better than to go in; they'd heard the stories, and they respected the warnings. But outsiders, drifters, and the curious—they often weren't so lucky.

No one knew exactly how it worked, but once you stepped inside *The Pub,* you couldn't leave. Not until you'd had your fill, and your fill was always too much.

One night in late October, when the wind had a bite and the trees were bare, a stranger arrived in Alderwood. His name was Tom, a city slicker with a big mouth and a bigger ego, who'd gotten lost on his way home from a late-night business meeting. When he saw the faint glow of *The Pub* in the distance, he felt a pang of relief. A stiff drink sounded like exactly what he needed to take the edge off.

He pushed open the door and stepped into the dim, warm interior, surprised by how quiet it was. The pub was small, cozy even, with a long wooden bar and a handful of tables scattered throughout. The lighting was low, the air thick with the scent of wood and stale beer, and there was a sense of timelessness about the place, as though it hadn't changed in a hundred years.

Behind the bar were two figures—a tall, wiry man with sharp features and hollow cheeks and a woman with dark hair pulled back in a messy bun, her face pale, her eyes unreadable. They looked up as Tom entered, exchanging a glance that seemed to hold a thousand secrets.

The man nodded in Tom's direction. "Evening," he said, his voice smooth but strangely empty. "What'll it be?"

"Whiskey," Tom said, sliding onto a barstool. He gave the woman behind the bar a quick nod, but her gaze was unsettling, cold, her expression impossible to read.

"That'll be the house special, then," the man said, grabbing a dusty bottle from the top shelf. "Name's Rob, and this here is Josie." He poured Tom a glass, sliding it across the bar with a small, almost knowing smile. "You're in luck. We pour strong here."

Tom smirked, lifting the glass in a mock salute. "Just what I need. Been one hell of a day."

He took a long, slow sip, savoring the warm burn of the whiskey as it slid down his throat. It was strong, smoother than he'd expected, with a faint, earthy undertone he couldn't quite place. He felt a tingling sensation spread through him, a warmth that settled deep in his bones, melting away the day's frustrations. It was, quite simply, the best drink he'd ever had.

Before he realized it, his glass was empty, and he found himself gesturing for another.

Rob poured him a second without a word, his face calm, his eyes sharp. Josie stood at the end of the bar, polishing glasses, her gaze never straying from Tom. There was something about her, something in her eyes that made his skin prickle, though he couldn't explain why.

As he downed his second drink, a strange thought crossed his mind—a feeling that he could drink all night, that he *wanted* to drink all night. The thought should have been alarming, but it wasn't. It felt natural, like an invitation he was happy to accept.

Hours passed, or maybe only minutes—Tom couldn't tell. All he knew was that the drinks kept coming, each one smoother and richer than the last. The room felt hazy, soft around the edges, and the faces of Rob and Josie blurred and sharpened in turn, their eyes seeming to glint in the dim light.

"Tell me," Tom slurred, his voice thick. "How... how long have you two been running this place?"

Rob's lips twitched, as though he found the question amusing. "Oh, a while," he said casually. "Long enough to see plenty of folks come and go."

Josie glanced over, her expression unreadable. "Some stay longer than others," she added, her voice a soft, lilting whisper that sent a shiver down his spine.

Tom tried to focus on her, his mind struggling to process her words, but the whiskey was fogging his brain, wrapping it in a warm, numbing haze. "I get it," he mumbled, chuckling to himself. "Good drinks. Good vibes. I could... I could stay here all night."

"That's the spirit," Rob said, pouring him yet another drink.

Tom lifted the glass, his hand shaking slightly, but his thirst was insatiable, a hunger that gnawed at him, driving him to drink, to fill the emptiness he hadn't known was there. With each sip, he felt a sense of warmth and comfort, a feeling that he was exactly where he was supposed to be.

But as he drained yet another glass, he felt a flicker of unease—a small, nagging thought that he had to leave, that he was losing himself, that he was forgetting something important. He tried to stand, but his legs felt heavy, his body anchored to the stool, as though something unseen held him in place.

"Where... where's my wallet?" he muttered, patting his pockets, but they were empty, and a wave of panic washed over him.

Josie's hand appeared on his shoulder, her grip gentle but firm. "There's no need for that here," she said softly, her gaze locking with his. "Just stay. Have another drink."

Her eyes seemed to shimmer, her voice a lullaby that washed over him, calming him, pulling him deeper into the fog. He sank back onto the stool, the thought of leaving slipping from his mind, replaced by a desperate need for another drink, for the warmth, for the oblivion that waited in the bottom of his glass.

As Tom drifted further into his whiskey-induced haze, he became aware of movement at the edges of the room. Shadows shifted in the corners, and he realized, with a start, that he wasn't alone. Other people sat at the tables, their faces hidden in shadow, their bodies slumped, their glasses empty. They looked... wrong, their skin pale, their eyes vacant, their expressions frozen in a grotesque mimicry of life.

A chill ran down his spine, but he couldn't look away, his gaze drawn to the figure at the nearest table—a man with hollow cheeks and sunken eyes, his face gaunt, his clothes rumpled and faded. He sat staring at an empty glass, his lips parted as though he were about to speak, but no sound came.

"Who... who are they?" Tom whispered, his voice thick with fear.

Rob smiled, but it was a cold, empty smile, his eyes gleaming with a strange light. "Regulars," he said simply. "Just folks who liked it here a little too much."

Tom felt his throat tighten, a sense of horror settling over him as he realized the truth. These people weren't patrons—they were prisoners, trapped in a loop of endless drinking, bound to the bar, their lives slipping away one drink at a time.

He tried to stand, his hands gripping the edge of the bar, but his legs wouldn't move, his body heavy, anchored by an unseen force. Panic clawed at his chest, his heart pounding as he turned to Rob, his voice a desperate whisper.

"Please... I need to go. Let me go."

Rob's gaze was steady, his expression calm, almost sympathetic. "It doesn't work like that," he said softly, pouring him another drink. "Once you sit down here, you stay. That's the rule."

Josie moved closer, her hand resting on his shoulder, her touch cold and unyielding. "Have another drink," she whispered, her voice soft but relentless. "It's what you came here for, isn't it?"

Tom's hand trembled as he lifted the glass to his lips, his mind screaming at him to stop, to fight, but his body betrayed him, the glass pressing against his lips, the warm, numbing liquid filling his mouth, washing over him, pulling him deeper into the darkness.

The faces around him grew dim, their eyes empty, their souls lost, bound to the pub, their lives sacrificed to the endless thirst that drove them, the hunger that consumed them. And as Tom took his last, desperate sip, he felt himself slipping away, his mind fading, his body growing cold, until he was nothing more than another face in the shadows, another forgotten soul in the pub down the block.

The next morning, the door to *The Pub* was closed, the neon sign dark. But by nightfall, it would light up again, flickering softly, waiting for the next lost soul to wander in, for the next patron to sit down, to take that first sip.

And behind the bar, Rob and Josie would be waiting, their faces calm, their eyes empty, their hands ready to pour another drink.

Because in *The Pub,* no one ever leaves.

The Pub had stood at the edge of Alderwood long before the town had a name, long before it had streets or sidewalks or houses. Stories circulated that it had once been a hunting lodge, a hideout for criminals, even a place of ritual where strange ceremonies were held under the cover of night. The original structure had been rebuilt and remodeled countless times over the years, its walls absorbing the secrets and shadows of every generation that passed through its doors.

And yet, no one knew the true origin of *The Pub,* nor the reason why no one ever left once they started drinking. It was as if the building itself had a hunger, a need that couldn't be satisfied. But perhaps the most unsettling mystery of all was how Rob and Josie had come to work there, bartenders bound to *The Pub* just as much as the poor souls who wandered in.

The story began in the early 1800s, when Alderwood was nothing more than a small settlement nestled in a dense forest. Back then, the establishment was simply known as *The Alderwood Inn,* a two-story building that offered weary travelers a place to rest and a hearty meal. The owner, Samuel Marsh, was a stern but fair man, proud of his establishment. But there was one thing he could never understand: why people who drank in his bar often stayed until dawn, empty-eyed, silent, nursing the same glass of whiskey over and over.

It was only after a series of deaths in the inn—each one eerily similar, each victim found slumped at the bar, their faces frozen in terror—that Samuel began to suspect something was terribly wrong.

Desperate for answers, he summoned a traveling medium named Eliza Mayfield, a woman known for her ability to communicate with the dead. She arrived on a misty autumn night, her dark eyes sharp, her demeanor somber as she walked through the doors of *The Alderwood Inn.*

Eliza spent hours in silence, moving through the rooms, studying the walls, the floors, as if listening to the secrets hidden within. At last, she sat Samuel down at one of the tables, her face pale, her voice low and urgent.

"There is something dark here, Mr. Marsh," she whispered. "Something... *hungry.*"

According to Eliza, *The Alderwood Inn* sat on cursed ground, the site of a long-forgotten tragedy that had left a mark on the land itself. She spoke of a massacre that had taken place centuries earlier, a ritual where travelers were lured to the site, sacrificed in the dead of night to satisfy a nameless entity that dwelled beneath the earth. The blood of the victims had seeped into the soil, binding the spirits to the land, turning it into a place that would forever demand payment.

"But why the drinks?" Samuel had asked, his face pale, his voice trembling.

Eliza's eyes were dark, her expression grim. "Drinking is a way of binding oneself to a place, a ritual in its own way. Here, every drink deepens the curse, pulling the drinker closer to the shadows. It isn't the whiskey that keeps them here—it's the ground, calling them back, binding them."

Desperate to break the curse, Samuel begged her for a solution, a way to cleanse the inn, to stop the endless cycle of death. But Eliza could only shake her head. "The only way to lift the curse is to satisfy it," she told him. "It demands souls, and it will take them... one by one."

Samuel closed the inn for a time, hoping the curse would weaken, that the land would grow quiet. But as the years passed, he fell into despair, haunted by whispers in the dark, shadows that moved when he wasn't looking. At last, he reopened the doors, resigned to the dark legacy he'd inherited, and travelers once again began to disappear into the inn, their souls claimed by the thirsty earth beneath.

In the early 1900s, *The Alderwood Inn* became *The Pub.* New ownership brought new renovations, fresh paint, and a change of staff, but the curse remained, lurking in the shadows, waiting for each new soul to wander in. It was around this time that Rob and Josie appeared, seemingly out of nowhere, two faces in a small town where everyone knew everyone else.

They were a strange pair—Rob, tall and sharp-featured, with a quiet, observant manner, and Josie, small and pale, with dark eyes that seemed to hold endless secrets. They claimed to be siblings, though there was an ageless quality to them, something that felt both ancient and timeless.

The townsfolk speculated about them endlessly. Some said they were relatives of Samuel Marsh, others claimed they were drifters who'd somehow made their way into Alderwood and never left. But no one could remember when they had arrived, and no one ever saw them outside the bar. And when they spoke, it was always in the same calm, steady tone, their words measured, their expressions unreadable.

In time, Rob and Josie became as much a part of *The Pub* as its dim lights and crooked neon sign, guardians of the cursed ground, bartenders who knew the secrets of every soul that walked through the door. They served drinks without question, never refusing a patron, never letting anyone leave until the curse had claimed its due.

One night, a local named Garrett—a man who fancied himself a bit of a ghost hunter—decided he'd had enough of *The Pub* and its dark legends. Determined to uncover the truth, he confronted Rob and Josie after last call, demanding to know why no one ever left, why the patrons disappeared, their faces frozen in terror.

Rob had only smiled, his expression calm, his eyes cold. "It's not us, Garrett. It's the land. We're just here to... facilitate."

"But why do you stay?" Garrett pressed, his voice shaking. "Why don't you leave like everyone else?"

Josie's gaze softened, her face unreadable. "We're bound to it," she said simply. "Once you pour for the lost, you belong to them. We are part of the offering, just as they are. The only difference is, we don't get to leave."

And as Garrett stumbled back, realizing the depth of the curse, the darkness that held *The Pub,* he saw the truth in their eyes—the quiet resignation, the endless watchfulness of two souls who had become part of the curse, bound to serve it, to draw others into its depths. They were no longer human, not fully. They were... caretakers, keepers of the curse.

He left that night, his heart heavy with the knowledge, never to speak of it again. And *The Pub* continued, unchanged, its doors open to all who wandered in, its curse unbroken.

Through the decades, *The Pub* became a legend, a place where locals dared not enter, where drifters and curious souls were drawn in only to disappear. And Rob and Josie remained, their faces unchanging, their eyes filled with a cold, ageless understanding, watching as the curse continued, as each drink pulled a new soul into the darkness.

It was a quiet, unending cycle—a deal struck centuries ago, a pact with the land that bound them all. And as the years wore on, *The Pub* became a place out of time, a forgotten corner of Alderwood, its dim lights and creaking door a lure for those seeking oblivion, a final resting place for the lost.

And on quiet nights, if you stood close enough, you could hear the whispers of those who'd been claimed—their voices rising from the floorboards, their empty glasses reflecting the faint light, calling out for one last drink, one final taste of life before the darkness closed in.

For Rob and Josie, it was a life without end, a duty bound to the land, to the curse they served, one drink at a time.

And so, they waited, always ready, always watching, as *The Pub* claimed another soul.

Hannah McCrae was tired of the city. She had left her job, her cramped apartment, and her toxic relationship all in the same week, throwing her things into her old car and setting out with no particular destination. When she spotted Alderwood on the map—a small dot just outside the sprawling city—she figured it was as good a place as any to catch her breath and regroup.

After driving for hours through empty roads and quiet suburbs, she saw it: *The Pub*, glowing dimly at the end of Alderwood's narrow main street. The crooked red neon sign flickered weakly in the dusk, the "P" buzzing and fading in and out. The place looked like a forgotten relic, and the sight of it sent a tingle down her spine, but Hannah pushed the feeling aside. She just needed a drink, something strong to dull the ache of the past few months.

She parked her car, straightened her jacket, and walked toward the door. As she pushed it open, a faint chill swept over her, like a cold breeze blowing from the depths of an ancient cellar. She shivered, but forced herself to step inside.

The interior of *The Pub* was dim and cozy, lit by low, flickering lamps that cast long shadows across the wooden walls. The smell of old wood and faint tobacco smoke filled the air, a comforting scent that seemed to wrap around her like a blanket. Hannah slid onto a barstool, taking in the quiet, timeless atmosphere.

Behind the bar stood two people—a tall, gaunt man with sharp features and a woman with dark hair and eyes that seemed to hold the weight of many lifetimes. They turned to look at her, exchanging a glance before the man gave her a polite nod.

"Welcome," he said, his voice deep, smooth. "What'll it be?"

"A whiskey," she replied, managing a small smile. "And maybe a story if you've got one."

The man smiled, though it didn't quite reach his eyes. "Whiskey it is. And stories? We've got plenty of those here."

He introduced himself as Rob, and the woman as Josie. As Rob poured her a drink, Josie drifted closer, her gaze fixed on Hannah with an intensity that made her shift uncomfortably.

"First time here, isn't it?" Josie asked, her voice soft.

"Yeah," Hannah replied, taking a sip of her whiskey. It was strong, smoother than anything she'd had in years, and the warmth spread through her, settling into her bones. "Never heard of this place, but... I'm glad I found it. Needed a break."

Rob's eyes flickered with something she couldn't quite place. "Lots of folks who come through here feel that way," he said, his voice soft, almost... sympathetic.

As she took another sip, Hannah became aware of other people in the room—silent figures sitting at tables in the shadows, their faces hidden, their gazes fixed on their empty glasses. A strange, uncomfortable sensation settled over her, but she shrugged it off, attributing it to her own exhaustion.

But as the minutes passed, she noticed something strange: no one moved. The other patrons sat frozen, their bodies still, their glasses untouched. She turned back to Rob, trying to ignore the growing knot of unease in her stomach.

"So... how long has this place been around?" she asked, forcing a casual tone.

Rob's lips curled into a slight smile. "Oh, a long time. Long enough to see many patrons come and go."

"Or stay," Josie added, her gaze piercing, her voice carrying a hint of something darker.

Hannah frowned, her fingers tightening around her glass. "Stay?"

Rob chuckled, his tone light, but his eyes were unsettlingly calm. "It's just a saying. People come in, they get comfortable... sometimes they find it hard to leave."

Hannah laughed nervously, though the unease in her chest grew. She looked at her glass, suddenly aware of how quickly she was drinking, how each sip seemed to draw her further into the quiet, hazy warmth of the bar, blurring the edges of her mind. She tried to slow down, to set her glass down, but she found herself reaching for it again, her hand moving almost against her will.

A chill settled over her as she looked up, catching Josie's gaze. "Is... is there something in the whiskey?"

Josie's expression didn't change, but her gaze softened. "The whiskey's just whiskey. It's the place that holds people."

The words hung in the air, filling her with a sense of creeping dread. Hannah looked around, taking in the silent, motionless patrons, the stillness that filled the room, the shadows that seemed to linger in the corners, watching.

"What... what is this place?" she whispered, her voice barely audible.

Rob leaned forward, his face calm, his voice low. "It's *The Pub*, Hannah. It's exactly what it appears to be... and exactly what it's not."

Hannah tried to stand, her body suddenly feeling heavy, as though the air itself were pressing down on her, holding her in place. She struggled, panic clawing at her chest as she looked back at Rob and Josie, the truth beginning to settle over her.

"Please," she said, her voice shaking. "Let me go. I... I didn't know."

Josie's face softened, her expression filled with a strange, sorrowful understanding. "No one knows," she murmured. "They just come in, drawn by something they can't explain. And once they're here... they stay."

"But why?" Hannah demanded, her voice growing desperate. "Why can't you just let them leave?"

Rob's gaze was steady, his voice calm. "It's not up to us. The pub... it has its own rules, its own... appetite. We just pour the drinks."

Hannah looked at her glass, horror settling over her as she realized what they meant. Every sip, every drink was binding her to the place, pulling her deeper into its grasp. She was part of the curse now, another soul added to the pub's collection.

"Isn't there a way out?" she asked, her voice trembling. "Anything?"

Josie hesitated, glancing at Rob, her gaze filled with a flicker of something Hannah couldn't quite place—pity, perhaps, or regret.

"There is one way," Rob said finally, his voice barely a whisper. "But it's... not easy. The pub lets you leave only if it has a replacement."

The meaning of his words sank in, and Hannah felt a wave of horror wash over her. "You mean... I'd have to bring someone else here? Trap them?"

Rob nodded, his expression solemn. "The pub demands a soul. It always has."

She looked down at her glass, the liquid inside suddenly feeling thick, poisonous, like it was pulling her deeper, claiming her with each sip. She knew she couldn't do it, couldn't bring someone else into this nightmare. But the thought of staying, of becoming one of the silent figures in the shadows, terrified her even more.

Desperate, Hannah looked back at Rob and Josie, her voice a whisper. "What about you? Can't you leave?"

They exchanged a glance, their expressions unreadable. "We're already part of it," Josie said softly. "The pub owns us, just as it owns everyone else who enters. We're its caretakers, bound to serve, to keep it... satisfied."

Hannah's mind raced, her thoughts a blur as she tried to find another way, a loophole, anything that would let her escape without sacrificing another soul. But as she looked around the room, at the silent patrons, the empty eyes, she realized the pub's power was absolute, unbreakable. The only way out was to play by its rules.

After a long, agonizing moment, she lifted her glass, her hand trembling as she took a final, resigned sip. The warmth of the whiskey filled her, spreading through her body, settling into her bones, binding her to the pub, to the darkness that lingered beneath its walls.

And as she looked up, she saw Rob and Josie watching her, their faces calm, their eyes filled with quiet understanding.

"You'll get used to it," Josie whispered, her voice soft, almost gentle. "We all do."

In the days that followed, Hannah became another face behind the bar, her mind foggy, her memories slipping away as she fell deeper under the pub's spell. The other patrons came and went, drawn by the pub's silent call, each one bound to stay until the curse claimed its due.

And Hannah, like Rob and Josie, became part of the pub's legacy, her soul tied to its dark power, her voice fading into the quiet, endless rhythm of pouring drinks, watching as new patrons took their seats, each one falling under the pub's inescapable pull.

The neon sign outside flickered, the "P" buzzing as it waited, always ready for the next lost soul to wander in, to take that first, fateful sip.

And in the shadows, the pub waited, hungry, eternal, its thirst unending.

The End

2

HOME IS WHERE THE HEART IS

Thanksgiving Day dawned cold and gray in the quiet suburb of Millwood Pines. Families filled the neighborhood streets, bustling between cars with dishes covered in tin foil, greeting each other with laughter and warm hugs. The Owens family was no exception. They had traveled from all over—Rebecca from Seattle, Mark and his family from Dallas, and Daniel from the city, a quick two-hour drive. They came back to their childhood home every year, to the old, familiar street with its tidy lawns and neatly painted houses.

For the Owens siblings, Thanksgiving meant warmth, family, and home-cooked food. But this year, there was something different in the air, something almost... wrong. They couldn't quite place it, brushing off the feeling as they unpacked their cars and gathered around the dining room table to reminisce and laugh.

Across the street, from the window of a dimly lit house, their elderly neighbor, Mr. Calhoun, watched them closely. He had lived in the neighborhood for over forty years, but few really knew him. He was a solitary figure, an older man who kept mostly to himself, tending meticulously to his lawn and garden, keeping his house perfectly painted, his hedges perfectly trimmed. He had a face that was hard to remember—average in every way, the kind of face you could pass on the street and forget immediately. That suited him just fine.

As the Owens family settled in, Mr. Calhoun took a slow, steady breath, then turned away from the window, his gaze drifting down the dim hallway that led to his basement door.

"Is everyone here?" Mrs. Owens called, bustling around the kitchen, checking the timer on the oven for the third time. Her voice was filled with the usual holiday cheer, the kind that settled into everyone like the smell of baking bread.

Rebecca smiled, nodding. "All accounted for, Mom." She hugged her younger brother Daniel, pulling him in close. "It's good to see everyone."

Daniel grinned, nodding to his mother and their father, who was pouring drinks in the living room. "It's good to be home," he said, his voice warm. "After all these years, this place still feels... I don't know, comforting?"

Mark's wife, Lena, set down a casserole dish and smiled. "It's like nothing ever changes here. Just like it was when I first met you, Mark," she said, glancing at her husband with a laugh.

As they exchanged stories, laughter filled the Owens household, drifting out through the windows, out into the street where the neighbors could hear it. But none of them noticed the shadowed figure standing just inside his own doorway, listening, watching. Mr. Calhoun's lips curled into a thin smile as he stepped back from the window, his eyes reflecting something cold and calculating, a hunger that had been brewing for years, waiting for the right moment.

The family across the street had no idea that this Thanksgiving, he would be closer than ever before.

The Owens family was in the middle of a lively conversation when there was a knock on the door. It was odd—most of their neighbors didn't come by unannounced, especially during a family holiday. Mr. Owens raised his eyebrows and walked to the door, opening it with a polite, welcoming smile.

There, standing on the doorstep, was Mr. Calhoun, his hands tucked into his coat pockets, his face an expression of polite awkwardness. "Evening, Mr. Owens," he said, his voice smooth, steady. “I just wanted to wish you all a happy Thanksgiving. Saw all the cars outside—looks like you’ve got a full house this year.”

Mr. Owens smiled, relaxing slightly. “Thank you, Calhoun. Happy Thanksgiving to you too. You’re welcome to come in, have a drink with us.”

Mr. Calhoun’s eyes flickered, just for a second, a hint of something dark beneath his otherwise neutral expression. “Oh, I wouldn’t want to impose,” he said, though his gaze drifted past Mr. Owens, into the house, as though savoring the sounds of laughter, the smell of food.

“Nonsense!” Mrs. Owens chimed in, appearing beside her husband. “Come on in. It’s the holidays—nobody should be alone tonight.”

After a pause, Mr. Calhoun stepped inside, giving them a small nod. “Thank you,” he said, his eyes scanning the living room, taking in each member of the family. “I appreciate it.”

He lingered in the doorway, watching, as the family went back to their conversations. His eyes rested on each of them in turn, as though memorizing their faces. And then, slowly, he smiled, though no one seemed to notice the way it didn’t quite reach his eyes.

The Owens family had always believed that Thanksgiving wasn’t just about food—it was about tradition. They gathered around the table, raising glasses, each taking a turn to share what they were grateful for that year. Mr. Calhoun sat quietly at the end of the table, his hands folded, listening with a strange, detached interest.

"So, Mr. Calhoun," Rebecca said, her tone cheerful, "we don't know much about you. Have you lived in Millwood Pines long?"

He looked at her, his eyes expressionless. "Oh, yes," he replied, his voice low, almost a murmur. "A long time. Longer than most. Seen a lot of people come and go. Millwood Pines has been... good to me."

Mark raised an eyebrow. "What's kept you here all these years?"

Mr. Calhoun's gaze flickered, his smile widening slightly. "The people, mostly," he said, his voice carrying a hint of something dark. "Such a... *kind* community."

The Owens family exchanged polite smiles, though they couldn't shake the strange feeling that seemed to settle over the room. Something about Mr. Calhoun's presence was unsettling, a feeling they brushed off as paranoia.

The conversation turned back to familiar topics, and for a moment, the unease was forgotten. But Mr. Calhoun's eyes never left them, his gaze lingering on each member of the family with a look that felt oddly possessive, almost... hungry.

After an hour, Mr. Calhoun excused himself, thanking the Owens family for their hospitality. As he walked back to his house, he felt a deep sense of satisfaction, a thrill that ran through him as he thought about the laughter, the warmth of their home. It was always the same—these families, so trusting, so open, so willing to invite him in, never realizing the danger that lived right next door.

Inside his darkened house, he moved to the basement door, his fingers tracing the edge of the wooden frame. He opened the door, descending into the darkness, his steps slow, measured, each one carrying a sense of ritual. Downstairs, the air was thick, heavy with the unmistakable scent of formaldehyde.

As he reached the bottom, he flicked on a small lamp, illuminating a small room lined with shelves. And on those shelves, placed with careful precision, were dozens of glass jars. Inside each jar, suspended in cloudy liquid, was a heart. Some were small, some larger, each one a unique treasure.

Mr. Calhoun moved slowly, almost reverently, his gaze drifting over the rows of jars, his fingers tracing the cold glass, lingering on each heart. He could still remember each face, each voice, each life he had taken. Over the years, he had become more careful, more discreet. No one had ever suspected him, no one had ever looked beyond the friendly, unassuming mask he wore.

Until now.

His thoughts drifted back to the Owens family, to their laughter, their warmth, and he felt a thrill, a dark satisfaction that filled him with anticipation. It wouldn't be long now, he thought. They would be perfect additions to his collection.

And as he moved through the rows of jars, his fingers tracing each one, he murmured softly to himself, his voice low, filled with dark excitement.

"Home is where the heart is."

Mr. Calhoun sat alone at his kitchen table, a faint, eerie smile playing on his lips as he sipped his tea. The visit to the Owens house had left him with a renewed sense of purpose. It was almost... energizing, being around them. He could still hear the echoes of their laughter, feel the warmth of their home, so different from the cold silence that surrounded him here.

He had chosen the Owens family carefully, watching them over the years from his window, noticing the details, understanding their routines. Rebecca with her easy laugh, Mark's steady demeanor, Daniel's quiet charm. They were close-knit, a family that held each other dearly. But he knew their closeness would make it all the more satisfying to tear them apart.

It wasn't just about the hunt, the act itself—it was the *process* that thrilled him, the careful preparation. Mr. Calhoun was a man of precision, of ritual. And now, he had the perfect plan in mind.

Over the next few days, Mr. Calhoun made himself a fixture in the Owens family's daily lives. He stopped by with small gifts: a homemade apple pie for Mrs. Owens, a neatly potted plant for their front porch, small tokens to ingratiate himself further. His presence was as polite and non-intrusive as possible, always lingering just enough to make them comfortable, never too long to raise suspicion.

The Owens family, generous and kind-hearted, invited him in each time. To them, he was just a lonely old neighbor, a harmless man with few friends, grateful for the company. Rebecca even found herself softening toward him, feeling a twinge of pity for the man who seemed so isolated.

But Mr. Calhoun's eyes held a different story. Behind his gaze was a silent hunger, a need he had been stoking for years. Every encounter brought him closer to the moment when he would bring them down into his world, into the dark, hidden room in his basement, where his collection waited.

One evening, as he was preparing his next move, Mr. Calhoun decided it was time to test the waters further.

He prepared an invitation, scrawling out a note in careful, delicate handwriting:

Dear Owens Family,

I wanted to thank you for your warm hospitality on Thanksgiving. If you're free this weekend, please join me for dinner at my home. I'd love to return the favor. Warm regards, Calhoun.

He slipped the note under their door, his heart pounding in anticipation.

The following afternoon, Mrs. Owens found the note and called the family into the kitchen to read it aloud. They exchanged glances, a mix of surprise and curiosity.

"Should we go?" Mark asked, shrugging. "He's just a lonely old guy. Besides, what harm could it do?"

Daniel nodded. "It seems like he genuinely enjoyed Thanksgiving. It's probably been ages since he's had any company."

Rebecca hesitated. She couldn't quite explain why, but there was something about Mr. Calhoun that had started to unsettle her. The way his eyes lingered on each of them, the way his smile never quite seemed to reach his eyes... it felt off. But she pushed the feeling aside, telling herself she was overreacting.

"I suppose it couldn't hurt," she said, forcing a smile. "Maybe it would be good for him, you know? He probably just needs some company."

And so, it was decided: they would accept Mr. Calhoun's invitation.

On Saturday evening, the Owens family walked across the street to Mr. Calhoun's house. He greeted them at the door, a warm smile on his face, his eyes glinting with an unreadable intensity. His house was dimly lit, the rooms filled with heavy, dark furniture, the walls lined with old, faded wallpaper. A faint, unpleasant scent lingered in the air, something metallic and musty that made them wrinkle their noses. But they pushed it aside, attributing it to the age of the house.

"Please, make yourselves at home," Mr. Calhoun said, gesturing to the living room where a large, worn sofa sat. "It's not often I get such wonderful company."

Mrs. Owens noticed a strange collection of knickknacks on the mantle: small figurines, old picture frames with faded photos, and, curiously, a row of small glass jars with dark liquid inside. She felt an inexplicable chill as she looked at them, as though they were watching her. She quickly averted her gaze, brushing off the unease.

"Lovely home," she said, though the words felt hollow.

Mr. Calhoun's smile widened. "It's full of memories," he replied softly. "More than you could ever imagine."

They all sat in the living room, making small talk while Mr. Calhoun served them a tea he claimed was his own "special blend." Rebecca took a tentative sip, noting the bitter taste but forcing herself to be polite.

As they chatted, Mr. Calhoun's gaze drifted to each member of the family, his eyes lingering on their necks, their wrists, the faint pulse beneath their skin. They had no idea, he thought, smiling to himself. They had no idea they were sitting in a room that had seen more horror than they could ever imagine, a room that held the secrets of countless victims, each one lured here by the same invitation.

But tonight was different. Tonight, he wasn't just adding to his collection.

Tonight, he wanted *all of them.*

As the evening wore on, Mr. Calhoun's behavior grew stranger. He watched them intently, his fingers tapping rhythmically on the arm of his chair, his eyes never blinking, as though he were waiting for something. The family exchanged uneasy glances, feeling the tension thickening around them.

Daniel cleared his throat, forcing a casual tone. "So, Mr. Calhoun, where do you get all these... interesting decorations?" he asked, nodding to the shelves lined with odd trinkets and glass jars.

Mr. Calhoun's smile faded slightly, his gaze sharpening. "Oh, here and there," he replied, his voice low. "Every piece has a story. A memory. You could say that each one has a... *part* of someone I cared for."

A shiver ran down Rebecca's spine, her unease intensifying. She looked around the room again, her gaze settling on the glass jars. In the dim light, she noticed that they were not merely filled with liquid, but with something dark and organic floating inside, something almost... pulpy. She felt a sudden surge of nausea, a sense of dawning horror that made her heart race.

The realization struck her like a punch to the stomach.

Those jars held hearts. Real, human hearts.

She glanced at her family, panic flickering in her eyes. But before she could speak, Mr. Calhoun stood, his demeanor shifting, his friendly mask slipping to reveal something cold, something hungry.

"You're all so lovely," he murmured, his voice carrying an unsettling edge. "I think you'll fit in nicely with the others."

Mark stood up, his face pale. "What... what are you talking about?"

But Mr. Calhoun only smiled, reaching into his pocket and pulling out a small vial filled with a dark liquid. "I've been collecting memories for a long time. And tonight, I think it's time I add a few more."

Without warning, he flung the vial across the room, the liquid splattering against the walls and furniture, filling the air with a sharp, metallic scent. The family staggered back, coughing as the fumes filled their lungs, their vision blurring, their bodies growing heavy.

Rebecca's vision swam, her limbs tingling as she tried to push herself up, to move, but her body felt leaden, unresponsive. She looked up at Mr. Calhoun, her heart pounding as his face twisted into a dark, malicious smile.

"Don't worry," he whispered, his voice soft, mocking. "This will only take a moment."

As the darkness closed in, Rebecca caught one last glimpse of him standing over her, his gaze filled with satisfaction, with a dark, twisted joy.

Hours later, Mr. Calhoun moved through his basement, arranging new jars on the shelves, his hands steady, his mind calm. Each jar contained a single heart, carefully preserved, floating in formaldehyde, each one a reminder of the night he had taken them. He smiled as he placed the last jar, his eyes glinting with satisfaction.

"Home is where the heart is," he murmured to himself, his voice soft, echoing through the empty basement.

The Owens family would never be seen again, but their laughter, their warmth, their *essence*—he had captured it, preserved it, just as he had done so many times before. And as he moved through the basement, the faint hum of the refrigerator the only sound, he felt at peace, surrounded by the only family he had ever truly known.

The family of his *collection*.

When the Owens family failed to answer any calls the following day, neighbors grew worried. It wasn't like them to leave without notifying someone, especially during the holiday. Their house sat eerily still, blinds closed, no lights on, and no sign of life.

Across the street, Mr. Calhoun watched as police cruisers began pulling up to the Owens' driveway. He stayed hidden behind his curtains, his face expressionless as he observed the officers moving around, glancing in windows, knocking on doors. He'd seen it all before—the frantic worry, the helpless searching, the inevitable frustration as they tried to piece together what had happened to such a well-liked family. He knew what they would find: nothing.

By dusk, the neighborhood was buzzing with tension. Residents gathered in clusters, whispering anxiously, trading theories. "I saw them just last night," one neighbor said. "They seemed fine, just... gone, without a trace."

The police sealed off the Owens' house, treating it as a crime scene. Search parties were organized, volunteers combing through the neighborhood, the surrounding woods, even checking nearby highways. Mr. Calhoun watched it all with calm detachment, never once betraying a flicker of emotion.

Days turned into a week, and with each passing hour, the hope of finding the Owens family faded. It was as if they had been swallowed by the earth, leaving no trace behind. Their disappearance spread through the town, growing into a grim story, an unsolved mystery that haunted the community.

Then, just as people began to adjust to the shock, a young officer named Carla Mendez took a closer interest in Mr. Calhoun. Her keen instincts told her there was something off about him. He was the last known person to have seen the Owens family, and his behavior during the investigation was unsettling. While the neighbors shared stories, searched, and mourned, Mr. Calhoun remained silent, a quiet, unremarkable presence at the edge of every gathering, watching.

One afternoon, Officer Mendez visited him, clipboard in hand, her face a mask of professionalism. She knocked on his door, surprised when it opened before her second knock.

"Good afternoon, Mr. Calhoun," she said. "I'd like to ask you a few questions regarding the Owens family."

Mr. Calhoun's face betrayed nothing, his expression calm. "Of course, Officer," he replied smoothly, stepping aside. "Please, come in."

Inside, the house was dimly lit, the air stale with a faint, lingering metallic scent that pricked at her nose. The wallpaper was faded, the furniture worn, giving the place a feeling of strange, preserved emptiness. As Officer Mendez looked around, she noticed the odd collection on his shelves—small glass jars filled with dark liquid.

"What's in those jars?" she asked, her tone casual, though her stomach twisted at the sight.

Mr. Calhoun's gaze followed hers, his eyes glinting in the dim light. "Just an old man's hobby," he replied softly. "Memories, you could say."

A chill ran down her spine, but she forced a polite smile. "How long have you lived here, Mr. Calhoun?"

"Oh, quite a long time," he answered, his voice carrying a note of satisfaction. "Long enough to see families come and go. The Owens family, though... they were special. Always so welcoming."

He studied her reaction, his gaze unnerving. Mendez glanced away, her mind racing. She had no proof, but the way he spoke, the way his eyes lingered, there was something *wrong*.

"Did you notice anything unusual the last time you saw them?" she asked, forcing her voice to remain steady.

His smile widened, though it held no warmth. "No, Officer, nothing unusual at all. We had a nice dinner. They were good people... polite, trusting." His voice softened, his gaze fixed on the jars. "You know, it's a shame when good people go missing. So few understand the importance of... preserving the ones we care about."

The statement sent a chill down her spine, and Officer Mendez felt a wave of dread settle over her. She knew she needed to tread carefully. Thanking him for his time, she excused herself, promising to return if she had any further questions.

As she left, she felt his eyes following her, watching her retreat, an invisible weight pressing against her back.

That night, Carla Mendez lay awake, the memory of Mr. Calhoun's gaze lingering in her mind, unsettling and unshakable. She knew something was hidden within that house, something he wasn't telling them. She decided to take matters into her own hands.

The following night, just past midnight, she returned to Mr. Calhoun's house, her heart pounding as she parked a few doors down, making her way through the shadows. She couldn't shake the feeling that the answers to the Owens' disappearance were inside that house, locked away in its walls, hidden from sight.

She reached the back door, testing the handle, surprised to find it unlocked. With a deep breath, she slipped inside, moving through the darkened house, her flashlight cutting through the gloom. The living room was empty, the shelves lined with those eerie jars. She moved quickly, searching for a clue, something that would confirm her suspicions.

Then, her flashlight illuminated a door tucked away in the far corner of the kitchen. It was slightly ajar, leading down into the basement. The air grew colder, heavier, as she descended, her footsteps barely a whisper on the stairs.

The basement was dimly lit by a single, weak bulb, casting shadows that danced along the walls. And there, lining the shelves, were rows of glass jars, each one filled with a heart, floating in a thick, cloudy liquid. Carla felt her stomach turn, horror twisting through her as she realized the full, grim truth.

The hearts were real. Human.

Each jar had a small label on it, marked with a date and initials. She moved closer, her hand shaking as she read the names. Each jar bore the initials of a person who had gone missing in the last twenty years, their fates a mystery—until now.

Her gaze fell on three new jars at the end of the shelf, each one marked with fresh initials: *R.O., M.O., D.O.*

The Owens family.

A surge of horror washed over her, her breath coming in short, panicked gasps as she staggered back, the room spinning. But as she turned to leave, she froze.

Mr. Calhoun stood at the top of the stairs, his silhouette outlined in the dim light, his face hidden in shadow.

"Oh, Officer Mendez," he said, his voice soft, almost amused. "I wasn't expecting company at this hour."

Her heart pounded as she backed away, reaching for her radio, but he moved faster, descending the stairs with slow, deliberate steps, his face breaking into a cold, malevolent smile.

"You shouldn't have come here," he whispered, his voice carrying a dark satisfaction. "This room... it's only for family."

She tried to shout, to call for help, but his hand clamped over her mouth, his grip cold, unyielding. The last thing she saw was his face, twisted in dark triumph, as he dragged her into the shadows, her voice swallowed by the silence.

Days passed, and Officer Carla Mendez's absence became the latest mystery in Millwood Pines. The town searched, the police investigated, but no one thought to look in Mr. Calhoun's house, where her heart now floated beside the Owens family's, preserved forever in his dark, twisted collection.

Mr. Calhoun resumed his quiet, solitary life, his face unremarkable, his presence fading back into the background. The neighbors barely noticed him, too consumed by the town's latest tragedy. And as the days wore on, the Owens family's house remained empty, its windows dark, a constant reminder of the horror that lingered just beneath the surface of their perfect suburb.

And in his basement, Mr. Calhoun moved slowly through the rows of jars, his fingers tracing each cold glass surface, his gaze softening as he murmured to himself, his voice filled with a chilling tenderness.

"Home is where the heart is."

The End

3

OCTAMO LAKE

Oakville was a quiet town, nestled deep in the heart of the New England countryside. Thick forests surrounded it, their branches casting long shadows across the narrow roads that wound through town. Despite the quiet charm Oakville offered to outsiders, the locals knew that their town held a darker, almost forgotten secret—a secret that began and ended at Octamo Lake.

Octamo Lake was a small, murky pond hidden at the edge of Oakville, surrounded by a dense thicket of trees. The lake was rarely visited, its banks overgrown with weeds and reeds, its waters dark and still, like a mirror of the sky's darkest parts. Only a few fishermen still ventured there, though even they didn't dare stay past dusk. They whispered of strange sights—shadows that drifted across the surface without any source, voices carried on the wind, strange footprints appearing and disappearing in the mud along the shore.

As the legend went, Octamo Lake wasn't just any lake. Hundreds of years ago, before Oakville was even a mark on a map, this land had belonged to the Octamo tribe, who believed the lake held spiritual significance—a gateway between worlds. They'd used its shores as a burial ground, believing that the lake would protect and preserve their spirits. But as settlers arrived, the tribe was driven away, the burial grounds desecrated, the graves lost to time.

No one believed the stories anymore, of course. The lake was simply a dark, forgotten part of the landscape. But that didn't stop people from feeling uneasy near its banks, from walking a little faster if they found themselves close by. And this was especially true of the teenagers of Oakville High, who loved to trade ghost stories about the lake, each tale growing darker with every telling.

On this particular night, four friends—Mark, Emily, Connor, and Rachel—were gathered around a campfire near the edge of Octamo Lake, each of them daring the other to tell the scariest story they knew. The air was thick with the scent of burning wood and the quiet rustle of leaves as the wind moved through the trees. Their flashlights flickered, casting eerie shadows over their faces.

"You know," Mark said, grinning as he leaned forward, "they say if you listen closely, you can hear the spirits of the Octamo tribe whispering from the lake, warning us to stay away."

Emily rolled her eyes, though she glanced nervously at the dark, still water. "Come on, Mark, you know that's just a myth. I've been here a dozen times and never heard a thing."

Connor smirked, his flashlight casting a faint glow over the lake's edge. "Maybe that's because you never listen," he teased. "They say the lake only whispers to those who disturb it."

Rachel shivered, pulling her jacket tighter around her. "Disturb it? Like... how?"

Connor grinned, an unsettling gleam in his eyes. "Like this."

Before anyone could react, Connor stood, grabbing a nearby stick and hurling it into the water. It landed with a loud splash, the ripples spreading out across the lake's surface, shattering the glassy stillness. The group watched, their eyes fixed on the water as it slowly settled, the silence of the forest pressing down around them.

Emily let out a breathy laugh, the tension breaking. "See? Nothing happened. Just a creepy story."

But just as she spoke, a faint, low sound echoed across the lake—a whisper, barely audible, like the rustle of leaves, but deeper, darker. It was a single word, a name, drifting across the water as though carried by the wind.

"Octamo..."

The laughter died on their lips, each of them frozen, their gazes locked on the lake. The whisper came again, soft, insistent, like someone calling from far away, the voice carrying an old, haunting melody that stirred something deep within them, something primal.

"Did... did you guys hear that?" Rachel whispered, her face pale.

Mark swallowed, his voice tense. "It's probably just the wind..."

But deep down, none of them believed that.

The lake's surface seemed to shift, the darkness deepening, almost as though something were moving beneath the water, disturbing its stillness. Ripples began to form again, growing wider, more erratic, even though the air was completely still.

"Let's just go," Emily whispered, standing up, her face pale and drawn. "This isn't funny anymore."

But as they turned to leave, a loud splash erupted from the lake, the water surging up like something massive had struck it from beneath. They froze, their eyes fixed on the spot, dread settling over them like a suffocating fog.

And then, they saw it—a shape, rising slowly from the depths, breaking the surface of the water. It was dark, shadowy, a figure hunched and twisted, its form barely visible in the dim light. The figure stood at the water's edge, dripping with mud and algae, its head bowed, its arms hanging limp at its sides.

It looked human, but there was something wrong, something inhuman about the way it moved, jerky and unnatural. And as it lifted its head, its face emerged from the shadows, a mask of decayed flesh stretched tight over a skull, empty eye sockets staring out at them with an ancient, malevolent hunger.

Emily gasped, stumbling back, her voice barely a whisper. "Oh my god... what is that?"

The figure took a step forward, its movements slow and deliberate, leaving dark, wet footprints in the mud as it moved toward them. And then, it spoke, its voice low and raspy, like the sound of gravel scraping over stone.

"Leave... this place..."

The words hung in the air, thick with an ancient weight, a command that sent chills down their spines. But before they could react, the figure took another step, its hand reaching out, the fingers long and skeletal, the nails blackened and sharp.

"Go," it hissed, its voice rising to a bone-chilling wail. "Go, before you join the dead!"

In a blind panic, the friends turned and ran, their footsteps echoing through the trees as they bolted down the narrow trail that led back to town. The air around them felt heavy, charged, each shadow seeming to reach out for them as they fled. The whispers followed them, echoing through the trees, a chorus of voices calling their names, beckoning them back to the lake.

They didn't stop running until they reached the edge of town, their breaths ragged, their faces pale and drenched in sweat. They huddled together, each of them glancing back at the forest, at the faint glimmer of the lake in the distance.

"What... what was that?" Rachel whispered, her voice trembling.

Connor shook his head, his face pale. "I don't know... but we should never go back there. Ever."

But deep down, each of them felt a strange pull, an unspoken connection to the lake that filled them with a sick, twisted curiosity. They'd seen something impossible, something that defied reason, and though they'd escaped, the lake's whispers echoed in their minds, a haunting melody they couldn't shake.

And as they parted ways that night, each of them couldn't help but feel that this was only the beginning. That Octamo Lake had marked them, that the spirits within it had claimed them as their own.

For in Oakville, the dead didn't rest.

And neither would they.

Long before Oakville existed, before the settlers had carved their towns and roads into the landscape, the land was inhabited by the Octamo tribe, a people whose culture was deeply rooted in the surrounding forests, mountains, and rivers. They lived in harmony with the land, believing it to be a gift from the spirits of their ancestors. But there was one place they considered sacred above all others—a dark, still pond that would later be known as Octamo Lake.

To the Octamo people, the lake was more than just a body of water. It was a gateway between worlds, a place where the boundary between the physical realm and the spirit world was thin, fragile. They believed that the lake held the souls of their ancestors, who watched over them, guiding and protecting their descendants. For generations, they buried their dead along the lake's shores, each grave marked with stones, offerings, and carefully carved totems that represented the soul's journey through the spirit world.

But Octamo Lake was also a place of immense power, and with that power came darkness. The tribe's elders warned that the lake's energy could be dangerous if disturbed. They spoke of an ancient legend—a guardian spirit, a twisted, malevolent being that had once been human but had crossed too far into the spirit world, merging with the forces of death and decay. This guardian, known in their language as *Ahsaki*, or "The Shadow Keeper," was said to guard the lake, ensuring that only the spirits of the tribe were allowed to pass through.

Ahsaki's presence kept other spirits at bay, acting as a barrier that protected the Octamo tribe from dark forces. But the legend came with a warning: should anyone desecrate the burial grounds, Ahsaki would awaken from the depths, his wrath unleashed upon those who disturbed the sanctity of the lake.

For generations, the Octamo people honored this pact, treating the lake with reverence, never daring to upset its balance. But this changed in the early 1700s, when settlers arrived in Oakville, drawn by the land's rich resources and fertile soil. They were unaware of the lake's significance, of the lives and legends tied to it.

The settlers saw only land to be conquered and used. To them, the burial ground was nothing more than an obstacle. At first, the Octamo tribe attempted to warn them, speaking of Ahsaki, of the spirits that resided in the lake, of the curses that would fall upon those who dared disturb it. But the settlers dismissed their warnings as superstitions, relics of a "primitive" people they barely understood.

One cold autumn day, in an act that would forever change the fate of the lake, the settlers began clearing the land around Octamo Lake, removing the grave markers, disturbing the earth, and tossing aside the sacred stones and totems the tribe had placed. They saw them as little more than obstacles, relics of a culture they did not respect.

When the Octamo tribe saw what had been done, their sorrow and anger turned to desperation. The tribe's elders pleaded with the settlers, begging them to stop the desecration, but their pleas fell on deaf ears. Finally, in one last effort to protect the lake, the tribe's shaman, a woman named Naya, performed a ritual at the lake's edge, invoking the spirit of Ahsaki.

By the light of a full moon, Naya chanted, her voice rising and falling like the wind as she called upon the lake to protect itself, to unleash its guardian upon those who had defiled it. The other tribe members gathered along the shore, silent, watching as the water began to ripple, strange shapes forming in its depths. The air grew cold, a chilling mist rising from the lake, and then they saw it—a shadow, tall and twisted, emerging from the water.

It was Ahsaki, The Shadow Keeper.

His form was terrifying, like a man who had been twisted and stretched by the lake's dark magic, his eyes empty, hollow, yet burning with an unnatural fire. His body was covered in mud and algae, his fingers long and bony, sharp like claws, as though they were made to dig into flesh and bone. As he rose from the lake, the air filled with an unnatural silence, a heaviness that made it impossible to breathe, to move.

The settlers who had defiled the lake that night were the first to feel Ahsaki's wrath. They were found the next morning, scattered along the shore, their faces frozen in expressions of horror, their bodies cold and stiff, as though the life had been drained from them. But that was only the beginning.

Over the next few weeks, more settlers began to fall ill, plagued by feverish dreams of the lake, of shadows moving in the water, of hands reaching up to drag them down. The Octamo tribe warned them that Ahsaki would not rest, that the lake's anger would not subside until the burial grounds were restored and the dead properly honored.

But instead of heeding the warning, the settlers turned against the Octamo people, blaming them for the strange events. The tribe was forced from their land, driven away from the lake they had once worshiped, leaving behind their ancestral graves, their stories, their heritage.

As the Octamo people disappeared, so did the stories of the lake, buried along with the graves at its shores. But Ahsaki remained, bound to the lake, watching over the desecrated ground, waiting for the day he might reclaim it. The settlers continued to live near the lake, but they began to avoid it at night, speaking in hushed tones of strange figures seen on the shore, of whispers that drifted across the water, of footprints that appeared and disappeared along the banks.

Over time, the stories faded into ghostly rumors, half-remembered legends. But every generation would lose a handful of people to the lake—fishermen, wanderers, children dared by their friends to test its waters. They would disappear without a trace, the only evidence of their presence the ripples on the lake's surface and the faint whispers that followed.

In the years that followed, Oakville grew, and so did the lake's legend. The Octamo tribe was all but forgotten, but the lake's curse remained, a shadow over the town, a reminder of the desecration that had never been set right.

The elders of the Octamo had left behind one final prophecy, a warning that the lake would always demand a price. It was said that the lake would not rest until it was restored, that each time someone disturbed its waters, Ahsaki would rise again, more powerful, more vengeful. He would claim anyone who dared enter his domain, dragging them down into the depths, their souls trapped alongside the ancient spirits of the Octamo.

And now, generations later, Ahsaki's power was stronger than ever, fed by centuries of anger and betrayal. He lurked beneath the surface, waiting, watching, drawn to those who disturbed the lake's fragile peace. The spirits of the Octamo still lingered there, their voices joining his, echoing across the water like a haunting lullaby, a warning to those who ventured too close.

The townsfolk might have forgotten the full story, but the lake had not. It held onto its history, its anger festering beneath the surface like a wound, waiting to unleash its wrath on anyone who dared disturb the dead.

The morning after their night at Octamo Lake, Mark, Emily, Connor, and Rachel were plagued by strange dreams—visions of shadows moving in the water, voices whispering their names, skeletal hands reaching up from the depths. They tried to brush it off, but each of them felt an unshakable dread, a sense that something was watching them, waiting.

As the days passed, strange things began to happen. Mark found muddy footprints outside his bedroom window one morning, even though it hadn't rained. Emily noticed her reflection in the mirror behaving oddly, the face staring back at her somehow hollow, unfamiliar. Connor heard whispers at night, voices that drifted through his room like a cold breeze, each one calling him back to the lake.

Desperate to understand what was happening, they turned to the town's history, digging through old records and newspaper clippings, until they uncovered the truth—the story of the Octamo tribe, the desecration of the burial grounds, and the legend of Ahsaki, The Shadow Keeper.

They realized that their night at the lake, the splash Connor had made, had disturbed something ancient and angry. Ahsaki was awake, and he was coming for them, driven by a curse that could not be broken.

The only question now was whether they could find a way to appease him before it was too late.

Days after their unsettling night at Octamo Lake, Mark, Emily, Connor, and Rachel found their lives transformed by an unshakable sense of dread. Each had begun experiencing things that defied explanation, eerie signs that something far older and darker than they could imagine had taken an interest in them. The legend of Ahsaki, The Shadow Keeper, now haunted their every waking moment.

Mark was the first to experience Ahsaki's haunting presence in the mirror. One morning, as he brushed his teeth, he glanced up and noticed something strange about his reflection. His face was pallid, his eyes sunken, as though he hadn't slept in days. He tried to brush it off, leaning closer to inspect the unusual darkness around his eyes.

That's when he saw it—another figure in the background, a shadow lurking in the dimly lit bathroom. At first, it was a faint outline, like a smudge in the mirror, but as he stared, the figure became clearer, more defined. He saw it—a tall, twisted shape, cloaked in darkness, with empty, hollow eyes that seemed to pierce through him.

"Ahsaki..." the name slipped out of his mouth in a horrified whisper.

His reflection mouthed the word back to him, his own eyes dark and empty, mirroring the shadow's hollow gaze. Mark stumbled back, his pulse pounding, his mind reeling with terror. When he looked again, his reflection was normal, the shadow gone. But the fear lingered, a clawing dread that burrowed deep, a reminder that Ahsaki was watching him, waiting.

Emily's experience came the following night, in the form of a nightmare that felt disturbingly real. In her dream, she was standing alone at the edge of Octamo Lake, the night air cold and thick with mist. The water was black and still, reflecting the ghostly light of the moon. She felt the ground shift beneath her, like something stirring just below the surface.

Then she saw them—hands, skeletal and covered in mud, reaching up from the water, pulling themselves onto the shore. One by one, figures emerged from the lake, each one cloaked in shadows, their bodies twisted and decayed. She recognized them from the old records—the Octamo tribe, their faces hollow, their expressions twisted in agony. They moved in unison, their empty eyes fixed on her, and as they stepped closer, the smell of decay filled the air.

In the dream, Emily tried to scream, but no sound escaped her lips. She could feel their cold, wet hands reaching for her, dragging her toward the lake. And then, as she looked back toward the water, she saw him. Ahsaki.

He was taller than the others, his form shifting and dark, his skeletal face twisted into a mask of malice. His empty eye sockets bore into her, and when he raised his hand, she felt her body freeze, her limbs going numb as she was pulled toward him, helpless.

"Ahsaki... demands you," his voice rasped, a hollow, ancient sound that seemed to echo inside her head.

She jolted awake, gasping for breath, her sheets damp with sweat. But even as she sat in her room, safe and surrounded by the familiarity of her things, she couldn't shake the feeling of cold hands on her skin, the memory of Ahsaki's hollow eyes burned into her mind.

Connor's encounter came two nights later, when he was walking home after spending the evening with his friends, desperately trying to distract himself from the creeping fear that had been gnawing at him since the night at the lake. As he took the shortcut through the woods, he heard footsteps behind him, faint but steady, matching his every movement.

He stopped, his breath catching, and turned around. The path was empty, shadows stretching across the ground, the only sound the wind rustling through the trees. He shook his head, laughing nervously at himself, and kept walking.

But the footsteps continued, louder now, faster, echoing through the quiet night. He broke into a run, his heart racing as he tried to escape the invisible pursuer, but no matter how fast he went, the footsteps stayed close behind, relentless.

Then, in a moment of desperation, he turned back and saw it—a figure, tall and twisted, standing in the shadows, watching him with empty eyes. The figure's body was skeletal, its arms impossibly long, its fingers reaching out toward him.

"Connor..." a voice whispered, low and guttural, the sound grating against his ears. "You cannot escape me..."

Connor stumbled back, his vision blurring as he broke into a sprint, refusing to look back. He didn't stop until he reached his house, slamming the door shut behind him, his breath coming in ragged gasps. But even as he stood there, shaking, he could still hear the footsteps, faint but steady, fading into the night.

Rachel's encounter came in the dead of night, as she lay awake in bed, her mind racing with thoughts of the lake, of the spirits, of Ahsaki. She closed her eyes, trying to shake the images from her mind, but as she drifted into an uneasy sleep, she felt a presence, cold and heavy, pressing down on her.

When she opened her eyes, she found herself lying in a place that wasn't her bedroom. She was on the shore of Octamo Lake, the water dark and still, the moonlight casting an eerie glow across the landscape. She could see the shadows moving in the water, figures rising and falling, their faces twisted, their arms reaching out toward her.

Then, Ahsaki emerged, his form towering over her, his skeletal face hidden in shadow, his empty eyes gleaming in the darkness.

"Rachel..." he whispered, his voice a low, hollow murmur. "You have disturbed my rest... and now you must pay."

She tried to move, to run, but her body was frozen, trapped in his gaze. He reached out, his hand closing around her wrist, his grip cold and suffocating, pulling her toward the lake. She felt herself sinking, the water rising around her, cold and thick, pulling her down into the depths. She couldn't breathe, couldn't scream, couldn't escape.

When she woke, she was back in her room, her sheets soaked with sweat, her wrist throbbing with pain. She looked down and saw it—a dark, bruise-like mark on her wrist, the shape of Ahsaki's bony hand burned into her skin.

The group met the following evening, each of them pale and haunted, the marks of their encounters visible in their hollow eyes, their trembling hands. They shared their stories, each one more terrifying than the last, each one deepening the dread that had taken hold of them.

"We can't ignore this," Mark said, his voice shaking. "Ahsaki... he's coming for us. We have to do something."

"But what can we do?" Emily whispered, her face pale. "The lake... it's cursed. He's bound to it. He won't stop until he has us."

Connor clenched his fists, his jaw tight. "There has to be a way to break the curse, to appease him. The Octamo people... they must have known how to deal with him."

Rachel nodded, her hand absently rubbing the bruise on her wrist. "We need to find the Octamo burial ground, the one by the lake. Maybe if we return the offerings, restore what was taken... maybe he'll leave us alone."

The group agreed, their fear tempered by a desperate hope. They would go back to Octamo Lake, they would find the burial ground, and they would do whatever it took to break the curse.

That night, as they prepared for the journey back to the lake, they each felt a chill settle over them, a sense that they were being watched, that Ahsaki was waiting, lurking in the shadows, his hollow eyes fixed on them.

But they knew they had no choice. If they didn't confront him, if they didn't find a way to appease him, he would haunt them forever, dragging them down into the dark waters of Octamo Lake, their souls bound to the lake, trapped alongside the spirits of the dead.

And as they set out into the night, the whispers of the lake followed them, soft and haunting, echoing Ahsaki's warning:

"You cannot escape... the Shadow Keeper."

The next evening, under the cover of night, Mark, Emily, Connor, and Rachel made their way back to Octamo Lake, each of them gripped by an uneasy mixture of fear and determination. They had gathered supplies—candles, offerings from the local Native American museum, and anything else they thought might appease the restless spirits of the Octamo tribe. They hoped that by restoring the lake's sacred ground, they could satisfy the wrath of Ahsaki, the Shadow Keeper, and end his haunting pursuit.

The air was cold and damp, the kind of chill that seeped into their bones, prickling their skin with goosebumps. The forest was dark and silent, and as they walked along the narrow, winding path that led to the lake, they felt as though unseen eyes were watching them, observing their every step. Shadows stretched out between the trees, their forms twisting and shifting, and each time a branch snapped underfoot, they jumped, glancing nervously around.

When they reached the lake, they paused, standing at the water's edge, the dark, glassy surface reflecting the pale light of the moon. Octamo Lake was still and quiet, an unnatural silence filling the air, and the sense of dread only grew stronger as they looked upon its murky waters. It was as though the lake itself was waiting, aware of their presence, knowing why they had come.

Mark cleared his throat, breaking the silence. "Alright. We're here. Let's... let's get started."

They set their supplies down, laying out the offerings in a circle near the shore, placing small, carved stones and feathers from the museum that represented the spirits of the Octamo tribe. They hoped it was enough, that these tokens would restore the balance they had disturbed.

Emily lit the candles, their soft glow illuminating the offerings, casting flickering shadows across the ground. She took a deep breath, her voice trembling as she recited a prayer she had found in a book about Native American traditions, her words quiet, reverent.

"We come here to honor those who rest in this place, to offer respect, to restore what was lost..."

But as she spoke, a low, haunting whisper rose from the lake, filling the air with a deep, guttural sound that sent chills through each of them. It was Ahsaki's voice, ancient and unrelenting, echoing through the night.

"Too late... too late..."

The whisper grew louder, a chorus of voices joining Ahsaki's, their words overlapping, creating a cacophony of anger and sorrow. The friends covered their ears, trying to block out the voices, but they could feel them—like a physical weight pressing down on them, filling their minds with a sense of dread that made their skin crawl.

Suddenly, the lake's surface began to ripple, the water churning as though something massive were moving beneath it. The air grew colder, a bone-deep chill that made it hard to breathe, and the shadows around them seemed to stretch and twist, taking on strange, unnatural shapes.

Connor took a step back, his eyes wide with fear. "This... this isn't working. We need to get out of here—now!"

But as they turned to leave, the ground beneath them seemed to shift, rooting them in place, their feet sinking into the soft, muddy earth. It was as though the lake itself was holding them back, refusing to let them go.

Then they saw him.

Ahsaki rose from the water, his twisted, skeletal form emerging from the depths, his empty eye sockets gleaming with a malevolent hunger. His body was cloaked in shadows, his limbs elongated and distorted, his fingers long and sharp, like claws reaching out to grasp them. The spirit's presence was overwhelming, filling the air with a sense of dread so powerful it left them paralyzed, unable to move, unable to scream.

"Ahsaki..." Rachel whispered, her voice barely audible, her face pale with terror.

The Shadow Keeper stepped closer, his hollow gaze fixed on each of them in turn, his voice a low, echoing rasp that seemed to vibrate through the air.

"You have disturbed my rest... desecrated the ground of my people... defiled the lake that was once sacred."

Mark tried to speak, to explain, but his voice failed him, his words caught in his throat. He felt Ahsaki's gaze bore into him, a weight so intense it was as if his very soul were being stripped bare.

Ahsaki raised his hand, his skeletal fingers extending toward them, each digit tipped with sharp, blackened nails. The air grew colder still, the shadows around them deepening as the spirit's presence filled every corner of their minds.

"You must pay... in blood," he intoned, his voice echoing like a death knell.

The ground began to tremble, and the friends stumbled, their feet slipping in the soft mud. Dark shapes began to rise from the lake—figures of the Octamo dead, their faces hollow, twisted, each one bearing the marks of a life long lost. They moved slowly, their bodies swaying, their empty eyes fixed on the group, their hands outstretched as though reaching for something... or someone.

The friends huddled together, their backs to the lake as the spirits advanced, a slow, unstoppable tide of shadows and decay. Emily clutched the stones they had brought, holding them up as if they could shield her from the spirits' touch.

"Please!" she cried. "We're sorry! We didn't know! We're trying to make it right!"

But Ahsaki's gaze was merciless, his hollow eyes burning with a rage centuries in the making. He raised his hand again, and the ground beneath them began to split, dark tendrils of water and mud reaching up like skeletal fingers, wrapping around their ankles, pulling them down toward the lake.

"You have awoken the dead... and now you shall join them."

The spirits reached out, their hands cold and wet, their touch like ice against skin. Mark struggled, kicking and twisting, but the hands were relentless, dragging him closer to the water's edge, closer to Ahsaki, who loomed over him like a specter of death.

Connor's voice broke through the chaos, a desperate cry. "Wait! Please! We... we'll do anything! Just... tell us how to make it right!"

For a moment, Ahsaki paused, his gaze shifting to Connor, a flicker of something unreadable in his hollow eyes. He tilted his head, as though considering the plea, his voice a low, echoing murmur.

"Restore... the balance. Return... what was taken."

The friends exchanged a quick, terrified glance, unsure of what he meant, their minds racing as they tried to understand.

"What... what do you mean?" Rachel stammered, her voice barely a whisper. "What must we return?"

Ahsaki's gaze darkened, his hollow eyes fixed on her. "Blood... was shed. Life... was taken. A sacrifice must be made... to seal the lake's curse."

The words hung in the air, heavy with meaning, and the friends understood in an instant. A sacrifice—a life given in exchange for peace, to restore the balance that had been broken. One of them would have to stay behind, to join the spirits of the lake, to appease Ahsaki's wrath.

"No..." Emily whispered, her face pale. "There... there has to be another way."

But Ahsaki remained silent, his gaze merciless, his presence filling the air with an undeniable finality. This was the price, the only way to break the curse, to end his haunting pursuit.

Mark stepped forward, his face set, his eyes filled with a strange, resigned calm. "I... I'll stay."

The others turned to him, their faces filled with horror, but Mark held up a hand, stopping them. "We disturbed this place... we awoke him. This... this is the only way to make it right."

He looked at them, a faint smile on his lips, a quiet acceptance in his gaze. "Go. Go, and don't look back."

The friends hesitated, their hearts breaking as they watched him step toward the lake, but they knew there was no other choice. They turned, their steps slow and heavy, their faces wet with tears as they made their way back up the path, leaving Mark behind, his figure silhouetted against the dark waters of the lake.

As they reached the edge of the forest, they heard one final whisper, a haunting, sorrowful sound that echoed through the night.

"Thank you..."

They turned, catching a last glimpse of Mark as he vanished beneath the water, his form fading into the shadows, his sacrifice sealing the lake's curse, restoring the balance that had been broken.

And as they walked back to town, the whispers of Octamo Lake faded, leaving only silence—a silence that held the weight of what had been lost, what had been given, and the dark history that would forever linger in the lake's still, haunted waters.

The End

4

DAYLIGHT

There was no warning. The sun rose that morning like it had every other day, spreading its soft, golden light over the small town of Waverly. People went about their routines—making coffee, walking dogs, heading to work. But within minutes, an unimaginable horror unfolded.

Eli Mercer was one of the first to realize something was wrong. He'd stepped outside to grab the newspaper, his bare feet cold against the dewy grass. The morning was bright, the air crisp. The sunlight was spilling over the horizon, painting everything in warm, soft hues. He barely registered it at first, just another weekday morning, just another day.

But then, as his fingers touched the paper, he felt it—a sharp, searing pain spreading across the back of his hand. He yanked it back, staring in shock as his skin bubbled and blistered, the flesh turning an angry red, as though he'd plunged his hand into boiling water.

"Ahh!" Eli staggered backward, clutching his hand, his eyes wide with horror as he watched the skin peel away, melting before his eyes. The pain was like nothing he'd ever felt, a searing agony that twisted in his stomach, sending him stumbling back into the house.

In the span of a few seconds, he felt his heart racing, his mind reeling, as he stumbled to the sink and thrust his hand under cold water, trying to soothe the pain, but nothing seemed to help. The skin kept melting, kept peeling, like wax dripping from a candle, exposing the raw muscle underneath.

"Lydia!" he screamed, his voice thick with panic.

His wife appeared in the doorway, her face a mix of confusion and fear as she saw his hand, her mouth dropping open in horror.

"Oh my God, Eli! What happened?"

"I... I just went outside!" he stammered, his voice shaky, his eyes wild. "I just went to get the paper, and... the sun, it... it burned me. It's burning everything it touches."

Lydia stared at him, her mind struggling to process his words. But before she could respond, they heard a scream—a high-pitched, guttural sound, coming from the street outside.

Eli turned, rushing to the window, peering through the blinds. His heart dropped as he saw his neighbor, Mr. Bell, stumbling down his driveway, his skin bubbling, blistering, his face twisted in pain as he reached out, his arms flailing, his body steaming under the sunlight.

Another scream rang out, this time from further down the street. Then another, and another, each one sharper, more desperate, filling the air with a cacophony of terror that echoed through the neighborhood.

Lydia's face went pale, her hand covering her mouth as she looked at Eli, her eyes wide with fear. "What... what's happening?"

Eli shook his head, his mind racing, his breath coming in short, frantic gasps. "I don't know," he whispered, his voice barely audible. "But... we can't go outside. The sun—it's killing people."

They closed the curtains, locking out the sunlight, their minds racing with fear, with questions they couldn't answer. The screams outside grew fainter, replaced by an eerie silence that hung over the neighborhood like a shroud. Eli's hand throbbed, the pain searing, pulsing, a constant reminder of the horror they were facing.

Then, from the living room, they heard the faint sound of the radio crackling to life.

Lydia rushed over, her hands shaking as she turned up the volume, her face pale as she listened to the hurried voice of a news broadcaster, his tone filled with panic, disbelief.

"This... this is an emergency broadcast from WNXR News," the voice stammered, each word sharp, urgent. "Reports are coming in from across the country—people experiencing severe burns, melting flesh, even death upon exposure to direct sunlight. This is not isolated. It appears to be happening nationwide, possibly worldwide. All citizens are advised to stay indoors, avoid sunlight at all costs. Block your windows, do not attempt to leave your homes. Repeat, do not go outside."

The radio fell silent, the message looping, each word sinking into Eli and Lydia's minds, the full weight of the horror pressing down on them.

"It's everywhere," Lydia whispered, her voice filled with terror. "It's not just us."

Eli nodded, his mind racing, his body tense, his heart pounding. "We... we have to stay calm. We need to figure out what we can do to survive this."

But even as he spoke, he felt a gnawing fear growing inside him, a sense of helplessness that settled over him like a dark cloud. The sun, the very thing that had once brought life and warmth, had turned against them, becoming a silent, invisible killer.

Hours passed. The house grew darker as they blocked the windows with blankets, furniture, anything they could find. They moved in silence, their minds numb, the horror of the morning settling over them like a heavy fog. Occasionally, they heard faint cries from outside, distant, desperate voices calling for help, for rescue, for anyone who might listen.

But no one came.

By evening, the streets were silent, the neighborhood transformed, a graveyard of abandoned cars, empty houses, darkened windows. The once-familiar streets now felt like a nightmare, a place where light had become a weapon, where daylight was something to fear.

Eli and Lydia huddled in the living room, their only light a small candle, its flickering glow casting long shadows across the walls. They listened to the radio, the news reports growing more sporadic, more desperate, each broadcast a grim update on the horror unfolding around them.

"This is Sarah Mason, reporting from WNXR News. We... we're losing communication with other states. Reports indicate the same phenomenon—melting skin, catastrophic burns, fatalities. Hospitals are overwhelmed. There's been no word from the government... no response. We advise all listeners to remain indoors, to stay in the dark."

Her voice was thick with emotion, the terror unmistakable, the helplessness bleeding through every word.

And then, silence.

Eli glanced at Lydia, his face filled with fear, with an unspoken question. "How... how long can we last like this? With no sun, no food, no... no way to go outside?"

Lydia took a shaky breath, her eyes filled with tears, her voice barely a whisper. "I don't know. But we have to try. We have to find a way."

They sat in silence, the weight of their situation pressing down on them, each one lost in thought, in fear, in the gnawing sense of dread that filled the air.

The hours stretched on, the house growing colder, the darkness heavier. But as night fell, a strange thought began to form in Eli's mind, a glimmer of hope, a sense of possibility that cut through the fear.

"Lydia," he said, his voice low, urgent. "If the sun is what's causing this... then night is the only time we can go outside."

Lydia looked at him, her face pale, her eyes wide. "You mean... go out there? But what if it's not safe? What if... what if there's something else?"

Eli shook his head, his expression filled with a desperate resolve. "I don't know. But we can't stay in here forever. We need supplies—food, water, maybe even answers. There has to be something out there, someone who knows what's going on."

Lydia hesitated, her fear warring with the knowledge that he was right, that they couldn't survive in the house forever, not without the basics. "Alright," she whispered, her voice trembling. "But we go together. We stick to the shadows. And we come back before sunrise."

Eli nodded, his mind racing with the possibilities, the dangers. He knew it was a risk, but it was a risk they had to take. As the sun sank below the horizon, casting the world into darkness, they prepared for their journey, gathering flashlights, blankets, anything that might help them survive the unknown.

They opened the door, stepping out into the night, the air cold against their skin, the silence thick, oppressive, filled with a sense of dread that gnawed at their minds.

But as they ventured out, moving through the empty streets, they felt a strange, eerie presence, a sense that they were not alone, that something watched from the shadows, silent, waiting.

And in the distance, they saw it—a faint, flickering light, coming from the center of town, a glimmer of hope in the darkness, a sign that they were not the only ones left.

But as they moved toward the light, their footsteps echoing through the silence, they couldn't shake the feeling that something was watching, that the darkness held secrets, horrors, waiting to be uncovered.

And in the back of their minds, a single, terrifying thought echoed, a reminder of the horror they faced.

The sun would rise again.

The town of Waverly felt alien in the darkness, every street they'd known for years transformed into an eerie labyrinth. There were no streetlights, no glimmers of life from neighboring houses. Just an empty silence, thick and pressing. It was as if the town had been abandoned overnight, left to decay in the stillness.

Eli and Lydia moved cautiously, their flashlights off, the dim moonlight their only guide. They were careful to keep to the shadows, staying close to buildings, scanning every corner for movement. Each step felt heavier, the cold air biting against their skin, but they pushed on, driven by necessity and fear.

Ahead, a faint glow broke through the darkness, flickering from what looked like the center of town. The sight filled them with hope, but also a sinking dread. There had been no word of survivors on the radio since afternoon—only static and brief emergency broadcasts advising people to stay inside. If anyone was still out there, they'd have to be as desperate as they were.

"Do you think it's others?" Lydia whispered, her voice barely audible.

Eli glanced over his shoulder, his face tense. "Maybe. If anyone's left, that's where they'd go." But he didn't say what they were both thinking—that if other survivors were gathered there, they could be exposing themselves to dangers worse than isolation.

They rounded a corner, approaching the heart of town. What had once been the bustling center, a place of daily routines and familiar faces, was now filled with a chilling quiet. But then, as they neared the square, they heard it—a faint, rhythmic sound, barely perceptible over the silence. It was coming from the direction of the flickering light.

Lydia's grip tightened on Eli's arm, her breathing quickening. "What... what is that?"

He shook his head, his eyes scanning the shadows, his senses on high alert. "Let's get closer. Just stay low."

They crept forward, stopping behind an overturned bench as they reached the edge of the square. The light they'd seen was coming from a makeshift bonfire in the center, its flames casting eerie shadows over the empty buildings. Around the fire, a small group of people huddled close, their faces pale, their eyes hollow. They were silent, some with heads bowed, others staring into the flames as though in a trance.

Eli and Lydia exchanged glances, both of them feeling a surge of hope. Survivors. People who had made it through the day without succumbing to the burning light. But as they looked closer, a chilling realization set in.

The people around the fire weren't moving. They stood like statues, frozen in place, their faces twisted in expressions of horror and pain, their skin stretched and cracked, as though the flames were the only thing holding them together. And then, with a sickening twist in his stomach, Eli understood.

They had been burned. Some of them beyond recognition, their skin blackened and cracked, their bodies rigid. They weren't truly alive; they were caught somewhere between life and death, their forms preserved in horror, as though the fire had somehow granted them a twisted form of survival.

Lydia gasped, her hand flying to her mouth as she took in the scene. "What... what did this to them?"

Eli shook his head, his heart racing as he pulled her back into the shadows. "I don't know. But we need to keep moving. Whatever's out here with us, we can't stay close to it."

But before they could retreat, a soft voice called out from the other side of the square, a voice thick with desperation.

"Help... please."

They froze, their eyes scanning the darkness, trying to locate the source of the voice. Then, just beyond the firelight, they saw him—a man crouched behind a stack of crates, his face pale, his body trembling. He looked young, his eyes wide with fear, his clothes torn and dirt-streaked.

"Are you... are you like us?" Lydia whispered, stepping forward despite Eli's warning grip on her arm.

The man nodded, his face twisted in terror as he glanced toward the charred figures around the fire. "Yes... I don't know what happened to them, but they just stood there. They walked into the light and... it took them."

Eli felt a chill crawl down his spine, a dark, sickening feeling settling over him. "We can't stay here. Whatever this is... it's dangerous."

The man scrambled to his feet, wincing as he clutched his arm, his skin raw and red, as though he'd barely escaped the sun's deadly reach. "Please. I don't know how to survive this. I don't even know if anyone else is alive."

"We'll figure something out," Eli replied, his voice steadier than he felt. "Come with us. We're heading out of town, trying to find shelter until we know it's safe."

The man nodded, his face filled with gratitude and fear. "My name's Connor. Thank you. I... I was starting to think I was the last one."

As they retreated from the square, keeping to the shadows, a faint sound filled the air behind them, a low, rhythmic crackling. They turned to see the charred figures around the fire beginning to move, their bodies shifting, their limbs jerking in strange, unnatural movements.

Connor stifled a scream, his eyes wide with horror. "What... what are they doing?"

Lydia pulled him along, her own face pale with terror. "I don't know, but we need to keep moving. Now."

The figures began to shuffle toward them, their bodies jerking, their heads tilted at odd angles, as though sensing the presence of something living, something untouched by the fire's deadly embrace. Eli and the others ran, their footsteps echoing through the empty streets, the shadows stretching around them, each one filled with a creeping sense of dread.

They didn't stop running until they reached the edge of town, a series of abandoned warehouses looming in the darkness. Eli led them to a small, secluded building, its windows shattered, its walls covered in peeling paint. It was far enough from the square to give them some breathing room, a place where they could gather their thoughts, plan their next move.

Inside, the air was cold, stale, but it felt safe compared to the horrors they'd left behind. They sat in a circle, their faces illuminated by a single flashlight, their breaths coming in short, shallow gasps.

Connor's voice broke the silence, his words shaky, filled with fear. "What... what was that? Those people... they were dead, but they were moving."

Eli took a deep breath, his mind racing, trying to make sense of the madness they'd witnessed. "I don't know, but whatever it is, it's tied to the sunlight. The moment it touched them, it... it did something to them, kept them half-alive, or maybe something worse."

Lydia shivered, her gaze fixed on the floor, her voice barely audible. "It's like the sun's turned against us, like it's something evil, something that doesn't care if it leaves us burned or broken."

The group fell silent, each one lost in their own thoughts, their own fears. The only sound was the faint rustling of the wind outside, a reminder that morning was only a few hours away, that the deadly sunlight would soon return.

Eli looked at the others, his face filled with determination, though his heart was heavy with dread. "We'll keep moving at night, stay hidden during the day. We don't know if this is happening everywhere, but we have to try and survive. We have to find answers, or maybe even a way out."

Connor nodded, though his face was pale, his expression haunted. "But what if there's nowhere safe? What if the sun keeps burning, and we're left running until there's nowhere left to hide?"

Eli clenched his fists, his mind racing with questions, with fears that gnawed at his mind. But he knew they couldn't give up, not now. "Then we keep moving, keep searching. There has to be something out there. Someone who knows what this is."

And as they sat in the darkness, the first faint light of dawn broke over the horizon, casting a dim, ominous glow over the town, filling the streets with shadows, with the echoes of the horrors they had witnessed.

They knew they had to survive the daylight. But as the sunlight crept over the town, they felt a terrible realization settling over them.

The daylight wasn't just killing them.

It was hunting them.

As the first rays of dawn slipped over the horizon, Eli, Lydia, and Connor huddled in the warehouse, every sliver of light blocked by makeshift barricades of crates and tarps. The warehouse was suffused with shadows, a temporary sanctuary against the horror waiting outside.

In the pale light of a single flashlight, they planned their next move. Eli's mind raced, piecing together fragments of what they'd heard on the radio, what little they'd seen outside, and the terrible transformation they'd witnessed in the town square.

"We need to figure out what's causing this," Eli whispered, his voice barely above a murmur, though the warehouse was empty but for their small group. "It's not natural... sunlight doesn't just turn on us overnight. This has to be something else, something deliberate."

Connor nodded, his face drawn with exhaustion and fear. "There was talk of strange sunspots a few days back," he said. "I heard it on the news... the announcer said they'd never seen activity like this before. Do you think it's related?"

Eli considered this, his mind struggling to connect the dots. "If it was just sunspots, there would have been some kind of warning, some sign. This... this was like a switch being flipped. As if someone—or something—wanted it to happen all at once."

Lydia shivered, her gaze fixed on the floor. “So what if it wasn’t an accident? What if this is an experiment, or some kind of weapon?”

The idea settled over them like a dark cloud, filling the air with a tangible weight of dread. None of them spoke, each lost in their own thoughts, in the horrifying possibility that someone could have done this intentionally. Finally, Eli broke the silence, his voice resolute.

“There’s one place that might have answers,” he said. “The Waverly Institute. They’ve been researching solar energy for years, some kind of government partnership... maybe they know what’s happening.”

Connor’s eyes widened. “You mean the lab on the outskirts of town? That place is locked down tight. They never let anyone near it.”

Eli nodded. “I know. But if there’s a chance they know what’s causing this... we have to go there. We can’t just sit here waiting to be burned alive. We have to find answers.”

Lydia looked at him, her eyes filled with fear and resolve. “Then we go tonight. We’ll move as soon as the sun sets.”

The hours crawled by, each minute a test of endurance, of patience as they waited for the sun to dip below the horizon. They passed the time in tense silence, listening to the faint sounds outside—an occasional crackle, like the distant snapping of bones, and the eerie quiet that followed.

At last, dusk fell, and they slipped out of the warehouse, moving cautiously through the streets, sticking to the deepest shadows. The Waverly Institute was located two miles out of town, isolated and surrounded by thick woods, its remote location intended to keep prying eyes at a distance. The journey was silent, the air filled with tension as they moved, each footstep carefully placed to avoid drawing attention.

The institute was a dark silhouette against the night sky, its walls tall and foreboding, its entrance flanked by high fences and security cameras. But tonight, the cameras were still, their lights dark, as though abandoned.

Eli took a deep breath, scanning the grounds. "The place looks deserted. But we can't let our guard down... anything could be inside."

They climbed over the fence, the metal cold and rough against their hands, landing silently on the other side. The building loomed before them, its windows dark, its doors partially open as though inviting them in.

Inside, the institute was eerily silent, the air thick with the smell of antiseptic and dust. They moved through the empty corridors, their footsteps echoing faintly, each shadow seeming to shift and move, casting distorted shapes across the walls.

They passed through a series of labs, each one filled with high-tech equipment and strange, unfamiliar machinery, though all of it seemed to have been abandoned in haste. Papers lay scattered on the floors, monitors flickered with static, and the faint hum of machinery was the only sound in the otherwise silent building.

At the end of the corridor, they found a large room, its walls lined with screens displaying images of the sun, each one showing different parts of its surface. Strange symbols were scrawled across the walls, and on a large whiteboard, they saw a single word written in red marker:

HELIOX.

"What is that?" Lydia whispered, her eyes fixed on the word.

Eli moved closer, studying the whiteboard, his mind racing. "Heliox... I think it's an energy project. I heard something about it once, some experimental technology to harness solar power directly from the sun's surface."

Connor glanced around, his face pale. "So this Heliox project... it's connected to the sun somehow. Do you think they did something to it? Triggered this... this burning effect?"

Eli ran his fingers over the diagrams and symbols scrawled across the board, his mind struggling to make sense of the complex equations and notes. "If they tampered with solar energy directly, it could have changed the sunlight's properties. Maybe they activated something they couldn't control."

Lydia's voice was barely a whisper, her face filled with horror. "So you're saying they... they turned the sun against us?"

A cold silence settled over them as they absorbed the implications, the possibility that the very thing meant to power the world could now be its undoing. But as they stood there, staring at the symbols, they heard a faint noise—a soft, mechanical whirring, coming from a darkened corner of the room.

They turned, their flashlights illuminating a glass enclosure. Inside, a figure slumped against the wall, its form barely visible in the dim light. As they drew closer, their breaths caught in their throats, horror creeping into their minds.

It was a person, but their skin was raw, burnt, peeling in layers, their eyes open and unseeing, as though caught in a permanent state of pain and terror. They seemed barely alive, their body held together by tubes and wires, their chest rising and falling in shallow, labored breaths.

The figure's lips parted, and a faint, raspy whisper filled the room.

"Stop... the light... it's... alive..."

Eli stepped back, his mind reeling, his stomach churning as the figure's words sank in. "The light... alive? What does that mean?"

The figure's eyes flickered, the life in them fading, but they managed a few final, strained words. "They... they made it conscious... connected it to us... too late... the sun... it wants us..."

Their voice trailed off, their body going limp, their breathing ceasing as the monitors around them flatlined. The silence that followed was suffocating, each of them struggling to process the figure's final words.

Lydia's face was pale, her hands shaking as she looked at Eli. "The sun... it's aware? How... how is that even possible?"

Eli shook his head, his mind racing with horror, with disbelief. "If they turned the sun into some kind of sentient energy, it could be reacting to us like a threat. Maybe it sees us as intruders, as something to eliminate."

Connor's face twisted in terror. "Then... it's not going to stop, is it? The sun will keep burning, keep melting everything it touches... until we're all gone."

Eli clenched his fists, a fierce determination filling him. "Not if we find a way to stop it. If they started this, then there has to be a way to reverse it."

They gathered what they could from the lab, taking notes, diagrams, anything that might hold a clue to reversing the Heliox project. As they made their way back through the empty corridors, the truth settled heavily over them.

The sun was no longer just a source of light and life. It had become a sentient force, an entity with a mind of its own, one that now viewed humanity as a threat to be eradicated.

As they stepped outside, the first hints of dawn tinged the sky, casting an ominous glow over the town. They hurried back to their shelter, a new fear gnawing at them, a realization that even the darkness might not be enough to protect them for long.

Because now, the sun wasn't just a danger in the daylight.

It was a predator. And it wouldn't stop until it had claimed every last one of them.

As dawn's first light crept across the horizon, Eli, Lydia, and Connor huddled in their makeshift shelter, the weight of their discovery pressing down on them. The sun wasn't just killing them. It was actively hunting them, a sentient force turned against humanity, born from the reckless ambitions of the Heliox project.

The sun's consciousness, if that's what it was, had one objective: erasing any living thing it touched.

Eli paced the room, his mind racing through the scraps of information they'd managed to gather. "There has to be a way to shut down Heliox," he muttered. "If the project made the sunlight dangerous, reversing it might be our only chance."

Lydia leaned against the wall, her face pale and drawn. "But where would we even start? The institute was abandoned, and all we found were bits and pieces. We're running on fumes."

Connor spoke up, his voice hesitant. "What about the notes we found? There was something in there about a failsafe—some kind of 'reset' option."

Eli nodded, his fingers rifling through the crumpled pages they'd taken from the institute. "Yeah, I saw it too. If I'm reading this right, there's a secondary facility nearby where the main controls for the Heliox project might still be intact."

The realization brought a flicker of hope, though it was tempered with dread. "It's further out in the foothills," Eli continued, pointing to a marked spot on the map. "We'd have to travel on foot. If we leave at sundown, we might make it by dawn, but..." His voice trailed off, and the grim reality settled over them.

They'd have to return during daylight.

Lydia's voice was barely above a whisper. "So we're risking everything, betting on the chance that this secondary facility has a way to reverse all of this?"

Eli looked at her, his face filled with determination. "It's a long shot, but it's better than waiting here to be burned alive."

Connor nodded, his face grim. "Then we'll go. Tonight."

When the sun finally set, casting the town into blessed darkness, they left the shelter and made their way through the abandoned streets. Waverly was eerily silent, the emptiness a constant reminder of what was at stake. The world they'd known was gone, replaced by something hostile, something otherworldly.

They walked in tense silence, each step filled with the knowledge that the dawn would bring deadly light, that time was against them. The sky above was clear, the stars scattered like distant beacons in the vast darkness, but the promise of sunrise loomed over them, a ticking clock.

The foothills lay just beyond the edge of town, their steep, jagged terrain made more treacherous by the darkness. They climbed, their bodies tense, their breaths heavy as they pushed forward, each one driven by the faint hope that they might reach the facility in time.

After hours of navigating the winding paths, they spotted it—a small, unassuming building nestled between two ridges, its silhouette barely visible against the starry sky. The facility was heavily fortified, its doors flanked by cameras and security keypads, though the systems appeared to have been abandoned like the rest of the Heliox project.

They slipped inside, their flashlights casting faint beams across sterile white walls, rows of darkened computer screens, and a massive control panel at the far end of the room. The equipment looked advanced, intricate, far more complex than anything they'd seen at the other lab.

Connor approached the control panel, his hands shaking as he scanned the unfamiliar controls. "So... what now?"

Eli flipped through the notes they'd gathered, scanning for any clue on how to initiate the failsafe. "The reset function... if this thing really exists, it should be in here somewhere." He found a marked section in the notes, tracing his finger over the instructions.

"Here it is," he muttered, his heart pounding. "It's a reboot sequence. We just need to initiate it, and it should send a shutdown signal to the Heliox project's core systems. With any luck, it'll turn off whatever signal's making the sun... hostile."

Lydia looked over his shoulder, her face filled with a mixture of hope and fear. "So we just... press a button, and it all stops?"

Eli took a deep breath, his fingers hovering over the controls. "I don't know if it's that simple. The instructions mention that the reboot will take a few hours to complete. We'll have to start it and then survive until it's done."

Connor's face went pale. "But that means... the sun will be up before it's finished."

Eli's jaw tightened. "Then we'll have to find a way to keep ourselves safe. There's no other option."

He activated the sequence, his hands shaking as he entered the final command. The computers whirred to life, their screens flickering, displaying lines of code and a countdown timer—*2 hours 54 minutes.*

The realization settled over them: the reset wouldn't be complete until well after sunrise.

They moved through the facility, searching for any kind of cover, any materials they could use to protect themselves. They found metal sheets, thick tarp, and lengths of sturdy wire. They worked quickly, rigging makeshift barricades around the control room, reinforcing every window, every possible entrance against the deadly sunlight.

As the countdown ticked down, they huddled together, each one aware of the impending dawn, the horror that would come with it. The silence was thick, each minute dragging on as they waited, their breaths shallow, their nerves frayed.

Lydia broke the silence, her voice barely a whisper. "Do you think this will work? Do you think we'll survive this?"

Eli took her hand, his grip firm. "We have to believe it will. It's all we have."

The first light of dawn crept over the horizon, casting a faint glow that seeped through every crack, every seam in their barricade. The light was soft, almost gentle, but it held the promise of death, a reminder of the terror that waited just beyond the walls.

As the sunlight grew, the temperature inside the facility began to rise, the heat pressing down on them, filling the air with a stifling, oppressive weight. They could hear the faint hum of the Heliox systems, the countdown ticking down, each second an eternity.

The walls creaked, the light seeping through tiny gaps, each beam a deadly threat. The metal sheets they'd used to cover the windows began to warm, glowing faintly as the sunlight pressed against them, as though trying to force its way inside.

Connor whimpered, his face pale, sweat dripping down his forehead as he stared at the glowing seams. "How... how long do we have?"

Eli glanced at the timer, his heart sinking. *1 hour 10 minutes.*

They huddled together, the heat intensifying, the air growing thick, almost unbearable. The light pressed against the metal, brightening, searing, each beam a promise of pain, of death. They could feel the sun's malevolent force pressing against them, a sentient hunger waiting to claim them.

Minutes passed, each one an agonizing stretch of fear, of tension. The walls groaned, the heat intensifying, filling the room with a suffocating weight that threatened to crush them.

And then, just as the countdown reached its final minutes, a deep, rumbling hum filled the air, the sound vibrating through the walls, shaking the facility.

The light dimmed, the heat receding, the oppressive force lifting as the Heliox system shut down, its final signals dissipating, the reset complete. The sunlight outside softened, returning to a gentle warmth, the deadly force that had hunted them gone.

They slumped against the walls, their bodies drenched in sweat, their minds reeling with relief, with disbelief. The horror was over. They had survived.

Days passed, and as the world adjusted to the sudden, unexplainable disaster, news trickled in from other towns, other survivors who'd managed to endure the horror of the burning sunlight. People spoke of loved ones lost, of entire cities devastated, of the sun's once-gentle light turned deadly.

Eli, Lydia, and Connor returned to Waverly, the town forever changed by the trauma they'd endured. Survivors shared their stories, their grief mingling with a sense of gratitude for the life they'd been spared, for the light that had returned to normal.

But as the weeks passed, rumors began to circulate—strange occurrences in other labs, unusual solar activity that couldn't be explained, brief, random flares that melted away anything they touched. It was as if the sun still held a trace of the Heliox project's consciousness, a reminder of the force that had once hunted them, of the nightmare they'd barely escaped.

And every now and then, as the sun rose over Waverly, they could feel it—a faint, watching presence, a reminder that the day might come when the sun would awaken again, a sentient predator waiting, watching, for the chance to rise once more.

The End

5
THE BAG LADY

The house on Maplewood Lane had been empty for years, its windows dark and cracked, its front steps sagging with rot. Children from the neighborhood dared each other to run up to its door on Halloween, to knock three times, to listen for any sounds from within.

They all knew the story. They'd heard the whispers about her—the Bag Lady.

She was more than a rumor. A friend's cousin had sworn he saw her in the attic window one night, her shadowed figure framed by moonlight, a bag tied over her head, her face hidden beneath a shroud of dark cloth. They called her the Bag Lady, though none of them had ever actually seen her face. No one knew why she lived up there, why she only appeared after dark, why people said you could hear her muttering to herself from the street. But there was one rule, a warning passed from kid to kid, whispered in hushed voices on playgrounds and in alleys: *don't look her in the eyes.*

Seventeen-year-old Sam didn't believe in ghost stories. He'd heard the tales of the Bag Lady all his life, how she lived in the abandoned house, how she could freeze you with a look. He thought it was nonsense, something kids made up to scare each other. But one chilly October night, his friends dared him to go inside the house, to find her and prove she wasn't real.

Sam glanced back at his friends, their faces pale, their eyes wide with a mix of fear and excitement. They huddled near the edge of the driveway, unwilling to get any closer.

"All you have to do is step inside and come back out," Jake said, a nervous grin on his face. "Easy, right?"

"Come on, it's just an empty house," Sam scoffed, though a prickle of dread crept up his spine. He turned, stepping up to the front porch, the wood creaking under his weight, the wind whispering through the cracked windows.

The door was ajar, hanging open as though inviting him in, daring him to enter.

With a deep breath, Sam pushed it open, stepping inside. The house was dark, the air thick with the scent of mildew and dust. The faint light from the street cast eerie shadows across the peeling wallpaper, illuminating faded photos on the walls, furniture draped in old sheets, forgotten remnants of lives long gone.

The silence was almost overwhelming, a heavy, suffocating quiet that filled the air, pressing down on him. He glanced back at the door, at the faint outline of his friends peering in from the street, their faces half-hidden in shadows.

"See?" he called, his voice echoing through the empty halls. "Nothing here!"

But as he turned to leave, he heard it—a faint, shuffling sound, coming from above, from the attic.

He froze, his heart pounding, his breath catching in his throat. The sound was soft, almost like footsteps, moving slowly, deliberately, as though someone were pacing back and forth, just above him. He took a step back, his mind racing, but curiosity tugged at him, urging him forward, pulling him deeper into the house.

Ignoring the dread pooling in his stomach, he moved toward the staircase, his footsteps soft, barely a whisper against the floorboards. He placed one foot on the first step, then another, the creak of the wood echoing through the silence, each step bringing him closer to the attic, to the source of the sound.

The air grew colder as he climbed, each step filling him with a sense of foreboding, a chill that seeped into his bones, that settled in his chest, tightening around his heart. The attic door loomed above him, slightly ajar, a sliver of darkness visible through the crack.

With a deep breath, he pushed the door open, stepping into the attic. The room was dark, filled with boxes and old furniture, draped in sheets, shadows stretching across the floor, twisting into strange shapes that seemed to shift and move. The only light came from a small, dirty window at the far end of the room, casting a faint glow over the space.

And then he saw her.

She was standing in the corner, her back turned to him, her body hunched, her head covered by a large, dark bag, tied tightly around her neck. Her clothes were tattered, hanging loosely from her thin frame, her hands hidden in the folds of fabric.

Sam's breath hitched, his body frozen, his mind racing. She was real. The Bag Lady was real.

"Hello?" he whispered, his voice barely audible.

She didn't respond, didn't move, her form still, almost statuesque, her head tilted slightly, as though listening, waiting. And then, slowly, she began to turn.

Sam's heart pounded, his instincts screaming at him to run, to leave, but he couldn't move, his feet rooted to the spot as he watched her turn, as he saw the faint outline of her face beneath the bag, hidden in shadow.

Her movements were slow, deliberate, her head tilting to one side, her body twisting as she faced him. And then, she looked up, her eyes meeting his through the thin fabric of the bag, her gaze piercing, cold, filled with something dark, something that sent chills racing down his spine.

He tried to move, to run, but his body was frozen, paralyzed, his muscles locked in place. He couldn't look away, couldn't break the gaze, couldn't even blink as her eyes held him, as her stare bore into him, filling him with a sense of dread, of horror that he couldn't escape.

The Bag Lady's eyes seemed to shimmer, to glow beneath the bag, her gaze sharp, unyielding, as though she could see straight through him, into the deepest parts of his soul. Her lips parted, and she spoke, her voice low, raspy, a sound that filled the air, that echoed through the room, wrapping around him like a shroud.

"You came here... uninvited," she murmured, her words slow, deliberate, each one filled with a quiet menace. "You looked... you shouldn't have looked."

Sam's heart pounded, his mind screaming at him to run, to fight, but he was trapped, frozen in place, held by her gaze, by the power that radiated from her eyes, a force he couldn't resist, couldn't escape.

Her hand reached out, bony fingers emerging from the folds of her sleeves, stretching toward him, inching closer, closer, until they were just inches from his face, from his eyes. He could feel the chill radiating from her touch, a cold that seeped into his skin, that froze him to the core.

And then, in a single, swift movement, she reached up, gripping the edges of the bag over her head, pulling it back, revealing her face.

Sam's heart stopped, his mind reeling, as he saw her eyes, her face, twisted, distorted, her gaze unyielding, her mouth stretched into a dark, toothless grin, a smile that seemed to stretch across her entire face, her eyes empty, hollow, filled with a darkness that defied understanding.

He tried to scream, but no sound escaped his lips. He was frozen, trapped in her gaze, his mind overwhelmed, his body numb, as though he were sinking into a void, a darkness that wrapped around him, that pulled him deeper, deeper, until he could feel nothing, hear nothing, see nothing but her eyes.

And then, everything went black.

The next morning, Sam's friends returned to the house, their laughter fading as they saw that he hadn't come out, hadn't returned. They stood in silence, staring at the house, their faces filled with fear, with a terrible, gnawing dread.

They called his name, their voices echoing through the empty halls, but there was no answer, no sound, only the faint, eerie silence that filled the house, that pressed down on them, filling them with a sense of unease, of horror.

As they searched, one of them glanced up at the attic window, his breath catching in his throat as he saw something—a figure, half-hidden in the shadows, her head covered by a dark bag, her eyes fixed on him, watching, waiting.

He froze, his body tense, his heart pounding as he stared back, as he felt her gaze, as he felt the chill settling over him, wrapping around him like a shroud.

And then, she raised her hand, a slow, deliberate wave, a gesture filled with a dark, silent promise.

He stumbled back, his face pale, his mind racing, as he turned to his friends, his voice trembling.

"Sam's... he's gone. And she... she's still there."

The Bag Lady watched them from the window, her figure barely visible, her gaze piercing, unyielding, her presence a shadow that lingered, that haunted, a reminder that the house on Maplewood Lane was not empty, that it held secrets, that it held a darkness that would never fade.

And as the children fled, her gaze followed them, a silent warning, a promise that they would never be safe, that her eyes would always find them, that her darkness would always reach them.

The Bag Lady was real.

And she was waiting.

Word of Sam's disappearance spread quickly through the neighborhood, whispers of the Bag Lady growing more insistent, more chilling. Some said Sam had run away, tired of the small-town life. But his friends knew the truth—they'd seen her in the attic window, that shadowed figure staring down at them, the Bag Lady's hand lifting in that slow, ominous wave. Since that day, none of them could sleep, haunted by nightmares of her gaze, of Sam's frozen expression in their minds, locked in horror.

Jake couldn't shake the image of her from his mind. He'd been the last one to see her face, even if only from a distance, and every time he closed his eyes, he felt her watching, felt that suffocating cold settle over him, like she was still there, her eyes locked on him. But as scared as he was, he couldn't let it go. He needed answers. He had to know what had happened to Sam.

That evening, Jake sat on his bed, clutching his phone, scrolling through articles about the house on Maplewood

Lane, about disappearances tied to it from years ago, decades even. But no one had documented anything substantial. There were only vague accounts of "odd events," an urban legend about a woman who "froze people with a glance." But as he scrolled further, his screen flickered, and a single phrase caught his eye: *the curse of the Bag Lady.*

The article mentioned rumors from decades ago, stories that claimed a woman had once lived in the house—an outcast, shunned by the town, who wore a bag over her head to hide from the world. They said she had died alone, cursed to remain in the house forever, her gaze twisted into something dark, something deadly. And anyone who looked her in the eyes would be trapped, frozen in place, as her spirit drained them.

Jake's heart pounded as he read, the words filling him with a growing sense of dread. He couldn't shake the image of Sam standing in the attic, locked in that twisted gaze. And he knew what he had to do.

That night, he slipped out of his house, the cool autumn air biting at his skin as he made his way toward Maplewood Lane. He tried to keep his breathing steady, his footsteps silent, but every rustle of leaves, every whisper of wind sent chills racing down his spine. He felt as though the shadows themselves were alive, shifting, watching, waiting.

The house loomed before him, its windows dark, the air around it filled with an unnatural stillness. He paused at the edge of the yard, his heart pounding, his mind racing with fear, but he forced himself to move forward, to step up onto the rotting porch.

"Sam," he whispered, his voice barely audible, though he knew Sam couldn't hear him, wouldn't answer. He took a deep breath, his hand reaching for the doorknob, his fingers trembling as he pushed it open, stepping inside.

The house was dark, the silence heavy, pressing down on him, filling the air with a sense of foreboding. He moved slowly, his footsteps echoing through the empty halls, his flashlight casting long shadows that twisted and shifted with each step. The stairs to the attic loomed before him, their wood warped and creaking, leading up into the darkness, to where he knew she was waiting.

As he climbed, a faint sound reached his ears—a soft, whispering voice, drifting through the silence, filling the air with a chill that seeped into his bones. It was a voice unlike anything he'd ever heard, a rasping, echoing sound that seemed to come from everywhere at once.

"Come closer..."

He stopped, his heart pounding, his breath hitching as the voice filled the air, as though it were wrapped around him, pulling him forward, urging him closer to the attic, to the room where she waited. Every instinct screamed at him to turn back, to run, but he was frozen, unable to look away, unable to resist the pull of her voice.

With each step, the voice grew louder, filling his mind, drowning out everything else. He reached the attic door, his hand trembling as he gripped the handle, pushing it open, stepping inside.

The room was dark, filled with shadows that seemed to pulse and breathe, the only light coming from a small, broken window at the far end. And there, in the corner, he saw her.

She was hunched over, her back turned to him, her head covered by the bag, her body wrapped in tattered, dark clothing that draped over her frame, shrouding her in darkness. She didn't move, didn't make a sound, but he could feel her presence, heavy and cold, pressing down on him, filling him with a dread he couldn't shake.

"Sam?" he whispered, his voice trembling, barely audible.

And then, slowly, she turned.

Her movements were slow, deliberate, her head tilting to one side, her body twisting as she faced him, her bag-covered face turning toward him, her gaze piercing, unyielding, as though she could see straight through him, into the deepest parts of his soul.

Jake tried to look away, tried to move, but he was frozen, trapped in her gaze, unable to look away, unable to escape. Her eyes seemed to burn through the fabric of the bag, two dark, empty voids that filled him with a horror he couldn't understand, a fear that went beyond anything he'd ever felt.

"Why have you come here?" she whispered, her voice low, echoing, a sound that wrapped around him, that pulled him deeper into the darkness, into the cold, suffocating void that radiated from her gaze.

He couldn't speak, couldn't breathe, his body numb, his mind trapped, frozen, as her gaze held him, as her eyes bore into him, filling him with a sense of dread, of terror that he couldn't escape.

The Bag Lady took a step forward, her bony fingers emerging from the folds of her sleeves, reaching toward him, inching closer, closer, until they were just inches from his face. He could feel the chill radiating from her touch, a cold that seeped into his skin, that froze him to the core.

"You wanted to see him?" she murmured, her voice barely a whisper. "Then look."

She lifted her hand, pointing to the far corner of the attic, where the shadows shifted, revealing a figure—Sam, standing motionless, his eyes wide, his face pale, frozen in horror. His body was stiff, his limbs locked, his expression twisted in a silent scream, as though he'd been trapped in that moment of terror, unable to move, unable to escape.

Jake's mind reeled, his heart pounding as he realized the truth, as he understood what had happened to Sam, what would happen to him. He was trapped, frozen, held by her gaze, by the power that radiated from her eyes, a force that defied understanding, that held him in place, filling him with a terror that he couldn't escape.

The Bag Lady's face twisted into a smile, her eyes gleaming beneath the bag, her expression filled with a dark, twisted satisfaction.

"You came to find him," she whispered, her voice soft, mocking. "Now... you'll join him."

Her gaze held him, unyielding, her eyes piercing, cold, as his vision blurred, as the world faded to black, his body numb, frozen, trapped in the darkness, a darkness that stretched on forever, that held him, that consumed him, as though he were sinking into a void, a void filled with her eyes, her voice, her gaze.

And then, everything went silent.

By morning, rumors of Jake's disappearance spread through the town, whispers of the Bag Lady growing louder, more insistent. His friends spoke in hushed voices, their faces pale, filled with a growing sense of dread, a fear that settled over them like a dark cloud.

They'd all known the stories, the warnings, the tales of her cursed gaze, but they'd never believed, never thought it was real. But now, with both Sam and Jake gone, the truth settled over them, an undeniable horror that filled them with a terror they couldn't shake.

One by one, they began to see her, in the attic window, her shadowed figure barely visible, her eyes fixed on them, watching, waiting. And as night fell over the town, they felt her presence, a dark, unyielding force that filled the air, that whispered to them, calling them, drawing them closer, pulling them into the darkness.

The Bag Lady was real.

And she was watching.

The town was changing. Since the disappearances of Sam and Jake, an unsettling atmosphere had taken hold, a fear that seeped into every street, every home. Parents warned their children to stay indoors after dark. Neighbors glanced nervously at each other, exchanging murmurs of unease, as though saying her name aloud might summon her.

People claimed to see her everywhere. A faint shadow in the attic window, a glimpse of dark fabric moving through the trees, a faint voice drifting on the wind, low and raspy, as though calling to them. But the sightings were brief, fleeting, as if the Bag Lady was toying with them, haunting them from the edge of sight.

Rumors spread like wildfire. Some said she was a ghost, a restless spirit bound to the house. Others whispered that she was a curse brought on by the house itself, an ancient evil lurking in the walls. But one thing was certain: no one who went into the house ever came back.

The final straw came one chilly evening when Mrs. Halverson, the elderly woman who lived across the street from the Maplewood house, rushed into the town's small library, her face pale, her eyes wide with terror. She claimed to have seen the Bag Lady outside her window, standing on the sidewalk, watching her, her bag-covered face turned upward, her dark, unblinking gaze fixed on Mrs. Halverson's window.

"I saw her," she whispered, her voice shaking, her hands trembling. "She was just... standing there. Staring, as if she could see right through me."

Word of Mrs. Halverson's sighting spread through the town, each person who heard it feeling a cold dread settle over them. That night, the town council called an emergency meeting in the old church, the only place large enough to fit the concerned crowd that gathered, each person filled with a growing sense of fear.

Mayor Whelan, a thin, balding man with worry lines etched deep into his face, stood at the front of the room, his hands clenched tightly around a crumpled sheet of paper, his voice trembling as he addressed the crowd.

"We... we all know why we're here," he began, his gaze sweeping over the anxious faces before him. "Sam and Jake are still missing. We've heard the rumors, the stories about... about the woman in the Maplewood house. And while I don't personally believe in ghosts, we can't ignore what's been happening."

An uncomfortable murmur rippled through the crowd, people exchanging glances, fear flickering in their eyes.

"Something has to be done," called out a voice from the back of the room, an older man with a face set in grim determination. "This house has been haunting us for too long. Whatever's inside... it's taken our kids. We can't just sit back and do nothing."

Mayor Whelan nodded, his expression somber. "I agree. We need answers. Tomorrow night, I'm organizing a search team. We'll go into the house and find out once and for all what's inside."

The room fell silent, each person absorbing the weight of his words, the knowledge that they would confront the thing that had haunted their town for years.

Mrs. Halverson stood, her voice trembling. "But... but what if she's real? What if... if she's waiting for us?"

The mayor's jaw tightened, his face pale, his eyes filled with fear. "Then we'll face her. Together."

The following night, as the sun dipped below the horizon, the town gathered at the edge of Maplewood Lane. The house loomed before them, its windows dark, its walls weathered, draped in shadows. Mayor Whelan led the small group of volunteers, their faces tense, their bodies rigid as they stood at the gate, each one feeling the weight of what they were about to face.

"Let's get this over with," the mayor said, his voice barely more than a whisper.

They moved toward the house, their flashlights casting thin beams through the darkness, illuminating the cracked walls, the peeling paint, the broken windows that seemed to watch them as they approached. The air was thick with tension, each step filling them with a growing sense of dread.

As they reached the porch, the wood creaking beneath their feet, they hesitated, glancing at each other, their faces pale, their eyes wide with fear.

And then, slowly, the door opened, swinging inward with a soft, groaning sound, as though the house were inviting them inside, daring them to enter.

Mayor Whelan stepped forward, his flashlight trembling in his hand as he crossed the threshold, the others following close behind. The air was cold, thick with the scent of mildew and dust, the faint sound of whispers drifting through the darkness, filling the silence, wrapping around them like a shroud.

They moved through the house, their flashlights illuminating empty rooms filled with old furniture, faded photographs on the walls, relics of lives long forgotten. But as they reached the staircase, they stopped, their bodies tense, their breaths shallow as they heard it—a faint, shuffling sound, coming from above, from the attic.

Each one felt the weight of her presence pressing down on them, a cold, heavy dread that seeped into their bones, that filled them with a terror they couldn't shake. They exchanged glances, each one reluctant, but Mayor Whelan squared his shoulders, his jaw set in determination.

"We came here to find answers," he said, his voice steady, though his face was pale. "We're not leaving until we know what's up there."

They climbed the stairs, each step slow, deliberate, the creak of the wood echoing through the silence, each sound filling them with dread, with a fear that pressed down on them like a heavy weight.

As they reached the attic door, they stopped, their flashlights casting shadows across the dark, worn wood, each one feeling the cold, oppressive presence pressing against them, filling the air, wrapping around them.

Mayor Whelan took a deep breath, his hand trembling as he reached for the doorknob, twisting it, pushing the door open.

The attic was dark, filled with shadows that seemed to pulse, to breathe, the only light coming from a small, broken window at the far end of the room. And there, in the corner, they saw her.

She was hunched over, her back turned to them, her head covered by the bag, her body wrapped in dark, tattered clothing that draped over her frame, her hands folded in her lap. She didn't move, didn't make a sound, but they could feel her presence, cold and unyielding, filling the room, pressing down on them, filling them with a horror that went beyond anything they'd ever felt.

Mayor Whelan raised his flashlight, his voice barely a whisper. "Ma'am... we don't mean any harm. We just want to know what happened to those boys."

For a moment, she remained still, her form shrouded in shadow, her head tilted downward, her face hidden beneath the bag. But then, slowly, she began to turn.

Her movements were slow, deliberate, each motion filled with a strange grace, a quiet menace that held them frozen, trapped in place, unable to move, unable to look away.

She turned to face them, her bag-covered head tilting upward, her gaze piercing, cold, as though she could see straight through them, into their souls. And then, she lifted her hands, reaching for the edges of the bag, pulling it back, revealing her face.

The volunteers froze, their bodies locked in place, their minds reeling with horror as they saw her eyes—dark, hollow voids that seemed to pull them in, that held them, trapped, paralyzed.

Her gaze pierced each of them, her lips parting in a slow, toothless smile, her face twisted, distorted, filled with a darkness that defied understanding.

One by one, they felt their bodies go numb, their muscles locking, their breath caught in their throats as her gaze held them, as her eyes filled them with a horror that consumed them, that pulled them deeper, deeper into the void.

And then, everything went black.

By morning, the townspeople found the volunteers, each one frozen in place, their bodies locked in expressions of terror, their faces pale, their eyes wide, staring into the distance, as though caught in a moment of unimaginable horror.

They were unresponsive, unable to speak, to move, as though they'd been drained, as though their souls had been trapped in that house, held by her gaze, by the power that lingered in the attic.

And as the town gathered, as they stared at the volunteers' frozen forms, a cold dread settled over them, a knowledge that filled them with a terror they couldn't escape.

The Bag Lady was real.

And now, she had more to keep her company.

The town of Maplewood fell into a grim silence in the days following the failed search. The volunteers, those brave souls who had entered the Bag Lady's house, now lay in the town's small hospital, their bodies locked in a frozen state of terror. Eyes wide, lips parted in silent screams, they remained completely unresponsive, as if they were statues—trapped, haunted relics of their encounter. The doctors, baffled, could only watch over them in horror, as their vital signs remained steady but unchanging.

Rumors of the Bag Lady's curse spread faster than the morning papers. Parents forbade their children from going near the house, friends exchanged whispered theories, and even the most skeptical grew uneasy. In the stillness of night, residents claimed they could hear faint, raspy whispers, drifting through the streets, calling their names, beckoning them to come closer.

Pastor Timothy was among the few people who refused to give in to the spreading terror. A young, compassionate man who'd moved to Maplewood only recently, he couldn't believe that a single house—an old, decrepit building—

could hold so much fear over the townsfolk. The story of the Bag Lady seemed, to him, like an old tale spun wildly out of control.

But when he visited the hospital and saw the look of frozen horror on the faces of those volunteers, he felt something new. This was no ordinary fright; this was a fear that ran deeper, something primal. Determined to find a solution, he gathered a small group of people willing to face the Bag Lady once again, this time with a plan: they would consecrate the house, banish whatever spirit lingered there, and, they hoped, free their friends from the curse.

That evening, Pastor Timothy, accompanied by two locals—Mr. Donovan, a retired schoolteacher, and Sarah, a no-nonsense nurse from the hospital—prepared to confront the Bag Lady. Armed with candles, holy water, and old purification salts from the church, they approached the house with cautious determination.

"Remember," Pastor Timothy whispered as they reached the doorstep, "we stick together. Don't look directly at her face. We've been warned enough—keep your eyes low, and trust that we're here for the right reasons."

The others nodded, though their faces were pale, each one fighting a rising dread.

They stepped inside, the air thick with the familiar, oppressive silence. Shadows hung heavily over every corner, the rooms filled with stale air and a lingering scent of decay. They moved slowly, their flashlights flickering across the walls, the beams catching dust motes that drifted lazily in the heavy air.

They passed through the downstairs rooms, murmuring prayers, sprinkling holy water, marking the doorframes with salt. Pastor Timothy's voice was steady, his presence grounding, but as they climbed the stairs to the attic, the silence grew thicker, heavier, each step a struggle against the oppressive atmosphere that seemed to cling to them.

At the top of the stairs, they paused, each of them feeling a cold chill that seeped into their bones, a dread that whispered of things unseen, of horrors waiting in the darkness. The attic door stood before them, slightly ajar, as though inviting them in, daring them to step forward.

Pastor Timothy took a deep breath, his hand steady as he pushed the door open, his flashlight illuminating the dusty, cluttered space. The room was empty, save for the old furniture covered in sheets, the dusty boxes piled in the corner, and the faint, lingering scent of something rotten.

And then they saw her.

The Bag Lady stood in the far corner, her back turned to them, her hunched form shrouded in dark fabric, her head covered by the infamous bag, tied tightly around her neck. She was still, unmoving, but the weight of her presence filled the room, pressing down on them, a cold, unyielding force that seeped into their skin, into their minds.

Pastor Timothy began to speak, his voice steady, reciting an ancient prayer of exorcism, his words echoing through the silence, filling the room with a strange, pulsing energy.

But as he spoke, she began to turn.

Her movements were slow, deliberate, each motion filled with an unnatural grace, her head tilting to one side, her body twisting as she faced them. Her bag-covered face seemed to radiate a dark, sinister energy, an invisible force that held them frozen, unable to look away.

"Do not look," Pastor Timothy whispered, his voice trembling as he stared at the floor, fighting against the pull of her gaze. "Don't meet her eyes."

Mr. Donovan and Sarah obeyed, their eyes fixed firmly on the floor, their bodies tense, their breaths shallow, but the Bag Lady's presence filled the room, pressing against them, filling them with a dread that went beyond fear, a terror that gnawed at their minds, their souls.

Her voice broke the silence, a low, raspy whisper that seemed to seep into their bones, chilling them to the core. "You come here... uninvited," she murmured, her words echoing through the room. "You think you can rid me of my home?"

Pastor Timothy continued his prayer, his voice trembling but unwavering. "In the name of all that is holy, I command you to leave this place, to release your hold on those you have taken."

She laughed, a low, hollow sound that filled the air, her head tilting as though in amusement. "You cannot command me," she whispered, her voice soft, mocking. "This place is mine. They are mine."

Her hands lifted, pale and bony, reaching for the edges of the bag, her fingers curling around the fabric, pulling it back. Pastor Timothy clenched his eyes shut, his breath hitching, as he sensed the change in the room, as he felt the weight of her gaze pressing down on him, filling him with a terror he couldn't escape.

Sarah's voice was a faint, trembling whisper. "Pastor... we need to leave."

But it was too late.

The Bag Lady pulled the bag from her head, revealing her face—a face twisted, distorted, hollow eyes fixed on them, dark voids that seemed to pull them in, to hold them, freezing them in place, trapping them in her gaze. Mr. Donovan gasped, his body going rigid, his mouth open in a silent scream as her eyes met his, as her gaze held him, locked him in place.

Pastor Timothy felt the chill creep over him, the numbness settling into his bones, his voice faltering as he struggled to look away, to break free from her gaze. But her eyes held him, unyielding, filling him with a darkness that seeped into his mind, drowning him in a sea of fear, of despair.

The Bag Lady smiled, a slow, twisted smile that stretched across her face, her hollow eyes gleaming with satisfaction, with a dark, malevolent joy.

"You cannot take what belongs to me," she whispered, her voice soft, final. "This place... these souls... they are mine."

And then, everything went black.

When the townspeople found Pastor Timothy, Mr. Donovan, and Sarah the next morning, they were standing motionless in the attic, their faces frozen in terror, their eyes wide, staring into the darkness, trapped in that same, horrific state as the others who had entered the house before them.

News of the failed exorcism spread, each new detail adding to the growing sense of horror that filled the town. People avoided the street altogether, refusing to go near the house, even in broad daylight. Schools closed early, businesses shuttered, and an unspoken rule fell over Maplewood: stay away from the Bag Lady's house.

But the sightings continued. Children claimed to see her wandering the streets at night, her dark figure moving silently, her eyes fixed on them, watching, waiting. Others swore they heard her whispers drifting through the town, calling their names, filling the air with an eerie, oppressive presence that lingered long after the sun rose.

Some families left town, unwilling to stay in a place haunted by such a dark, malevolent force. Others huddled in their homes, praying, hoping that she wouldn't come for them, that they wouldn't be the next to disappear.

And in the heart of Maplewood, the Bag Lady watched from her window, her hollow eyes fixed on the town, her gaze unyielding, her presence a constant reminder of the darkness that lingered, that haunted every street, every home.

As night fell over the town, the whispers grew louder, filling the air, a haunting echo that drifted through the darkness, a reminder that she was still there, waiting, watching, her curse spreading like a shadow over Maplewood.

The Bag Lady had claimed her home, her souls, and she wasn't finished.

And as the people of Maplewood lay awake in their beds, dreading the sound of footsteps outside, the faint whisper of her voice, they knew one thing for certain.

The Bag Lady was real.

And she would never leave.

The terror gripping Maplewood was palpable, a thick, unseen presence that seeped into the very air. People spoke in hushed tones, casting nervous glances over their shoulders, avoiding the house on Maplewood Lane like the plague. But no matter how hard they tried, they couldn't escape the Bag Lady. She lingered in every darkened window, every creak of the floorboards at night, every chill that prickled the skin unexpectedly.

Desperation grew. Some residents pleaded with the town council to demolish the house, believing that destroying it might somehow release her hold over them. But each time they sent contractors or city workers, they would return, shaken and pale, claiming the house felt "wrong," as though it were somehow pushing them away, refusing to let them enter.

Amid the rising fear, there was one person who believed she might have answers: Mara Graves, an elderly woman who had lived in Maplewood for nearly eighty years. She was rarely seen outside her home these days, her body weakened by age, but she was known for her vast knowledge of the town's history—and for her strange connection to the Bag Lady's past.

When rumors spread that Mara might know something, a small group of the remaining residents gathered enough courage to approach her. They visited her on a quiet afternoon, the sky overcast, the town blanketed in a subdued, eerie silence. They found her sitting by the window, staring out at the street with a knowing look, her hands folded in her lap.

"You've come about her, haven't you?" Mara said, her voice soft, almost resigned.

The group exchanged wary glances, nodding.

Mara sighed, her gaze distant, her voice tinged with sorrow. "They called her Ethel Baker. But long before she became the Bag Lady, she was just a girl, lost and broken by this town."

According to Mara, Ethel had once been a resident of Maplewood, but her life had been filled with hardship. Her family was poor, her father a drifter and her mother frail. Ethel was ridiculed in school, mocked by her peers, whispered about by the townsfolk who claimed her family was cursed. She was lonely, withdrawn, a shadow in the background of the town's bustling life.

As a teenager, she fell in love with a young man, the son of a well-to-do family. But when his parents discovered their relationship, they forbade him from seeing her, and rumors spread quickly that she had "bewitched" him. People began to avoid her, crossing the street whenever she walked by, muttering about her in the church pews, casting her out like an unwelcome spirit.

Her life spiraled into despair. Isolated, her heart hardened, and over time, her presence in Maplewood became something of a ghost story. Children claimed they saw her lingering on street corners, muttering to herself, her eyes hollow and dark. Eventually, she moved into the house on Maplewood Lane, sealing herself away from the world.

But the final breaking point came one winter night when a group of townsfolk, fed up with her "haunting" presence, broke into her home. They dragged her out, shouting curses, calling her a witch. In their blind fury, they tied a bag over her head, leaving her stranded, humiliated, in the street as the townspeople watched.

Mara's voice trembled as she spoke, her eyes glistening with tears. "The next morning, Ethel was gone. No one saw her again. Some said she left town, others that she'd taken her own life. But the truth was far darker. She died that night, trapped by the hate and cruelty of those who had cast her out."

The room fell silent, the horror of Ethel's fate settling over them like a dark cloud. Mara's gaze turned hard, her voice a low whisper. "When she died, her spirit became bound to the house. She was filled with anger, with sorrow... with the darkness that the town had forced upon her. And now, her curse lingers, her spirit bound to the house, drawing in anyone foolish enough to enter."

One of the townsfolk, a young man named Peter, cleared his throat, his face pale. "But... is there a way to break it? To free her? So she'll stop... taking people?"

Mara's gaze shifted, her eyes filled with a mix of hope and sorrow. "There is one way. Her spirit seeks peace, to be remembered not as the monster they made her into, but as the girl she once was. If you can find her belongings—the things that meant something to her—and return them to the house with respect, with forgiveness, you may be able to appease her."

Determined to end the curse, a few brave souls from Maplewood set out to locate Ethel's belongings. Mara provided them with clues, mentioning that Ethel had kept a small diary, her most cherished possession, filled with poetry and thoughts she'd never shared with anyone. She'd also owned a locket, given to her by her mother, a delicate piece with a faded photograph inside.

The group split up, searching abandoned buildings, the town's archives, and old storage rooms. Days passed, and tensions grew as more people began to see the Bag Lady's dark figure in their windows, standing silently in the streets, her gaze unblinking, as if waiting.

Finally, after countless hours of searching, they found the diary in an old box in the town library, hidden among dusty books and forgotten papers. The locket took longer, but they eventually located it in a box of belongings left in an old storage closet of the town's church.

With these items in hand, the group prepared to return to the house, hopeful that this would be enough to end the Bag Lady's haunting.

On a moonless night, a small group gathered outside the house, Mara among them, her hands steady despite the gravity of what they were about to attempt. She directed them on how to proceed: place the diary and the locket in the attic, where Ethel had spent her last days, and light a candle for her, offering her the peace she had been denied.

They moved through the house, their steps soft, respectful, each one feeling the weight of her story, of her sorrow. As they reached the attic, they arranged the items carefully on the floor, placing the diary beside the locket, lighting a candle to honor her memory.

Mara's voice trembled as she spoke, addressing the Bag Lady directly. "Ethel... we know what happened to you. We're sorry. You didn't deserve the hate, the fear. Please, find peace."

A hush fell over the room, the air thick with anticipation, with a sense of quiet that felt almost sacred. The candle flickered, casting long shadows over the walls, illuminating the space with a soft, warm glow.

And then, in the corner of the attic, a figure appeared.

The Bag Lady stood there, her head still covered by the bag, her body hunched, her presence filling the room. But something had changed. Her form seemed less solid, almost ethereal, her posture less threatening, her gaze softer. She moved forward, reaching out to the items they had left for her, her hand trembling as she touched the locket, as she traced her fingers over the worn cover of her diary.

For a moment, the room was silent, the air filled with a quiet reverence as the townsfolk watched, their hearts pounding, their breaths shallow.

And then, slowly, she lifted her head, her hollow eyes meeting theirs. There was no malice in her gaze, only sorrow, a deep, aching sadness that filled the room, that seeped into their hearts, as though she were sharing her pain, her suffering, for the first time.

She turned, her form dissolving into shadows, the darkness lifting, dissipating, as though her spirit were finally at peace, finally freed from the chains that had bound her to the house.

The candle flickered one last time, then went out, leaving them in darkness, a silence that felt different—lighter, almost peaceful.

In the days that followed, the Bag Lady's presence faded from Maplewood. The sightings stopped, the whispers quieted, and the house on Maplewood Lane became just another empty building, no longer haunted by the shadows of the past.

People spoke of Ethel with compassion, remembering her not as a ghost, but as a girl lost to the cruelty of a fearful town. They honored her memory, leaving flowers at the house, ensuring she was never forgotten.

And as the years passed, the legend of the Bag Lady faded, her story becoming part of the town's history, a reminder of the darkness that can be born of hatred, and the peace that comes from understanding, from forgiveness.

The house remained empty, but it was no longer feared. And Ethel, the girl who had once been known as the Bag Lady, was finally at rest.

The End

6
THE FACE MELTERS

The quiet suburban neighborhood of Cedar Grove was cloaked in a blanket of calm, the warm, orange glow of house lights flickering behind closed curtains as families gathered for evening meals. The air was thick with the smell of roasting meats, simmering sauces, and the faint clink of dishes being set. It was an unremarkable night, and in the Whitmore household, a dozen guests sat around a long dining table, sharing laughter and stories over an elaborate spread of food.

Margaret Whitmore, the hostess, was in her element. She loved hosting these gatherings—the wine, the ambiance, the chance to share her culinary creations. She hovered at the head of the table, beaming with pride as she poured another round of wine into the guests' glasses, her eyes gleaming with satisfaction.

"To good friends, good food, and many more nights like this!" Margaret toasted, lifting her glass. The guests followed suit, smiling and clinking glasses as they joined in her cheer.

Plates were filled, and conversation flowed easily, laughter and warmth filling the air as everyone dug in, savoring the delicate flavors. Frank Russell, a real estate agent with a quick wit and an appetite to match, took a hearty bite of the roast. He smacked his lips in appreciation, nudging his wife, Diane.

"Now *this* is what I call a meal," Frank said, wiping his mouth. "Margaret, you've really outdone yourself."

Margaret blushed, waving off the compliment as she took her seat. "Oh, please! It's nothing. I'm just glad you're all enjoying it."

But just as she settled in, a peculiar silence fell over the table. Across from her, Diane had stopped chewing, her fork hovering mid-air as her face twisted in a strange expression. Her eyes darted around the table, confused, her fingers clutching the edge of her napkin.

"Is... is anyone else feeling a little... off?" Diane murmured, a tremor in her voice.

Several guests paused, glancing at each other. Margaret felt her heart skip a beat. "Diane, what do you mean? Are you okay?"

Diane didn't answer. Instead, she reached up, touching her cheek, her fingers coming away with a strange, viscous substance. She stared at her hand, her eyes widening as she registered the sticky, red substance glistening on her fingertips. A low gasp escaped her lips as she touched her face again, feeling something wet and soft—*too* soft.

"Frank...?" she whispered, her voice trembling. "Something's wrong."

Frank's eyes went wide as he looked at his wife's face, and in that moment, the room erupted into a symphony of gasps, choked cries, and horrified whispers. One by one, the guests reached up to their own faces, their expressions morphing from confusion to terror as they felt it—flesh loosening, slipping beneath their fingertips, like wax melting under intense heat.

"Oh God!" one of the guests, David, choked, clutching his face as he stumbled back, his chair scraping against the floor. His hand came away from his cheek, covered in a layer of red and pink tissue, the raw bone of his cheekbone glistening under the dining room lights. He turned to his wife, Helen, his voice thick with panic. "Helen... what's happening?"

Margaret's mind raced, her stomach turning as she watched her guests writhe, their fingers clawing at their faces in horror, desperate to stop the strange, sickening effect spreading across their skin. Diane's mouth hung open in a silent scream as her cheeks slid downward, the muscle and skin separating from her face, exposing the white gleam of her jawbone.

Frank stumbled to his feet, his hand reaching out to his wife, his own face slick with red as his flesh melted away, clinging to his shirt in thick, sticky strings. "Diane! Someone—*please!* Help us!"

Margaret's own skin felt hot, almost tingling, as if an invisible flame was licking at her face. Her heart pounded, and her breath came in short, frantic gasps. She could feel something wet at the corner of her mouth, and when she reached up to touch it, her fingers came away bloody, pieces of her own lip clinging to her hand.

"No... no, no, no," she whispered, backing away from the table as her vision swam. Her beautiful dining room, once filled with laughter and light, was now a tableau of horror, her friends and neighbors transformed into grotesque, skeletal figures, their faces melting like candles left too close to a flame.

"Margaret," Diane whimpered, her voice hoarse and wet, her throat exposed as the skin slipped down her neck in red, meaty clumps. "What's happening to us?"

Margaret stumbled, her mind racing, her gaze fixed on the doorway as if expecting someone to burst in, to explain, to *help.* But no one came. The only sounds were the gurgling, muffled screams of her guests, each one clawing at their own face in a desperate, futile attempt to halt the decay.

Then, just as suddenly as it had begun, the silence returned, thick and absolute.

Margaret forced herself to look around the table, her vision blurred with tears and pain. The guests had stopped moving, their bodies slumped in their chairs, their hands limp at their sides. What remained of their faces were bare skulls, the flesh and muscle melted away, exposing empty eye sockets and grinning, skeletal jaws.

A wet sob escaped her lips as she staggered back, the horror of it all pressing down on her, suffocating. Her dining room, her guests... all of them reduced to macabre figures, a horrific sight out of some nightmare.

Margaret's knees buckled, and she fell to the ground, her mind reeling as she tried to comprehend the impossible. She could feel her own face, raw and burning, the skin slipping away with each brush of her fingers, her own cheekbones now cold and exposed.

The silence was broken by a single, muffled noise—a low, mechanical hum coming from the kitchen. Margaret's breath hitched as she recognized it, the sound both familiar and sinister in the stillness.

The *microwave.*

She forced herself to stand, her legs shaking as she stumbled toward the kitchen. The hum grew louder, more insistent, like a living thing, pulsing with a strange energy. She reached the doorway, her eyes wide with horror as she took in the sight.

The microwave door was open, the interior glowing with a sickly green light. Inside, a strange, thick liquid bubbled and hissed, the fumes rising in a hazy mist. Margaret's stomach churned as she realized the smell—it was the same stench that filled the dining room, the smell of burning flesh, of something rotting and foul.

She covered her mouth, suppressing a scream as the light intensified, pulsing with a sickly, hypnotic rhythm that seemed to echo in her mind. And then, as suddenly as it had started, the hum stopped, the light flickering out, leaving the kitchen shrouded in darkness.

Margaret staggered back, her mind a whirl of terror and confusion. She looked down at her hands, at the blood and flesh that clung to her fingers, and a single, horrifying thought settled in her mind.

Whatever had happened to her guests, to *her,* it had come from *inside the house.*

And whatever it was... it was only just beginning.

Margaret's dining room looked like a scene from a nightmare, a grotesque display of death frozen in stillness. The twelve guests—her friends, her neighbors, people she'd known for years—were unrecognizable. Their flesh, once warm and full of life, had melted away to reveal bare, grinning skulls and hollow eye sockets that seemed to watch her in silent accusation.

Her mind was numb, her thoughts fractured and chaotic as she tried to make sense of the horror before her. Her own face still felt raw, throbbing with an unbearable heat. She staggered to the hallway mirror, her heart pounding as she lifted a trembling hand to her cheek.

What she saw made her stomach turn.

The skin around her mouth and nose was red, raw, and blistered, pieces hanging loose where they'd started to peel away. She could feel the air against her exposed cheekbones, the sensation as foreign and wrong as if someone had peeled back the layers of her soul. Her reflection, the half-bare skull staring back at her, was something from a fevered nightmare.

Her breath came in ragged gasps, each one filled with the stench of rot and decay. She stumbled away from the mirror, unable to bear the sight any longer. Her vision blurred as she turned back to the dining room, desperate for some explanation, some reason for the unthinkable horror that had unfolded here.

And then she saw it—the faint, green glow coming from beneath the door of her basement. It pulsed rhythmically, like a heartbeat, filling the hallway with an eerie, unnatural light. The microwave had been just the beginning. Whatever was causing this... it was somewhere down there, hidden in the shadows of her own home.

Margaret took a shaky breath, her mind torn between a primal need to flee and a desperate urge to understand. She had to know what had caused this, what had turned her friends into skeletal remains, what was turning *her* into one as well.

With trembling hands, she reached for the basement door, her fingers slick with sweat as she twisted the knob. The door creaked open, revealing the dark stairwell that descended into the depths of her house. The green light flickered and pulsed, beckoning her, daring her to step forward.

She hesitated, fear gripping her heart, but a sick curiosity propelled her onward. Slowly, she descended the stairs, each step creaking under her weight. The air grew colder, denser, filled with the metallic tang of something unnatural, something that didn't belong in this world.

As she reached the bottom of the stairs, she saw it—a strange, humming machine sitting in the center of the room, connected by a series of thick cables to her electrical panel. The machine was covered in dials and gauges, its surface slick with condensation, the green light pouring from its base in ghostly waves. It looked like something out of a mad scientist's laboratory, a device built with no purpose other than to invoke fear.

Her stomach turned as she took a step closer, her eyes fixed on the pulsing green light. She had no idea how the machine had gotten there, no memory of ordering or installing anything like this. It seemed to have appeared overnight, like a parasite embedding itself in her home.

But as she drew closer, a memory flickered in her mind—an ad, one she'd seen just a few weeks ago on the TV. *"Revolutionary new cooking device! Enhance flavor, texture, and more! Safe for home use. The future of culinary technology!"* She had ordered it without much thought, eager to impress her guests with the latest cooking trends.

She hadn't even remembered the name. But now, staring at it, she felt a wave of nausea wash over her. *The Face Melter.* The words blazed in her mind, mocking her, as if they'd been waiting to reveal themselves all along.

Margaret covered her mouth, bile rising in her throat as she pieced it together. The machine—*this machine*—had caused the unimaginable horror upstairs. It hadn't just cooked the food. It had done something far worse, something beyond human understanding.

Her thoughts raced, and she felt the bile rise again as she glanced at the machine's dials. One of them was labeled *Resonance Frequency.* Another read *Cellular Breakdown,* its needle still quivering in the red zone, as if whatever effect it had caused wasn't yet finished.

She felt a dark thrill of horror as the truth began to settle over her. This device, whatever it was, hadn't just cooked their food. It had emitted something, some kind of frequency or energy that had broken down their faces, disintegrating their skin and flesh from the inside out.

A low hum began to fill the room, growing louder, more insistent. Margaret took a step back, her hand reaching out to steady herself as the machine's dials started to flicker, the green light intensifying, casting grotesque shadows on the walls. It was as if the machine were coming to life, responding to her presence, its pulsing light filling her mind with a sickening dread.

She stumbled back, her heart racing as she turned to flee, desperate to escape the horror that had taken root in her home. But just as she reached the stairs, the hum grew louder, almost deafening, filling her mind with a single, overpowering command:

FEED ME.

Margaret froze, her mind reeling as the words echoed in her head, relentless and consuming. She turned slowly, her body moving as if guided by some unseen force, her gaze fixed on the machine's green glow. It was hungry, demanding, and it wouldn't stop until it was satisfied.

Her breath hitched as she realized the truth. The machine wasn't just a device. It was alive, sentient, feeding off the people it lured in. The dinner party had been its feast, a grotesque banquet that had left her friends reduced to skeletal husks.

"No," she whispered, her voice trembling. "No, this can't be real."

But the machine hummed louder, its dials spinning wildly, as if mocking her, taunting her. And then, as if to confirm her worst fears, the words appeared on a small, digital screen embedded in the device:

INITIATE SECOND COURSE?

Margaret's heart stopped. She knew instinctively that she was the next course, that the machine wouldn't stop until it had finished what it had started. Her skin burned, her face raw and throbbing, and she felt a strange pull, as if her body were being drawn toward the machine, compelled by some dark, magnetic force.

She gritted her teeth, forcing herself to move, to fight the compulsion that urged her closer. Her eyes scanned the room, searching for anything that could help her destroy this thing, to end the nightmare once and for all. Her gaze fell on a heavy crowbar leaning against the wall, and without thinking, she lunged for it, her fingers closing around the cold metal.

With a cry of desperation, she swung the crowbar at the machine, the metal clanging against its surface with a sickening crunch. The green light flickered, the hum stuttering, as if the machine itself were wounded. Margaret felt a surge of adrenaline, her grip tightening as she struck again, over and over, her rage and fear pouring into each swing.

The machine sparked and sputtered, the green light fading as its dials cracked and shattered. The hum grew weaker, dying with each blow, until finally, with one last swing, the machine went silent, the green light winking out, leaving the basement in complete darkness.

Margaret collapsed to her knees, her body trembling, her breaths coming in ragged gasps. She could still feel the burn on her face, the rawness of her skin, but she knew it was over. Whatever horror she had unleashed was finally gone.

She staggered to her feet, making her way up the stairs, her mind numb with exhaustion and grief. The sight that awaited her in the dining room brought fresh tears to her eyes—her friends, still seated around the table, their skeletal faces frozen in silent screams, a testament to the nightmare she had unleashed.

Margaret stumbled out of the house, her feet carrying her away from the scene of horror, her heart heavy with guilt and horror. She didn't look back as she disappeared into the night, her mind filled with the memory of that green glow, the hum that had echoed through her mind, demanding to be fed.

But somewhere, deep in the recesses of her mind, a new fear took root—a fear that the machine wasn't truly gone, that it had simply gone dormant, waiting for its next feast, its next course.

And as Margaret vanished into the darkness, she knew one thing for certain.

This was only the beginning.

The aftermath of the dinner party horror rippled through Cedar Grove like a shockwave, transforming the quiet suburban neighborhood into a hive of police activity. Emergency vehicles lined the street in front of Margaret Whitmore's house, their flashing lights casting eerie shadows over the pristine lawns. Neighbors gathered at their windows, whispering in hushed voices, speculating about what had happened behind those closed doors.

Detective Adrian Cole arrived at the scene just past midnight, his tired eyes scanning the crowd of onlookers and the unsettling stillness that seemed to hang over the house. He had seen his share of horrific crime scenes, but something about the atmosphere here sent a chill through him. There was a strange energy, an oppressive heaviness in the air that made his skin prickle.

Cole tightened his coat around him as he walked up the driveway, nodding at the officer stationed by the door. "What's the situation, Andrews?"

Officer Andrews looked pale, his eyes wide and darting as if he were struggling to process what he'd seen. He shook his head, swallowing hard. "I... I've never seen anything like it, sir. Twelve people. All of them dead. And... it's their faces."

Cole raised an eyebrow. "Their faces?"

Andrews nodded; his expression haunted. "Or... what's left of them. It's as if the flesh just... melted away, right off the bone."

Cole's stomach tightened. He'd heard of various causes of skin and flesh deterioration, but nothing like what Andrews was describing. "Has anyone spoken to the homeowner?"

"Ms. Whitmore?" Andrews cleared his throat, his gaze shifting nervously. "She... she ran. Witnesses say they saw her leave, but we haven't found her yet. Honestly, I can't say I blame her. You'll see what I mean."

With a curt nod, Cole stepped inside, bracing himself as he entered the dining room. But no amount of preparation could have prepared him for what he saw.

The dining table was set as if for a holiday feast, each place meticulously arranged with fine china, polished silverware, and delicate wine glasses, all untouched. But the twelve figures seated around the table were frozen in grotesque poses, their skulls exposed, hollow eye sockets staring into the void. Bits of flesh clung to the bones, congealed blood pooling around their collars, their hands slack and limp in their laps. The remains of the meal lay scattered before them, untouched, as if time had stopped in the middle of their last bite.

Cole's breath caught in his throat as he scanned the scene, his mind racing to comprehend the horror before him. It was as though some unseen force had stripped the faces from these people, leaving them transformed into ghastly skeletons, frozen forever in that macabre dinner party.

Detective Lisa Tran, his partner, appeared beside him, her face pale as she took in the scene. "Jesus," she whispered, her hand covering her mouth. "What the hell could have done this?"

Cole shook his head, his mind racing through possibilities. "I don't know. Chemical exposure, maybe, or some sort of extreme allergen. But this..." He trailed off, gesturing to the dining room, "I've never seen anything like it."

Lisa leaned in closer, her gaze drawn to the fragments of flesh still clinging to the bones. "It's almost as if... the flesh liquefied somehow. Look at this." She pointed to a trail of what appeared to be viscous, partially coagulated blood pooling around the base of each chair.

Cole frowned. "Something triggered this. Something in this house."

As they circled the room, trying to piece together the mystery, a forensic technician, Karen Rodriguez, entered, her equipment slung over her shoulder. She glanced at the bodies, her face growing taut with discomfort. "We'll start with tissue samples, but I can already tell you... this doesn't look like anything biological."

"What do you mean?" Cole asked, watching her as she approached the first skeleton.

She pulled out a swab, carefully collecting a sample from the exposed jawbone. "This doesn't appear to be any kind of conventional decomposition. It's more like accelerated erosion, or... breakdown on a cellular level." She glanced at Cole, her brow furrowing. "Like they were dissolved from the outside in, but in real-time. Rapidly."

Cole's mind buzzed with questions. "What about the kitchen? Anything unusual?"

Rodriguez nodded. "We found an odd device down in the basement. It looks like some kind of industrial microwave or prototype cooking unit. It was smashed to pieces, though—it's hard to say what it even did. But it was giving off weird energy readings before it was destroyed. We're taking it back to the lab."

Lisa shot Cole a concerned look. "Could the device be responsible?"

"It's the only lead we have." He shook his head, a chill creeping down his spine. "Let's hope it tells us something."

As Rodriguez left, Cole's gaze wandered to a single empty chair at the table. "One of these chairs was empty. Someone was here, and they got away."

"Margaret Whitmore," Lisa replied, glancing at her notes. "The hostess. Neighbors said she left the house right after dinner. Ran down the street covered in blood, and no one's seen her since."

Cole clenched his jaw. "We need to find her. She's our only witness—and maybe our only suspect."

The search for Margaret Whitmore stretched late into the night, officers canvassing the neighborhood and beyond, interviewing anyone who might have seen her. The few people who had noticed her described her as frantic, distraught, her face partially melted, skin hanging loosely as if scorched by an invisible fire.

It wasn't until dawn that they finally found her.

She was crouched in a narrow alley several blocks from her house, her body hunched, shivering violently. Her face was a ghastly sight, the skin blistered and raw, patches missing to reveal bone and muscle beneath. She was muttering to herself, her eyes wide and unseeing, as though trapped in some waking nightmare.

Cole and Lisa approached her slowly, careful not to startle her.

"Margaret?" Cole said softly, crouching down to her level. "It's Detective Cole. We're here to help you."

Her gaze snapped up, wild and terrified. She didn't seem to register his words, her hands twitching as she clawed at her own face, her fingers trembling as they brushed against the exposed bone.

"He... he wanted us to eat," she whispered, her voice choked, her eyes wide with horror. "He was *hungry.* The machine... it said it wanted... *more.*"

Cole felt a chill settle over him, her words cryptic and unsettling. "Margaret, who is 'he'? Are you talking about the machine?"

She nodded, a shudder running through her. "It... it whispered to me, told me to serve... told me it wanted a feast. I thought... I thought it was just for cooking. But it wasn't. It *ate* them. It melted them, devoured them." Her voice trailed off, her gaze turning distant.

"Margaret, we found the machine. It was in your basement. Can you tell us how you got it?"

Her eyes flickered with a faint recognition, but then a strange, hollow laugh escaped her lips. "An ad... I saw an ad... said it would change everything. But it changed us, didn't it? It *took* them. Took me." She glanced down, her fingers brushing over her face, the skin sloughing off under her touch.

Lisa looked at Cole, her eyes wide with shock. "This sounds like some kind of... experimental technology gone wrong. But why would it... *do* that?"

Margaret's laugh turned into a sob. "It's not a machine. It's a *thing.* It has a will of its own. It's *alive.* And it's still hungry..."

Her words dissolved into gibberish, her mind unraveling as the horror of the night overtook her. Cole motioned for the medics to move in, watching as they carefully lifted her onto a stretcher, her body limp, her eyes glassy with terror.

As they loaded her into the ambulance, Cole turned to Lisa, his mind racing. "Whatever that machine was, it didn't just malfunction. It was designed to do this, to feed on these people. And Margaret's not crazy—it left her alive for a reason."

Lisa shivered. "So what do we do? How do we even begin to understand this?"

Cole's gaze darkened. "We start with the machine. And we find out who created it, who sold it. If this thing is still out there... we need to destroy it before anyone else gets hurt."

As the sun rose over Cedar Grove, Cole and Lisa stood in the quiet, deserted street, the weight of what they had seen settling heavily on their shoulders. Whatever horror had unleashed itself in Margaret Whitmore's home was still out there, lurking in the shadows, waiting for its next victim.

And as they made their way back to the station, Cole knew one thing for certain: they were facing something far beyond their understanding, something that defied logic and reason.

Something that *hungered.*

Detective Cole sat in his cramped office, the dim light from his desk lamp casting long shadows over the stacks of case files and photos scattered in front of him. His eyes lingered on the picture of Margaret Whitmore—her face frozen in terror, her expression hollow and wild. He could still hear her voice in his head, the tremor, the hysteria: *"It wanted us to eat... It's still hungry..."*

Across from him, Lisa sat tapping away on her laptop, her brow furrowed in concentration as she scanned through pages of data on the mysterious device recovered from Margaret's basement. It was no ordinary cooking gadget; the lab report had made that clear. The device operated on frequencies and technology far outside the norm, designed to manipulate matter in ways no consumer product should.

"This isn't some kitchen gimmick," Lisa murmured, scrolling through the lab analysis. "It emits high-intensity microwave bursts paired with something called *thermal resonance fields*. I don't even know what that means. The lab tech said it's the kind of equipment you'd expect to see in a government lab... or an experimental weapons facility."

Cole shook his head, an icy chill creeping down his spine. "If it's that advanced, how did it end up in Margaret Whitmore's house?"

Lisa pushed a printout across the desk, her expression darkening. "It was custom-built by a company called Neuronex Dynamics. They're known for creating high-tech prototypes—experimental weapons, AI, and some pretty hush-hush biotechnology." She paused, glancing at him with a troubled look. "But get this—the product wasn't for sale.

The ad she saw? It wasn't even part of a legitimate campaign."

Cole's jaw tightened. "Someone must have set it up for her to find."

Lisa nodded. "Exactly. Whoever designed that ad wanted her to buy it. It was targeted—almost like she was chosen."

Cole ran a hand over his face, the pieces beginning to fall into place. "So we're dealing with something more sinister than a cooking device gone wrong. This was orchestrated. But why target Margaret?"

Lisa's fingers danced across the keyboard as she pulled up Margaret's purchase records. "I've got a contact at Neuronex Dynamics," she said, a hint of hesitation in her voice. "Dr. Evan Markham. He's one of their engineers. If anyone knows the origins of this device, it would be him."

Cole didn't need any more convincing. "Let's pay him a visit. If this machine came out of his company, he may be our best shot at understanding what the hell is going on."

They arrived at Neuronex Dynamics' headquarters later that afternoon, a sleek glass structure looming above the city with reflective walls that seemed to swallow the light. Inside, the building was cold and sterile, filled with labs and offices manned by people in crisp lab coats, moving through the halls with quiet efficiency. It felt detached, alien—a place more suited to secret experiments than a cooking device.

A receptionist led them through a maze of corridors to a lab tucked away at the back of the building. There, Dr. Evan Markham was waiting for them, his face thin, gaunt, and shadowed with exhaustion. He looked up as they entered, his gaze wary, as if he already suspected what they'd come to ask him.

"Detective Cole, Detective Tran," he said, nodding in greeting. "I heard you wanted to discuss one of our prototypes. The lab informed me about the incident involving Margaret Whitmore. Unfortunate, to say the least."

Cole cut straight to the point. "Unfortunate? Doctor, twelve people are dead because of that device. Margaret's face melted off, her skin stripped like wax. You call that unfortunate?"

Dr. Markham's face remained impassive, though his fingers tapped nervously against his clipboard. "Believe me, Detective, we're as disturbed as you are by what happened. But I should clarify—Neuronex Dynamics didn't authorize any commercial sale of this product. It was part of a classified project we were developing for... specialized applications. Someone took it and modified it for consumer use, in a way that it was never intended for."

Lisa's eyes narrowed. "Modified? You're saying it was altered to function as a regular kitchen appliance?"

Dr. Markham nodded. "Yes. We developed the initial technology to affect cellular structures—only in non-human applications. The machine's capabilities are theoretically boundless. But in the wrong hands, it could... well, clearly, it's capable of what you witnessed."

Cole folded his arms, his patience wearing thin. "Who would do that, Doctor? Who would take your machine, twist it into some household death trap, and release it to the public?"

Markham sighed, his shoulders slumping as he leaned against the lab bench. "A rogue engineer, a former colleague of mine named Gabriel Lawson. He was... brilliant, obsessed with the boundaries between technology and biology. But his work grew increasingly experimental, unethical. He believed he could manipulate matter, break it down, rebuild it in new forms. We had no idea he'd take it this far."

Lisa looked at him, disbelief etched on her face. "So you're saying this Lawson designed the machine to... *consume* people?"

Markham nodded, a haunted look in his eyes. "It's what he wanted. He talked about the machine as if it were alive, a creature with its own hunger. He believed that if he could feed it the right energy, the right... *life force*, it would evolve into something beyond technology. He called it *The Face Melter*. And now, it appears he's testing it on unsuspecting people."

Cole felt a chill settle over him. This wasn't just murder; it was something darker, an experiment in pain and horror. He needed to find this Lawson before anyone else fell victim to his twisted creation.

"Where is he now?" Cole asked, his voice steely.

Markham shook his head, regret darkening his gaze. "We don't know. Lawson left the company six months ago, right around the time the prototype went missing. We thought he'd vanished, disappeared. But it seems he's been here, watching his creation wreak havoc."

Cole took a step closer, his voice low. "Give us everything you have on Lawson. Any addresses, known contacts—whatever we can use to track him down."

Markham nodded, scribbling down an address on a piece of paper. "I heard he kept a storage unit across town. It's the last known location he was seen. I'll have our security team provide you with everything we have."

Cole took the paper, his mind racing. "One more thing. Is there any way to destroy the machine? A way to reverse what it's done?"

Markham hesitated, his face pale. "The device is self-sustaining. It operates on an algorithm Lawson designed, something he called *The Circuit.* It's... adaptive, a feedback loop that grows stronger with each activation, feeding off the energy it consumes. Destroying it might be impossible... but if you could disable the Circuit, it might shut it down permanently."

Cole nodded, grim determination settling over him. "Then we'll start there."

The storage unit was in a decaying industrial district on the outskirts of town, a shadowy maze of rusted metal and forgotten buildings. The air was thick with the smell of oil and rot, the scent clinging to their skin as they approached Lawson's last known hideout.

The unit was old, its door covered in grime and rust. Cole forced it open, the door screeching as they stepped inside, the dim light from a single hanging bulb casting flickering shadows across the space.

The storage unit was filled with workbenches covered in tools, blueprints, and small prototypes—versions of the device Margaret had unknowingly used in her home. But the thing that caught Cole's eye was a large metal box in the corner, covered in wires and circuit boards, humming faintly.

Lisa approached it cautiously, her flashlight illuminating a small plaque bolted to the side. The words were etched with clinical precision, cold and unsettling: *Mark 1 Prototype: Biomass Consumption Device.*

Cole's stomach twisted. "Biomass consumption? This... this thing was always meant to feed on people."

Lisa nodded, her face pale. "This wasn't an accident. Lawson designed it with intent."

As they sifted through the blueprints, Cole's gaze landed on a sheet covered in scrawled, manic handwriting. Words like *life energy*, *cellular breakdown*, and *energy circuit* jumped out at him. But in the margin, in small, precise letters, was a final, ominous note:

FEED UNTIL TRANSFORMATION COMPLETE.

Lisa's hand trembled as she read the note over his shoulder. "What transformation? What does that mean?"

Cole shook his head, dread thickening in his chest. "I don't know. But whatever it is, Lawson believed this machine would evolve into something worse."

They gathered the files, stuffing them into bags as they scanned the blueprints, piecing together Lawson's twisted vision. But as they turned to leave, the faint hum of the device grew louder, filling the room with an eerie, almost human whisper.

Cole's blood ran cold as the machine powered up, the hum morphing into a low, throaty hiss.

Feed me.

The words seemed to pulse in the air, thick with hunger, filling the small space with an unbearable pressure.

Without another word, they bolted from the unit, slamming the door shut behind them, the machine's hunger echoing in their minds as they stumbled back into the night.

They knew now that this was more than a rogue experiment. Lawson's machine was alive, a creature born of circuits and malice, evolving with each victim it consumed.

And somewhere out there, Lawson was waiting, watching, feeding his creation with the lives of the unsuspecting, pushing it toward its final, terrible form.

The engine of Detective Cole's unmarked car hummed softly as he and Lisa sped down the empty streets, the files they had taken from Lawson's storage unit sprawled across the back seat. The words scrawled on those pages were burned into Cole's mind: *"Feed until transformation complete."* He couldn't shake the feeling that they were racing against the clock, that with each passing minute, Lawson's device was edging closer to some horrific transformation.

"We need to know more about Lawson," Cole muttered, gripping the wheel tightly. "If he's been monitoring the machine, there has to be a pattern. Some way he's picking his targets."

Lisa glanced at her laptop, her fingers flying over the keys as she accessed police and medical records. "I'm pulling up any incident reports over the past few months that might match these... effects." Her brow furrowed. "There's been a string of unexplained deaths in neighboring towns. People were found with severe tissue damage, skin lesions, and even skeletal exposure, but the causes were labeled as undetermined."

She turned the screen toward him. "Look at this—it goes back further than Margaret's dinner party. There are reports from nearly six months ago. But nothing caught the connection because the victims were all from different areas."

Cole clenched his jaw. "Lawson's been running tests. Each time refining the machine, making it deadlier."

Lisa nodded, her face grim. "These records show a clear escalation. The earlier cases were isolated, almost controlled—smaller breakdowns, like trials. But now it's spreading. The machine's output is growing more... aggressive."

They pulled into the parking lot of a small motel on the outskirts of town. This was the last known address they had for Lawson, a tip they'd dug up from his financial records. The place looked run-down, the neon sign flickering erratically above a line of battered doors.

As they stepped out of the car, the air felt thick, charged, as if the entire area were holding its breath. Cole and Lisa approached the door to Room 15, the paint peeling, the door slightly ajar. Cole exchanged a glance with Lisa before pulling his gun, his voice low.

"Stay behind me," he murmured, pushing the door open with his shoulder.

Inside, the room was a chaotic mess of discarded blueprints, wires, and electronic parts. It looked like a makeshift lab, with half-built circuits and strange, metallic contraptions covering every surface. The walls were lined with scribbled notes, formulas, and calculations, all scrawled in a frenzied hand. But it was the photographs tacked to the wall that made Cole's stomach lurch.

They were of Margaret Whitmore, taken at various places around Cedar Grove: her home, the grocery store, the park. Beside them were photos of her guests, each one marked with dates and times. The final photograph was of Margaret in her dining room, taken moments before the dinner party. Below the photo, a single line was written in red ink:

"Feast begins at dusk."

Lisa's face paled as she scanned the wall. "He's been watching them. Stalking them. Margaret's dinner party was just a test... a controlled experiment. He knew exactly what the machine would do."

Cole felt a surge of anger as he looked at the twisted documentation of Lawson's experiment. "This was never about technology or progress. He's using this machine to feed his own sick fascination."

He scanned the room, his eyes landing on a small, cracked journal sitting on the desk. He picked it up, flipping through the pages. Most of it was incomprehensible—mathematical equations and sketches of human anatomy mixed with cryptic symbols. But one passage caught his eye, written in careful, deliberate script:

"The machine is more than a tool. It is alive, evolving with each life it consumes. Soon, it will reach the threshold, becoming something beyond comprehension. The human form is weak, limited. This device... it will give me the body I deserve."

Lisa's eyes widened as she read over his shoulder. "He doesn't just want to experiment on others. He wants to become... something else."

The words sent a chill through Cole. "That's why he calls it *The Face Melter.* It's not just about stripping flesh. It's about breaking down human bodies and reshaping them. But into what?"

They stood in stunned silence, the gravity of Lawson's intentions settling over them like a shroud. This wasn't just a murder spree; it was a twisted pursuit of some form of evolution.

A sudden thud echoed from the back of the room, snapping them out of their horror. Cole and Lisa turned, guns drawn, as they moved toward a closet at the far end of the room. The door rattled, and a faint, muffled voice sounded from within.

"Help... please..."

Lisa moved forward, pulling the closet door open. Inside, huddled in a corner, was a man in his early thirties, his face bruised and pale, his wrists bound with a tangled mess of wires. His eyes were wide with fear as he looked up at them, his voice hoarse.

"Are... are you the police?"

Cole nodded, holstering his gun. "We are. Who are you? Did Lawson do this to you?"

The man shuddered, his face etched with terror. "Yes... my name's Carl Hughes. I used to work with him, back at Neuronex. I had no idea what he was building until it was too late. He said he needed my help to finish the device, but once I saw what it was doing, I tried to leave. That's when he... he trapped me here."

Lisa crouched beside him, carefully removing the wires around his wrists. "Carl, can you tell us anything about the device? Is there any way to stop it?"

Carl's face contorted with fear and regret. "I... I designed part of the Circuit. It's an adaptive feedback loop—feeding on energy, growing stronger with each activation. Gabriel believed it would evolve, become something... organic. I thought he was crazy, but he said he'd proven it... by feeding it."

Cole felt his stomach turn. "He's using people as fuel."

Carl nodded, his hands shaking. "Yes. And the more it consumes, the closer it gets to a critical point. Soon, it won't need to be plugged in; it'll sustain itself, independent. It'll be unstoppable."

Lisa exchanged a look with Cole, dread tightening in her chest. "Then how do we stop it?"

"There's a failsafe built into the Circuit," Carl whispered, his voice barely audible. "If you can access the core of the device and overload it, it'll short-circuit, shut down permanently. But... but Gabriel removed the failsafe. He knew I'd try to disable it."

Cole's hands clenched into fists. "Where is he, Carl? Where would he go if the device was close to... whatever he thinks it's going to become?"

Carl swallowed, his gaze drifting to the corner of the room where another set of blueprints lay. "There's one more place he always talked about. An old warehouse where he kept the earliest prototypes. If he's trying to force the device to evolve, he'll be there, somewhere he can monitor it as it reaches... whatever he's hoping for."

Cole's jaw tightened. "Then that's where we're going."

He helped Carl to his feet, guiding him to a chair. "Stay here. Call for backup, tell them what you know, and stay out of sight until we get back."

Carl's face was ashen, but he nodded, a look of desperation in his eyes. "Be careful. If you see the machine... don't get too close. The field it emits... it draws you in, like it's pulling your very cells apart."

Cole and Lisa left the motel room, a renewed sense of urgency propelling them forward. As they drove to the warehouse, the sun had dipped below the horizon, casting the sky in hues of bruised purple and deepening black. The city's lights flickered on, illuminating streets that now felt empty, haunted by Lawson's twisted experiments.

When they reached the warehouse, it was shrouded in darkness, looming over them like a sleeping beast. Cole felt his pulse quicken as they approached, his instincts screaming that whatever lay within those walls was something no one should ever have created.

Inside, the warehouse was cold and silent, the air thick with an electric tension that prickled at their skin. At the center of the room, bathed in a sickly green light, was the device. Larger than any previous version, it pulsed and hummed, as if alive, as if waiting.

And standing beside it, his face twisted with dark satisfaction, was Lawson.

He looked up as they entered, his smile widening. "Detectives," he said, his voice a chilling whisper. "Just in time. The machine is almost ready. Soon, it will transcend... and so will I."

Cole raised his gun, his voice steely. "It's over, Lawson. Step away from the machine, and come with us."

Lawson only laughed, his gaze flickering with a fanatical gleam. "Over? This is just the beginning! Don't you see? This machine is my life's work. It will remake me. *Perfect* me."

Lisa moved to the side, her gun aimed steadily at Lawson. "Your work is murder, Lawson. You can't escape this."

Lawson's smile twisted, his eyes flashing. "Maybe not... but I'll live on. In this machine, in everything it touches." He pressed a button on the device, the green light intensifying, filling the room with a sickening hum.

Cole and Lisa felt it immediately—the heat, the pull of the machine's energy, as if their very cells were being tugged toward it. The sensation grew stronger, a creeping warmth that turned to searing pain.

But Cole forced himself to raise his gun, aiming for the Circuit—the core of Lawson's twisted creation. In one swift move, he fired, the bullet hitting the device's exposed center. Sparks flew, the green light flickering wildly as the machine sputtered, struggling against the damage.

Lawson screamed, lunging toward the device, his hands scrambling to repair it. But Lisa fired again, hitting the core, shattering it completely.

The machine let out a piercing scream, a sound that tore through the warehouse as the green light imploded, pulling inward, consuming itself. Lawson's face contorted in terror as the energy he had tried to control enveloped him, dissolving his flesh, stripping him down to the bone.

Within seconds, the machine went silent, leaving nothing but smoke, the faint smell of burnt ozone, and Lawson's skeletal remains.

Cole and Lisa stood in stunned silence, the weight of the nightmare settling over them. The machine was destroyed, its creator gone, but the memory of its hunger would haunt them forever.

They left the warehouse, the city now quiet, knowing that the horror Lawson had unleashed would leave scars that might never fade.

The End.

7
PUMPKIN HILL

Every town has its secrets, but Pumpkin Hill was the kind of mystery that drew people in, no matter how many warnings surrounded it. Tucked away at the edge of Ridgemont, the hill rose above the sleepy suburban houses, a quiet, looming presence that seemed to watch the town from its perch. And every October, as the air grew crisp and the leaves turned, the pumpkins appeared—hundreds of them, scattered like ghostly lanterns across the hill, their rough orange skins practically glowing in the misty twilight.

This year, a group of neighborhood kids decided it was time to explore Pumpkin Hill for themselves. They'd heard the stories, of course—about the farmer who'd gone mad and planted pumpkins on the graves of his enemies, about strange lights flickering on the hilltop, about shadows moving among the pumpkins at night. But in the daylight, with the breeze carrying the sweet smell of fall through the air, it all seemed harmless enough.

At least, that's what they told themselves.

Owen was the ringleader, a lanky fourteen-year-old with an adventurous streak. He had convinced his friends, Charlie, Emma, and Sam, that they could handle the hill. After all, they'd been up there before—only during the day, of course, but this time, he had a flashlight, and he wasn't going to let a bunch of stories scare him off.

The sun was starting to dip below the horizon when they made their way up the narrow path, the crunch of leaves underfoot the only sound. Owen led the way, his flashlight casting a thin beam of light across the ground, illuminating the scattered pumpkins around them. Some were small, barely more than lumps on the ground, while others were massive, twisted and gnarled, their shapes unsettling in the dim light.

"Are you sure about this, Owen?" Emma asked, glancing nervously at the shadows stretching between the pumpkins. "My mom said people shouldn't come here at night. She says it's... haunted."

Owen scoffed, though he felt a twinge of doubt himself. "Come on, Emma, those are just stories. There's nothing haunted about a bunch of pumpkins. Besides, don't you want to see what's at the top? I heard there's this old stone altar or something."

Charlie, the youngest of the group, gave a nervous laugh. "Maybe it's where they sacrificed people! You know, like in those horror movies."

"Stop it, Charlie," Sam muttered, rolling his eyes. "You're just trying to freak us out."

The group pressed on, the path growing narrower, the pumpkins thicker and more twisted, as if they were watching the kids with their hollow, unseen eyes. The hill grew steeper, and with each step, the air felt colder, sharper, the sweet smell of the pumpkins fading into something else, something earthy and rotten.

Halfway up the hill, Emma stopped, clutching Owen's arm. "Wait—did you hear that?"

They all froze, straining their ears. At first, there was only silence, the thick, oppressive kind that made it hard to breathe. But then they heard it—a faint whisper, barely audible, like the rustling of dead leaves, drifting through the air.

"What... what was that?" Charlie whispered, his eyes wide.

Owen shook his head, trying to brush off the prickling sense of fear creeping up his spine. "Probably just the wind," he said, though he didn't quite believe it himself.

But as they stood there, the whispering grew louder, filling the air around them, a sound that was too rhythmic, too deliberate to be mere wind. It seemed to come from the pumpkins themselves, a soft, eerie murmur that made their skin crawl.

Emma took a step back, her face pale. "Let's go back, Owen. This... this doesn't feel right."

But Owen was already moving forward, his flashlight trained on the ground, his curiosity overtaking his caution. "It's just a sound. We've come this far, haven't we?"

Reluctantly, the others followed, their steps slower, their gazes darting nervously between the pumpkins, as if expecting something to lunge at them from the shadows.

After what felt like an eternity, they reached the top of the hill, emerging into a small clearing bathed in pale, silvery moonlight. In the center stood a large stone slab, weathered and cracked, its surface etched with strange, faded symbols. The ground around it was littered with pumpkins, each one larger and more twisted than the last, their dark, shadowed forms casting eerie shapes across the clearing.

Owen moved closer, his flashlight flickering as he examined the stone slab. "See? I told you there was something up here," he said, his voice filled with excitement. "It's like... like some kind of altar."

But as he stepped closer, he noticed something strange—dark, dried stains covering the stone, spreading out in rough, jagged patterns. He felt his stomach churn, a sickening realization settling over him.

"Guys... do you think this is... blood?"

Emma clapped her hand over her mouth, her eyes wide with horror. "Owen, we need to go. Now."

But before they could turn to leave, the whispering returned, louder this time, filling the clearing, echoing off the stone and swirling around them like a sinister chant. The pumpkins seemed to shift, their twisted forms casting shadows that stretched and moved, closing in around them, as if the hill itself were alive.

The air grew colder, the smell of rot thickening, and suddenly, Charlie cried out, stumbling back as his foot sank into the earth. He looked down, his face contorted in terror as he saw what he had stepped on—an exposed hand, half-buried in the soil, its fingers frozen in a final, desperate grasp.

"Oh my God," Sam whispered, his voice shaking. "There are... there are bodies up here."

They stared at the ground, horrified, as they realized the truth. The pumpkins weren't growing in ordinary soil—they were growing in graves. The entire hill was filled with the bodies of those who had come before them, their remains feeding the pumpkins, their voices lingering in the air, whispering, calling out to them.

"Run!" Owen shouted, his voice breaking as he stumbled back, his flashlight flickering wildly.

The group turned to flee, their hearts pounding as they tore through the pumpkins, their footsteps echoing through the darkness. But as they ran, the whispering grew louder, filling their minds, drowning out everything else, each word a dark promise, a chilling warning.

One by one, the pumpkins began to split open, revealing dark, pulpy interiors, something shifting, writhing within, as if the hill itself were coming alive, as if the pumpkins were more than just fruit. The hill had awakened, and it wasn't letting them go.

The path twisted and turned, the pumpkins looming larger, their forms distorted, their thick vines curling across the ground, reaching for the kids as they ran, their movements slow, creeping, as though savoring the chase. Emma stumbled, letting out a scream as a vine wrapped around her ankle, pulling her back, dragging her toward a massive pumpkin that split open, revealing a hollow, pulsing cavity within.

Owen grabbed her hand, pulling her free, but his strength was waning, his heart racing, his mind filled with the terrifying realization that they might not make it out.

"Don't look back!" he shouted, his voice filled with desperation.

But Charlie glanced over his shoulder, his eyes widening as he saw shadows moving among the pumpkins, figures emerging from the darkness, their faces pale, their eyes empty, their mouths open in silent screams. They were the lost souls of Pumpkin Hill, bound to the land, trapped in an endless nightmare, forever feeding the monstrous harvest that grew from their graves.

The whispering grew louder, a dark chant that filled the air, drowning out their screams, filling their minds with a single, terrifying thought.

You belong to the hill.

Just as they reached the bottom, the chanting stopped, the air heavy with silence, the vines receding, the pumpkins returning to their still, silent forms, as though nothing had happened, as though the hill had merely let them go.

But they knew the truth. Pumpkin Hill was alive, fed by the bodies of the dead, bound by a curse older than any of them could imagine. And it would wait, silently, patiently, for the next souls to stumble into its grasp.

Back in the safety of their homes, the kids huddled together, their faces pale, their minds haunted by what they had seen. They swore never to speak of it, never to return to the hill, but they knew the horror would stay with them forever.

As they lay awake that night, listening to the wind rustling through the trees, they could still hear the faint whispering, drifting through the darkness, a haunting reminder of the hill that waited just beyond the edge of town.

And in the silence, a single, chilling thought lingered in their minds:

Pumpkin Hill never lets go.

The events of that night lingered like a shadow over the kids. Emma had nightmares of whispering voices and dark, gnarled hands reaching up from the soil. Charlie couldn't sleep without the light on, while Sam spent hours trying to forget the sight of the bodies, half-buried beneath the earth, feeding the monstrous pumpkins. Only Owen was determined to get to the bottom of what had happened.

There had to be an explanation, he thought. And, late one night, he decided he'd find it, dragging his friends back into the mystery, telling them it was the only way they'd ever be free from the horror they'd experienced on Pumpkin Hill.

Reluctantly, they agreed, and the next day, they set out on a mission to uncover the origins of the hill.

The local library was quiet, a place few of the townsfolk visited outside of school hours. The town's archivist, Mrs. Hargrove, had worked there for decades, a small, wiry woman with thick glasses and an unsettlingly sharp memory. She'd lived in Ridgemont her entire life, her roots deeply intertwined with its history. If anyone knew about Pumpkin Hill, it would be her.

When the kids arrived, Mrs. Hargrove eyed them suspiciously. "Now, what's got you kids so interested in the town's history all of a sudden?" she asked, her voice a low rasp. "I thought you'd all be out playing or trick-or-treating."

Owen cleared his throat, trying to hide his nerves. "Actually, Mrs. Hargrove, we wanted to know more about Pumpkin Hill. Like... where it came from. And... if anything strange ever happened there."

Her eyes narrowed, her gaze piercing as she studied them. "Pumpkin Hill? Strange things always happen on Pumpkin Hill, don't they?" She hesitated, glancing around as if to make sure no one was listening. "Why the sudden interest?"

Charlie swallowed, his voice barely a whisper. "We... we saw things up there. Something bad. Something... alive."

A flicker of understanding crossed Mrs. Hargrove's face, and she nodded slowly, leading them to a back room filled with dusty books and old records. She pulled a yellowed file from one of the shelves, handing it to Owen with a solemn look.

"These records go back over a hundred years," she said, her voice dropping to a whisper. "The town doesn't like to talk about it, but Pumpkin Hill has always been... cursed. In the late 1800s, it was owned by a farmer named Edgar Belden. His family farmed that land, growing crops, raising livestock. But one year, something went terribly wrong."

She opened the file, revealing black-and-white photos of the hill, grainy images of pumpkins scattered across a barren landscape. In one photo, a grim-faced man stood in front of a field, a gaunt figure with a haunted look in his eyes. "That's Belden," she said, pointing at the man. "He was obsessed with his crops, determined to grow pumpkins bigger and better than anyone else in the county. But when his crops began to fail, he turned to dark methods."

The kids leaned in, captivated, a chill settling over them.

"Belden was said to have struck a deal," Mrs. Hargrove continued. "With whom, no one knows. Some say it was a witch who passed through town, others claim it was the devil himself. Whatever it was, he promised Belden a thriving harvest, but it came at a steep price: he had to offer something... personal, something of his own flesh and blood."

Emma shivered. "What did he give?"

Mrs. Hargrove's face darkened. "He gave the hill his family. One by one, they disappeared—first his wife, then his children, and then the farmhands. People began to notice, and soon enough, rumors spread that the pumpkins were being grown in the soil enriched by their bodies. And they were right."

She showed them more photos, faded but unmistakable—images of open graves, strange symbols carved into the soil, pumpkins growing over the remains of the missing.

"Belden was shunned," Mrs. Hargrove continued. "He became the town's dark secret, his land left to rot. People tried to burn it, to tear up the soil, but the pumpkins always came back, as though they were tied to the hill by something... unnatural. Belden himself vanished, and no one ever saw him again."

The kids exchanged uneasy glances, the weight of the story settling over them.

"But it didn't end there," Mrs. Hargrove said, her voice barely a whisper. "Every fall, when the air grows cold and the veil between worlds is thin, the pumpkins reappear. And each year, someone goes missing—wanderers, thrill-seekers, children who go up the hill at night, never to be seen again. The curse demands a harvest, and if it doesn't get one, it takes what it's owed."

As they left the library, the kids walked in silence, each one haunted by what they had learned. The pumpkins weren't just plants—they were part of something darker, something that demanded a sacrifice. And now, they knew they had barely escaped becoming part of that dark harvest.

"We have to do something," Owen said, his voice trembling. "We can't just leave the hill... like that. If we don't stop it, other people will go up there, and it'll happen again."

Emma shook her head. "But how? What can we possibly do against... whatever that is?"

Charlie's face was pale, his voice barely a whisper. "Maybe... maybe we have to destroy the pumpkins. Burn them. If they're part of the curse, maybe we can break it by getting rid of them."

Sam nodded, though his face was etched with fear. "But we have to be careful. It might... it might try to stop us."

They made a plan to return to the hill at dusk, armed with matches and gasoline, their minds filled with a grim determination. They knew the risks, but they couldn't leave it, couldn't let the curse claim anyone else.

The sun was setting as they made their way back up the hill, the sky streaked with shades of orange and purple, casting an eerie glow over the pumpkins scattered across the ground. They moved quickly, their flashlights flickering as they poured gasoline over the pumpkins, covering as much of the hill as they could.

Owen struck a match, his hands shaking as he held it over one of the largest pumpkins, its twisted form casting a long, dark shadow across the ground. "This is for everyone who's lost," he whispered, dropping the match.

The pumpkin burst into flames, the fire spreading quickly, licking across the dry vines, casting an orange glow over the hill. But as the flames grew, the air filled with an eerie, high-pitched wail, a sound that seemed to come from the very ground beneath their feet. The pumpkins began to shake, to twist, their forms splitting open, revealing dark, pulpy interiors, something alive and writhing within.

A shadow rose from the ground, a figure that seemed to take shape within the smoke and flames—a gaunt, ghostly form with hollow eyes, staring at them with a hatred that chilled them to the bone. It was Belden, his spectral form tethered to the hill, his expression twisted in anger as he moved toward them, his voice a hollow, echoing rasp.

"You can't end this," he hissed, his eyes gleaming with dark fury. "The hill demands a harvest... and it will have it."

They stumbled back, the fire spreading around them, the pumpkins igniting one by one, filling the air with the smell of burning earth, of rot and decay. The ground trembled beneath their feet, the earth splitting open as dark, twisted vines reached up, clawing at their ankles, pulling them back, as though trying to drag them into the soil.

But as the fire grew, as the hill was consumed in flames, the ghostly figure began to fade, his form dissolving into smoke, his voice fading into a whisper.

"The hill... will always... demand a harvest..."

And then, he was gone, his form dissipating into the night, leaving only the flames and the smoldering remains of the pumpkins, their ashes scattering in the wind.

When the fire finally died, the hill was quiet, the ground charred, the pumpkins reduced to ashes. The kids stood together, their faces pale, their hearts pounding, the weight of what they had done settling over them. They knew the curse was gone, that Belden's twisted harvest had finally been destroyed.

But as they walked back down the hill, the wind rustling through the trees, they couldn't shake the feeling that something still lingered, a whisper in the air, a reminder of the darkness they had faced.

And every fall, when the air grew cold and the pumpkins ripened, they would remember the night they had faced Pumpkin Hill, and the curse that had haunted their town for generations.

The hill was quiet now. But they knew it would never truly be gone.

The townspeople awoke the next morning to the sight of Pumpkin Hill, charred and smoldering. Smoke still rose from the blackened earth, and the once-bright orange pumpkins were nothing more than ash and twisted, blackened vines. News spread quickly through Ridgemont; people gathered at the base of the hill, whispering, wondering who would burn it and why.

Emma, Owen, Charlie, and Sam stayed silent, exchanging worried glances as they watched the townsfolk speculate. Some people were relieved, whispering that maybe the curse of the hill was finally gone, that maybe they could be rid of the dark legend once and for all. But others seemed uneasy, sensing that something deeper, something darker still lingered over the town.

For the kids, their relief was short-lived. In the days following the fire, each of them felt an unsettling presence, as though they were being watched, as though something had followed them down the hill. At night, they could still hear the faint whispering, like leaves rustling in the wind, calling their names.

One evening, as they gathered in Owen's basement to talk about the events on the hill, they heard a familiar voice—Mrs. Hargrove, the archivist, calling out from the top of the stairs. She'd arrived without notice, her face pale, her eyes sharp, brimming with worry.

The kids looked at her in surprise. Mrs. Hargrove had never come to their homes before. She was always a figure of the library, someone rooted in the town's history but distant, unchanging. Yet here she was, standing in Owen's basement, her expression grim.

"I warned you not to go back to that hill," she said, her voice low, trembling with urgency. "Burning it was dangerous—if you don't end a curse correctly, sometimes... sometimes it leaves behind *shadows*."

Emma's stomach dropped. "Shadows? What do you mean?"

Mrs. Hargrove closed her eyes for a moment, gathering her thoughts. "Pumpkin Hill's curse wasn't just about Belden's harvest. That hill has always been a place where things don't stay dead, a place where the line between our world and the next is thin. Burning those pumpkins might have disrupted the curse, but it also left it... fractured."

"Fractured?" Owen repeated, his face pale. "So... we didn't get rid of it?"

Mrs. Hargrove shook her head. "You may have weakened it, but you didn't destroy it. Belden's spirit still lingers, looking for a way to restore the curse, to pull souls back to the hill. And now, his hatred is fixed on you."

The kids exchanged terrified glances. They'd thought it was over, that the burning had been enough. But now, they realized they had only stirred the hill's anger.

"What do we do?" Sam asked, his voice shaking.

Mrs. Hargrove took a deep breath, her gaze fixed on them. "You'll have to finish it. There's one last way—a ritual to sever the hill's connection to the spirit world, to stop

Belden from reclaiming the curse. But it's dangerous. You'll have to face him one last time."

Mrs. Hargrove instructed them to return to the hill on the next full moon, when the veil between worlds was at its thinnest. They were to bring a few items: salt to create a protective circle, iron nails to break the lingering power of the curse, and something to represent their own lives—a lock of hair, a bit of blood, something personal.

When the night of the full moon arrived, the kids made their way back up the blackened hill, their hearts pounding, their hands shaking as they prepared to face the darkness once more. The moon hung high above them, casting a cold, silvery light over the hill, illuminating the ash and twisted remains of the pumpkins.

They created a circle with the salt, each of them taking their place within it, clutching their items. The air grew colder, thicker, the scent of rot filling their noses as they chanted the words Mrs. Hargrove had given them, calling out to Belden, daring him to come, to end this once and for all.

At first, there was only silence, the soft whisper of the wind. But then, the ground trembled, the air growing heavy, thick with the dark, oppressive energy they had felt that night on the hill. Shadows gathered around them, dark shapes flickering at the edges of their vision, figures twisted and gaunt, eyes hollow, watching them with a hunger that sent chills through their bones.

And then, he appeared.

Belden's ghostly form rose from the ground, his eyes blazing with anger, his figure twisted and contorted, as though he were more shadow than man. His gaze fixed on the kids, his mouth twisting into a dark, malevolent grin.

"You think you can break my curse?" he hissed, his voice echoing through the night, filled with rage. "This hill is mine, fed by my blood, my soul. You will never escape it."

The kids held their ground, reciting the words of the ritual, their voices shaking but determined, their minds focused on ending the curse, on stopping Belden from reclaiming the hill. The shadows drew closer, reaching for them, clawing at the edges of the salt circle, but they pressed on, their voices growing louder, stronger.

Belden let out a terrible scream, a sound that seemed to shake the earth itself, his form flickering, dissolving, his face twisted in hatred as he fought against the ritual, against the binding that held him.

"You... will... pay," he rasped, his voice fading, his form dissipating, until he was nothing more than a wisp of smoke, a shadow fading into the darkness.

As his figure vanished, the shadows around them faded, the hill falling silent, the air growing still. The ritual was complete, the curse broken, the hill finally free from Belden's grasp.

In the days that followed, the hill remained quiet, its earth charred and blackened, the pumpkins gone, the shadows lifted. Word of the fire spread, but people soon forgot the hill's dark history, treating it as an unfortunate accident, a strange but harmless mystery.

But the kids knew the truth. They'd faced the darkness, seen the curse with their own eyes, and now, they felt a strange peace, a sense of closure that settled over them, knowing they had freed their town from Belden's twisted grip.

As fall turned to winter, the hill grew barren, a quiet reminder of the horror that had once haunted it. And every Halloween, as the air grew cold and the pumpkins ripened, the kids would remember the night they had faced the hill, the night they had ended the curse of Pumpkin Hill.

And though they'd broken the curse, they'd never forget the shadows that had lingered there, the whispers that had haunted them, a reminder that some things never truly die—they simply wait, buried beneath the earth, hidden in the darkness, waiting for someone to bring them back to life.

The End

8

THE GARBAGE MAN

The city of New York was alive, pulsing with the noise of traffic, the hum of streetlights, and the never-ending flow of people. But beyond the bustling streets and glaring lights, there were places few ever ventured, places thick with shadows and stench—alleys littered with debris, forgotten by all except those forced to live in them.

Derek knew these places well. He'd been on the streets long enough to recognize the alleys that even the desperate avoided. As he made his way down one such alley near the Lower East Side, he caught a whiff of something foul, even worse than the usual stink of rot and garbage.

It was the smell of decay, of something left to fester and seep into the city's underbelly. Derek wrinkled his nose, clutching his coat tighter around him as he scanned the shadows. The alley was littered with scraps—plastic bags, old food, rusted metal. But there was something else tonight, something that made his skin crawl.

The shadows seemed to ripple, shifting in unnatural ways, as if hiding something that was waiting just beyond his line of sight. The sound of faint, raspy breathing drifted toward him, echoing through the narrow passage, barely audible over the distant rumble of traffic.

Derek froze, his heart pounding. He'd heard rumors, whispered stories about a creature that lurked in the alleys at night. They called him *The Garbage Man*—a twisted figure that moved through the city's refuse, collecting things left behind. People, animals, even memories. They said he only came out in the darkest hours, that he was something ancient, something that belonged to the night.

He told himself it was just an urban legend, something to scare the rookies and keep the homeless from wandering alone after dark. But here, in the cold, rotten silence of the alley, Derek wasn't so sure.

He took a step back, his eyes darting to the exit, but the shadows seemed to deepen, thickening around him, closing off his escape. A strange scraping sound echoed from behind the dumpster to his right, a slow, deliberate noise, like metal dragged across concrete.

"Hello?" he whispered, his voice hoarse, trembling. "Who's there?"

Silence.

Derek's fingers tightened around his coat as he took another cautious step back, but his foot caught on something soft. He looked down and his blood ran cold. Half-buried in a pile of garbage was a shoe. Just one, covered in dirt and grime. It looked new, like it hadn't been there long.

He knew he should run, that every instinct was screaming at him to turn and bolt, but something kept him rooted in place, his gaze fixed on the shoe. Slowly, he reached down and lifted it, feeling a heavy weight inside. With a grimace, he tilted the shoe, and a small, broken bone slid out, clattering against the ground with a hollow, sickening sound.

His heart hammered, and his breath came in short, panicked gasps. That wasn't just trash. It was a piece of someone.

Just then, a soft, shuffling sound drifted from the end of the alley. Derek's head snapped up, his eyes widening as he caught sight of a figure emerging from the shadows. It was tall, hunched, its body hidden beneath layers of tattered, filthy cloth that dragged along the ground. In one twisted hand, it held a large, grimy sack, the bottom sagging with something heavy, something that squelched as it hit the ground.

The creature's face was obscured, but Derek could see its eyes—two gleaming pinpricks of white staring at him from deep within the shadows of its hood. They didn't blink, didn't waver, fixed on him with a hungry intensity that made his skin crawl.

"Y-you need help?" Derek managed, his voice barely a whisper. He tried to take a step back, but his feet felt glued to the ground, his entire body paralyzed by fear.

The figure tilted its head, the movement slow and deliberate, almost curious. And then it opened its mouth.

A long, rasping hiss escaped its throat, echoing through the alley like the scraping of metal against bone. The sound was low, grating, filled with a sick, gurgling wetness that made Derek's stomach turn. He could smell it now, a rancid odor of decay and filth that hung around the creature like a shroud, the smell of rotting meat mixed with something sharp and metallic.

It lifted its hand, long fingers extending toward him, the nails cracked and filthy, glinting faintly in the dim light. Derek's pulse quickened as he watched the hand move closer, every instinct screaming at him to run, but his body refused to listen.

"Please..." he whispered, his voice shaking.

The creature's fingers hovered inches from his face, and Derek could see them clearly now. They weren't fingers at all. They were twisted pieces of bone, jagged and broken, bound together with scraps of flesh and sinew, each one ending in a sharp, pointed tip. The creature's hand smelled of rot, the scent filling his nostrils as it moved closer, reaching for him.

"Mine..." it hissed, its voice a low, guttural rasp that sent chills down Derek's spine.

The creature's fingers brushed against his cheek, cold and wet, and Derek felt his mind spiral into panic. He forced himself to move, to break free from the creature's gaze, and stumbled backward, his foot slipping on the damp pavement.

He fell to the ground, gasping for breath, his heart pounding as he scrambled to his feet. But the creature didn't move, didn't lunge. It just watched him, its eyes glinting in the shadows, its head tilted as if studying him.

And then, slowly, it took a step back, fading into the darkness, its raspy breathing growing softer until it was nothing more than a faint echo, swallowed by the shadows.

Derek didn't wait to see if it would return. He bolted from the alley, his footsteps echoing through the empty streets as he ran, the image of the creature's skeletal fingers burned into his mind. He didn't stop until he reached a well-lit street, his body trembling, his mind racing.

But even as he caught his breath, safe in the neon glow of the city lights, he knew one thing for certain.

The Garbage Man was real.

And somewhere, hidden in the alleys, he was waiting.

Derek couldn't shake the encounter. His mind replayed every horrible detail: the raspy hiss, the gleaming white eyes, the feel of the creature's bone-like fingers grazing his skin. The next day, he wandered the streets in a daze, the fear gripping him tightly, wrapping around his thoughts like thick chains. He glanced into every alley, every darkened corner, as if expecting to see the hunched figure lurking there, watching him with those empty, hungry eyes.

As evening approached, he made his way to a makeshift encampment near the old warehouse district, a spot where the homeless gathered for safety. Tonight, though, the crowd was unusually small. Only a few familiar faces huddled around, their eyes shadowed with exhaustion.

"Hey, Derek!" called a thin, wiry man named Lonnie. He was bundled up in layers, his face weathered from years on the street, but his sharp eyes took in every detail. "You look like you've seen a ghost, man. You alright?"

Derek swallowed, his mind flickering back to the sight of the Garbage Man, the touch of that clammy, skeletal hand. "I don't know what I saw, Lonnie," he murmured, lowering his voice. "Last night, in the alley over on 7th... there was something there."

Lonnie's face twisted into a wary frown. He leaned in, his voice dropping to a whisper. "Don't tell me you saw him. The Garbage Man."

The others perked up, glancing nervously at Derek. A few crossed themselves; others exchanged uneasy looks. The name alone seemed to drain the warmth from the air.

Derek nodded, his throat dry. "I don't know what he was, but he looked... wrong. Like he was made out of trash and bones. He just... stared at me."

Lonnie exhaled sharply, his face darkening. "You're lucky he didn't take you. Folks been disappearing, and it's been getting worse lately. Just last week, Mario vanished. Was sleeping over by the bridge, and then—poof. Gone."

Derek's skin prickled. Mario had been a regular face, a kind man in his fifties who'd always offered food to those in need. "Gone? Like, no one's seen him since?"

"No one," Lonnie muttered, looking around. "And he's not the only one. Margo, Ray, that kid with the tattoos—Ryan. All gone. Left their stuff, too, just... disappeared."

A silence settled over the group. Derek could feel the weight of their fear. He wasn't the only one haunted by the Garbage Man. This creature wasn't just an urban legend. It was real, and it was hunting people like them.

One of the others, an older woman named Ruth, spoke up, her voice shaking. "I heard he only comes out late at night, around midnight, when it's quiet. He's looking for people... people nobody else would miss." Her eyes glistened with tears, the unspoken truth hanging in the air. *People like us.*

Derek clenched his fists, feeling a spark of anger mixed with his fear. "So what, we just sit here and wait to be taken? There has to be a way to stop him."

Lonnie shook his head, his face grim. "I don't think he can be stopped. He's been here longer than we have, longer than the city itself, maybe. They say he's as old as the bones of the earth, that he feeds on the forgotten, the discarded."

Ruth shivered, clutching her blanket closer. "He leaves something behind. Every time someone goes missing, there's always... something. A shoe, a scrap of clothing. A reminder."

Derek's stomach twisted as he remembered the shoe he'd found the night before, half-buried in the garbage. He'd picked it up, felt the weight of it in his hand. *The broken bone inside.*

As the sun sank below the horizon, a chill settled over the encampment. Derek felt it seep into his bones, his skin prickling with an instinctive dread. He knew the creature was out there, lurking in the shadows, waiting for the night to fall.

"I'm not sitting around," he said finally, his voice tense. "If he's taking people, then there has to be a way to find him before he finds us."

Lonnie's eyes widened, and he shook his head. "Derek, don't. Don't go looking for him. People say he lives off the fear of those he hunts. The more you think about him, the closer he gets. Like he's pulled to you."

But Derek was already standing, his mind made up. The thought of waiting, of letting himself be hunted like prey, made his skin crawl. He'd rather face the creature head-on, know what he was dealing with, than spend every night glancing over his shoulder, wondering if he'd be next.

Lonnie sighed, his face drawn. "If you're really going, take this." He reached into his pocket, pulling out a small, rusted knife. It wasn't much, but in the dim light, it looked sturdy. "Just in case."

Derek nodded, accepting the knife. The weight of it felt solid in his hand, a sliver of reassurance in an otherwise terrifying night.

As he turned to leave, Ruth called after him, her voice trembling. "Be careful, Derek. And remember—if you hear him... don't look back."

Derek walked away from the encampment, his heart pounding as he ventured back toward the alley where he'd seen the Garbage Man. The city was quiet now, the streets dark, the only light coming from the flickering streetlamps casting long, twisted shadows across the pavement.

He passed by dumpsters overflowing with trash, bags split open, their contents spilling out in putrid heaps. The smell was worse tonight, a sickly-sweet stench that hung heavy in the air, like something long-dead hidden just out of sight. It reminded him of the Garbage Man's breath, that rancid, metallic scent that clung to him like a curse.

As he approached the alley, a faint sound reached his ears—a low, rhythmic scraping, like metal being dragged along concrete. His pulse quickened, his grip tightening on the knife. He took a deep breath, forcing himself to move forward, his footsteps silent as he crept toward the source of the noise.

There, in the shadows, he saw it.

The Garbage Man was hunched over a pile of garbage, his skeletal hands sifting through the refuse with a grotesque precision. He moved slowly, deliberately, as if searching for something specific. His head was bowed, hidden beneath the tattered hood, but Derek could see the twisted fingers, the bones protruding, thin strips of flesh clinging to them like rotting fabric.

Derek's breath caught in his throat. He wanted to look away, to run, but he forced himself to stay, to watch. If he was going to survive, he needed to understand what he was dealing with.

The Garbage Man paused, his head tilting slightly, as if sensing Derek's presence. Slowly, he lifted his head, and his empty, white eyes locked onto Derek's.

A sick smile spread across his face, revealing teeth that were cracked and jagged, each one sharp enough to tear through flesh. He stood up slowly, his body unfolding in jerky, unnatural movements, the sound of bones popping and cracking echoing through the alley.

"Mine," he rasped, his voice a low, guttural whisper that sent a shiver down Derek's spine. "You don't belong here."

Derek took a shaky step back, the knife trembling in his hand. "I... I'm not afraid of you," he said, his voice barely more than a whisper.

The Garbage Man's grin widened, his eyes gleaming with a sick pleasure. "You should be."

Before Derek could react, the creature lunged, moving faster than anything he'd ever seen. Derek stumbled back, his heart pounding as he raised the knife, but the Garbage Man was upon him in an instant, his cold, bony fingers closing around Derek's wrist, squeezing with a strength that felt like iron.

Derek cried out, pain shooting up his arm as he struggled to break free. The creature's grip tightened, the sharp bones digging into his flesh, drawing blood. The stench was overpowering, a wave of rot and filth that made him gag.

He thrashed, kicking wildly, and his foot connected with the creature's knee, forcing it to stumble back. The knife fell from his hand, clattering to the ground as he scrambled to his feet, gasping for breath.

The Garbage Man straightened, his eyes fixed on Derek, a twisted grin on his face. "Run, little rat," he hissed, his voice filled with a dark amusement. "I'll find you. I always do."

Derek didn't need to be told twice. He turned and sprinted down the alley, his footsteps echoing through the night. The sound of the Garbage Man's raspy breathing followed him, growing fainter as he put distance between them, but he knew it wouldn't be long before the creature found him again.

As he reached the end of the alley, he glanced over his shoulder, and his blood ran cold.

The Garbage Man stood there, watching him with those empty, gleaming eyes, his body shrouded in shadow, his twisted fingers raised in a mock wave. And then, just as quickly as he'd appeared, he melted back into the darkness, leaving only the faint scent of decay hanging in the air.

Derek stumbled into the street, his heart racing, his body shaking with adrenaline. He had escaped, but he knew it was only a matter of time before the Garbage Man found him again.

Because in the city's forgotten corners, where the shadows were deepest and the stench was thickest, the Garbage Man was always watching, always waiting.

And he wasn't done with Derek yet.

Derek's legs carried him through the darkened streets without direction, each alley and shadowed doorway setting his nerves on edge. He kept glancing over his shoulder, half-expecting to see the Garbage Man lurking behind him, his skeletal hand reaching, his raspy voice echoing in Derek's mind: *You don't belong here.*

It wasn't until he reached a small, dimly lit park that he stopped, his breaths ragged. He dropped onto a bench, his entire body trembling as the weight of the night pressed down on him. The Garbage Man was real, and he was hunting people like Derek. The knowledge churned in his gut, bringing a wave of nausea with it.

The park was empty, silent except for the distant hum of traffic. Derek rubbed his hands over his face, trying to erase the twisted grin, the lifeless eyes, the stench of rot that had seemed to seep into his very bones.

Then, a voice broke the silence, low and rough. "Rough night, huh?"

Derek looked up to see a man sitting on the other end of the bench, his face mostly hidden beneath a hood, his hands shoved deep into his pockets. Derek hadn't noticed him before and, instinctively, his muscles tensed.

"Yeah... something like that," Derek replied, his voice cautious.

The man chuckled, a dry, humorless sound. "Let me guess. You saw him."

Derek's blood ran cold. He didn't need to ask who the man meant. He nodded slowly, his gaze fixed on the stranger. "You've seen him too?"

"Oh, yeah," the man muttered, his face shadowed and unreadable. "We all have. Anyone who spends enough time out here, in the alleys, the forgotten places... we all see him sooner or later."

Derek's stomach twisted. He glanced around, feeling a chill creep down his spine. "Who are you?"

The man shifted, his hood falling back slightly to reveal tired, bloodshot eyes. "Just call me Paul. I've been out here a long time, long enough to know that you don't cross paths with the Garbage Man and walk away unchanged. He's... drawn to certain people, people the world's left behind. Like us."

The words hit Derek like a punch to the gut. "So, what? We're just... stuck here? Waiting for him to come for us?"

Paul looked down, his expression hardening. "Not if you know where to go." He glanced at Derek, his eyes sharp and calculating. "There are places he doesn't go, places even he won't touch. But to find them... you have to know where to look."

Derek felt a flicker of hope, fragile and fleeting. "Where? Where do I go?"

Paul hesitated, glancing around as if checking for anyone listening. "There's a spot—deep below the city, in the old subway tunnels near 14th Street. The station's been shut down for years, but it's not entirely abandoned. People say it's... different down there. They call it the Hollow."

"The Hollow?" Derek repeated, the name sending a chill through him.

"Yeah," Paul whispered, his voice low and secretive. "Some say it's a sanctuary. Others say it's a trap. Either way, the Garbage Man won't go near it. I think it's the one place in the city he can't reach, the one place where we might have a chance of finding answers... maybe even a way to stop him."

Derek's mind raced. He didn't know if he trusted Paul, but he knew one thing for certain—he couldn't spend another night running, waiting for the Garbage Man to appear. “How do I get there?”

Paul slipped a crumpled piece of paper from his pocket and pressed it into Derek’s hand. “Meet me at midnight. Near the abandoned station entrance, just off 14th Street. If you’re really serious about this, that’s where you’ll find me.”

Before Derek could respond, Paul rose from the bench, slipping back into the shadows, his figure melting into the night. Derek stared at the paper, his heart pounding as he read the instructions scrawled in smudged ink. Beneath the address, a single line was written:

Do not look back.

The next night, Derek found himself standing outside the boarded-up entrance to the old subway station. The street was deserted, the distant hum of the city barely reaching him as he stared at the broken concrete steps leading down into the darkness. Graffiti covered the walls, faded and cracked, the colors dulled by years of grime and neglect. A small, rusted sign reading *14th St. Hollow* hung above the entrance, its letters barely visible.

Paul was waiting for him, his face hidden beneath his hood, his expression unreadable. He nodded when he saw Derek, a faint smile tugging at his lips.

“You came,” he said, his voice low. “Good. That means you’re serious.”

Derek swallowed, his hands clenched at his sides. “What is this place?”

Paul gestured for him to follow, leading him down the crumbling steps. The air grew colder as they descended, the stench of mildew and rust filling Derek’s nostrils. Flickering lights cast eerie shadows on the walls, illuminating faded posters and broken glass scattered across the floor.

They reached the platform, which was dark, silent, and empty. Shadows pooled in the corners, thick and heavy, clinging to the walls like they had a life of their own. In the distance, Derek could hear the faint sound of dripping water, echoing through the empty space.

"This is where they come," Paul whispered, his gaze fixed on the shadows. "People like us, people who've seen him. They come here for answers... or for a chance to disappear."

Derek glanced around, feeling a strange, oppressive weight settle over him. The shadows seemed to move, swirling like smoke, stretching and shifting, almost as if they were watching him.

"Why doesn't he come here?" Derek asked, his voice barely more than a whisper.

Paul shook his head, his expression distant. "No one knows. Some say this place is cursed, a place of forgotten souls. Others think it's some kind of sanctuary, a barrier against whatever he is. All I know is that he doesn't come here. And if we're lucky, maybe we can use that to our advantage."

They walked deeper into the tunnel, the air growing colder, thicker with each step. Derek's heartbeat echoed in his ears, his nerves on edge as he tried to process what he was seeing. The graffiti-covered walls seemed to pulse with an unnatural light, flickering in time with his heartbeat.

At the end of the platform, Paul stopped, his eyes fixed on a doorway partially hidden by debris. The door was covered in strange markings, symbols Derek didn't recognize, each one scratched into the metal with something sharp, each one filled with a darkness that seemed to pulse and writhe.

"This is it," Paul said, his voice barely audible. "If we're going to find answers, they're in there."

Derek hesitated, his gaze fixed on the door. The symbols seemed to pulse, drawing him in, filling his mind with images he couldn't place—dark tunnels, endless shadows, faces twisted in agony, whispers that echoed through his thoughts like a chorus of despair.

He took a deep breath, steeling himself. Whatever lay beyond that door, it was better than waiting, better than being hunted.

Together, they stepped through the doorway, the darkness swallowing them whole. The air was thick and cold, pressing down on them as they moved deeper into the tunnel. Shadows flickered at the edges of his vision, the whispers growing louder, filling his ears with words he couldn't understand.

And then he saw them.

Figures drifted through the shadows, their faces pale and gaunt, their eyes hollow, staring straight ahead with expressions of numb despair. They moved silently, their feet barely touching the ground, their bodies shrouded in darkness. Derek realized, with a sickening jolt, that they were people—people who had once been like him, people who had come here looking for answers.

People who had never returned.

He wanted to turn back, to run, but Paul gripped his arm, his gaze fixed on a figure standing at the edge of the shadows. The figure's face was twisted, contorted with pain and fear, its eyes wide and unseeing. It reached out, its fingers curling, its mouth opening in a silent scream.

Derek felt a cold, sickening dread settle over him as he realized what he was seeing.

These were the Garbage Man's victims, souls trapped in a purgatory of darkness and silence, forever bound to the shadows.

"This is what he leaves behind," Paul whispered, his voice trembling. "This is what happens when he finds you."

Derek took a shaky step back, his mind reeling as he stared at the silent figures drifting through the tunnel. He could feel their pain, their terror, pressing down on him, filling his mind with a suffocating darkness.

"We need to go," he whispered, his voice barely audible. "Now."

But as they turned to leave, a low, rasping hiss echoed through the tunnel, filling the air with a sense of impending doom. Derek's blood ran cold as he realized the truth.

The Garbage Man was here.

They hadn't escaped him.

They'd walked straight into his lair.

The hiss reverberated through the tunnel, a low, grating sound that sent chills crawling up Derek's spine. He felt the air thicken, as if the very walls were closing in, trapping him in the heart of darkness. The figures around them—the hollow-eyed, silent remnants of the Garbage Man's victims—stared ahead, unseeing, their faces frozen in expressions of terror and pain.

Derek's pulse pounded in his ears. He could feel it now, a presence lurking in the shadows, watching him, closing in. It was as if the walls themselves were alive, pulsing with a malevolent energy that sought to pull him deeper.

Beside him, Paul was breathing hard, his face pale and drawn. "We have to keep moving," he whispered, his voice shaking. "If he's found us here, then... then this place isn't safe anymore."

They stumbled through the dark, moving deeper into the Hollow. The shadows grew denser, the air colder with each step. The faint greenish glow from the old lights barely illuminated the path ahead, casting long, twisted shadows that seemed to stretch out, grasping for them.

They reached a fork in the tunnel. Paul hesitated, his gaze darting between the two paths, his expression tense. "Left," he muttered, almost to himself. "We need to go left. It's the only way out."

But just as they took a step, the low hiss returned, filling the air with a sound that was both alive and dead. It was a rasping whisper, thick with decay, echoing off the walls and filling the space with a sense of unspeakable dread.

"Leaving so soon?" the voice rasped, dripping with malice. It was a voice Derek recognized instantly, a sound that had haunted his dreams since the night he first saw him. The Garbage Man.

Derek felt the urge to bolt, but Paul grabbed his arm, his eyes fierce. "Stay calm. If we panic, he'll have us. We have to keep moving."

They took the left path, their footsteps echoing through the empty tunnel, the sounds bouncing back at them in distorted, twisted echoes. But the hissing voice followed, growing louder, sharper, like metal scraping against bone.

"You don't belong here," the Garbage Man's voice slithered through the air, as cold and cutting as ice. "This is my world, my domain. And you have brought fear into it... how delicious."

The shadows shifted, twisting around them, and Derek's heart hammered as he caught a glimpse of a figure moving just beyond the edge of his vision. It was tall and hunched, shrouded in darkness, its face hidden beneath a filthy hood, but he could see the gleam of bone-white fingers stretching toward him.

They ran, their footsteps pounding through the Hollow, breath hitching with every step. The tunnel twisted and turned, each passage looking more like the last, each shadow darker and deeper. The world around them felt endless, labyrinthine, stretching on with no end in sight.

As they rounded a corner, Derek felt the cold, skeletal hand of the Garbage Man graze his shoulder, icy and wet, sending a shock through his body. He stumbled forward, his heart pounding as he scrambled to put distance between them. The creature's laughter echoed behind him, a sound that was both gurgling and hollow, filling the tunnel with an oppressive dread.

They reached a large chamber, its ceiling high and lost in shadows, the floor littered with scraps of metal and debris. The walls were covered in the same strange symbols Derek had seen on the door, but here they seemed to pulse, each one radiating a faint, sickly green light that illuminated the space with an otherworldly glow.

"This way!" Paul shouted, his voice filled with desperation. He pointed to an old iron ladder leading up the far wall, barely visible in the dim light. "If we can get up there, we might be able to reach the surface!"

Derek didn't hesitate. He grabbed hold of the ladder, his hands shaking as he climbed, his legs aching with every step. Paul followed close behind, the sounds of their labored breaths mingling with the ever-present hiss of the Garbage Man, still echoing below.

Halfway up the ladder, Derek risked a glance down. His blood froze.

The Garbage Man was standing at the base, his head tilted back, staring up at them with those empty, gleaming eyes. He reached out, his bony hand wrapping around the lowest rung of the ladder, and began to climb, his movements slow, deliberate, each step accompanied by the sickening sound of bones popping and flesh shifting.

"Faster!" Derek shouted, his voice hoarse with terror. He climbed faster, his fingers slipping on the cold, rusted metal, his body trembling as he pushed himself upward.

But the Garbage Man was gaining on them, his skeletal form stretching, his movements grotesque and unnatural. He reached out, his fingers inches from Derek's ankle, and let out a low, rasping hiss.

"You can't escape," he whispered, his voice filled with a twisted glee. "You belong to me now."

Derek's heart pounded, his hands slick with sweat as he climbed, his every nerve on edge. He could feel the Garbage

Man's cold breath on his skin, the stench of rot filling his lungs as he scrambled up the ladder, desperate to reach the top.

With one final push, he reached the ledge, pulling himself up and out of the tunnel. He collapsed on the ground, gasping for breath, his body shaking with exhaustion and fear.

Paul followed seconds later, his face pale and drawn. He slammed a rusted grate over the opening, jamming a piece of metal into it to hold it in place. They could still hear the Garbage Man's voice below, his hissing laughter filling the air, taunting them.

"This isn't over," he rasped, his voice filled with malice. "You can run, but you'll never escape."

The sound faded, leaving them in silence, the echoes of the Garbage Man's laughter lingering in their minds like a curse.

For a long moment, they just lay there, breathing heavily, the weight of what they had just survived settling over them. Derek's mind raced, images of the Hollow, the trapped souls, the Garbage Man's twisted grin flashing through his thoughts.

Paul sat up, his face etched with grim determination. "This is worse than I thought," he said, his voice hoarse. "The Hollow... it's not just a place he avoids. It's part of him. That's why we couldn't get out. It's like he's anchored to it."

Derek shivered, the realization settling over him like a heavy weight. "So, there's no way to escape him? He's just... always going to be there?"

Paul's eyes narrowed. "No. There's a way to end this. But it's going to be dangerous. And we can't do it alone."

He glanced around, his gaze distant, as if searching for something just beyond his reach. "There are others," he murmured. "People who've seen him, survived him. If we can find them... if we can bring them together... maybe we can weaken him."

Derek's pulse quickened. "You really think that will work?"

Paul met his gaze, his eyes hard and unyielding. "It has to. If we don't stop him, he'll keep taking people, dragging them down into the Hollow, trapping them in his darkness."

They stood in silence, the enormity of their task hanging over them like a dark cloud. Derek could feel the weight of it, the sense that they were about to walk into something far darker and more dangerous than they could imagine.

But he knew one thing for certain: he couldn't go back. Not now. Not after everything he'd seen, everything he'd felt. He had to end this, to face the creature that had haunted his nights, that had stolen the lives of so many.

Together, he and Paul turned and made their way back to the city, their minds filled with a single, terrifying goal.

They were going to hunt the Garbage Man.

And this time, they would make sure he never returned.

The weight of the city seemed to settle heavier on Derek's shoulders as he and Paul emerged from the Hollow, the first rays of dawn filtering weakly through the thick, smoggy air. Everything felt surreal, as though they had stepped back into a reality that no longer recognized them.

The regular world went on as it always had, blind to the terror lurking just below its surface.

Derek's mind buzzed with questions and fears, images of the Hollow and the Garbage Man flashing through his thoughts. The trapped souls, the skeletal hand reaching up the ladder—he couldn't shake them. And Paul's words echoed in his mind: *There are others.*

"Do you really think we can find them?" Derek asked, his voice barely louder than a whisper. "People who've... who've seen him and survived?"

Paul gave a slow nod, his expression distant, wary. "They're out there. I know of a few already, people who left the city when he started coming for them. Others might still be around, but they keep to themselves. The fear stays with you, keeps you hidden." He met Derek's gaze. "It's going to be hard getting them to trust us."

"But they'll know we're telling the truth," Derek murmured, a bitter edge to his voice. "They'll have the scars, too."

Paul's eyes darkened. "Exactly."

They spent the day planning, pooling their scant resources, scraping together what little money they had for a burner phone and a handful of supplies. Paul jotted down names on a scrap of paper—names he'd heard over the years, rumors of people who had escaped the Garbage Man, sightings of those who had vanished and then reappeared, seemingly haunted and forever marked by their ordeal.

By nightfall, they had a plan. It was far from perfect, but it was a start.

Their first stop was the outskirts of the city, near an abandoned warehouse where, according to Paul, a man named Calvin had been spotted off and on for years. Calvin was one of the "long-haunters"—someone who'd managed to survive the Garbage Man's pursuit by keeping to the shadows, staying invisible. Paul had only heard whispers about him, but he was certain Calvin had seen the Garbage Man and lived to tell the tale.

The warehouse loomed dark and silent, its broken windows staring blankly out onto the empty street. The air around it felt thick and stagnant, heavy with the scent of rust and damp concrete. Derek hesitated, his heart pounding as he gazed up at the dilapidated building.

"Do you think he'll talk to us?" he asked.

Paul shrugged, his expression unreadable. "If he's even here, we'll have to convince him. Calvin's probably more scared of the Garbage Man than anyone else."

They stepped inside, their footsteps echoing through the vast, empty space. The smell of mildew and decay hung in the air, mixing with the faint scent of something burnt. Their flashlight beams sliced through the darkness, illuminating scattered debris, rusted machinery, and empty crates that looked like they hadn't been touched in years.

"Calvin!" Paul called, his voice echoing off the walls. "It's safe. We're here to talk."

For a moment, there was only silence. Then, a faint shuffling sound came from the far end of the warehouse, near a cluster of crates stacked haphazardly against the wall. Derek's grip tightened on the flashlight as he followed the sound, his pulse racing.

A figure emerged from the shadows, hunched and wary, his eyes darting around like a cornered animal. He was gaunt, his skin pale and stretched over his bones, his clothes tattered and filthy. But his eyes were sharp, filled with a mixture of fear and suspicion as he looked them over.

"Who are you?" the man asked, his voice rough, raw. He looked past Derek, his gaze lingering on Paul. "Why'd you bring him here?"

Paul took a slow step forward, hands raised in a gesture of peace. "Calvin, right? My name's Paul, and this is Derek. We're... survivors. We've seen him too."

Calvin's eyes narrowed, his body tense. "You're talking about the Garbage Man, aren't you?"

Derek nodded, feeling a strange sense of relief that he wasn't alone in his terror. "Yes. We've seen him, and we're trying to find a way to stop him."

Calvin let out a bitter laugh, his gaze hard. "Stop him? You think you're the first? People have been trying for years. Every time, he finds them. He drags them down into the Hollow, just like all the others. You're wasting your time."

Paul took a deep breath, his expression resolute. "We don't have any other choice. If we don't do something, he'll keep taking people. We want your help, Calvin. Whatever you know about him, whatever you've learned."

Calvin shook his head, his face twisted with anger and fear. "I survived because I stayed hidden. Kept to myself, moved around. He doesn't chase what he can't find." His eyes flickered to Derek, a glimmer of something almost like pity in his gaze. "You're marked, aren't you? He's already found you."

Derek nodded, feeling the weight of that truth settle over him. "Yeah... and I think he'll keep coming until he has me."

Calvin stared at him for a long moment, his face a mixture of frustration and resignation. Finally, he let out a heavy sigh. "Fine. I'll tell you what I know. But after this, I'm gone. For good. And you're on your own."

Derek felt a flicker of hope. "We just need anything you can tell us. Anything at all."

Calvin sat on an overturned crate, rubbing his hands together, his eyes fixed on a distant point in the darkness. "The Garbage Man... he's not like us. Not like anything I've ever seen. People think he's just a monster, something that comes out of the shadows and drags people away. But he's more than that. He's tied to the city, like he's part of it. Wherever there's trash, decay... he's there."

Paul frowned, his gaze intent. "Why? Why does he take people?"

Calvin's lips twisted into a grim smile. "You think I know that? I've tried to understand, tried to figure out why he hunts us. The best I can tell, he's drawn to certain people—those who've been left behind, those society's forgotten. The lost, the unwanted. Maybe he thinks we're like him."

A chill ran through Derek as he listened. It made a sick kind of sense. The Garbage Man was a predator, but he was also a collector, gathering the discarded souls of the city.

"Is there any way to stop him?" Derek asked, his voice barely above a whisper.

Calvin was silent for a long time, his gaze distant. "There might be. There are stories, rumors. People say there's a place even he can't go, a place buried deep below the city, where the oldest roots are, the darkest shadows. They call it the Core."

"The Core?" Paul repeated, his voice a mix of fascination and fear.

Calvin nodded. "It's a place of pure darkness, a place no light can touch. Some say it's where he came from, that he crawled out of it like some kind of disease spreading through the city. Others say it's where he's bound, trapped by something even older than him. If you could get there, maybe... maybe you could break the bond."

Derek's mind raced, his thoughts spiraling. "And if we break the bond?"

Calvin's face was grim. "Then maybe he'll disappear. Maybe he'll finally leave us alone. But it's a risk. If you go to the Core and fail, he'll own you. You'll be trapped, just like the others."

Silence settled over them, the enormity of what lay ahead pressing down on them like a weight.

Paul met Derek's gaze, his eyes dark with determination. "This is our chance, Derek. If there's even a small chance we can end this, we have to take it."

Derek took a deep breath, feeling a surge of fear and resolve rise within him. He'd come this far; there was no turning back now.

Calvin stood, his face pale. "If you're going to the Core, be ready. He'll know. He always knows when someone's getting close." He reached into his pocket, pulling out a small, tattered notebook. "Take this. It's everything I know about him, everything I've learned over the years. Maybe it'll help."

Derek accepted the notebook, feeling the weight of it in his hand. It was worn, the pages filled with sketches, notes, descriptions of sightings. Each page felt like a small piece of a larger puzzle, one that might finally lead them to the truth.

Calvin turned, his figure melting into the shadows. "Good luck," he muttered, his voice barely audible. "You'll need it."

And then he was gone, leaving Derek and Paul alone in the darkness, the notebook their only guide.

They exchanged a look, the fear and determination mirrored in each other's eyes. They knew what they had to do.

They were going to find the Core.

And they were going to confront the Garbage Man once and for all.

The descent to the Core began in silence, each step taking Derek and Paul deeper into the heart of the city's darkness. The notebook Calvin had given them was clutched tightly in Derek's hands, its worn pages their only guide through the labyrinthine tunnels beneath New York. The air was thick, stale, carrying the scent of mold and damp earth. It was as if they were walking into the city's buried soul, a place long forgotten, where light and life had no reach.

The directions were scattered throughout the notebook, scrawled in broken sentences and jagged lines, as if written in moments of sheer desperation. Calvin's words echoed through Derek's mind: *If you go to the Core and fail, he'll own you.*

The journey twisted through narrow passages, forgotten subway lines, and tunnels choked with debris. Each tunnel seemed darker than the last, the walls covered in strange symbols, markings that pulsed faintly in the dim light of their flashlights. Derek's skin crawled as he brushed past the markings, feeling as if unseen eyes were watching, judging their every step.

Finally, they reached a gaping opening—a cavernous space that stretched out like the mouth of some ancient beast. The Core. The air was colder here, thick with a silence so profound it felt like it was pressing in on them. Derek's heart hammered, his body tensed as they crossed the threshold, stepping into a place that felt as if it had never known light.

A single word, etched in bold letters at the top of one of Calvin's final notes, burned in Derek's mind: *Sacrifice.*

"What... what do you think it means?" Derek whispered, his voice barely more than a breath.

Paul's face was pale, his eyes fixed on the darkness ahead. "I don't know. But if Calvin's right, the Core is where he came from. This place is like a tether, a bond that keeps him here. Maybe sacrifice is the only way to break it."

Derek shivered, his thoughts racing. "What... kind of sacrifice?"

Paul didn't answer. Instead, he took a shaky step forward, his flashlight casting a feeble glow that barely penetrated the shadows. Derek followed, his heart pounding as they moved deeper into the Core, their footsteps echoing through the oppressive silence.

Then, a faint rustling sound broke the stillness, like the dry whisper of paper against stone. Derek stopped, his breath hitching as he scanned the darkness.

From the far end of the cavern, the Garbage Man stepped into view, his skeletal form hunched, his bony fingers twitching with unnatural eagerness. His eyes gleamed, hollow and white, filled with a terrible, malevolent joy.

"You have come," he rasped, his voice dripping with satisfaction. "Finally, you understand."

Derek felt his body go cold, every nerve screaming at him to turn and run. But he held his ground, his fists clenched as he faced the creature that had haunted him, hunted him, from the shadows.

"We're here to end this," Paul said, his voice steady but tinged with fear. "This is where you're bound, isn't it? The Core. This is where you draw your power."

The Garbage Man tilted his head, his grin widening. "Yes. This place is mine, as much a part of me as your fear, your despair." He took a step closer, his footsteps slow, deliberate. "You cannot sever the bond. This city... its shadows, its waste... it sustains me."

Derek's hand tightened around the notebook. He flipped through the pages, his gaze landing on one of Calvin's last entries, a scrawled sentence that sent a chill down his spine: *Only one soul can break the bond, but that soul will never leave.*

He glanced at Paul, a sickening realization settling over him. The sacrifice Calvin had mentioned... it wasn't just symbolic.

The Garbage Man watched them with growing anticipation, his eyes gleaming with hunger. "Are you afraid?" he hissed, his voice a low, mocking whisper. "Good. Fear is the only thing that matters here."

Derek took a shaky breath, forcing himself to stand tall, to face the creature head-on. "Maybe we're afraid," he said, his voice trembling. "But we're not going to let you keep doing this. If this place ties you to the city, then maybe we can bind you here forever."

The Garbage Man's smile faltered, a flicker of doubt crossing his twisted face. Paul stepped forward, his jaw set with grim determination. "If one soul can break the bond," he said quietly, "then one soul will."

Before Derek could react, Paul lunged forward, stepping between Derek and the Garbage Man, his gaze fixed on the creature with fierce defiance.

"Paul, no!" Derek cried, reaching for him, but Paul shook his head.

"This is the only way, Derek," he murmured, his voice soft. "You're young. You still have a chance. I've been running from him long enough. It's time I ended this."

He turned to face the Garbage Man, his body rigid, his fists clenched. "Take me. I'm your sacrifice. Bind yourself to this place, and release the others. No more hunting, no more shadows. End it here."

The Garbage Man let out a low, guttural laugh, his eyes gleaming with savage delight. "Very well," he whispered, his voice thick with satisfaction. "One soul, bound forever to the Core."

Derek watched, helpless, as the Garbage Man reached out, his skeletal fingers wrapping around Paul's shoulder, pulling him closer. Paul's face twisted with pain, but he didn't resist, his gaze unwavering, his jaw set in grim determination.

As the Garbage Man's grip tightened, Paul's body began to change, his skin paling, his eyes glazing over as if drained of life. Derek could see his friend fading, becoming one with the darkness, his form melting into the shadows, disappearing into the Core.

"No!" Derek cried, his voice breaking as he reached for Paul. But it was too late.

With a final, echoing hiss, the Garbage Man and Paul vanished, leaving only silence and darkness in their wake.

Derek collapsed to his knees, his heart pounding, his chest tight with grief and horror. He was alone, the Core stretching out around him like an endless, empty void. But the shadows felt... still, as if something heavy, something ancient, had finally been put to rest.

He rose to his feet, his body trembling as he turned to leave. The weight of Paul's sacrifice hung over him like a shroud, filling him with a mixture of sorrow and gratitude. He knew he'd never forget what his friend had done, that he'd carry this moment with him forever.

As he made his way back through the tunnels, a strange feeling settled over him—a sense of peace, of finality. The city's shadows felt less oppressive, the darkness less consuming. He knew, somehow, that the Garbage Man was gone, bound to the Core by Paul's final act of defiance.

When Derek finally emerged into the morning light, he took a deep breath, the fresh air filling his lungs, cleansing him of the horrors he had endured. He looked back at the city, the towering buildings, the bustling streets, and felt a weight lift from his shoulders.

For the first time, he was free.

Months later, Derek found himself wandering the city's alleys, the familiar streets now holding a new, quiet beauty. He no longer looked over his shoulder, no longer felt the oppressive weight of something lurking just beyond his sight.

But one night, as he walked past the entrance to the old subway station, a faint sound reached his ears—a soft, distant whisper, like the rustling of paper against stone. He froze, his heart skipping a beat as he glanced toward the darkness.

And in the distance, faint but unmistakable, he thought he saw a figure, hunched and shadowed, watching him with hollow eyes.

He turned and walked away, never looking back, but the whisper stayed with him, drifting through the night, a reminder of the darkness that lay just beneath the surface of the city.

A reminder that, in some corners of the world, the shadows never truly sleep.

The End

9

THE MIDNIGHT FEAST

Midnight was approaching, and the streets were still. The city of West Haven was a place most people avoided after dark, its abandoned buildings casting long shadows across cracked sidewalks and empty lots. No one really knew what went on in the darker corners of the city, but they all heard the rumors—the stories of people who disappeared without a trace, and the strange, shuffling sounds that echoed through the night.

Dean pulled his coat tighter, trying to ward off the biting chill. He'd been living on the streets for years, and though he'd heard his share of stories, he'd never put much stock in them. Hunger and cold were real enough. Monsters and ghosts were things the others talked about to pass the long hours, nothing more.

But something was different about tonight. The air felt thick, charged with an electricity that made the hair on his arms stand on end. The wind had died down, and a strange, suffocating silence filled the streets, pressing down on everything like a heavy weight.

Then, somewhere in the distance, came a soft, scraping sound—like nails dragging across pavement.

Dean froze, his eyes scanning the dark alleyways. At first, he thought it was one of the other homeless, maybe even a rat scavenging for scraps. But then he saw it, just beyond the glow of a flickering streetlamp. A figure, hunched and misshapen, lumbering slowly out of an alley.

Its movements were wrong—jagged and stiff, as if its limbs were being pulled by invisible strings. It dragged one foot behind it, its body twisting at odd angles. Dean squinted, heart pounding, trying to make sense of what he was seeing. The figure stepped into the light, and his stomach twisted.

The man's skin was pale, almost gray, hanging loosely over a bony frame. Large chunks of flesh were missing, exposing sinew and bone beneath, and his face was contorted into an expression of agonized hunger. Milky white eyes, empty and lifeless, locked onto Dean.

Dean's breath caught in his throat. He wanted to scream, to run, but his feet felt like they were glued to the ground.

More shapes shuffled out of the shadows behind the first figure, each one as mangled and decayed as the last. The smell hit him next, a nauseating stench of rotting flesh and earth. These weren't people. They weren't alive.

They were dead.

Dean stumbled back, nearly tripping over his own feet, his heart hammering as he tried to make sense of what he was seeing. One of the creatures tilted its head, jaws hanging open, teeth bared in a horrific grin. Without warning, it lunged forward, moving with an unnatural speed that belied its stiff, broken body.

Dean turned and ran, the sound of shuffling footsteps and low, guttural groans echoing behind him. He dashed down the alley, his breath coming in short, panicked gasps, feet slipping on the damp pavement. He ducked behind a dumpster, pressing himself against the cold metal, hoping the shadows would hide him.

But the groans grew louder, closer, until they filled his ears. He peeked around the corner, his heart dropping as he saw a swarm of the creatures moving down the alley, pale and ravenous, eyes fixed forward. Their fingers clawed at the ground, and their mouths opened and closed in jerky, repetitive motions, as if already tasting their prey.

Dean held his breath, heart pounding in his throat. He'd never felt fear like this before—raw, icy terror that left him shaking uncontrollably. He could hear them breathing, or something close to it, the sound a raspy, rattling wheeze as they sniffed the air.

Then one of them stopped, head twitching as it caught his scent. Its eyes snapped to his hiding place, its jaw cracking open in a sickening grin as it let out a bone-chilling hiss. The others turned, and for a brief, horrifying moment, they were all staring directly at him.

Dean's instincts kicked in, and he bolted, tearing down the alley as fast as his legs would carry him. The creatures screeched, their voices guttural and angry, and he could hear them close behind, their feet dragging along the pavement, their arms outstretched, grasping for him.

He darted into another alley, his mind racing, searching for any place he could hide. But there was nowhere to go. They were closing in, and the footsteps were getting louder, the smell of rot filling his nostrils.

Just as he thought it was over, a hand reached out from the shadows, grabbing his arm and yanking him into a narrow doorway. He struggled, but a gruff voice hissed in his ear, "Quiet, or they'll hear you!"

Dean bit his tongue, forcing himself to stay silent as the hand dragged him deeper into the darkness. He could hear the creatures just outside, their groans growing louder, their bony fingers scratching at the walls as they searched for him.

Then, just as quickly as they had appeared, the sounds faded. Dean let out a shuddering breath, his body shaking with relief and terror. He turned to his rescuer, squinting to see in the darkness. A man, ragged and dirty, stared back at him with wide, haunted eyes.

"You have no idea what you're dealing with," the man whispered, his voice trembling. "They come out every night... and they won't stop until they've fed."

Dean swallowed hard, the horror of what he'd just witnessed sinking in. "What... what *are* they?"

The man's face twisted into a grimace, his eyes hollow and tired. "They're the dead. And if you don't want to end up like them, you'd better learn how to survive the night."

Dean's heart still pounded, the terror lingering like a taste of bile in his throat. The man who had saved him gestured deeper into the shadowed hallway. Dean had no choice but to follow, his body still trembling with fear as he crept along the narrow corridor, lit only by the dim glow of a flickering bulb overhead. The man guided him down a set of rickety stairs, into what looked like an abandoned basement.

Dean glanced around, taking in the space. It was cluttered with torn blankets, empty cans, and broken furniture—clearly a makeshift shelter, a last refuge for those trying to survive the night. A few others were huddled in the shadows, their eyes wide and haunted, casting wary glances at Dean as he entered.

The man, noticing his fear, nodded gravely. "You're new to the streets, aren't you?"

Dean gave a hesitant nod, not trusting his voice.

The man sighed, scratching at the stubble on his chin. "Name's Jonas," he said, extending a hand. "You picked the wrong place to be homeless, my friend."

Dean shook his hand, noting the rough calluses and the strength in his grip. "I... I thought the stories were just rumors," he muttered, his voice barely more than a whisper. "But those... things... they're real."

"Oh, they're real," Jonas replied, his eyes dark. "Every night after midnight, they crawl out of their graves, hungry and lost. They've got no souls, no memories—just a need to feed."

Dean swallowed hard, the words hanging heavily in the air. He glanced at the others in the room, their hollow faces, the fear in their eyes. He wasn't the only one who had come face-to-face with death tonight.

"Why don't they go after everyone? Why just the homeless?" Dean asked, a bitter edge in his voice.

Jonas's expression grew grim. "I don't know. Maybe it's easier for them to pick us off—no one's looking out for us, no one cares if we disappear." He paused, glancing at the others. "And the ones who know what's happening? They stay away from this part of the city after dark. We're the ones left behind."

Dean felt a cold, twisting knot in his stomach. He wanted to leave, to get as far from this place as possible, but he knew he'd never make it past the undead waiting just beyond the walls. He sank down against the cold, crumbling bricks, rubbing his face with shaking hands.

"I don't even know how to survive this," he admitted, his voice hollow.

Jonas placed a hand on his shoulder, firm and steady. "Stick with us. We've managed to make it this far, but it's getting worse. They're getting smarter, more organized, like they're learning." His voice dropped to a whisper. "And lately... some of them have started to remember."

Dean's head snapped up. "Remember? What do you mean?"

"Sometimes, they call out names," Jonas said, his voice barely audible. "People they knew in life, people they lost. As if something in them recognizes us, remembers what it used to be. But don't be fooled—there's nothing human left in them. It's just a cruel echo, something that makes it easier for them to lure us out."

A chill ran down Dean's spine. He closed his eyes, trying to process what Jonas was saying. His mind flashed back to the thing that had chased him down the alley—the way it had looked at him, as if recognizing him, reaching for him with that awful, grinning skull.

Suddenly, a sound echoed through the basement, making everyone jump. A scraping, scratching noise, like nails dragging against concrete. Dean's heart stopped, and he exchanged a horrified glance with Jonas. They were here.

"Everyone, keep quiet," Jonas hissed, motioning for them to huddle against the far wall, away from the door. The others crouched in silence, eyes wide with fear.

The scratching grew louder, closer, a sickening drag of bone and flesh against stone. And then came the voice—a low, guttural whisper that drifted through the cracks in the wall.

"D...ean..."

Dean's blood ran cold. He stared at the door, his heart pounding painfully against his ribs. That voice, hollow and broken, sounded like his mother's. He hadn't thought of her in years, not since she had passed away. But this was impossible. She was gone, buried a thousand miles away, far from this city. And yet...

"Dean... it's me..." The voice, faint and pleading, filled the room, a terrible mimicry of his mother's once-soft tone.

He squeezed his eyes shut, pressing his hands over his ears, trying to block it out. It wasn't real, he told himself. It was a trick, just like Jonas had said. But the voice grew louder, each word clawing at his sanity.

"I've missed you, Dean... come to me..."

Dean shook his head, struggling against the wave of emotions flooding him. He felt a hand on his shoulder and looked up to see Jonas's grim expression. "Don't listen to it," Jonas whispered. "They'll say anything to get you to open that door."

Dean nodded, forcing himself to stay still, ignoring the voice that continued to whisper, the sound twisting into a low, guttural snarl.

And then the door shook, rattling violently as something clawed at it, pounding against the wood with inhuman strength. The entire room fell silent, every breath held as they watched the door, waiting for it to splinter under the force.

But after a few tense seconds, the banging stopped. The scraping sounds receded, fading back into the night as the undead moved on, searching for another weak soul to lure into the darkness.

Dean let out a shaky breath, his entire body trembling. He looked around at the others, their faces pale and drawn, each of them clinging to the fragile hope that they'd survive until dawn.

Jonas patted him on the back, a weary but determined look in his eyes. "Welcome to the night, Dean. This is just the beginning."

Dean swallowed, a flicker of defiance sparking within him. If he was going to survive, he would have to become like them—ruthless, unyielding, willing to face the nightmares that lurked in the shadows. And maybe, just maybe, he'd find a way to stop the creatures that wore the faces of the dead.

As he sat there in the darkness, Dean knew one thing for certain: he wouldn't be leaving West Haven until he understood what had turned the city's forgotten souls into monsters.

The dawn brought a bleak gray light to the basement, casting long shadows across the concrete floor. The quiet of morning offered little comfort to the survivors huddled together in the stale air, still shaken from the night's terror. Dean hadn't slept at all, his mind replaying the image of that grotesque, decaying face clawing at the door, calling his name in his mother's voice. He could still hear her, that hollow, warped echo drifting through his memory, *"Come to me, Dean..."*

Jonas stirred beside him, his face grim. He caught Dean's eye and gave a slow, weary nod. "Not everyone makes it through their first night," he muttered, almost like it was a small victory. "You did good."

Dean wasn't so sure. Every muscle in his body was tense, every nerve on edge. He felt like a caged animal, trapped in the basement with strangers, knowing those things were waiting outside. The thought made him shiver, and he rubbed his hands over his arms, trying to dispel the chill.

As the day wore on, the small group of survivors began to emerge from their fearful silence, talking in hushed tones about their plans for food, water, and another night of survival. Dean listened quietly, feeling like an outsider, his mind still buzzing with a mix of dread and confusion.

Jonas leaned closer, his voice barely a whisper. "Tonight, I'll take you out there. You've got to see what we're dealing with if you're going to survive."

Dean looked at him, fear flickering in his eyes. "Out there? Why can't we just stay here?"

"Because hiding isn't enough," Jonas replied, his expression hardening. "They're learning. Sooner or later, they'll find a way to break down that door. We've got to keep moving."

Dean took a shaky breath, nodding. As much as he hated to admit it, Jonas was right. Those things were growing stronger, smarter. He'd felt it in the way they'd targeted him, calling his name, dragging out his worst fears to lure him closer. It was only a matter of time before hiding stopped working.

As dusk settled, a heavy silence filled the basement once again. The air grew thick with anticipation, the taste of fear almost tangible. Jonas checked a battered old watch on his wrist, his lips pressed into a grim line.

"It's time."

Dean's heart pounded as he followed Jonas to the basement door, his every instinct screaming at him to turn back, to run. But he pushed forward, telling himself he needed to know what lay out there, what horrors waited in the shadows.

Jonas slowly opened the door, and they crept into the street, their breaths clouding in the cold night air. West Haven's streets were silent, the streetlamps flickering above like dying stars. Dean could see faint shadows flitting between the buildings, slipping in and out of sight, like phantoms haunting the empty alleys.

They moved carefully, keeping close to the walls, skirting around piles of garbage and broken glass that littered the ground. Dean's nerves were stretched taut, every small sound causing his pulse to spike. The night seemed to close in around them, suffocating and thick.

As they rounded a corner, Jonas grabbed Dean's arm, pulling him into the shadows. He raised a finger to his lips, and Dean nodded, his stomach churning with unease.

Ahead, a figure emerged from the darkness, staggering into the street. Dean's breath caught in his throat as he recognized the telltale jerking, unnatural movements. The creature's flesh hung in loose, decaying strips, its face a nightmare of torn muscle and exposed bone, its mouth hanging open in a silent scream. Milky eyes stared ahead, unseeing, but its nose flared as if scenting the air.

Jonas tensed beside him, his hand clamping down on Dean's arm. "Stay perfectly still," he whispered. "It's hunting."

Dean held his breath, willing his body not to move. His heart thundered in his chest, each beat feeling louder than the last. The creature sniffed the air, its head swiveling unnaturally as it searched for the scent of fresh prey.

Slowly, a low, rattling sound began to escape its throat—a wet, inhuman growl that made Dean's blood run cold. He could see its fingers twitching, nails caked with dried blood and dirt, ready to rip and tear.

The creature's head snapped toward them, and Dean's heart stopped. He felt Jonas's grip tighten, and he forced himself to stay still, even as the creature began to stagger in their direction, its bony fingers twitching hungrily. The smell of rot filled the air, nauseating and thick.

Then, in an instant, another noise shattered the silence—a can clattering to the ground farther down the alley. The creature's head snapped toward the sound, its milky eyes narrowing as it focused on the new distraction. With a low snarl, it turned and shuffled away, disappearing back into the shadows.

Dean let out a shuddering breath, his body trembling. "Why... why didn't it just come for us?"

Jonas shook his head, his face pale. "They're getting stronger, but they're not smart enough to track us by sight yet. Sound and scent are all they have. But it's enough. We're lucky to be alive."

Dean wanted to respond, but his voice caught in his throat. They crept forward, moving quickly and quietly, but every alley and doorway seemed to hold a new threat. Shadows shifted, and every flicker of movement set Dean's nerves on edge. He could feel them all around, stalking them, an invisible presence lingering just out of sight.

As they approached the edge of the city, Jonas stopped, motioning for Dean to look up.

And there, silhouetted against the moonlight, was a sight that would haunt Dean forever.

A horde of them, dozens of pale, decaying bodies clawing their way out of the ground, their limbs tangled and broken, their faces frozen in expressions of primal hunger. They emerged from shallow graves, their hands clawing at the dirt, pulling themselves up with sickening determination. The air was filled with the sound of snapping bones and tearing flesh as they ripped free from the earth, rising to join the others.

Dean felt bile rise in his throat as he watched. One by one, the creatures turned, their heads jerking in unison as they caught the scent of life. His life. Their eyes—empty and hollow—locked onto him with a hunger that seemed to radiate from the darkness itself.

"Run," Jonas whispered, his voice barely audible.

Dean didn't need to be told twice. He turned and sprinted, his footsteps pounding against the pavement as he raced through the streets. He could hear the creatures behind him, their guttural growls and hisses filling the air, their footsteps growing louder with each passing second.

They rounded another corner, and Dean stumbled, his body aching with terror and exhaustion. He looked back, his heart sinking as he saw the horde closing in, their pale faces grinning with malicious delight, their arms outstretched, ready to drag him down.

Just as one of them lunged, a pair of strong arms yanked him into a doorway, slamming the door shut just as the creature's claws scraped against the wood.

Dean collapsed against the wall, gasping for air, his body shaking with adrenaline. Jonas leaned over him, his face dark and serious.

“They’re not going to stop until they’ve fed,” he said quietly. “Tomorrow, we plan. But if we’re going to survive this, you’re going to have to be ready to fight.”

Dean looked up at him, fear and determination warring in his gaze. He had never been a fighter, never thought he would need to be. But as he listened to the undead scratching and snarling just outside the door, he realized he had no choice.

Because the dead were hungry, and they weren’t going to rest until they had their fill.

The morning light was weak and gray, barely filtering through the grime-covered windows of the abandoned building where Dean, Jonas, and a few others had spent the night. The air inside was thick and damp, the stench of decay seeping through the walls as if even daylight couldn’t purge the horrors of the night. Every time Dean closed his eyes, he saw them—their hollow eyes, their bloodied hands reaching, grasping, desperate to feed.

He shivered, pulling his jacket closer as he sat with his back against the wall. Jonas stood nearby, pacing in slow, tense strides. He looked worn, his eyes dark with exhaustion, but his movements were brisk, focused. There was a fire in him that Dean couldn’t ignore—a determination that seemed to grow stronger with every encounter.

“Listen up, everyone,” Jonas said, his voice low but carrying through the silent room. The others—about eight in total—gathered closer, their expressions grim. Dean recognized the haunted look in their eyes. They'd all seen it. They all knew the terror that waited in the darkness.

"We can't keep running," Jonas continued. "It's only a matter of time before they find us here, too. They're getting faster, stronger. If we're going to survive, we need a plan. We need to find a way to stop them."

"How?" a voice called from the back, shaky and doubtful. It belonged to Lena, a wiry woman with a scar across her cheek and a hard look in her eye. She crossed her arms, her gaze fixed on Jonas. "We don't even know what they are. How do we kill what's already dead?"

Jonas looked down, his jaw clenched. "That's what we need to figure out," he said. "They're feeding on us because we're vulnerable, because we're scattered. But if we come together, if we plan our moves, maybe we can at least buy ourselves some time."

Dean cleared his throat, his voice barely above a whisper. "You said they're... remembering things. Does that mean they're not just mindless monsters?"

The room fell silent, and everyone stared at Jonas, waiting for his answer. He glanced around, his expression darkening.

"It's true," he said finally. "Some of them... they have these moments. Like a flash of who they used to be. It's quick—usually when they're hunting. Sometimes they'll say names or words that seem like memories." He paused, his gaze distant. "But don't mistake it for humanity. Whatever they are, they're not alive, and they're not... us."

Dean's stomach twisted. He wanted to argue, to hope that maybe there was some remnant of a soul, something that could be reasoned with. But deep down, he knew it was a fantasy. He'd seen the hunger in their eyes, the mindless need to consume, to destroy.

"What about the graves?" Dean asked suddenly. "If they're coming from the ground... shouldn't we go there? See if we can figure out what's causing it?"

Jonas's eyes narrowed thoughtfully, and the others exchanged nervous glances. It was a dangerous idea, but they all knew it was the only way to get answers.

"The cemetery," Jonas said, nodding. "The problem started there, so maybe the solution lies there too. But we'll need supplies—anything we can use to defend ourselves. Weapons, flashlights, food. Once we leave here, there's no coming back."

The group murmured their agreement, a sense of unity, however fragile, settling over them. They gathered what few belongings they had—mostly scraps of food, some knives and pipes scavenged from abandoned buildings, and a few flashlights with flickering batteries. It wasn't much, but it was all they had.

As they prepared, Dean's pulse quickened. Every step forward felt like a step closer to death, yet a strange resolve filled him. He wasn't going to die cowering in a corner, waiting for those things to find him. If he was going down, he'd do it fighting.

When night fell, they set out under the cover of darkness, moving like shadows through the empty streets. The city was deathly quiet, the only sound the faint rustling of leaves in the wind. Every dark alley, every empty window felt like a pair of eyes watching them, waiting.

As they neared the cemetery, Lena froze, her eyes widening in horror. She pointed toward the far side of the fence, where several fresh graves lay disturbed, the earth churned up and scattered. The group halted, tension crackling in the air as they stared at the exposed dirt, each grave looking as if something had clawed its way up from below.

"Look," Jonas whispered, gesturing toward the headstones. Dean squinted, his breath hitching as he realized what was carved into the stone.

Each headstone bore the name of one of the homeless, people who had gone missing in recent months, whose disappearances had been brushed aside. He recognized some of the names—Tommy, Hazel, Mitch. Friends. Faces he hadn't seen in weeks, faces he'd assumed had simply moved on.

His blood ran cold. These were the people who'd come back, twisted and decayed, hunting the living. And if they weren't stopped, he knew he'd be next.

"This is it," Jonas murmured, his eyes flashing with grim determination. "They're coming back because they can't rest. Something's keeping them here, bringing them back... forcing them to hunt."

A cold wind swept through the cemetery, sending chills down Dean's spine. He glanced around, the shadows lengthening as the darkness grew deeper, pressing in from all sides.

Then, a faint rustling sounded nearby.

Dean turned, his flashlight shaking in his hand as he aimed it toward the source of the sound. The beam cut through the darkness, landing on the hunched form of a decayed figure, its flesh hanging in tattered ribbons, its eyes hollow and dead. It stared back at him, lips pulling back in a grin that stretched too wide, too tight, revealing rotted teeth.

"Get back!" Jonas shouted, but it was too late.

The creature lunged, moving with unnatural speed, its bones cracking and twisting as it hurtled toward them. Dean staggered back, his flashlight falling from his hand, plunging them into darkness.

He could hear the others screaming, the sounds of struggle and the sickening crunch of flesh and bone. Hands grabbed at him, clawing at his jacket, pulling him toward the ground. He kicked wildly, feeling his foot connect with something soft and yielding.

Another flashlight beam cut through the night, and Dean saw Jonas swinging a piece of rebar, smashing it against the creature's head. It stumbled, its skull caving in with a sickening crunch, but it kept moving, its hands outstretched, fingers snapping as they tried to grasp at Jonas's throat.

With a guttural scream, Dean grabbed a nearby rock and slammed it into the creature's head, over and over, until its body finally went limp, collapsing in a heap at his feet. He stumbled back, his chest heaving, his hands slick with something warm and sticky.

They regrouped, breathing heavily, the weight of what had just happened settling over them like a shroud. Each of them was battered, bloodied, their eyes wide with horror and fear.

"What... what are we doing here?" Lena whispered, her voice barely audible. "We're going to die out here."

"No," Jonas said, his voice firm. "We're not dying tonight. Not like this."

He turned to the graves, his face set with grim determination. "We dig. We find whatever's binding them here, and we end this."

One by one, they moved toward the graves, the flickering flashlight beams illuminating the dark earth. They dug with bare hands and broken tools, tearing into the soil, ignoring the pain, the cold, the exhaustion.

Finally, Dean's fingers hit something solid, cold and unyielding. He wiped the dirt away, his heart pounding as he realized what he was holding.

A small, rusted amulet, shaped like a skull, lay in his hand, the metal icy to the touch. A wave of dread washed over him, a feeling of darkness so deep it seemed to reach into his very soul.

Jonas stared at the amulet, his eyes wide. "This... this is it," he whispered. "This is what's keeping them here."

He raised the amulet above his head, preparing to smash it against a rock. But just as he brought his hand down, a low, inhuman wail filled the night, echoing from all around them. The shadows began to shift, the air growing thick and heavy as the undead rose from the darkness, dozens of them, their eyes locked onto the amulet, their faces twisted in rage.

Dean's breath caught in his throat as he realized the truth. They hadn't come here to end the curse.

They'd come to wake the dead.

The night erupted in chaos.

As soon as Jonas's hand crushed the amulet against the rock, a deafening wail tore through the air, so loud and unearthly that it sent every one of them to their knees, clutching their heads. The sound vibrated deep into Dean's bones, like the cry of a thousand souls, agonized and furious.

Around them, the earth began to tremble. The graves they had disturbed seemed to open wider, the soil churning as more twisted figures emerged, skeletal hands clawing their way out of the dark, pulling bodies from the earth. Dean's vision swam with horror as he watched the dead come alive—faces he recognized, friends who had once shared his fate, now twisted and empty, pale eyes fixed on him with a hunger that sent his blood cold.

"Run!" Jonas screamed, grabbing Dean by the arm and pulling him toward the edge of the cemetery. The others scattered, their flashlights bobbing wildly as they sprinted through the darkness, desperate to escape the clawing hands reaching from every direction.

Dean's legs pumped beneath him, the cold air stinging his lungs as he raced after Jonas, barely able to keep up. Behind him, he could hear Lena's frantic footsteps, her breaths coming in gasps, but the undead were close—too close.

A guttural snarl erupted from the darkness, and Dean risked a glance over his shoulder. One of the creatures was almost on top of him, its mouth hanging open in a ghoulish grin, jagged teeth exposed as it reached for him. Its skin was stretched tight over its bony face, bits of flesh hanging in strips, eyes wide with a twisted kind of joy at the hunt.

He stumbled, his foot catching on an exposed root, and he hit the ground hard. The creature pounced, fingers digging into his arm, nails biting into his skin. Dean screamed, his free hand scrabbling in the dirt for anything to use as a weapon. His fingers found a rock, and he swung it blindly, feeling the sickening crunch as it connected with the creature's head.

It barely slowed down. The thing snarled, its mouth snapping inches from his face, hot, rancid breath washing over him. Dean pushed back, the creature's weight pressing down on him, his muscles straining as he held it at bay.

Then, suddenly, the pressure lifted. Jonas had yanked the creature off him, hurling it to the ground before plunging a broken piece of metal into its chest. The creature writhed, hissing and clawing, but the fight slowly drained from it, its movements growing sluggish until it lay still, eyes staring blankly into the night.

"Come on!" Jonas shouted, pulling Dean to his feet. "They won't stay down for long!"

They bolted, sprinting through the graves, dodging hands that reached from the ground, faces that snarled and snapped at them from the shadows. The cemetery gates loomed ahead, their rusted iron bars twisted and broken, offering little comfort from the horrors clawing their way out of the earth.

But it was their only hope.

They burst through the gates, crashing into the open street. Jonas stopped, breathing heavily, his eyes scanning the dark alleys and empty buildings. "We need somewhere to hide," he said, his voice tense. "They'll keep coming—they can smell us, hear us. And now, we've got them all awake."

Dean shivered, the weight of what they'd done settling over him like a heavy shroud. The amulet—he'd thought destroying it would end the curse, but it had done the opposite. They hadn't freed the souls trapped in the cemetery; they'd unleashed them.

A scream pierced the air, high-pitched and desperate. Dean looked up to see Lena sprinting toward them, her face twisted in terror. Behind her, a dozen of the undead swarmed, moving with terrifying speed, their movements jerky and unnatural, their faces contorted into hungry snarls.

"Inside!" Jonas shouted, shoving Dean toward an old, abandoned church across the street. They dashed up the steps, throwing open the heavy wooden doors and slamming them shut just as Lena reached the entrance, her eyes wild with fear.

The undead crashed against the doors, their fists pounding on the wood, scratching, clawing, their voices rising in a cacophony of snarls and guttural wails. The door shuddered under the weight of their assault, but it held—for now.

The church was dark, silent except for the muffled sounds of the dead outside. Dean's breath came in short, panicked gasps as he leaned against the wall, his body trembling with adrenaline.

Jonas lit a small, dusty oil lamp he found near the altar, casting an eerie glow across the room. The stained-glass windows threw distorted colors across the floor, painting the walls with twisted images of saints and martyrs, their faces staring down with hollow eyes.

Lena clutched her arms, her face pale. "What the hell just happened out there?" she demanded, her voice shaking. "We were supposed to stop them, not... not *this*!"

Jonas looked down, his jaw clenched. "The amulet... it didn't break the curse. It just... woke them up."

Dean stared at him, his mind racing. "Then how do we stop them?"

Jonas shook his head, his expression grim. "I don't know. But whatever bound them to that place, whatever started this... it's older, darker than anything we can understand. It's like they're tied to something, something that won't let them rest."

A sudden, bone-rattling crash shook the door, splintering the wood. The undead were relentless, their pounding growing stronger, more frenzied. Dean took a step back, his pulse racing.

"They're going to get in!" Lena cried, her eyes wide with panic. "We have to do something!"

Jonas turned to her, his expression steely. "There's nowhere left to run, Lena. We're going to have to fight."

Dean's heart pounded, the reality of their situation settling over him like a cold, damp blanket. He picked up a heavy metal candlestick from the altar, gripping it tightly. His hands were shaking, but he forced himself to steady his breathing. If they were going to survive the night, they couldn't afford to be afraid.

Another crash, and the door splintered further, the hands of the undead clawing their way through the gaps, reaching, hungry. Their faces pressed against the cracks, leering, their mouths gaping open as they hissed and snarled.

The door burst open, and the first of the undead staggered into the church, its bony fingers outstretched, its eyes fixed on Dean with a terrible hunger. He swung the candlestick with all his strength, feeling it connect with the creature's skull, the impact sending a jolt up his arm. The creature reeled, but it didn't go down, its empty gaze locked onto him as it lunged forward again.

Jonas leaped in, ramming a piece of broken wood into the creature's chest. It shuddered, emitting a guttural hiss before it crumpled to the floor. But there were more—dozens more—flooding into the church, their mouths open in silent screams, their eyes burning with the madness of the cursed.

Lena screamed, swinging a rusted pipe at the nearest creature, her face twisted in terror and fury. Dean fought beside her, each swing of his candlestick met with sickening crunches and snarls. They fought in a frenzy, their movements desperate, every breath filled with the stench of rot and decay.

But the dead kept coming, relentless, unstoppable.

Dean's muscles ached, his breaths coming in short gasps, but he didn't stop. He couldn't stop. The undead surrounded them, a sea of pale, twisted faces, their hands reaching, grasping, pulling him down.

Just as he thought it was over, a strange sound filled the air—a low, deep hum that vibrated through the walls of the church. The undead froze, their heads turning as one, their bodies swaying in rhythm with the sound.

Jonas's eyes widened. "Do you hear that?" he whispered, his voice filled with awe and terror.

The hum grew louder, more intense, as if something ancient and powerful were awakening beneath the earth. The undead turned, shuffling back toward the door, their eyes blank, their movements almost mechanical. One by one, they filed out of the church, disappearing into the night, leaving the three of them standing in stunned silence.

"What... what just happened?" Dean asked, his voice trembling.

Jonas shook his head, a look of horror in his eyes. "Something called them back. Something even they're afraid of."

A chill ran down Dean's spine as he realized the truth. They hadn't survived by luck or by strength.

Something far darker, far older than the undead had saved them.

And it was still out there, waiting in the shadows.

The quiet that followed the undead's retreat felt oppressive, like the heavy silence before a storm. Dean leaned against the altar, his breath coming in shallow gasps, his muscles quivering from the night's ordeal. The others—Lena and Jonas—stood nearby, equally shaken, their faces pale under the flickering glow of the oil lamp.

Outside, the night was still, but it wasn't comforting. Instead, the silence hung with an unnatural weight, as if the city itself was holding its breath. The hum that had driven the creatures away lingered in Dean's memory, vibrating faintly in his bones. He didn't know what had called them back, but he knew, somehow, that they hadn't escaped danger. Not yet.

"We can't stay here," Lena said, her voice barely a whisper. She stared at the doorway, her gaze darting nervously to the dark street beyond. "Whatever sent them away... it'll come back. I know it."

Jonas nodded, his face grave. "Agreed. We need to keep moving, find somewhere safe. But first..." He turned to Dean, his eyes filled with a dark intensity. "We need to figure out what we're dealing with. Something's controlling them."

Dean swallowed hard, the memory of the amulet heavy in his mind. "You think that amulet... whatever it was, you think it's connected to all this?"

Jonas gave a slow nod. "It's not just the undead. Something powerful, something ancient, is using that amulet, calling them to it. And it won't stop until it has what it wants."

Dean shivered, glancing at the broken amulet still lying on the ground by the door, its metallic surface glinting faintly in the dim light. He didn't know much about curses, but he could feel the weight of it, the lingering darkness that seemed to seep from the tiny object.

"Then what *does* it want?" Lena asked, her voice cracking. "Why does it keep raising the dead, making them hunt us?"

Jonas shook his head, his expression troubled. "I don't know, but I'd bet it has something to do with the city itself—

something buried here, something that never should have been disturbed."

Dean's gaze drifted toward the darkened street, his pulse racing as he recalled the eerie feeling of being watched, of something ancient and unseen lurking just beyond the reach of the light. "Maybe it's... waiting for us to find it," he murmured. "Maybe that's why it's calling to us."

Jonas looked at him, a spark of understanding dawning in his eyes. "You might be right," he said slowly. "If it's using the undead to draw us in, it must want us to find something... or someone."

The three of them exchanged a tense glance, the realization settling over them like a shroud. Whatever was behind the undead, whatever force had awakened in the night, it was playing a game, guiding them into its grasp. And they were walking right into it.

Jonas checked his watch, his face tense. "It's almost dawn," he said, his voice low. "We've got a few hours of daylight. If we're going to figure this out, we need to start now."

They gathered what supplies they could find—a few broken pieces of wood for makeshift weapons, a flashlight that flickered weakly, and a few scraps of food scavenged from the church's storage closet. It wasn't much, but it was better than nothing.

Together, they stepped into the street, moving in silence, their eyes scanning every shadow, every dark alley. The city was quiet, the usual hum of traffic and distant voices replaced by an eerie stillness. It was as if the entire world had stopped, waiting for the next move.

They followed Jonas's lead, winding through narrow alleyways and deserted streets, the buildings looming above them like silent sentinels. The air grew colder as they approached the cemetery, a chill that seemed to seep into their bones, settling over them like a shroud.

Finally, they reached the cemetery gates. The graves lay in eerie silence, each headstone casting long, crooked shadows across the ground. The earth looked freshly disturbed, the soil churned and broken, as if something had clawed its way out.

Dean's breath hitched as he took in the scene, the memory of last night's horrors flashing through his mind. But this time, the graves were empty, their inhabitants nowhere in sight.

"What now?" Lena asked, her voice barely a whisper.

Jonas scanned the area, his eyes sharp. "Look for anything that stands out—a marking, a symbol, anything that could tell us what's going on."

They split up, each moving carefully among the graves, their eyes searching for any sign of the dark force that had raised the dead. Dean's pulse quickened as he moved through the rows of headstones, his flashlight casting an eerie glow across the names etched into the stone.

And then he saw it.

At the edge of the cemetery, hidden behind a gnarled tree, lay a small, crumbling tomb, half-buried in the earth. The door was ajar, a faint, sickly green light seeping from within, casting twisted shadows across the ground.

"Jonas!" he called, his voice trembling. "Over here!"

The others hurried to his side, their eyes widening as they took in the sight of the tomb. Lena stepped back, her face pale. "This is a bad idea," she muttered. "A really bad idea."

But Jonas was already moving forward, his face set with grim determination. "If this is where the power's coming from, we have to face it. We've come this far."

Dean swallowed hard, steeling himself as he followed Jonas into the tomb, the cold air thick with the stench of decay. Inside, the walls were covered in strange symbols, twisted shapes carved deep into the stone. The faint green light seemed to pulse, flickering in rhythm with some unseen heartbeat.

And then, at the center of the tomb, they saw it—a figure, hunched and cloaked, sitting in a throne-like chair carved from bone. Its eyes were empty sockets, hollow and dark, its face hidden beneath a shroud. But its bony fingers clutched something in its lap, something that gleamed with an unnatural light.

Another amulet.

Dean's stomach twisted as he realized what it was. The amulet in the figure's hands was identical to the one Jonas had shattered, only this one was whole, its surface unmarred, glowing with a sickly, hypnotic light.

The figure's head lifted, its empty eyes fixing on them with a terrible, knowing gaze. And then it spoke, its voice a low, raspy whisper that echoed through the tomb, filling every corner with a sense of dread.

"You have come... at last."

Dean felt his heart skip a beat, his body frozen in place. The creature's voice was like nails scraping against stone, ancient and malevolent, filled with a darkness that seemed to press down on him, suffocating.

"Why... why are you doing this?" Jonas demanded, his voice shaking. "What do you want from us?"

The figure's mouth twisted into a grin, revealing rows of jagged teeth. "I am the one who binds them," it rasped. "I am the one who calls them forth. They are mine, bound to my will... and now, so are you."

Dean's blood ran cold as the figure lifted the amulet, the green light growing brighter, pulsing in time with his own heartbeat. He could feel it pulling at him, drawing him closer, his body moving against his will. He struggled, trying to resist, but the pull was too strong.

"No!" Lena cried, lunging forward, grabbing Dean's arm, pulling him back. The creature's eyes narrowed, its bony fingers tightening around the amulet.

"You cannot escape," it hissed, its voice filled with venom. "You are bound, just as they are. You belong to me."

The ground began to tremble, the walls shaking as the symbols carved into the stone began to glow, filling the tomb with an otherworldly light. Dean could feel the power coursing through the air, dark and ancient, pressing down on him, suffocating.

"We have to destroy it!" Jonas shouted, his voice barely audible over the rumbling. "The amulet—if we break it, maybe we can stop this!"

Dean gritted his teeth, summoning every ounce of strength as he lunged forward, his hand reaching for the amulet. The creature snarled, its fingers tightening around the object, but Dean was faster. He wrenched it free, feeling the cold, unnatural energy pulsing through his hand.

With a yell, he hurled the amulet to the ground, smashing it beneath his heel. The tomb shook violently, the light fading as the amulet shattered, pieces scattering across the stone floor.

The figure let out an ear-piercing scream, its form disintegrating into a cloud of ash and shadow, swirling around them before vanishing into the darkness. The tomb fell silent, the only sound their ragged breathing, their bodies trembling with the aftermath of terror.

"It's... it's over," Lena whispered, her voice barely audible.

But as they staggered out of the tomb, the first rays of dawn breaking over the cemetery, Dean couldn't shake the feeling that it wasn't over. That the darkness was still there, lurking just beyond the light, waiting for its chance to return.

And as they walked back into the city, leaving the ruins of the tomb behind, he knew one thing for certain.

They had disturbed something that would never rest.

The dawn was bleak, casting a pale, washed-out light over the city. The streets were empty, but the air felt heavy, as if the night had left a lingering stain that even daylight couldn't erase. Dean, Jonas, and Lena made their way through the silent streets, the weight of the night's horrors pressing down on them.

They were exhausted, each step a painful reminder of the bruises, cuts, and fear they had endured. But the amulet was destroyed, the creature vanquished. It *should* have felt like a victory.

And yet, deep down, Dean felt an unsettling quiet—the kind that suggested something unfinished, like the silence that settles in just before a storm. He glanced over at Jonas, who wore a similarly grim expression, his eyes dark and distant.

"What now?" Lena whispered, breaking the silence. She looked back at the cemetery, now a hazy silhouette against the rising sun. "Are they... gone?"

Jonas shook his head, his lips pressed into a thin line. "Gone? I don't know. I wish I could say for sure, but after what we saw..." His voice trailed off, and he didn't need to finish. They'd all felt it—the presence that lingered, like an unseen shadow waiting just beyond the edges of reality.

As they walked, the sound of distant footsteps caught their attention. A lone figure stood at the end of the street, watching them with an unnerving stillness. Dean squinted, his heart hammering as he recognized the figure's outline.

It was one of the undead.

But unlike before, this one didn't lunge, didn't snarl or bare its teeth. Instead, it simply stared at them, its pale, empty eyes filled with something Dean couldn't place. Sadness? Longing?

Lena took a step back, fear flashing across her face. "I thought... I thought we destroyed the amulet," she whispered. "Why is it still here?"

The creature didn't move, didn't make a sound. Slowly, more figures appeared in the street, their forms emerging from the shadows, one by one. Each of them wore a similar expression, empty and hollow, yet somehow... mournful.

Dean felt a chill settle over him as he realized what they were seeing.

"They're not here to hunt," he murmured. "They're... waiting."

Jonas's eyes narrowed. "Waiting for what?"

The creature at the front of the group raised its head, its eyes meeting Dean's. And then, in a voice barely more than a whisper, it spoke.

"*Help us...*"

The words echoed through the street, carried by a soft breeze that seemed to chill the air. Dean felt his chest tighten, a wave of dread washing over him. The voice was filled with pain, with sorrow—and something else. Something ancient, a longing for peace that they couldn't achieve alone.

"They're trapped," Jonas muttered, understanding dawning in his eyes. "The amulet was only part of it. There's something deeper keeping them here, something binding them to this world."

Dean's mind raced, the memories of last night flooding back. The tomb, the creature, the strange symbols carved into the walls. He thought of the way the undead had risen, as if summoned by a force that went beyond a simple curse.

"It's the city itself," he said quietly. "Something happened here... something that tied their souls to this place."

The undead continued to watch them, their faces pale and gaunt, their eyes hollow but not hostile. They didn't move, didn't lunge. They just stood, waiting in the silence, their forms swaying slightly, like reeds in a ghostly wind.

Jonas exhaled, his shoulders slumping. "There's only one thing we can do," he said, his voice heavy with resignation. "We have to release them, once and for all."

Lena looked at him, her expression bewildered. "How? The amulet is destroyed. The creature in the tomb is gone."

Jonas's gaze was somber as he looked at the ground. "I don't know, but I think... I think we have to give them closure. Acknowledgment. Maybe they're waiting for someone to see them, to honor them."

Dean took a step forward, his eyes locked on the creature that had spoken. He could see it clearly now—a man, or what had once been a man, his face weathered and lined, his eyes reflecting a lifetime's worth of suffering. Dean felt a pang of sadness, a strange empathy that cut through his fear.

"We're sorry," he said softly, his voice trembling. "For whatever you went through, for whatever kept you here."

The creature's expression softened, and its head tilted slightly, as if listening.

Dean took a deep breath, speaking louder now. "You don't have to stay here anymore. Whatever happened... it's over now. You're free to go."

The silence that followed was thick and heavy, filled with a sense of anticipation. Slowly, the undead figures began to shift, their bodies turning toward the cemetery, their eyes empty but somehow at peace.

One by one, they shuffled away, their forms fading into the morning mist, disappearing into the shadows. Dean watched them go, his heart pounding as he felt a strange warmth settle over him, a sensation of release, of relief. The figures melted into the fog, leaving the street empty, silent, as if they had never been there.

When the last of them was gone, Jonas let out a shaky breath, his face a mixture of relief and exhaustion. "It's done," he whispered, his voice filled with awe.

Dean nodded, the weight of the night lifting from his shoulders. They stood there in silence, watching as the first rays of sunlight broke through the clouds, bathing the empty street in a soft, golden light. For the first time since the nightmare had begun, Dean felt a sense of peace, a calmness that settled over the city like a gentle lull.

They walked away from the cemetery, leaving the horrors of the past behind them. As they moved through the quiet streets, the buildings seemed brighter, the air lighter, as if the city itself had been cleansed of the darkness that had haunted it for so long.

But as they reached the edge of town, Dean felt a final shiver run down his spine. He glanced back at the cemetery, a faint, fleeting image catching his eye—a lone figure, watching them from the shadows, its face hidden beneath a hood, its eyes glinting with an otherworldly light.

And then, in an instant, it was gone.

Dean took a deep breath, turning away. He knew the past was never truly gone, that the shadows would always linger. But for now, the dead could rest.

The End

10
THE SKELETON PEOPLE

The small town of Raven's Hollow was the kind of place where nothing much ever happened. Nestled in a valley surrounded by dense forests and rocky hills, it was the kind of town where the people were quiet, where everyone knew everyone else, and where strange things rarely happened. But that all changed one cold October night when people began to vanish without a trace.

It started with strange sounds—scratching noises in the dark, faint whispers that floated through the town's empty streets. People brushed them off at first, blaming the wind or some wandering animal. But as the days passed, the sounds grew louder, more insistent, filling the air with a sense of unease that no one could shake.

Then, the disappearances began.

The first to vanish was Old Man Grayson, a retired watchmaker who lived on the edge of town. His neighbors said they heard him shouting in the middle of the night, his voice echoing through the stillness, but by the time anyone arrived, he was gone. The only trace left behind was his cane, lying abandoned on his front porch.

A week later, young Emily Cartwright was reported missing. Her parents found her bedroom window wide open, the curtains fluttering in the cold night breeze, her bed empty. A search party combed through the woods, but there was no sign of her—just a series of deep scratches along the tree trunks near her house, marks that looked almost like claw marks, though no one could explain what animal could have made them.

By the time a third person, a local schoolteacher named Miss Hensley, went missing, the town was gripped by fear. The people of Raven's Hollow began to lock their doors at night, to avoid going out after dark, but the sense of dread only grew, spreading through the town like a sickness.

That night, as the cold wind howled through the streets, seventeen-year-old Ethan Hawke sat alone in his bedroom, staring out the window at the dark, empty street below. He was one of the few who had seen something—something strange, something he couldn't explain.

It had happened just the night before, as he was walking home from a friend's house. He'd taken a shortcut through the alley behind Main Street, his footsteps echoing through the narrow passage, the streetlights casting long shadows along the walls. And that's when he'd heard it—a soft, scratching sound, coming from somewhere in the darkness.

He'd paused, his heart pounding, his eyes scanning the shadows, and then he saw it.

A figure stood at the end of the alley, half-hidden in the shadows, its form tall and thin, its body wrapped in tattered clothing that hung loosely from its frame. But what struck him most was its face—or rather, the lack of one. The figure's skin was stretched taut over bone, pale and skeletal, its hollow eye sockets fixed on him, unblinking.

Ethan had frozen, his breath caught in his throat, his body paralyzed with fear. The figure tilted its head, as though studying him, its mouth stretching into a wide, toothless grin, a soundless laugh that sent chills racing down his spine. And then, just as quickly as it had appeared, it melted back into the shadows, disappearing as though it had never been there.

He hadn't told anyone. Not his parents, not his friends. He'd convinced himself it was a trick of the light, a shadow cast by something harmless. But as he sat in his room, staring out into the dark street, he couldn't shake the feeling that something was out there, watching, waiting.

The next morning, the townspeople gathered in the town square, their faces drawn and fearful, their voices hushed as they exchanged worried glances. Sheriff Tom Riley stood on the steps of the town hall, his expression grim as he addressed the crowd.

"I know you're all scared," he began, his voice steady but tense. "We've lost three good people, and we still don't know why. But I promise you, we're doing everything we can to find them and to keep this town safe."

The crowd murmured, but their fear was palpable, a tension that hung in the air like a storm about to break. Ethan stood near the back, his heart pounding as he listened, his mind racing with memories of the skeletal figure he'd seen, the figure that now haunted his dreams.

As the sheriff spoke, Ethan noticed a group of strangers standing near the edge of the crowd, their faces partially hidden beneath dark hoods. They were tall, their bodies thin, their skin pale and stretched tight over their bones, almost like... no, it couldn't be. His mind must be playing tricks on him.

But then one of them turned, his hollow gaze meeting Ethan's, and for a moment, he felt a chill run down his spine, a sense of recognition that made his stomach twist. It was the same look, the same unblinking stare, and he knew, deep down, that these people—if they could even be called people—were connected to the disappearances.

The sheriff continued to speak, but Ethan's attention was fixed on the strangers, his mind racing with questions, with a growing, terrible suspicion. He could feel their eyes on him, watching, studying, as though he were the next one on their list.

As the crowd began to disperse, Ethan slipped away, his thoughts racing. He had to know the truth. He had to understand what was happening in Raven's Hollow and who—or what—these strangers were.

That night, as the wind whipped through the trees and the moon cast a pale glow over the town, Ethan snuck out of his house, his footsteps silent as he made his way to the abandoned church at the edge of town. He'd heard rumors that strange things happened there at night, that it was a gathering place for shadows and secrets. He didn't know what he was looking for, but he knew he couldn't stay silent any longer.

The church was dark, its windows shattered, its walls covered in ivy, a relic of the town's past that had been left to decay. He pushed open the heavy wooden doors, stepping inside, his flashlight cutting through the darkness, illuminating the rows of empty pews, the broken altar.

And then he saw them.

The figures stood at the front of the church, their bodies shrouded in darkness, their faces hidden beneath their hoods. But as he approached, he saw their faces—skeletal, skin stretched thin over hollow cheeks, empty eyes fixed on him with a cold, calculating stare. They watched him in silence, their heads tilting in unison, a movement that sent chills racing down his spine.

"Ethan," one of them whispered, his voice low and hollow, a sound that seemed to echo through the empty church. "You shouldn't have come here."

He took a step back, his heart pounding, his mind reeling with fear and confusion. "Who... who are you?" he stuttered; his voice barely audible.

The figure smiled, a thin, chilling smile that stretched across his face, his skin taut and lifeless. "We are the ones who walk between worlds," he murmured, his voice filled with a strange, eerie calm. "The Skeleton People. We come when the time is right, when the darkness calls us. And now... it's your time."

Ethan's mind raced, his body frozen with fear as he watched the figure step closer, his bony fingers reaching out, his hollow eyes fixed on him with a hunger that defied understanding.

He stumbled back, his flashlight falling from his hand, clattering to the floor as he turned and ran, his footsteps echoing through the empty church, his breath coming in short, frantic gasps. The Skeleton People followed, their movements slow but relentless, their hollow eyes watching, waiting, their presence filling the air with a cold, suffocating dread.

Ethan burst through the doors, the night air cold against his skin, his heart pounding as he ran, his mind reeling with terror. But even as he reached the edge of town, he could still feel their eyes on him, could still hear the soft, relentless whisper that followed him through the darkness.

"Ethan... we'll be waiting."

He made it home just as dawn was breaking, his body trembling, his mind haunted by the memory of the Skeleton People, of their hollow eyes, their chilling whispers. He knew he couldn't stay silent anymore. The town had to know the truth, had to understand the danger that lurked in the shadows.

But as he sat alone in his room, his heart pounding, he couldn't shake the feeling that the Skeleton People were still out there, watching, waiting, a presence that would never truly leave him.

And as he closed his eyes, he heard them once more, their voices a faint whisper in the back of his mind.

"Soon, Ethan... soon."

Ethan didn't sleep that night. His mind raced, replaying every horrifying detail he'd seen in the abandoned church. The image of the Skeleton People, their hollow eyes, the way they moved as if their very bodies were held together by darkness, haunted him. When morning finally broke, he felt a strange sense of relief, as though the daylight might somehow protect him from whatever lurked in the shadows.

But he knew he couldn't hide from them forever. He had to warn the town, had to tell someone. Yet, he hesitated, the words caught in his throat as he imagined how his story would sound to others. People would think he'd lost his mind, that he was just another teenager with an overactive imagination.

After hours of pacing and restless thoughts, he made up his mind to tell his best friend, Jake. If anyone would believe him, it would be Jake.

Later that afternoon, Ethan met Jake at their usual spot by the creek just outside of town. It was quiet there, away from the bustling sounds of people and cars, a place where they often went to escape and talk about everything and nothing.

Ethan took a deep breath, his mind racing with how to start. But before he could speak, Jake looked at him, his expression worried.

"You look like hell, man," Jake said, trying to sound casual but failing. "What's going on?"

Ethan glanced around, his voice barely above a whisper. "I saw something last night. Something in the church... the people who've been disappearing—I think I know who's behind it."

Jake's face shifted from worry to confusion. "Wait, you think you know what's going on with the disappearances?"

Ethan nodded, his voice shaking as he described the figures he'd seen, the skeletal faces, the hollow eyes, and their chilling whispers. As he spoke, Jake's expression changed from disbelief to something darker, a look of growing horror.

"So... you're saying there's some kind of... of skeleton cult?" Jake asked, his voice uncertain.

"No, Jake, it's worse than that." Ethan took a breath, trying to steady himself. "They're not people. They're like... these creatures, these beings that shouldn't exist. They called themselves the Skeleton People, and they knew my name, Jake. They knew who I was."

Jake looked down, his hands fidgeting, as though trying to make sense of it all. "So what are we supposed to do? Tell the sheriff? Tell someone in town?"

Ethan shook his head, his voice low. "They're not going to believe us. Not without proof."

There was a pause as both boys stared at the creek, their minds racing, trying to process the gravity of what Ethan had seen.

"So... we need proof," Jake finally said, his voice filled with a mix of determination and fear. "We go back to the church tonight. We get pictures, recordings, something."

Ethan's stomach churned at the thought of going back, of facing the Skeleton People again. But he knew Jake was right. If they wanted anyone to believe them, they needed evidence.

"Alright," he said, swallowing his fear. "Tonight. We'll meet at the edge of the woods by eight."

As darkness fell over Raven's Hollow, Ethan and Jake made their way to the abandoned church, their flashlights casting thin beams of light through the trees. The air was thick, cold, a silence filling the forest that was unnerving, unnatural. The closer they got, the heavier the atmosphere felt, as though something unseen was pressing against them, weighing them down.

When they reached the church, they hesitated, their footsteps faltering as they stared at the dark, looming structure. It seemed different in the moonlight, its walls casting long, twisted shadows, its windows dark and uninviting.

"You ready for this?" Jake asked, his voice barely a whisper.

Ethan nodded, though his heart pounded in his chest. "Yeah. Let's go."

They pushed open the doors, the old wood creaking, the sound echoing through the empty church. Their flashlights cut through the darkness, illuminating the rows of broken pews, the scattered debris on the floor. But the Skeleton People were nowhere to be seen.

Jake raised his camera, snapping photos as they moved through the building, each step slow, cautious. But as they reached the altar, they heard it—a faint, whispering sound, drifting through the air, surrounding them.

"Ethan... Jake..."

The boys froze, their flashlights shaking as the whispers grew louder, filling the church, each word thick with an unnatural resonance that seemed to seep into their bones.

"They know we're here," Ethan whispered, his voice barely audible.

Then, from the shadows, a figure emerged. It was one of the Skeleton People, tall and skeletal, its skin stretched tight over hollow bones, its empty eyes fixed on them with a chilling, unblinking stare. Another figure joined it, then another, until the boys were surrounded, their flashlights casting eerie shadows over the figures' skeletal forms.

Jake raised his camera, his hands trembling as he snapped picture after picture, desperate to capture the evidence they needed. But as he did, one of the Skeleton People tilted its head, its hollow eyes narrowing, its mouth stretching into a wide, silent grin.

"We do not like intruders," it whispered, its voice low, echoing, a sound that seemed to come from somewhere deep within the shadows.

Ethan felt a surge of panic, his mind racing as he took a step back, his flashlight flickering. "What... what do you want?"

The figure's grin widened, its face twisting into a grotesque mockery of human expression. "We want to walk among you," it murmured, its voice filled with a strange, twisted delight. "To take what is ours. You cannot stop us."

Without warning, the creatures surged forward, their skeletal forms moving with an unnatural speed, their hollow eyes fixed on the boys, their fingers reaching, stretching, clawing at the air. Jake and Ethan turned, sprinting toward the door, their breaths coming in frantic gasps, their footsteps pounding against the floor as they fled.

They burst out of the church, their hearts racing as they ran through the woods, the cold night air sharp against their skin, their minds reeling with terror. But even as they ran, they could still feel the presence of the Skeleton People, could still hear their voices, a faint, mocking whisper that followed them through the darkness.

By the time they reached the edge of town, both boys were breathless, their faces pale, their hands shaking. They stumbled onto Main Street, drawing the attention of a few late-night stragglers, their wide-eyed expressions filled with shock and fear.

"What's going on?" a man called, his voice laced with concern. "You boys alright?"

Ethan took a deep breath, his voice trembling as he looked up at the man. "We... we saw them. The people who've been disappearing... they're taking them. The Skeleton People. They're real, and they're coming."

The man's face twisted with disbelief, but as he looked at the boys, he could see the terror in their eyes, the sincerity in their voices. Slowly, others gathered, the townspeople exchanging anxious glances, murmurs of fear spreading through the crowd.

"What do we do?" someone asked, their voice filled with desperation.

Ethan glanced at Jake, a sense of determination settling over him. "We have to warn everyone," he said, his voice steady despite the fear that gripped him. "We can't let them take any more of us."

As the crowd grew, the sheriff arrived, his face grim as he listened to the boys' story. He was skeptical, but as he looked around at the frightened faces, at the fear that had taken hold of the town, he knew he couldn't ignore it.

"We'll keep watch tonight," he said, his voice filled with a resolve that masked his own uncertainty. "Everyone stay inside, lock your doors, keep your lights on. We'll face whatever's out there together."

The townspeople nodded, their fear tempered by a sense of unity, of shared purpose. They dispersed, each one returning to their homes, to their families, their minds filled with the image of the Skeleton People, of the creatures that lurked in the darkness, waiting.

Ethan and Jake stayed with the sheriff, watching as the night deepened, as the town fell silent, the only sound the faint rustle of leaves, the occasional creak of old wood. The streetlights cast a dim glow over Main Street, their beams barely penetrating the darkness, a fragile line of defense against the shadows.

But as the hours passed, they felt it—the chill that settled over the town, the presence that filled the air, pressing against them, suffocating. And then, from the shadows, they appeared.

The Skeleton People moved through the streets, their forms blending into the darkness, their hollow eyes fixed on the town, on the houses, on the lights. They moved slowly, deliberately, their mouths stretched into silent, chilling grins, their fingers reaching out, trailing along the walls, as though marking their territory.

Ethan watched, his heart pounding, his mind filled with a terrible, unshakable realization.

The Skeleton People were not just hunting them.

They were claiming Raven's Hollow as their own.

And as the first light of dawn broke over the horizon, casting its pale glow over the town, Ethan knew that this was only the beginning.

The Skeleton People had come.

And they would not leave until they had taken everything.

As the sun rose over Raven's Hollow, the sense of relief was short-lived. The Skeleton People had melted back into the shadows at dawn, but they left behind an eerie silence, a stillness that seeped into every street, every home. The townsfolk whispered anxiously to one another, their fear only growing as they realized this was no longer a nightmare to wake up from. The Skeleton People were real, and they were here.

Sheriff Tom Riley, a man who had always kept his calm in the face of disaster, looked more worn than anyone had ever seen him. His eyes were bloodshot, his expression haunted as he addressed the town from the steps of the town hall.

"They're watching us," he said, his voice carrying through the square. "Last night, they prowled the streets. They didn't take anyone, but they wanted us to see them. They're letting us know they can come anytime they want."

The crowd murmured, their fear mingling with anger, frustration. They were used to living in peace, in safety. And now that peace was shattered.

"What do we do, Sheriff?" a woman called from the crowd, clutching her child close.

Sheriff Riley took a deep breath, his voice steady but grim. "Tonight, we'll fight back. We'll form a guard, take shifts, patrol the streets. We need every able-bodied person to join. We can't let them take us without a fight."

Ethan and Jake stood at the edge of the crowd, listening, their faces pale but resolute. They knew they had been the ones to see the Skeleton People first, to bring the warning. And now, more than ever, they felt a responsibility to protect their town.

Ethan turned to Jake, his voice low. "We should join the patrol tonight. Whatever they are, we have to face them."

Jake nodded, though his expression was filled with fear. "Yeah... if we don't, they'll just keep coming."

As the townspeople dispersed, each one filled with a mixture of fear and resolve, Ethan and Jake made their way to the sheriff, volunteering for the night patrol. The sheriff nodded, gratitude in his eyes, though his face betrayed his own fears. He handed them flashlights, heavy wooden batons, and a supply of salt—an old trick he hoped might work against the supernatural.

"Salt's always had a way of keeping evil out," the sheriff muttered, more to himself than to the boys. "Let's hope it works against... whatever those things are."

As dusk fell over Raven's Hollow, a group of townsfolk gathered, each one carrying flashlights, batons, and salt bags slung over their shoulders. The streets were empty, every window darkened, every door locked tight. A tense silence hung over the town, broken only by the occasional rustle of leaves or the distant hoot of an owl.

The patrol split into pairs, each group assigned a section of the town. Ethan and Jake were paired with Sheriff Riley, their route covering the abandoned church and the woods nearby. The sheriff moved with quiet confidence, though his eyes betrayed his fear, his body tense as he scanned the shadows.

They walked the empty streets, their flashlights casting thin beams through the darkness, illuminating the twisted branches and the worn facades of the old buildings. The silence was suffocating, pressing against them, making every sound seem louder, every shadow seem alive.

And then they heard it—a soft, scratching sound, coming from somewhere up ahead, a sound that sent chills racing down their spines. It was faint, almost like nails scraping against stone, the kind of sound that didn't belong in the quiet night.

The sheriff motioned for them to stop, his flashlight trained on the darkness ahead. "Stay close," he whispered, his voice barely audible.

They moved forward, their footsteps silent, their breaths shallow as they approached the source of the sound. And there, just beyond the edge of the light, they saw them—the Skeleton People.

They stood in a loose circle, their forms tall and thin, their hollow eyes fixed on the patrol, their skeletal faces twisted into grotesque smiles. Their movements were slow, deliberate, each one moving with an unnatural grace, their bones visible beneath pale, stretched skin. The sight was nightmarish, their very presence filling the air with a cold, unyielding dread.

One of the creatures took a step forward, its mouth opening in a soundless scream, its bony fingers stretching, reaching, its hollow eyes fixed on Ethan.

The sheriff raised his baton, his voice filled with a fierce determination. "Stay back!"

But the Skeleton People didn't stop. They moved closer, their bodies shifting, almost blending into the shadows, their hollow eyes gleaming with a dark, insatiable hunger.

"Salt!" the sheriff yelled, grabbing his own pouch and throwing a handful toward the advancing figures.

As the salt hit the creatures, they recoiled, their bodies twisting, their faces contorting in anger. The sheriff seized the opportunity, throwing more salt around them, creating a barrier that forced the Skeleton People back, their forms flickering, as though caught between two worlds.

But the creatures did not retreat fully. They stopped just beyond the salt line, their faces twisted into mocking grins, their hollow eyes fixed on the patrol, a silent promise that they would not be held back for long.

By dawn, the townspeople gathered in the square once again, sharing stories of encounters, of strange sounds and sightings. Some had seen the Skeleton People lurking outside their windows, others had heard scratching at their doors, but the salt barriers had held, keeping the creatures at bay.

But they all knew it was only a temporary solution.

Ethan listened as the sheriff recounted their encounter near the church, the way the salt had forced the Skeleton People back, how they'd seemed almost weakened by it. But there was a look in the sheriff's eyes, a fear that couldn't be ignored.

"They're not going to stop," the sheriff said, his voice filled with grim certainty. "We've bought ourselves some time, but it won't be enough. We need something stronger, something that can send them back for good."

The townspeople murmured, fear and frustration mingling in their voices. They had used up most of the salt, had fortified their homes, but they knew it wouldn't hold forever.

Then, an elderly woman named Mabel stepped forward, her face lined with age, her eyes sharp and determined. She held a worn, leather-bound book, the pages filled with faded ink and strange symbols.

"I found this in my grandmother's things," she said, her voice steady. "It's a book of old rituals, things she used to keep the evil spirits at bay. There's one ritual in here—a banishment ritual. But it requires a place of power, somewhere the spirits are drawn to."

The crowd fell silent, each person considering her words, their faces a mix of fear and hope. And then Ethan spoke up, his voice firm.

"The church," he said. "They gather there every night. That's where we have to do it."

The sheriff nodded, his face grim. "Then tonight, we go to the church. We take whatever we can—salt, fire, this ritual. We drive them out once and for all."

As night fell once again over Raven's Hollow, the townsfolk gathered at the edge of the woods, their faces set with determination. They were armed with flashlights, bags of salt, torches, and Mabel's book, each person bracing themselves for the fight to come.

They made their way to the church, moving in silence, their footsteps muffled by the thick underbrush, their breath visible in the cold night air. The church loomed before them, its dark silhouette casting long shadows, the windows empty and lifeless.

Inside, they formed a circle around the altar, laying out the salt, lighting the torches, and reciting the words from Mabel's book. The air grew heavy, thick with the power of the ritual, each word filling the room with a strange, pulsing energy.

And then, they felt it—a cold breeze, a darkness pressing against them, and from the shadows, the Skeleton People appeared.

They moved through the walls, their forms flickering, blending with the darkness, their hollow eyes fixed on the circle of townsfolk. The Skeleton People advanced, their movements slow, menacing, each step filled with a twisted grace, their faces twisted into expressions of rage, of hunger.

The sheriff raised his torch, his voice steady as he addressed them. "This ends tonight!"

The Skeleton People hissed, their forms writhing, their bodies stretching as they reached for the townsfolk, their fingers clawing at the air, their hollow eyes filled with fury.

Ethan and Jake joined hands with the others, their voices joining in the chant, each word a barrier, a wall that held the creatures at bay. The torches blazed brighter, the salt forming a glowing line around them, a force that pushed the Skeleton People back, weakening them, forcing them to retreat.

One by one, the creatures faltered, their forms flickering, dissolving into shadows, their hollow eyes dimming as the ritual forced them out, banished them back to the darkness from which they had come.

And as the last of the Skeleton People faded, a heavy silence fell over the church, a stillness that felt like a sigh of relief, a release from the curse that had plagued the town.

The townsfolk lowered their torches, their breaths coming in short, relieved gasps, their faces filled with exhaustion, with disbelief.

They had survived. Raven's Hollow was safe.

But as they left the church, their footsteps echoing through the empty building, Ethan couldn't shake the feeling that something lingered in the shadows, a presence that watched, waited, a reminder that the darkness was never truly gone.

And as the first light of dawn broke over the town, he knew that they would never forget the Skeleton People, the creatures that had haunted their nights, a silent promise that Raven's Hollow would always be a place where shadows lingered, where the past never truly faded.

The End

11
THE HOUSE ON MAPLE STREET

The house on Maple Street had been the source of rumors in Briar Glen for as long as anyone could remember. It sat at the edge of town, a looming, decaying Victorian with peeling paint and boarded-up windows, its presence an ominous silhouette against the northern sky. No one dared approach it after dark, and even during the day, few lingered near its crumbling steps. Parents warned their children to stay away from it, yet the dare to visit its eerie halls was irresistible to every generation of teenagers who grew up in the town.

But for years, that was all the house on Maple Street had been—a haunting fixture in the town's lore, the subject of whispered stories and old superstitions. Until the night of October 23rd.

Jason Carter had lived in Briar Glen his whole life. He was no stranger to the stories about the house. He'd heard them all—the tale of the woman who had died in the attic, her spirit still trapped in the rafters, and the rumor about the children who had vanished from their beds only to be found weeks later on the house's front porch, lifeless, with no signs of what had taken them.

But Jason didn't believe in ghosts or haunted houses. He was seventeen, bold, and as he told his friends, "not afraid of a pile of rotting wood." So when they dared him to spend a night in the house on Maple Street, he accepted without a second thought. It was meant to be just another thrill, a quick scare, and maybe a funny story to tell at school the next day.

He arrived at the house just before midnight, a flashlight in hand, its beam flickering as he stepped through the overgrown yard. The autumn air was cold and damp, the kind that seemed to cling to your skin, and the wind howled softly, sending shivers down his spine. But he ignored it, pushing open the creaking gate and making his way up the crumbling stone path.

When he reached the front door, he hesitated, his hand hovering over the rusted doorknob. The wood was splintered, the faint smell of mildew wafting through the cracks. His heart pounded, but he forced himself to turn the knob, the door opening with a groan that echoed through the empty rooms.

The air inside was colder, thicker, carrying an odd, metallic tang. Dust hung in the air like a cloud, and the walls were lined with peeling wallpaper, the faint outlines of flowers barely visible beneath the layers of grime. As he stepped further in, he felt an unsettling stillness settle over him, as though the house itself were watching him, waiting.

He shook off the feeling, moving further into the house, his flashlight cutting a narrow path through the darkness. The silence was oppressive, thick, broken only by the faint creaks of the old floorboards beneath his feet. He wandered through the rooms, finding each one empty, abandoned, their windows boarded up, letting in only thin, jagged slivers of moonlight.

He reached the stairs, their wooden steps worn and splintered, leading up to the second floor. Jason hesitated, his hand on the banister, a strange sense of dread creeping over him. But the dare was to explore the entire house, and he wasn't about to back down now.

As he climbed the stairs, he heard it—a faint sound, like whispering, drifting down from above. He stopped, his breath catching, straining to listen. The whispers grew louder, clearer, as though someone were speaking just out of sight, their words indecipherable, a hushed litany that sent chills racing down his spine.

"Hello?" he called out, his voice sounding small, uncertain in the vast emptiness of the house. The whispers stopped, leaving a heavy silence in their wake. He swallowed, his hand gripping the flashlight tightly as he forced himself to keep going, each step heavier than the last.

At the top of the stairs, he found a long hallway stretching out before him, its walls lined with faded portraits, their frames tilted, their faces obscured by dust and grime. He shone his flashlight over them, his pulse quickening as he noticed the faint outlines of faces staring back at him, their eyes hollow, lifeless, their expressions twisted into masks of sorrow and fear.

As he moved down the hall, he heard another sound—a faint scratching, coming from one of the rooms to his left. He paused, his heart racing, listening as the sound grew louder, more frantic, like nails scraping against wood. Gathering his courage, he pushed open the door, his flashlight casting a pale glow over the room.

Inside, he saw a small, dusty nursery, a crib sitting in the corner, its sides splintered and broken. The walls were lined with faded wallpaper, once bright and colorful but now peeling and yellowed with age. And in the crib, something moved.

He froze, his breath catching as he watched a small figure crouch in the shadows, its back turned to him, its head bent low, its shoulders rising and falling with each ragged breath. The scratching continued, the figure's hand moving slowly, rhythmically, dragging its nails along the edge of the crib.

"Hello?" he whispered, his voice barely audible, a tremor running through him. The figure stilled, the scratching stopping, and for a long, agonizing moment, there was nothing but silence.

Then, slowly, the figure began to turn.

Jason took a step back, his heart pounding as he watched the figure shift, its head tilting upward, revealing a face pale and hollow, its eyes wide and empty, its mouth twisted into a hideous grin. It stared at him, unblinking, its gaze piercing, hungry, as though it could see straight into his soul.

Jason stumbled back, his flashlight slipping from his hand and clattering to the floor, casting long, flickering shadows across the walls. The figure rose slowly, its movements jerky, unnatural, its limbs bending at odd angles, its grin widening as it took a step toward him.

Panicking, Jason turned and ran, his footsteps echoing through the empty halls as he bolted down the stairs, his breath coming in short, frantic gasps. The whispers returned, louder now, filling the house with a chorus of voices, their words overlapping, drowning out his thoughts, pressing in on him from every direction.

He reached the front door, fumbling with the lock, his hands shaking, his heart racing as the whispers grew louder, angrier, surrounding him, filling his mind with a suffocating dread. He finally managed to throw the door open, stumbling out into the cold night air, collapsing onto the ground.

As he lay there, gasping for breath, he looked back at the house, his heart pounding as he saw a figure standing in the doorway—a tall, shadowy form, its hollow eyes fixed on him, its mouth twisted into that same, unnatural grin.

And then, as he watched, it raised its hand, beckoning him back inside.

He scrambled to his feet, his body trembling as he turned and ran, his mind reeling, his heart racing, the image of the figure burned into his memory.

From that night on, Jason was never the same. He told his friends about what he'd seen, but they laughed it off, convinced he was trying to scare them, just another ghost story about the house on Maple Street. But Jason knew the truth. He could still hear the whispers in his mind, the faint scratching that haunted his dreams, the memory of that hollow, grinning face.

Because once the house had marked him, it would never let him go.

The Dark History of the House

In the quiet town of Briar Glen, the house on Maple Street was known by many names—The Devil's House, The Widow's Curse, and more recently, The Haunt. But its official name, carved into the stone above the grand wooden doors, was *The Ashburn House*, named for the family who had once owned it nearly a century ago.

The story began in 1904, when Alexander Ashburn, a wealthy businessman from the city, decided to build his grand estate in Briar Glen, a place he claimed had "peaceful charm and a lack of distraction." He brought his young wife, Eleanor, to the town, hoping that a quieter life would ease her frail health. The townsfolk remembered her as beautiful, almost ethereal, with large, haunted eyes and a melancholic air, as though a dark cloud hung over her no matter where she went.

Alexander, however, was a different story. People described him as cold, distant, and calculating, a man who kept to himself and demanded silence and respect wherever he went. He was known for his sharp tongue and his unforgiving nature. Rumors circulated that his business dealings had been less than honest, with whispers of exploitation and shady practices. But no one dared confront him—Alexander Ashburn was not a man to be crossed.

For the first few years, the couple lived quietly, the house on Maple Street standing proud and beautiful, its lights glowing softly each night, visible even from a distance. But soon, strange events began to darken the house's reputation.

One autumn evening in 1909, Eleanor vanished without a trace.

Alexander claimed she had run away, leaving him with nothing but a hastily scribbled note. He showed the note to the town sheriff, insisting she had chosen to leave him. But something about his story didn't sit right with the townsfolk. Eleanor had been frail, shy, and deeply attached to her home—no one could believe she'd simply up and leave without a word to anyone. Her friends, those few she had made in the town, claimed she would never leave willingly. And yet, there was no sign of a struggle, no clues as to where she might have gone.

Weeks passed, and Alexander continued his life as though nothing had happened, but the house was no longer the same. Neighbors reported hearing strange sounds at night—muffled voices, the sound of weeping, and, most unsettling of all, the faint sounds of a lullaby drifting through the stillness, as though someone were singing to a child.

The townsfolk grew wary of the Ashburn House, avoiding it after sunset, but the sounds persisted, becoming more frequent, more disturbing. Those who dared pass by the house at night claimed to see the faint outline of a woman in the upstairs window, her figure barely visible in the darkness, her face obscured by shadow. Some swore they heard her crying, others said she whispered their names, calling them to the house.

Then, in 1911, tragedy struck again. Alexander was found dead in his study, his body contorted, his face twisted in horror. The official cause was listed as heart failure, but the sheriff noted that his fingers were frozen in a clawed position, as though he'd been reaching for something—or someone—that wasn't there. A single candle had burned down to a stub on his desk, casting a flickering light over his lifeless face, illuminating a single phrase scrawled on a piece of paper beside him:

She will not forgive me.

After Alexander's death, the house on Maple Street was abandoned, left to rot, its doors sealed, its windows shuttered. But the rumors only grew. Over the years, people began to speak of "The Widow," a spirit who haunted the house, her anger and sorrow woven into its very walls. Those who ventured near claimed to feel a cold presence, a sensation of being watched, as though unseen eyes followed their every move.

By the 1930s, the house had gained an infamous reputation, and locals swore that anyone who entered it would be marked by Eleanor's curse. Stories began to circulate of those who had gone inside, only to fall ill shortly after, plagued by feverish dreams of a shadowy figure standing at the foot of their bed, whispering secrets, calling them back to the house.

But the strangest and most disturbing rumors concerned the attic.

It was said that Eleanor had spent most of her time in the attic, where she had set up a small nursery in the hope of having a child—a child who had never come. After her disappearance, people claimed that the attic had been left untouched, that her things were still there, covered in dust, preserved as though waiting for her return. And in the years that followed, those who entered the house at night swore they could hear the faint sounds of a music box drifting down from the attic, playing a soft, haunting lullaby.

A local historian named Edwin Pierce became obsessed with the house in the 1970s, convinced that the spirits of Alexander and Eleanor were bound to the property, unable to move on due to some unfinished business. He moved into the house, determined to discover the truth. But after only three nights, he fled, his face pale, his hands shaking, muttering incoherently about a woman in white and "the eyes in the walls." He left town shortly after and never spoke of the house again.

By the turn of the century, the house had become a rite of passage for the town's teenagers, a test of bravery for those daring enough to explore its haunted halls. They would sneak in through broken windows, daring each other to go as far as they could—some to the basement, others to the attic. And those who ventured too far often returned with stories of whispers, cold drafts that seemed to breathe against their skin, and fleeting glimpses of a shadowy figure moving through the darkness.

But the most chilling account came from a boy named Travis Whitman, who dared to spend a night in the attic in 1999. He claimed he'd heard someone crying softly, rocking back and forth in the corner, her shadow stretching across the floor. When he looked closer, he saw her face—pale, hollow, her eyes filled with a bottomless sorrow. She'd reached out to him, her hand cold and skeletal, whispering, "Help me... he won't let me rest."

Travis had fled, and by morning, he had developed a high fever, his mind fevered with dreams of a dark figure standing over Eleanor, his face hidden in shadow, his hand reaching for her throat.

As he recounted the story to his friends, they noticed a thin, red mark on his wrist—a handprint, small and faint, as though left by someone with cold, frail fingers.

Present Day

As Jason Carter recovered from his terrifying night in the house on Maple Street, he couldn't shake the feeling that he was being followed. The image of the figure in the nursery haunted him, its twisted grin burned into his memory. And though he tried to brush it off as a prank, a trick of the shadows, he couldn't ignore the whispers he still heard at night, faint and persistent, calling his name.

His friends laughed at his story, shrugging off his experience as a figment of his imagination, a result of too many ghost stories. But Jason knew better. He could feel it—the house had marked him. And as the days went on, he began to notice strange things: shadows shifting in his peripheral vision, cold drafts brushing against his neck, and the faint sound of a music box playing a haunting melody just as he drifted off to sleep.

Desperate for answers, he visited the town's archives, digging through old records, trying to learn more about the Ashburns, about Eleanor and Alexander, about what had happened in that cursed house. The more he read, the clearer it became—the house was a trap, a place where the dead lingered, bound by anger, sorrow, and a desire for vengeance.

Jason realized with a growing sense of dread that he had disturbed something in that house, something that wouldn't rest until it had what it wanted.

As he left the archives that day, a cold wind swept through the street, carrying with it the faint scent of decay, a smell that clung to him, filling his lungs, making his skin crawl. He turned, glancing back at the house on Maple Street, its dark windows watching him, waiting.

And in that moment, he understood the truth:

The Ashburn House wasn't just haunted.

It was hungry.

Jason couldn't shake the feeling that the house on Maple Street was somehow tied to him now, its shadow reaching out across town, pressing into his mind even when he was miles away. Since his terrifying encounter, the whispers had intensified, lingering on the edge of his hearing, calling him back to the house. And in the quiet hours of the night, he could still see that twisted, grinning face, watching him, waiting.

Driven by an unsettling urge to understand what had happened, Jason returned to the town archives. This time, he focused on any mention of Alexander and Eleanor Ashburn's lives in Briar Glen. The records were sparse, but buried deep in a forgotten drawer, he found something that stopped him cold—a journal, bound in cracked leather, labeled simply with the initials *E.A.*

The handwriting was delicate and precise, written by someone who had once taken care with each word. But as Jason flipped through the pages, he noticed the entries becoming erratic, desperate, the words scrawled across the page in uneven, frenzied strokes. It was Eleanor's journal, and it contained her last words before she vanished.

Excerpts from Eleanor's Journal

August 23, 1909

"I have felt it again. The cold draft that brushes against me, as if a hand reaches from the shadows to touch me. Alexander doesn't believe me—he laughs, tells me my nerves are frail, that it is all in my mind. But I know the truth. Something lurks in this house, watching, waiting. The servants feel it too; they avoid the attic, muttering under their breath when they pass the stairs. And sometimes, late at night, I hear someone weeping. I follow the sound, but there is no one there."

September 15, 1909

"I dared to go into the attic today, though every instinct told me not to. The nursery, the one we'd prepared in hope of a child, remains untouched, frozen in time. There, I found a small music box on the windowsill, the one I'd bought in happier days. But it was different. Its song—once cheerful—now played slower, sadder, a tune I had never heard before. It filled me with dread, as though the song were a warning. I feel as if I am not alone here... as though someone else waits in this house."

October 1, 1909

"Alexander is not himself. He is colder, distant, barely speaking to me. His gaze has changed; there is something in his eyes that chills me to my core. He speaks of dreams he has had, dreams of a figure watching him from the shadows, and a voice calling him to the attic. He refuses to go up there now, claiming it is cursed, that 'she' waits for him. But who is 'she'? I am beginning to fear that whatever haunts this house has begun to haunt him as well."

October 20, 1909

"Tonight, he locked me in my room, saying I was 'too curious for my own good.' But I can feel it—the presence growing stronger. I know now that it is not just the house that holds this darkness. Alexander... he has been marked by it. He is becoming part of it. The look in his eyes, the way he stares at me—no longer my husband, but something else. I must escape, find a way out before it is too late..."

Jason's hands shook as he closed the journal, his mind racing. Eleanor's fear was unmistakable, a tangible force captured in her words, and the final entries hinted at a horror that went beyond the ordinary. It wasn't just Alexander who had changed—the house itself seemed to exert a sinister influence, bending those who lived there to its will.

But one line stayed with him more than any other: *"I know now that it is not just the house that holds this darkness. Alexander... he has been marked by it."*

Jason swallowed, the weight of those words settling heavily in his mind. He'd felt it too, that sense of being marked, claimed by something dark and relentless. And as the days had passed, that feeling had only grown stronger, the whispers more insistent, a constant pull drawing him back to the house.

That night, despite every instinct screaming at him to stay away, Jason found himself standing once more at the foot of the crumbling path leading up to the house on Maple Street. The air was colder here, thick with a silence that pressed against him, stifling every sound. He shivered, his breath visible in the frigid air, and for a moment, he almost turned back.

But the journal had left him with more questions than answers, and he knew he couldn't rest until he understood what had happened to Eleanor—and to Alexander. He took a deep breath, gripping the flashlight in his hand as he made his way up the steps, pushing open the heavy door.

The inside of the house was as he remembered it—silent, shadowed, the walls lined with faded portraits and peeling wallpaper. But this time, he felt something more—a presence, thick and oppressive, as though the house itself were alive, watching him with a silent, patient malice.

He moved cautiously, his footsteps echoing through the empty rooms as he made his way to the staircase. The whispers had returned, faint but persistent, drifting down from the upper floors, growing louder with each step. And as he climbed, he felt a strange pressure settle over him, a sensation of being pulled forward, guided by unseen hands.

At the top of the stairs, he found himself in front of the attic door, its wood warped and splintered, as though it had been forced open many times before. He reached out, his hand trembling as he turned the knob, pushing the door open and stepping inside.

The attic was as Eleanor had described—a nursery, frozen in time, filled with dust and decay. A crib sat in the corner, its wood darkened and cracked, the small mobile above it swaying gently, though there was no breeze. And there, on the windowsill, sat the music box, its lid open, the tiny ballerina inside slowly turning, playing a haunting, melancholy tune that filled the room.

Jason felt a chill crawl down his spine as he stepped closer, his gaze fixed on the music box. The melody was familiar, yet strange, the notes warped, distorted, as though echoing from a great distance. He reached out, his fingers brushing against the cold metal, and as he did, the music stopped.

The silence that followed was thick, almost tangible, pressing down on him like a weight. And then, he heard it—a soft, breathy whisper, barely more than a murmur, coming from the far corner of the room.

"Help... me..."

Jason froze, his heart pounding as he turned, his flashlight casting a faint, flickering glow over the corner. There, he saw her—a figure, pale and ghostly, her form barely visible in the darkness. Her eyes were wide and hollow, her face drawn with sorrow, her hand outstretched, as though reaching for him.

"Eleanor?" he whispered, his voice shaking.

The figure nodded, her gaze fixed on him, pleading, desperate. "He won't let me rest," she whispered, her voice filled with an endless sadness. "He... he has trapped me here, bound to this house. And now, he's marked you too."

Jason took a step back, his pulse racing, his mind reeling with terror. "Who? Alexander?"

Her face twisted, a shadow passing over her features. "Not Alexander... not anymore. He has become something else, something... darker. He is bound to this house, feeding on those who enter, keeping them here, trapped, their spirits bound to him."

Jason felt a cold wave of fear wash over him, the weight of her words sinking in. “How... how can I stop him?”

Eleanor’s gaze darkened, her expression shifting to one of sorrow and resignation. “There is only one way—to burn it. The house, the walls... they are his prison, his sanctuary. Destroy it, and you may release us all.”

Jason stared at her, his heart pounding, a mix of fear and determination welling up inside him. But before he could respond, the attic door slammed shut behind him, the sound echoing through the room, and the figure of Eleanor began to fade, her form dissolving into shadows.

And then, he heard it—a low, sinister laugh, echoing from the darkness, filling the room with a chilling, oppressive presence.

“Leaving so soon, Jason?” a voice murmured, deep and menacing. “I thought you came to stay...”

The laughter grew louder, filling the room, and as Jason turned to the door, he saw a shadowy figure blocking his way, its face twisted into a grotesque grin, its eyes burning with a dark, unnatural light.

He backed away, his heart racing, his mind consumed with terror as the figure advanced, the walls seeming to close in around him, the air growing colder, thicker, until he could barely breathe.

But even as the darkness pressed in, he held onto Eleanor’s words, the final hope that burned in his mind.

He would destroy the house. He would set them free.

If he could escape it alive.

Jason felt his heart hammering in his chest as the shadowy figure moved closer, blocking his only way out.

The figure—Alexander, or what had become of him—seemed to absorb the darkness, his form twisting and shifting, his eyes gleaming with a hungry, malevolent light. Jason backed up, his mind racing with Eleanor's last words: *Burn it. Destroy the house. Release us all.*

But standing here, trapped in the attic, he wasn't sure he'd make it out alive.

"Leaving so soon?" the voice repeated, its tone mocking, a twisted, hollow echo of Alexander's voice. "No one ever truly leaves..."

Jason gripped the flashlight in his hand, searching for anything, any object he could use as a weapon. His fingers brushed against the cold metal of the music box on the windowsill, its lid slightly ajar. In a moment of panic, he grabbed it, hurling it at the figure with all his strength. The box clattered against the shadow's chest, its haunting melody echoing faintly as it fell to the floor.

The figure paused, its form flickering, as though the sound had unsettled it. Jason seized the moment, pushing past, shoving open the attic door and stumbling into the hallway. He could hear the furious, inhuman growl of the shadow behind him, its rage palpable, reverberating through the walls as it pursued him.

The hallway stretched before him, dark and twisted, each door slightly ajar, each room filled with shadows that seemed to watch him, waiting. He raced down the stairs, his breath coming in sharp, ragged gasps, his heart pounding as he bolted toward the front door.

Just as he reached it, the door slammed shut, the old, rusted lock clicking into place. Jason rattled the handle, but it wouldn't budge. Behind him, he heard the ominous creak of footsteps, slow and deliberate, echoing through the empty hall.

He turned, his eyes darting around, searching for another way out. His gaze landed on the dining room window, its glass cracked, spiderwebbed with age. Without a second thought, he picked up a heavy candlestick from a nearby table and swung it at the window, shattering the glass with a deafening crash.

The cold night air rushed in, and he climbed through the window, stumbling over the jagged shards and dropping into the overgrown yard outside. As he hit the ground, he looked back at the house, its dark silhouette looming over him, the broken window staring back like an unblinking eye.

For a brief moment, he felt relief wash over him, the night air cool against his skin, his heart pounding with the thrill of escape. But then, he felt it—the same suffocating pressure, the same cold, oppressive presence seeping from the house, reaching out toward him.

And from the broken window, he saw it—a shadowy face, hollow-eyed, grinning, its twisted smile lit by the faint glow of candlelight. Alexander's form, barely visible, was watching him, a sinister promise in his gaze.

"This isn't over, Jason," the voice whispered, low and menacing, filling the night air. "You are mine."

Jason backed away, the words ringing in his mind as he turned and fled, his footsteps echoing down the empty street. But even as he put distance between himself and the house, he couldn't shake the feeling that the shadows were following him, stretching through the night, keeping him tethered to the Ashburn House.

Jason didn't stop running until he was home, his mind reeling, Eleanor's voice still echoing in his head: *Burn it. Destroy the house. Release us all.* The house was a prison for the spirits trapped within its walls, bound by Alexander's malevolent power. He knew now that he had to follow through, that the only way to end the haunting was to destroy the Ashburn House once and for all.

The next night, Jason returned to the house, this time prepared. He had gathered a small container of gasoline, a handful of matches, and a sense of steely determination that he clung to like a lifeline. He knew it was reckless, but he couldn't let fear control him. Not now. Not with Eleanor's soul, and perhaps his own, at stake.

The house loomed before him, silent and watchful, its windows dark and unblinking. He made his way up the crumbling stone steps, pushing open the front door with a sense of grim purpose. The air inside was thick, oppressive, the shadows stretching across the walls, flickering as though alive.

He moved quickly, pouring the gasoline along the floorboards, splashing it over the furniture, each step a silent prayer to Eleanor and the souls trapped within. His hands shook, but he pushed through, lighting a match, the small flame flickering in the dim light. He dropped it onto the gasoline-soaked floor, watching as the fire sprang to life, spreading across the floor in a burst of orange and red.

The flames grew, licking at the walls, casting long, twisted shadows across the room. The air filled with the acrid scent of smoke, the crackling of wood, the roar of the fire consuming the house. Jason stepped back, his gaze fixed on the growing inferno, his heart pounding as he watched the flames consume the dark, haunted space.

But then, from the depths of the fire, he heard it—a scream, high-pitched and desperate, echoing through the house. The sound was filled with agony, a torment that reached into his soul, twisting his insides. It was Eleanor.

"Jason!" her voice called, desperate, pleading. "Free me... please!"

He felt a surge of panic, his mind racing. Had he been too late? Was she suffering, trapped in the very fire meant to release her? He moved toward the flames, but the heat forced him back, the fire blazing, casting long shadows across the walls as it consumed the house.

And then, from the center of the flames, he saw him—Alexander, his form twisted, darkened, his eyes filled with a rage that transcended death. His voice was a guttural, unearthly roar, echoing through the burning room.

"You will never escape me, Jason," he hissed, his voice filled with venom, hatred. "You are mine, now and forever."

The flames climbed higher, consuming the walls, the ceiling, filling the house with smoke and fire. Jason backed away, watching as Alexander's form writhed in the flames, his face contorted with anger, hatred, his twisted spirit bound to the very walls he had used to trap Eleanor and the others.

But as the flames grew, he felt a shift in the air—a lightness, a release, as though something dark and oppressive had lifted. And then, amid the flames, he saw her—a faint figure, pale and ethereal, her expression soft, peaceful. Eleanor.

She looked at him, her eyes filled with gratitude, her form shimmering in the firelight. "Thank you," she whispered, her voice a soft echo in his mind. "You've freed us."

Jason felt a wave of relief wash over him, his heart pounding as he watched her fade, her spirit finally released, free from the house's dark grasp. And as he turned to leave, he could hear the final, furious screams of Alexander, his twisted form writhing in the flames, consumed by the very house he had cursed.

The house on Maple Street burned through the night, the flames casting a warm, haunting glow over Briar Glen. The townsfolk gathered to watch, murmuring in awe and fear as the fire consumed the house, reducing it to ashes, the shadows finally vanquished.

Jason watched from a distance, his heart filled with a strange, bittersweet satisfaction. He knew he had done the right thing, that he had freed Eleanor, and the others trapped within those cursed walls. But he also knew he would never forget the face of Alexander Ashburn, the twisted grin of a man who had become something monstrous, bound forever to the darkness he had embraced.

As the final embers died down, Jason turned and walked away, leaving the ashes of the Ashburn House behind him. But in the silence of the night, he could still hear Eleanor's voice, soft and grateful, a reminder that he had, in the end, done what she could not.

The house on Maple Street was gone, reduced to dust and memory, its dark history burned away.

But even as Jason walked home, a faint whisper lingered in the air, carried on the wind, as though some part of Alexander's spirit still clung to the ashes, waiting, watching.

And in that moment, Jason understood that while the house itself was gone, its shadow might never fully leave Briar Glen.

The End

12
THE SKIN WALKERS

The village of Black Hollow was isolated, nestled between dense woods and high mountains, cut off from the outside world by miles of winding dirt roads. It was the kind of place where everyone knew everyone else, where doors were left unlocked, and where the people lived simple, quiet lives. But lately, an unsettling shadow had settled over the village, and the nights had grown quieter than usual.

The rumors started when a group of hunters failed to return from the woods, leaving nothing but an abandoned campsite and whispers of strange footprints in the snow—large, elongated prints, as if made by something almost human, but not quite.

They were first spotted just beyond the village, moving through the trees in the dead of night—creatures with a human shape but no skin, their bodies raw and glistening, their muscles exposed, their veins pulsing in the moonlight. The few villagers who caught a glimpse of them claimed that the creatures moved silently, watching from the shadows, their heads tilting in a way that suggested some form of twisted intelligence.

No one dared venture into the woods after dark, not anymore.

The first true encounter happened on a night when the fog was thick, heavy as wool, clinging to the ground and muffling all sound. Old Man Wilkes, who had lived in Black Hollow his entire life, had stayed late at the village tavern, stumbling home in the mist, his breath clouding in front of him. He was a man who had seen many things over the years, and he wasn't easily frightened. But as he walked, he heard something behind him—a soft, rhythmic scraping, like wet flesh dragging across stone.

He paused, glancing over his shoulder, peering into the dense fog. But there was nothing there, only the pale glow of the moon and the faint outline of trees. He chuckled to himself, muttering about too much whiskey, and continued on his way.

But then, the sound came again, louder this time, closer.

Wilkes stopped, his heart beginning to pound, a chill crawling down his spine. Slowly, he turned, his breath catching in his throat as he saw it—a figure standing just a few yards away, half-shrouded in the mist.

It was human in shape, but its body was all wrong. It was tall, with long, sinewy limbs and a torso that seemed stretched, twisted, its muscles visible, raw and glistening as though freshly skinned. The creature's head tilted to one side, its empty eye sockets fixed on him, its mouth opening in a silent, horrifying grin.

For a moment, Wilkes was frozen, trapped in the creature's gaze, his body paralyzed by a fear he had never known. The creature took a step toward him, its movements slow, deliberate, each step accompanied by the sickening sound of flesh scraping against bone.

Wilkes stumbled back, a strangled cry escaping his lips as he turned and ran, his feet pounding against the dirt path, his breath coming in short, frantic gasps. But the creature was fast—he could hear it behind him, its steps unnaturally silent, the only sound the faint, wet rasp of its exposed flesh moving through the air.

He didn't stop until he reached his door, throwing it open and slamming it shut, his heart racing, his hands trembling. He peered out the window, his eyes scanning the fog, but the creature was gone, vanished back into the mist as though it had never been there at all.

The next morning, he told his story to anyone who would listen, his face pale, his voice shaking. But the villagers only half-believed him, brushing it off as the ramblings of an old drunk, a story told to frighten children. They didn't understand, couldn't understand, what he had seen in the fog.

But that night, everything changed.

In the early hours of the next morning, a scream echoed through the village, piercing the quiet, waking everyone from their slumber. The villagers gathered in the town square, their faces pale, their eyes wide with fear as the sound filled the air—a high-pitched, guttural shriek that seemed to come from everywhere at once.

They found the source of the scream at the edge of the village, near the woods where the hunters had disappeared. There, lying in the grass, was a woman named Elsie, her body twisted, her skin stretched and torn, as though something had tried to peel it away. Her eyes were open, wide with terror, her mouth frozen in a silent scream.

But there was something else—something that made the villagers draw back, horror twisting in their stomachs. Around her body, drawn in the dirt, were strange symbols, crude, twisted shapes that seemed to pulse with a dark energy, each one dripping with blood. The symbols formed a circle around her body, a boundary that seemed to shimmer in the morning light.

Sheriff James Bradford was called to the scene, a stoic man known for his calm, steady presence. But even he couldn't hide the tremor in his hands as he examined the body, his face pale, his jaw clenched.

"This... this isn't human," he muttered, glancing at the villagers gathered around, their faces filled with fear, their eyes darting to the edge of the forest. "No animal does this. And no person... no person could do something like this."

The village was on edge, the horror of Elsie's death hanging over them like a dark cloud. Rumors spread like wildfire, whispers of the creatures in the woods, of the skinless figures seen lurking in the mist. Some said they were spirits, the restless dead, others claimed they were demons, summoned by dark magic, by a curse cast upon the village.

But no one knew the truth.

And as the sun set that night, casting the village in shadow, an uneasy silence fell over Black Hollow, a silence broken only by the faint, haunting sound of something moving through the woods, something that watched, waited.

Martha and Sam Blackwood lived on the edge of the village, their small cabin surrounded by trees, the forest pressing in on all sides. They had heard the rumors, had seen the fear in their neighbors' eyes, but they tried to push it away, to hold on to the quiet life they had built.

But that night, as the wind howled through the trees, they heard something scratching at their door.

At first, they thought it was a branch, brushing against the wood, but the sound grew louder, more insistent—a rhythmic, deliberate scraping, as though something were clawing at the door, trying to get inside.

Martha clutched Sam's arm, her face pale, her eyes wide with fear. "Do you think it's... them?"

Sam shook his head, though his expression was tense, his jaw set. "It's probably just the wind. Don't worry, I'll check."

He grabbed a flashlight, his hands trembling as he approached the door, his heart pounding with a fear he tried to suppress. He took a deep breath, steeling himself, and opened the door.

For a moment, there was nothing but darkness, the trees swaying in the wind, the night air cold and still. He scanned the shadows, his flashlight sweeping over the ground, his eyes straining to see.

Then, he saw it.

A figure stood at the edge of the trees, its body tall, hunched, its skinless form glistening in the moonlight, each muscle, each tendon exposed, raw and pulsing. It tilted its head, its hollow, eyeless gaze fixed on him, its mouth opening in a silent, unnatural grin.

Sam stumbled back, his flashlight clattering to the floor, his voice caught in his throat as the figure took a step forward, its movements slow, deliberate, its body swaying with each step, as though testing the ground, feeling its way.

Martha screamed, slamming the door, her hands shaking as she locked it, her breath coming in short, panicked gasps. They huddled together, their backs pressed against the wall, their ears straining, waiting.

But the creature didn't leave.

They heard it outside, its footsteps soft, silent, moving along the walls, circling the cabin, its claws scratching against the wood, a slow, rhythmic sound that filled the air, filled their minds, a sound that promised pain, death.

And then, just as suddenly as it had come, the sound stopped, the silence filling the room, heavy and suffocating.

Sam and Martha didn't sleep that night, their ears tuned to every creak, every whisper of the wind, their minds haunted by the image of that creature, its hollow gaze, its twisted grin.

They knew, deep down, that it would come back.

The following morning, Sheriff Bradford called a meeting in the town square. The villagers gathered, their faces drawn and tense, their voices hushed as they exchanged fearful glances.

"We all know something's out there," Sheriff Bradford began, his voice steady, but the fear in his eyes unmistakable. "These creatures—whatever they are—they're hunting us. They took Elsie, and last night, they nearly got Sam and Martha."

A murmur of fear rippled through the crowd, the villagers clutching their loved ones, their gazes shifting to the forest, to the dark, dense trees that seemed to watch them, waiting.

"What are we supposed to do?" someone shouted, their voice filled with desperation. "We can't just sit here, waiting for them to come for us."

Sheriff Bradford took a deep breath, his gaze sweeping over the crowd. "I don't know what they want, or why they're here, but I know one thing: they don't belong in Black Hollow. We're going to fight, we're going to defend our homes."

But as he spoke, a chill settled over the crowd, a feeling of dread that gnawed at them, deep and unrelenting.

Because even as they tried to rally, to find hope, they knew, deep down, that the creatures lurking in the woods were more than just animals. They were something darker, something unnatural, something that no weapon, no strength could hold back.

They were the Skin Walkers.

And they were just getting started.

Long before the village of Black Hollow was settled, the land was wild and untouched, a vast expanse of dense forests, towering mountains, and shadowed valleys. It was a place of strange energy, sacred to the indigenous tribes who lived in harmony with the land, who believed it held powerful forces, both light and dark. One particular part of the forest, an area they called *Nįkicįna*, meaning *"the place of lost faces,"* was said to be inhabited by spirits that could peel away a person's very essence, leaving them hollow, stripped of their soul.

To protect their people, the tribe avoided the cursed area, performing rituals to keep the malevolent spirits bound within the woods. But in the mid-1800s, settlers arrived, drawn to the lush, fertile valley and the promise of new land. They dismissed the tribe's warnings as superstition, breaking the sacred ground to build what would become the village of Black Hollow.

Among the settlers was a man named Elijah Crane, a dark, reclusive figure, known as much for his intellect as for his obsession with the occult. A self-proclaimed mystic, Crane was fascinated by the legends surrounding *Nįkicįna* and ignored every warning from the tribes and his fellow settlers. Driven by a twisted curiosity, he ventured deep into the cursed forest one night, alone, determined to uncover the truth of the land's dark power.

Days passed without any sign of Elijah, and the village began to assume he had perished. But on the seventh night after his disappearance, he returned, stumbling out of the woods, his face hollow and pale, his eyes wide with terror. He wouldn't speak of what he'd seen, of what had happened to him, but there was something different about him—something that chilled the villagers to their core.

He began to spend hours in the woods, alone, performing strange rituals, chanting in languages no one understood. Those who ventured too close claimed to hear a soft, eerie singing, as though a choir of voices drifted through the trees, voices that didn't belong to any living creature. And in the weeks that followed, animals started disappearing—first livestock, then pets, only to be found days later, their bodies twisted, their skin missing, their empty eyes wide with terror.

The village was on edge, the strange occurrences growing more frequent, more violent, and Elijah Crane's behavior only fueled the fear. Some claimed he was cursed, marked by the spirits of *Nįkicįna*, that he had angered forces beyond understanding. But others whispered that he had done something darker—that he had made a pact with the spirits, sacrificing his own soul in exchange for something far more sinister.

Late one autumn night, a group of villagers gathered their courage and followed Elijah into the woods, determined to put an end to his rituals. They tracked him deep into the forest, past the boundary of *Nįkicįna*, to a clearing bathed in moonlight. There, they found Elijah kneeling before a makeshift altar, a circle of stones arranged around him, and on each stone was a small animal, skinned and lifeless, its body arranged in a twisted, unnatural posture.

Elijah's face was a mask of ecstasy, his hands slick with blood, his voice a low, guttural chant as he called upon the spirits of the forest, the entities that had haunted the land long before human memory. The villagers watched, frozen with horror, as a shadowy form began to emerge from the ground—a figure with no skin, its body raw and glistening, its eyes hollow, its mouth twisted into a hideous grin.

The creature reached out, its elongated fingers brushing Elijah's face, and as it did, his skin began to stretch, to peel away, as though drawn by some unseen force. He screamed, his voice echoing through the forest as his skin peeled back, his flesh exposed, raw and glistening, his body writhing as the creature absorbed his very essence.

The villagers fled, their minds reeling with terror, their hearts pounding as Elijah's screams faded into the darkness. They returned to the village, swearing never to speak of what they had seen, to bury the truth of Elijah Crane's fate. But as the weeks passed, they realized that his pact had left a stain, a darkness that lingered in the woods.

It started with strange sightings—shadowy figures moving through the trees, creatures with elongated limbs and eyeless faces that seemed to watch from the shadows. The villagers tried to ignore them, to convince themselves it was a trick of the light, a figment of their imagination. But the disappearances began soon after, each one more brutal than the last.

One winter night, a group of villagers went missing. Their bodies were discovered days later, scattered around the clearing where Elijah had once performed his rituals. Each one had been skinned, their bodies left in twisted, unnatural postures, their eyes frozen wide in terror. And beside each body was a single, bloody handprint, as though marking them, claiming them.

The elders of the village, desperate for answers, consulted the few remaining members of the tribe, who told them of *Nįkicįna*, of the spirits bound to the land. They explained that the spirits Elijah had awakened were not like ghosts; they were ancient, primal entities, born of the forest, bound by blood and darkness. They craved flesh, skin, a form to inhabit, and in Elijah's twisted pact, they had found a way to manifest in the physical world.

Now, these entities roamed the woods as Skin Walkers, humanoid figures that retained fragments of their former lives, their human memories twisted into something dark and unrecognizable. They could never regain their humanity, but they craved it, hungered for it, moving silently through the forest, watching, waiting.

And worst of all, they could mimic the voices of those they had claimed, calling out from the shadows, luring unsuspecting villagers into the woods with cries that sounded eerily familiar, echoing with fragments of lost souls. Those who followed the voices were never seen again, their bodies found days later, their skin peeled away, their eyes wide with horror, their souls bound to the curse that had claimed them.

Over the years, Black Hollow became a place of whispers, of fear and suspicion, the villagers haunted by the knowledge that something ancient, something insatiable, lurked just beyond their homes. The Skin Walkers watched from the shadows, their eyeless faces fixed on the village, their bodies moving with a twisted grace, always searching, always waiting.

It was said that those who caught a glimpse of a Skin Walker would be marked, their scent lingering in the air, drawing the creatures closer, like wolves drawn to the scent of blood. The mark was invisible, a feeling more than a sign, a sensation of being watched, of cold fingers trailing over one's skin, a reminder that once seen, the Skin Walkers would not forget them.

As the years passed, the villagers began to see the creatures as a dark legend, a story told to children, a superstition. But in the depths of winter, when the nights were long and the forest was silent, they knew better. They could feel it, a presence lurking at the edge of the village, the faint sound of skinless footsteps moving through the trees, the occasional glimpse of a figure with no face, watching them from the shadows.

And though they tried to live normal lives, to forget the curse that haunted them, the truth remained, buried deep in the heart of Black Hollow.

The Skin Walkers were waiting.

And they would come, again and again, until their hunger was satisfied.

The village of Black Hollow was never the same after the Skin Walkers' first appearance. Those who had seen them, who had felt their hollow gazes from the edge of the forest, knew they were marked. And once marked, the Skin Walkers would not relent. They were like shadows, drawn to their prey by some dark, insatiable hunger. The villagers avoided the forest, locked their doors tightly, and prayed the creatures would pass them by. But no one understood the curse better than Samuel.

Samuel had been a child when he first saw one of the Skin Walkers. His father had taken him hunting in the woods, warning him to stay close, to keep quiet, to respect the forest's dark power. But the curious boy had wandered too far, drawn by the faint sound of someone calling his name, a whisper that seemed to drift through the trees, soft and familiar. He had followed the voice, deeper and deeper into the forest, until he found himself alone, the trees looming above him, their branches casting twisted shadows on the ground.

And then he saw it.

Standing just beyond a cluster of trees was a figure, tall and lean, its skinless body glistening in the faint light, its eyeless face turned toward him, its mouth twisted into a silent grin. The creature tilted its head, reaching out with one long, sinewy arm, its fingers stretched, clawed, dripping with a dark, thick liquid.

Samuel had frozen, paralyzed with fear, his mind unable to comprehend what he was seeing. The Skin Walker took a step toward him, its movements slow, deliberate, its fingers twitching, reaching. But then, just as it was about to touch him, his father appeared, grabbing him, pulling him away, shouting words Samuel couldn't understand, his voice filled with a terror Samuel had never heard before.

They fled back to the village, his father's face pale, his eyes haunted, his voice barely a whisper as he told Samuel never to speak of what he'd seen, never to tell anyone. But even as a child, Samuel knew he had been marked. He could feel it, a cold sensation that lingered on his skin, a faint pressure on his chest, as though some invisible hand were pressing against his heart.

Years passed, and Samuel tried to forget, to live a normal life. But the memory of that creature haunted him, lurking in the back of his mind, a constant reminder that he was not safe, that the Skin Walkers would come for him one day.

The winter of Samuel's twenty-fifth year was harsh, the nights colder than he had ever known, the snow heavy and thick, blanketing the village in silence. The trees stood bare, their branches skeletal against the dark sky, and the villagers stayed inside, huddled by their fires, the old stories coming back to life, whispered in low voices as the wind howled outside.

And then, on the coldest night of the year, the Skin Walkers returned.

Samuel was walking home from the tavern, his coat pulled tightly around him, his breath visible in the icy air. The village was quiet, the streets empty, the only sound the faint crunch of snow beneath his boots. But as he walked, he felt it—the sensation he had known since childhood, a presence pressing against him, heavy and cold, as though a pair of unseen eyes were watching him from the darkness.

He quickened his pace, his heart pounding, his mind racing with memories of that day in the forest, of the creature's twisted grin, its outstretched hand. The sensation grew stronger, more intense, and as he rounded the corner to his street, he saw them.

Three figures stood at the edge of the village, their bodies tall and lean, their skinless forms glistening in the moonlight, each one turned toward him, their hollow faces staring, waiting. They stood motionless, their limbs stretched, their heads tilted, their mouths twisted into silent, mocking grins.

Samuel felt his blood run cold, his body frozen, trapped in their gaze. He could feel the mark on him, a dark, invisible stain that drew them closer, that bound him to them, his fate intertwined with theirs. He took a step back, his breath coming in short, panicked gasps, his mind screaming at him to run, to escape.

But the Skin Walkers began to move, their movements slow, unnatural, each step silent, their bodies swaying as they advanced, their eyeless faces fixed on him, their mouths opening in a soundless scream.

Samuel turned and ran, his footsteps echoing through the empty streets, his heart pounding as he stumbled through the snow, the cold air burning his lungs. He could hear them behind him, their steps unnaturally silent, each one closer than the last, their presence pressing against him, suffocating, relentless.

He reached his home, throwing open the door and slamming it shut, his hands trembling as he locked it, his breath coming in ragged gasps. He pressed his back against the wall, his mind racing, his body shaking with fear.

But the Skin Walkers did not stop.

He could hear them outside, their bodies moving along the walls, their fingers scratching against the wood, slow and deliberate, a reminder that they would not be denied. They circled the house, their movements a haunting rhythm, each scrape, each whisper a promise, a warning.

"Samuel," a voice called, soft and familiar, drifting through the air like a breath. It was his father's voice, a voice he hadn't heard since the old man had passed years ago, a voice filled with pain, longing. "Come to us..."

Samuel's eyes widened, his heart pounding as he pressed his hands over his ears, trying to block out the sound, to convince himself it wasn't real. But the voice grew louder, more insistent, the tone shifting, warping, turning guttural, inhuman.

"Samuel... we've been waiting for you."

He stumbled back, his body shaking, his mind reeling with terror. He could feel them pressing against him, their presence filling the room, as though the walls themselves were alive, breathing, watching him. He backed into the corner, his eyes wide, his breath coming in short, frantic gasps as he searched for something, anything to protect himself.

But there was no protection. There was only the mark, a curse he could not escape, a bond that tied him to the Skin Walkers, drawing them closer, binding them to his soul.

The next morning, Samuel gathered the elders of the village, his face pale, his eyes haunted. He told them of his encounter, of the voices, of the creatures that had haunted him since childhood. The elders listened in silence, their faces grave, their expressions filled with fear and sorrow.

One of the oldest elders, a woman named Agnes, spoke up, her voice a low, trembling whisper. "The Skin Walkers are bound to this land by Elijah Crane's curse. They are spirits without rest, bodies without skin, drawn to those who carry the mark. They will not stop, Samuel. They will follow you, haunt you, until you are one of them."

Samuel felt a chill settle over him, the weight of her words pressing down on him like a dark, heavy shroud. "Is there no way to break the curse? To remove the mark?"

Agnes shook her head, her gaze fixed on him, filled with a sorrowful understanding. "The mark cannot be removed. But there is one way to protect yourself... a ritual, ancient and dangerous, one that could bind them, trap them within the land. But it requires a sacrifice, Samuel. A life given willingly to the spirits, an offering of flesh and blood."

The villagers stared at him, their faces a mixture of fear and hope, the knowledge that his sacrifice could save them, could end the curse, written in their eyes.

Samuel took a deep breath, his mind racing, the image of the Skin Walkers burned into his memory, their twisted grins, their hollow, soulless faces. He knew what he had to do, knew that his life was bound to the creatures, that he could not escape them, but he could stop them. For a moment, he felt a sense of calm, a strange peace, knowing he could protect his home, his people, even if it cost him everything.

"I'll do it," he said, his voice steady, filled with a quiet determination. "Tell me what I need to do."

The villagers gathered around him, the air filled with the weight of his decision, the knowledge that his sacrifice could bring them peace. And as night fell over Black Hollow, Samuel prepared himself, the ritual burning in his mind, a promise to protect his people, to end the curse.

But as the darkness crept in, and the Skin Walkers' hollow whispers filled the air, he knew that this was only the beginning, that the true terror had yet to come.

Because the Skin Walkers would not rest. And as they closed in, their bodies raw, skinless, their fingers reaching for him, he felt the weight of their hunger, the darkness of their curse, pressing against his soul, a reminder that the forest would claim him, that the land would take its sacrifice.

And in the silence of the night, his final scream echoed through Black Hollow, a sound that would haunt the village for generations to come, a reminder that in the heart of the forest, some spirits would never find peace.

The village of Black Hollow had known relative peace after Samuel's sacrifice. For years, the Skin Walkers had not returned. The villagers had built new lives, raising children, harvesting crops, and keeping to themselves, their lives punctuated only by the occasional whisper of the past. Samuel's scream was a memory, a ghostly echo that haunted only the oldest among them, and many of the younger villagers grew up dismissing the stories as nothing more than folklore.

But as the elders passed on, so did the respect for the ritual that had bound the Skin Walkers to the forest. One by one, the protections faded, and those who remembered the sacrifices made by the marked men and women were gone. The next generation was less cautious, less reverent, more curious. And when a group of teenagers dared each other to venture into the cursed forest on a cold autumn night, the fragile peace shattered.

Marcus, Anna, Liam, and Sophie were bored. Black Hollow was no place for excitement, especially in the late fall when the nights were long, and the woods whispered tales of old curses. They had heard about the Skin Walkers—their parents and grandparents had warned them not to go near *Nįkicįna*, the place of lost faces. But they were teenagers, daring each other to do what everyone else had feared. They laughed at the old stories, telling each other they were nothing but old wives' tales, meant to scare children.

"Come on," Marcus said, his voice steady but laced with a thrill. "Just a quick look. Whoever makes it to the clearing first wins, no turning back."

The others exchanged nervous glances, the eerie forest looming behind them, silent and watchful. Finally, Anna nodded, her face set, determined. "Fine. We go in, but we go together."

They entered the forest, the light of their flashlights barely piercing the thick darkness. The air grew colder, each step drawing them deeper into a silence that seemed to press in from all sides. The trees rose like skeletal fingers reaching up toward the night sky, their branches casting twisted shadows across the ground.

As they ventured further, Liam felt a prickle along his spine, a chill that seeped into his bones. "Anyone else getting a weird feeling?" he asked, his voice a nervous whisper.

"Stop it, Liam," Marcus said, forcing a chuckle. "It's just trees."

But he too could feel it—a presence, a dark, oppressive weight, like unseen eyes following them through the shadows. He brushed it off, refusing to show his fear. They were almost to the clearing, almost to their goal. They were close.

Then, just as they reached the heart of the forest, Sophie stopped, her flashlight beam illuminating something on the ground. Her face went pale as she pointed. "Look."

There, half-buried in the dirt, were bones—small, brittle, their shapes twisted and cracked, scattered as though left behind by something that had no respect for the dead. The others crowded around, their faces filled with a mixture of fear and disgust.

"These aren't animal bones," Anna whispered, her voice trembling. "These... they look human."

Before they could react, a faint sound drifted through the trees—a whisper, soft and breathy, echoing through the darkness, surrounding them. It was a familiar voice, one they each recognized—a voice that shouldn't be there, that couldn't be there.

"Marcus... come home..."

Marcus's heart stopped, his blood running cold. It was his mother's voice, distant, calling to him from somewhere deep within the forest. He spun around, his eyes wide, searching for her, but there was nothing, only the trees, their shadows long and twisted, stretching out toward him.

Then the voice came again, louder this time, more urgent, calling his name with a desperate, haunting tone. "Marcus... come back..."

The others looked at him, their faces pale, fear etched into their expressions. "This... this isn't real, right?" Liam stammered, his voice shaking. "It can't be..."

But the voices multiplied, each one familiar, each one calling them by name. Anna heard her father's voice, distant and echoing, telling her to come home, to leave the forest. Sophie heard her grandmother, whispering her name, pleading with her to turn back.

They turned to run, but the forest was no longer familiar. The trees seemed to shift, their branches stretching, twisting, forming a maze of shadows that surrounded them, trapping them, each path leading them deeper into the cursed land. The voices grew louder, overlapping, merging into a haunting chorus that filled the air, drowning out their thoughts, pulling them further into the darkness.

And then, they saw them.

Figures moved between the trees, barely visible in the dim light, their bodies tall and twisted, skinless and raw, their muscles exposed, glistening in the moonlight. The Skin Walkers moved with a strange, unnatural grace, their hollow eyes fixed on the teenagers, their mouths twisted into silent, hideous grins.

Marcus stumbled back, his breath coming in short, ragged gasps as he watched the creatures close in, their bodies swaying, their heads tilting, their empty eye sockets watching with a twisted curiosity. One of them reached out, its fingers long and bony, the exposed muscles pulsing, its hand extending toward him with a slow, deliberate movement.

"Run!" Anna screamed, grabbing his arm, pulling him back, her voice filled with terror. The group turned and fled, their footsteps echoing through the silent forest, the Skin Walkers following, moving through the trees like shadows, their forms barely visible, a constant presence that loomed over them, relentless and unyielding.

They stumbled through the darkness, their breaths coming in frantic gasps, their minds racing with terror, but no matter how far they ran, the Skin Walkers were always there, moving silently, effortlessly, their hollow faces twisted into those horrifying grins.

They burst from the forest into the clearing, their lungs burning, their bodies shaking, but the Skin Walkers did not stop. The creatures stepped into the clearing, their raw, exposed bodies catching the moonlight, their forms twisted, elongated, monstrous. They watched the group, their empty eyes gleaming with a dark, terrible hunger.

Liam tripped, his hand hitting something half-buried in the ground, and he froze, his eyes widening as he realized what it was—an old, brittle bone, the remains of someone who had never escaped. He scrambled to his feet, his heart pounding, the horrifying realization settling over him: the bones they had found earlier had been the last people to venture into the cursed forest.

The Skin Walkers advanced, their movements slow and deliberate, their eyeless faces fixed on the group, their mouths opening in soundless screams. Marcus could feel their cold presence pressing against him, their twisted bodies filling the air with the stench of decay, their hollow faces watching him with a dark, malicious joy.

But just as the Skin Walkers reached them, a figure appeared at the edge of the clearing—an elderly woman, her face lined with age, her eyes filled with sorrow and a fierce determination. She raised her hand, her voice a low, steady chant, words in a language the teenagers didn't understand, but the Skin Walkers halted, their bodies frozen, their twisted forms wavering, as though caught in some invisible force.

The woman's chant grew louder, each word ringing through the clearing, filling the air with a strange, powerful energy. The Skin Walkers began to retreat, their hollow eyes narrowing, their grins fading as they melted back into the forest, their bodies dissolving into the shadows, disappearing one by one.

The teenagers stood in silence, their breaths coming in short, gasping sobs, their bodies trembling as they watched the creatures vanish. The woman turned to them, her gaze hard, her voice low.

"You shouldn't have come here," she said, her tone filled with a quiet fury. "You broke the pact. The Skin Walkers are awake now, and they will not rest. Not until they've claimed what they were promised."

Anna took a shaky step forward, her face pale, her voice trembling. "Who... who are you?"

The woman's face softened, a look of sorrow crossing her features. "I am Agnes, the last of the elders who remembers the curse, the price that was paid to keep these creatures bound. Your recklessness has broken the spell that held them. And now, they will come for you, for all of us."

The teenagers exchanged horrified glances, the weight of her words sinking in, the knowledge that their actions had unleashed something ancient, something that could not be stopped.

"What... what do we do?" Marcus whispered, his voice barely audible.

Agnes looked at them, her expression grim. "You go home. You warn the others. Tell them that the Skin Walkers have returned, that the darkness is awake once more. And you prepare... because they will not stop. They will come, again and again, until Black Hollow is theirs."

And as the teenagers fled the clearing, the weight of their mistake pressing down on them, they knew that the peace Black Hollow had known was over. The Skin Walkers were free, bound no longer by the ancient pact, hungry for the souls of those who dared to trespass on their land.

And as they ran, they could hear the faint sound of footsteps following, silent and relentless, a reminder that once marked, the Skin Walkers would never stop.

When the teenagers returned to the village that night, they did so with terror etched across their faces. They gathered the villagers in the town square, Agnes standing by, her face pale and determined. She watched as Marcus, Anna, Liam, and Sophie recounted their story—the bones, the voices, and the creatures that had followed them back, creatures more terrifying than the darkest village legends.

The townsfolk listened in a hushed silence, fear creeping into their eyes as they understood the gravity of what had happened. The tales of the Skin Walkers had lingered as ghost stories, whispers of old curses and ancient rituals, until tonight. Now, the curse was awake, and they were all in danger.

Agnes stepped forward, her voice carrying through the crowd, steady and filled with purpose.

"The pact has been broken. The Skin Walkers are free, and they will come for all of us," she said, her gaze sweeping over the villagers. "But there is a way to bind them once more. The ritual requires a new pact, a sacrifice to appease the spirits."

A murmur rippled through the crowd, dread spreading as Agnes continued. "This ritual is our only hope of surviving. We must do what our ancestors did—prepare an offering, give what they demand. But the sacrifice must be... willing."

Silence fell over the crowd as her words hung heavy in the cold night air.

Agnes took it upon herself to prepare the villagers, spending the next day arranging everything they needed for the ritual. She gathered herbs, symbols, and stones marked with ancient symbols passed down through her family, each one imbued with protective power. She marked the boundaries around the village, laying wards that would delay the Skin Walkers' approach, but she knew they would only hold for so long. At sundown, the ritual would begin, a fragile hope against the terror that waited beyond the trees.

Meanwhile, the villagers gathered, their faces tense and fearful as they whispered about who would volunteer for the sacrifice. No one dared to step forward, the fear of death and the unknown too powerful to overcome. The teenagers who had broken the pact felt the weight of guilt pressing on them, knowing that this horror had been unleashed by their actions.

As the sun began to set, Agnes led the group into the clearing on the edge of the forest, the very place where Elijah Crane had first summoned the Skin Walkers. She stood in the center, arranging the stones, each one etched with the symbols of binding, the markings that would close the gap between their world and the spirit realm. The air was thick with tension, the villagers' breaths visible in the cold, their faces pale in the fading light.

At last, Agnes spoke, her voice filled with both urgency and sorrow. "One among us must be the offering, a life given willingly to the spirits. This sacrifice will restore the balance, return the Skin Walkers to their realm. It is our only hope."

A heavy silence followed, the villagers' gazes dropping to the ground, each one weighed down by fear and doubt. Then, to everyone's surprise, Marcus stepped forward, his face pale but resolute.

"I was the one who led us into the forest," he said, his voice steady. "This is my fault. I... I will be the sacrifice."

Anna, Liam, and Sophie gasped, their faces filled with shock, but Marcus held his ground, meeting Agnes's gaze with a quiet determination.

Agnes nodded, respect and sorrow in her eyes. “You are brave, Marcus. Your courage will protect us all.”

As darkness fell over Black Hollow, the villagers formed a circle around Marcus, each one holding a candle, their faces shadowed, their expressions somber. Agnes began the chant, her voice low and resonant, the ancient words carrying through the clearing, filling the air with a strange, powerful energy. She sprinkled herbs over the stones, their smoke rising into the air, forming a thin, protective veil around Marcus.

But then, from the depths of the forest, the Skin Walkers appeared, emerging from the shadows like phantoms. Their skinless forms glistened in the moonlight, each one taller and more twisted than the last, their empty eyes fixed on the ritual, their mouths stretched into twisted grins.

The villagers shrank back, their breaths hitching as they watched the creatures draw closer, their movements slow and deliberate, as though savoring the terror that filled the air. Marcus stood in the center, his body tense, his heart pounding as he faced the Skin Walkers, the creatures who had haunted his nightmares, the monsters that had been waiting, watching.

Agnes continued the chant, her voice rising, her hands steady as she scattered more herbs around Marcus, marking the ground with symbols of binding, sealing him within a protective circle. The Skin Walkers paused, their bodies swaying, their hollow eyes narrowing as they sensed the power of the ritual, the force that bound them to the land.

One of the Skin Walkers stepped forward, its body tall and sinewy, its face twisted into a mockery of a human expression, its mouth opening in a silent scream. It reached out, its fingers long and bony, dripping with a dark, viscous fluid, its hollow eyes fixed on Marcus with a hunger that transcended the physical.

Agnes turned to Marcus, her voice soft, filled with a quiet sorrow. "Are you ready?"

He nodded, swallowing hard, his gaze steady as he faced the Skin Walkers, his mind filled with memories of his family, his friends, the life he had known. He took a deep breath, closing his eyes, a sense of peace settling over him as he accepted his fate.

Agnes raised her hands, her voice ringing out in the final words of the ritual, the chant echoing through the forest, filling the air with a powerful, binding energy. The Skin Walkers froze, their bodies stiff, their faces twisted into expressions of rage and fear as they felt the pull of the binding, the force that would draw them back into the darkness.

But just as Agnes completed the ritual, a terrible sound filled the air—a high-pitched, guttural scream, a sound that seemed to come from the very depths of the forest, filled with anger, hatred, and an insatiable hunger.

The Skin Walkers began to writhe, their bodies twisting, contorting, as though fighting against the binding, their hollow eyes filled with fury. The ground trembled beneath them, the air thick with a dark, suffocating energy, and the villagers watched in horror as the creatures began to advance, their movements jerky, unnatural, their bodies resisting the pull of the ritual.

Agnes's face paled, her voice faltering as she realized the truth—the ritual wasn't enough. The curse had grown too strong, fed by years of neglect, by the blood that had been spilled in the forest. The Skin Walkers had become something more than spirits; they were entities of pure darkness, bound not by the land, but by the hatred and suffering that had festered in Black Hollow.

The creatures broke through the circle, their movements frantic, desperate, their hollow eyes fixed on Marcus with a hunger that could not be denied. They reached for him, their fingers clawing at his skin, tearing, ripping, their faces filled with a dark, twisted satisfaction as they absorbed his essence, his sacrifice feeding their insatiable need.

The villagers screamed, backing away, their faces filled with horror as they watched Marcus vanish beneath the Skin Walkers, his body consumed, his spirit absorbed into the darkness. Agnes fell to her knees, her face wet with tears, her voice a broken whisper as she realized the terrible truth.

The Skin Walkers were not bound to the forest. They were bound to the people of Black Hollow.

And they would never rest.

With the ritual broken, the Skin Walkers turned to the villagers, their bodies swaying, their hollow eyes fixed on the crowd with a dark, malevolent hunger. The villagers scattered, running toward the town, their hearts pounding, their minds reeling with terror. The Skin Walkers moved after them, their bodies blending into the shadows, their forms flickering in and out of sight, like phantoms.

Agnes staggered to her feet, her mind racing, the weight of her failure pressing down on her like a heavy shroud. She knew now that the curse could not be broken, that the Skin Walkers would hunt them, haunt them, until every last soul in Black Hollow was claimed.

And as the screams of the villagers filled the air, echoing through the forest, she whispered a final, desperate prayer, a plea to whatever forces might hear, to spare them from the darkness that had been unleashed.

But there was no answer, only silence, and the cold, unyielding presence of the Skin Walkers, their hollow eyes gleaming with the knowledge that they had won, that Black Hollow was theirs.

And as the night closed in, the village was consumed by darkness, the shadows creeping over every home, every street, the Skin Walkers moving through the night, relentless, unstoppable, their hunger never-ending, their curse eternal.

The village of Black Hollow was transformed. Once a quiet place of simple lives and close-knit families, it was now a shadow of itself, haunted and hollow. The Skin Walkers had emerged from the woods each night, leaving no home untouched, no street unscathed. Those who had survived so far knew the creatures' patience was unyielding and their hunger insatiable.

For days, the villagers cowered in their homes, hoping the creatures would pass them by. But each night, the Skin Walkers returned, their hollow eyes and twisted forms lingering outside windows, their hands scraping against doors. The haunting whispers filled the air, echoing through the streets, pulling the villagers into a fear so deep it felt like it would never end.

But with every night, their numbers dwindled, and their hope faded. In desperation, they turned to Agnes, the last elder, the woman who had tried to bind the Skin Walkers. Her face was lined with guilt and fear, her heart heavy with the knowledge that her ritual had failed, that the curse was beyond her control. But she knew she could not let the village fall without a fight.

In a last act of defiance, Agnes called a meeting in the town hall, gathering the remaining villagers in a tight, silent circle. Her voice trembled as she spoke, but there was a fierce determination in her eyes, a resolve that had not been there before.

"The Skin Walkers are bound to us by the blood, by the darkness we disturbed," she began, her gaze sweeping over the frightened faces before her. "But there is one way we can weaken them. They are drawn to fear, to suffering. If we unite, if we stand together, we can keep them at bay."

The villagers murmured nervously, the fear etched into their faces. But as they looked around, they saw the same terror mirrored in each other's eyes, the same desperation to survive. And with that shared fear came a flicker of hope, a spark of resilience that Agnes fanned with her words.

"We have to draw them out," Agnes continued. "We can no longer hide and hope they leave. We must face them, together, with fire and salt, with anything that can cleanse this darkness. If we fight together, we might weaken them enough to drive them back into the woods."

She outlined the plan, simple but desperate. They would gather in the town square that night, a circle of torches and salt lines, a barrier that would keep the Skin Walkers at bay, if only for a short time. The villagers were to stand side by side, a united force, their combined courage the only thing left to challenge the Skin Walkers' hunger.

As the sun set over Black Hollow, the villagers gathered in the square, each one clutching a torch, their faces grim, their bodies tense. Agnes and a few others had laid a ring of salt around the square, forming a barrier that would slow the creatures' approach. The air was thick with anticipation, the only sound the crackle of flames and the occasional murmur of prayers whispered under breath.

The first sign of the Skin Walkers was the chill that settled over the square, a cold that seemed to seep into their bones, leaving them shivering despite the warmth of the torches. The shadows lengthened, stretching across the ground, moving with a life of their own, creeping toward the ring of light, of salt, and stopping just beyond it.

Then, from the darkness, the creatures appeared.

There were dozens of them now, their skinless forms glistening in the torchlight, their bodies twisted and elongated, their hollow eyes fixed on the villagers with a hunger that defied understanding. They moved with an unnatural grace, each step silent, their forms blending into the shadows, shifting, as though part of the darkness itself.

Agnes stepped forward, her torch held high, her voice steady as she addressed the creatures. "You cannot have us," she said, her words ringing through the silent square. "We will not give in. We will not be yours."

The Skin Walkers paused, their heads tilting, their hollow eyes narrowing as they regarded her, their twisted grins widening, as though amused by her defiance.

One of the creatures stepped forward, its mouth opening in a silent scream, its body stretching, twisting, its bony fingers reaching out, stopping just inches from the salt barrier. It seemed to be testing it, feeling the force that held it back, its mouth twisting into a sneer as it met Agnes's gaze.

But the villagers did not break. They stood together, torches held high, their faces set, their bodies trembling but united. And as they held their ground, something remarkable happened.

The Skin Walkers hesitated, their movements slowing, their hollow eyes flickering with a strange, unfamiliar light—a hint of frustration, of confusion, as though they could feel the strength of the villagers' unity, the power that came from their shared defiance.

For a moment, it seemed as though the creatures would retreat, as though the villagers' courage had somehow weakened them. But then, the largest of the Skin Walkers, a figure taller and more twisted than the rest, stepped forward, its hollow eyes fixed on Agnes, its mouth stretching into a hideous, mocking grin.

It lifted its hand, clawed and skeletal, and pointed at her, its gesture a silent promise, a challenge.

The villagers tightened their circle, their torches blazing brighter, their voices joining in a low, steady chant, a prayer for protection, for strength, a chant that filled the air, that echoed through the square, a sound that cut through the darkness, pushing back the creatures' shadows.

But the Skin Walkers began to advance, their bodies moving in unison, their hollow eyes gleaming with a dark, relentless hunger. They pressed against the salt line, their forms flickering, stretching, testing the barrier, their mouths open in silent screams, their bodies writhing as they pushed forward, inch by inch.

Agnes knew that the Skin Walkers would not relent, that the salt line would only hold for so long. The villagers were strong, but their strength was fading, their courage wavering as the creatures closed in, their forms pressing against the light, their shadows reaching toward the circle, relentless.

With a heavy heart, Agnes made a decision.

She took a step forward, breaking from the circle, her torch held high, her voice steady as she addressed the Skin Walkers. "You want a soul?" she called, her voice carrying through the square. "Then take mine. Take it and leave Black Hollow in peace."

The villagers gasped, their voices rising in protest, but Agnes silenced them with a look, her face filled with a quiet determination, a resignation that broke their hearts.

"Agnes, no!" Anna cried, her voice filled with anguish. "You can't!"

Agnes smiled, a sad, weary smile, her gaze soft as she looked at Anna, at the villagers who had been her family, her friends. "This is the only way. I am the last elder, the last who remembers the pact. My life is the only thing that can end this."

Before anyone could stop her, Agnes stepped beyond the salt line, into the darkness, her body bathed in the faint glow of the torches, her face calm, her voice steady as she met the gaze of the Skin Walkers, her expression filled with a fierce, unyielding courage.

The largest of the Skin Walkers moved forward, its hollow eyes fixed on her, its mouth twisted into a grotesque grin, its hand reaching out, its fingers long and skeletal, dripping with a dark, thick fluid.

Agnes did not flinch, did not look away. She held her ground, her gaze steady, her voice calm as she whispered a final prayer, a last, desperate plea for peace, for freedom.

And then, the Skin Walker touched her.

The villagers watched, their faces pale, their hearts breaking, as Agnes's body shuddered, as her spirit was drawn into the darkness, consumed by the Skin Walkers' hunger, her life given willingly, a final, desperate sacrifice to end the curse.

The Skin Walkers froze, their bodies wavering, their forms flickering as though caught in some invisible force, their hollow eyes filled with a strange, terrible light, a moment of satisfaction, of fulfillment, as Agnes's spirit merged with theirs.

And then, one by one, they began to fade, their forms dissolving into shadows, melting back into the darkness, their hunger sated, their curse fulfilled.

The villagers stood in silence, their torches flickering, their hearts heavy as they watched the Skin Walkers disappear, taking Agnes with them, leaving behind only a silence that was both mournful and peaceful, a reminder of the sacrifice she had made.

Black Hollow was forever changed. The villagers mourned Agnes, honoring her memory, her courage, her final act of love for them. They rebuilt, they healed, but they never forgot the price of breaking the ancient pact, of disturbing the spirits bound to their land.

And on cold autumn nights, when the wind whispered through the trees, they could still feel her presence, a gentle, protective force that watched over them, that guarded them from the darkness that lingered at the edge of the forest.

The Skin Walkers were gone, but their memory remained, a silent reminder that some curses could only be broken through sacrifice, that some evils could never truly be destroyed, only appeased.

And so, the village of Black Hollow endured, haunted by shadows, but united in the memory of Agnes, the last elder, the woman who had given everything to protect them, her spirit forever woven into the fabric of their lives, a guardian against the darkness that would never fully fade.

The End

13
THE STRAY'S

The city of Belmont had always had its share of stray cats—sleek black ones slipping between parked cars, skinny tabbies lounging on crumbling brick walls, mangy gray tomcats prowling the alleys. For years, they had been little more than a background feature of the city, their sleek bodies darting through shadows, scavenging for scraps, dodging headlights, and the occasional toss of a booted foot. People often left out bowls of food, scraps from dinner, tossed into dark corners where the cats would gather, their yellow eyes gleaming in the night.

But recently, something had changed.

The cats were no longer just scavengers; they'd grown bolder, moving in groups, hunting with precision. Locals began noticing that the usual stray behavior—the skittish glances, the darting movements—had shifted to something far more unsettling. These cats no longer fled at the sight of people; instead, they watched. And their eyes, once full of wary curiosity, now held a cold, predatory hunger.

It started small. At first, just the odd whisper of a missing person here, a homeless man gone from his usual post by the river. Then the disappearances grew more frequent, each one casting a shadow of dread over the city's late-night streets. The cats, though numerous, were still considered harmless, even as strange rumors began to circulate in Belmont's underbelly. But tonight, the residents of Belmont would discover just how wrong they had been.

Charlie Mendoza leaned against the graffiti-splattered wall of a narrow alley, his hoodie pulled low over his face, cigarette smoke curling from his mouth as he checked his phone. The night was cold, the kind that sent shivers down your spine, even in heavy layers. The streets were empty, the dim streetlights casting thin, weak patches of light on the pavement, and the air was filled with a silence that felt thick, almost unnatural.

He was waiting for his buddy Mike, who'd texted him twenty minutes ago saying he'd be right there. But Mike was late, and in the dead silence of the night, even a minor delay felt unnerving. Charlie glanced down the empty street, fidgeting, his cigarette trembling slightly between his fingers.

Then he noticed something odd—a faint rustling coming from behind a dumpster a few feet away. Charlie's eyes narrowed as he took a step closer, his curiosity piqued despite the chill running down his spine.

"Hello?" he called out, his voice echoing softly in the night.

Nothing but silence.

Then, suddenly, a pair of eyes appeared in the dark space between the dumpster and the wall—bright, yellow eyes, glinting in the faint glow of the streetlights. Charlie froze, the hairs on the back of his neck standing up as he recognized the shape of a cat, its body slinking forward, the eyes fixed on him with an unsettling intensity.

"Shoo," he muttered, waving his hand dismissively. But the cat didn't move. It remained perfectly still, its gaze locked onto his, its body tense, poised.

Charlie shifted uncomfortably, his heart beginning to race. "Get lost, ya creepy furball," he muttered, kicking a small rock in its direction. But as the rock clattered to the ground, the cat's gaze didn't waver. And then, as he stared back at it, another pair of eyes appeared beside it, then another, and another, until a whole line of glowing yellow eyes watched him from the shadows.

A wave of fear washed over him as he realized that he was no longer alone. Cats—dozens of them—began to emerge from the darkness, their bodies sleek and muscular, their eyes glinting with a hunger he'd never seen in an animal before. They moved in silence, forming a circle around him, their tails flicking back and forth, their bodies crouched low, ready to pounce.

Charlie's heart pounded as he backed up, pressing himself against the wall, his eyes wide with terror. "What... what the hell?"

The cats took a step forward, their movements eerily synchronized, like they were following some unspoken command. Charlie tried to shout, to scream, but his voice caught in his throat as one of the cats—a large, black tom with a scarred face—let out a low, rumbling growl, its eyes never leaving his.

The cats closed in, their bodies sleek and silent, their eyes glowing with a terrible intelligence, a calculated cruelty. Charlie's mind raced, trying to make sense of the nightmare unfolding before him. But before he could react, the first cat lunged, its claws slashing across his ankle, sharp and swift, sending a burst of pain up his leg.

He stumbled, his back pressed harder against the wall as he tried to kick the cat away, but more of them sprang forward, their claws sinking into his skin, their teeth biting down on his legs, his arms. He thrashed, trying to shake them off, but it was no use—the cats moved with a predatory grace, their teeth and claws tearing into him with savage precision.

In the last moments before darkness closed in, Charlie looked up, his gaze meeting the unblinking eyes of the black tom, who watched him with a cold, detached satisfaction. He saw a flash of sharp, white teeth, felt the pressure of claws on his chest, and then... nothing.

The alley returned to silence, the only sound the faint rustle of fur against concrete. One by one, the cats retreated into the shadows, their yellow eyes disappearing into the night, leaving nothing but a dark, still shape slumped against the wall, lifeless.

Detective Erin Hayes arrived at the scene just as the sun was rising, the early morning light casting long, eerie shadows across the alley. She had seen her fair share of strange cases in Belmont, but something about this call had set her nerves on edge. The dispatcher's voice had been tense, strained, as if he couldn't quite believe what he was saying.

She crouched by the body, her gloved fingers gently brushing away the edges of the torn clothing to reveal the wounds beneath. They were jagged, irregular, as though inflicted by dozens of small, sharp claws. Her heart pounded as she surveyed the scene, her mind racing to piece together an explanation.

"What could've done this?" asked Officer Ramirez, his face pale as he looked down at the body, his expression a mix of horror and confusion.

Hayes shook her head, her gaze fixed on the strange, almost surgical precision of the wounds. "I don't know. But whatever it was, it wasn't human."

She stood, scanning the alley, her eyes catching a faint, bloody paw print on the pavement, leading back toward the dumpster. She followed the trail, her mind spinning, her instincts telling her that something was deeply, terribly wrong.

When she reached the edge of the alley, she froze, her gaze drawn to a group of stray cats gathered on a nearby rooftop, their yellow eyes fixed on her, unblinking. They watched in silence, their bodies still, their gazes cold and detached, almost... calculating.

A chill ran down her spine as she realized they weren't just watching—they were observing, studying her, as though deciding whether she, too, might become their next target. The cats didn't scatter, didn't flee at her approach. Instead, they remained where they were, their eyes glinting with a strange, predatory intelligence that sent a wave of fear through her.

One of the cats, a large black tom with a scarred face, let out a low, rumbling growl, its gaze locked onto hers, a silent challenge. Hayes felt her breath catch, her pulse quicken, as she backed away, her mind grappling with the impossible truth.

The strays of Belmont were no longer just cats.

They were hunters.

And they were hungry.

Detective Erin Hayes couldn't shake the image of the cats from her mind. The look in their eyes—cold, calculating, almost human—haunted her, a vision that lingered long after she left the crime scene. She'd seen many strange things in Belmont, but the way those cats had watched her felt like something out of a nightmare. And the wounds on Charlie Mendoza... they weren't random. There had been precision to the attack, an almost surgical cruelty that left her deeply unsettled.

That afternoon, she sat in her small, dimly lit office, files spread across her desk as she sifted through reports of disappearances in the city. Most of them were homeless people or individuals with little family, people who might vanish without much attention or follow-up. But the pattern was unmistakable—the victims all disappeared near alleys, parks, or forgotten backstreets frequented by the city's stray cats.

A sharp knock on her door snapped her out of her thoughts. Officer Ramirez stepped in, his face pale, holding a file. "Detective, you're going to want to see this."

He handed her the file, which contained photos from a second crime scene—another body found in an alley not far from where Charlie had been discovered. The wounds were nearly identical—small, jagged claw marks, bites that tore through flesh with a ferocity unlike anything Hayes had ever seen.

"Another one?" she asked, a sinking feeling twisting in her stomach.

Ramirez nodded grimly. "Same thing as before. The body was practically torn to pieces. And get this—the witnesses said they saw a group of cats near the alley right before the attack. But by the time anyone realized what was happening, the cats were gone."

Hayes's hand tightened around the edge of the file. "It's impossible. Cats don't attack people like this... not even in a group."

Ramirez hesitated, shifting uncomfortably. "Look, I know it sounds insane. But... you saw those cats this morning. They weren't acting like strays. It was almost like they were organized... like they were waiting for something."

The words hung in the air, heavy with a truth neither of them wanted to acknowledge. Hayes could feel her rational mind pushing against the thought, but every instinct told her that something was terribly, horribly wrong.

"We need to get a hold of animal control," she said finally, forcing herself to think practically. "Tell them to round up as many strays as they can find. And see if anyone around the city has been feeding these cats—sometimes people leave food out, and they might have noticed something strange."

Ramirez nodded and left, but not before giving her one last, uneasy look. She watched him go, a chill creeping up her spine. The cats were up to something, and she could feel it in her bones. But why? And how?

The city of Belmont was blanketed in fog, the streetlights casting a dull, hazy glow that barely cut through the thick mist. It was the kind of night where even the bravest of souls would hurry home, driven by an unspoken fear of what might be lurking in the shadows.

Mr. Jennings, an elderly man who had lived in Belmont for over forty years, walked his usual route from the corner store, a bag of groceries in hand. He'd never been one to believe in ghost stories or rumors, and despite the strange news of missing people, he brushed it off as city talk. He was almost home when he noticed something unusual—a group of cats gathered in the middle of the sidewalk, blocking his path.

"Shoo!" he said, waving a hand dismissively.

But the cats didn't move.

He stopped, frowning as he looked closer. There were at least a dozen of them, their eyes glinting in the faint light, their bodies motionless. They stared at him with an intensity that made his skin crawl, their tails flicking back and forth in perfect synchronization.

Mr. Jennings took a step back, clutching his bag a little tighter. "Come on now... get out of here!"

One of the cats—a large gray tom with a scar over its eye—took a slow, deliberate step toward him. Its mouth opened, and it let out a low, rumbling hiss, the sound deep and resonant, filling the quiet street. The other cats followed, their bodies moving in eerie unison as they advanced, their eyes fixed on him, unblinking.

Jennings stumbled back, his heart pounding as he tried to make sense of the nightmare unfolding before him. "No... this can't be..."

He turned to run, but the cats were faster. They moved like a wave, surging forward, their bodies sleek and powerful, their claws flashing in the dim light. He felt a sharp pain as they leaped at him, their claws sinking into his skin, their teeth tearing into his flesh. His screams echoed through the foggy street, muffled by the mist, unheard by anyone nearby.

The cats attacked with a ferocity that was chillingly coordinated, their bodies moving as one, their claws and teeth working in perfect harmony to bring him down. As his vision blurred, he saw the gray tom staring down at him, its eyes glinting with a dark intelligence, a predatory satisfaction.

Then, everything went dark.

The next morning, Detective Hayes was called to the scene. The sight that awaited her was even worse than she'd imagined. Mr. Jennings's body lay on the ground, his clothes torn, his skin covered in deep scratches and bite marks. Blood stained the pavement, and a trail of bloody paw prints led back into the foggy alley.

Ramirez stood beside her, his face pale. "That's three victims now, Detective. Three people... torn apart by cats."

She stared down at the bloody paw prints, her mind racing. "This doesn't make sense. Cats don't hunt like this. They're solitary hunters, not pack animals. And even feral cats avoid people... they'd never attack like this."

Ramirez looked around nervously, his gaze drifting toward the shadowed corners of the alley, as though expecting something to leap out at them. "I don't know what's going on, Detective, but it feels like these cats... they're acting on orders. Like someone—or something—is controlling them."

Hayes didn't respond. Instead, she knelt beside the bloody paw prints, her fingers hovering just above the faint outlines. She noticed something strange—each print was perfectly formed, each one distinct, almost as if the cats had left them there deliberately, a silent warning.

"We need to set a trap," she murmured, standing up and brushing the dirt from her hands. "These cats are acting with intent, and I need to see it for myself."

That night, Hayes and Ramirez set up their trap in one of Belmont's narrow alleys, near a spot where several sightings had been reported. They left out food as bait, small plates filled with scraps, hoping to draw the strays in. Hayes hid behind a dumpster, her heart pounding, her breath coming in slow, steady draws as she waited.

The street was silent, the fog thick and heavy, wrapping around the buildings like a shroud. Then, just as Hayes was beginning to think they might have set up in the wrong place, she heard it—the soft padding of paws on concrete, the faint rustle of fur brushing against the ground.

One by one, the cats emerged from the shadows, their bodies sleek and muscular, their eyes glowing in the darkness. They moved slowly, cautiously, their heads low, their tails flicking back and forth as they approached the food. Hayes held her breath, her eyes fixed on them, every nerve in her body on high alert.

Then, from the back of the group, the gray tom appeared, his scarred face twisted into a snarl, his eyes glinting with an intelligence that sent chills down her spine. He lifted his head, sniffing the air, and for a moment, Hayes felt as though he was looking directly at her, aware of her presence, sensing her fear.

The gray tom let out a low growl, and the other cats froze, their bodies tense, their eyes fixed on him, waiting.

Then, in a blur of movement, they turned, their eyes snapping to Hayes's hiding spot. The alley filled with the sound of hissing and growling, their bodies coiled, ready to pounce.

Hayes's blood ran cold as she realized that the cats weren't just animals—they were something else, something far darker, something that was aware, calculating, and unafraid of her. She scrambled to her feet, backing away, her heart pounding as the gray tom advanced, his eyes gleaming with a predatory hunger.

"Ramirez, run!" she shouted, her voice breaking the silence.

They bolted down the alley, the sound of paws thundering behind them, the cats chasing them with a terrifying speed and coordination. Hayes felt their claws swipe at her heels, their snarls echoing in her ears as they closed in, relentless, unstoppable.

Just as they reached the edge of the alley, the cats stopped, their bodies frozen in the shadows, their eyes watching, waiting. The gray tom sat at the front, his gaze cold and unblinking, his expression almost... disappointed.

Hayes stumbled to a stop, her chest heaving, her mind reeling with terror and disbelief. She could feel the tom's gaze following her as she backed away, his eyes filled with a dark promise, a silent vow that this wasn't over.

The cats retreated into the shadows, disappearing as quickly as they had appeared, leaving Hayes and Ramirez shaken, their minds racing with questions, their hearts filled with dread.

The next morning, Detective Hayes sat in her office, the blinds drawn, the room shrouded in shadows. She could still feel the phantom of their claws, the cold, calculating stares of those cats. No part of it felt natural. These cats were coordinated, with a dark purpose she couldn't understand.

She'd been hunting killers for years, but this... this felt like something beyond anything she'd faced before.

The sound of her phone vibrating on the desk snapped her out of her thoughts. She glanced at the caller ID—an unknown number. Reluctantly, she picked up.

"Detective Hayes."

"Detective," a voice whispered on the other end, raspy and almost trembling. "My name is Eliza. I... I think I know what's been happening with the cats."

Hayes's heart skipped a beat. "How did you get this number?"

There was a pause, then a shuddering breath. "I used to be part of a small group... people who took care of Belmont's strays. But things... things changed. The cats... they aren't just cats anymore. They've become something else."

"Where can I meet you?" Hayes asked, her pulse quickening.

"Meet me at St. Bridget's," Eliza replied, her voice dropping to a faint whisper. "Come alone. And don't... don't bring anyone else."

The line went dead, leaving Hayes with the chilling realization that the truth she'd been chasing might be darker than she'd expected.

St. Bridget's Church was an old, crumbling building on the outskirts of Belmont, half-forgotten and overgrown with ivy, its stained glass darkened by layers of dust. Hayes walked up the steps, the faint morning light casting long shadows across the empty pews. At the front of the church, a woman waited, cloaked in a dark, hooded coat, her hands wringing nervously.

"Eliza?" Hayes called, her voice echoing softly in the empty church.

The woman nodded, pulling her hood back to reveal a gaunt face framed by graying hair. Her eyes were sharp, haunted, as though she had seen things that could never be unseen.

"You're here because of the cats, aren't you?" Eliza whispered, glancing around as though afraid the very walls were listening.

Hayes nodded. "They're attacking people. It's not natural. And the way they looked at me... it was like they knew who I was."

Eliza shivered, her gaze fixed on Hayes. "They do know who you are. Those cats... they're more than strays now. They're... they're something that was called forth, summoned."

Hayes's eyes narrowed. "Summoned? What are you talking about?"

Eliza swallowed, her voice shaking. "There's an old story—one most people have forgotten. Decades ago, when Belmont was just a small town, there was a man named Isaac Gale. He was an outcast, a recluse who lived on the outskirts and had an odd kinship with the cats. People said he could control them, command them to do his bidding."

"Like some kind of... dark magic?" Hayes asked, skepticism warring with her growing sense of dread.

Eliza nodded, her eyes wide. "He was shunned, mocked by the townsfolk, until one day he snapped. He performed a ritual, binding his soul to the cats, claiming that they would do his bidding, even beyond death. And since then, every generation of cats in Belmont has carried a piece of Isaac's spirit, a part of his anger, his hatred for the people who cast him out."

Hayes felt a chill creep down her spine. "And you believe he's controlling them now?"

"I know he is," Eliza whispered, her hands trembling. "I've seen it. A few years ago, I was part of a group that tried to help the cats—to feed them, care for them. But as we spent more time with them, we realized something was wrong. They weren't just strays; they were watching us, observing. I saw the black tom you mentioned—the one with the scarred face. He's... he's their leader, a vessel for Isaac Gale's spirit."

Hayes gripped the edge of the pew, her mind racing. "So how do we stop it? How do we break the connection?"

Eliza's face paled, her eyes full of fear. "There's only one way. We have to find the place where Isaac performed the ritual, where his spirit was bound to the cats. It's somewhere deep in the city's old alleys, where the strays gather. If we find it, if we destroy it... we might sever the bond."

Hayes took a deep breath, nodding. "Then we find it. And we end this."

Later that evening, Hayes and Eliza made their way to Belmont's oldest district, a maze of narrow alleys and abandoned buildings long forgotten by most of the city. The streets were quiet, the shadows deep, and as they ventured deeper into the heart of the district, Hayes could feel a prickling sensation along her skin, as though something dark and unseen were watching them.

Eliza led the way, her movements cautious, her gaze darting nervously from side to side. "This is where Isaac was rumored to have lived, hidden away from everyone. The cats still gather here sometimes... it's as if they're guarding something."

As they rounded a corner, Hayes caught sight of them—a group of cats, gathered in a tight circle, their eyes fixed on a spot in the alley where a single, worn stone lay embedded in the ground. They didn't react to her presence, didn't flinch or scatter. They merely watched, their eyes gleaming with a silent, eerie intensity.

"That's it," Eliza whispered, her voice barely audible. "That's where he bound himself."

Hayes took a step forward, her heart pounding, but as she moved closer, the cats parted, forming a path, their gazes never leaving her. She knelt by the stone, her fingers brushing over its rough surface, feeling a strange warmth beneath her hand, a pulse of energy that seemed to throb with an ancient rage.

"Eliza, how do we destroy it?" she asked, glancing over her shoulder.

But Eliza's face had gone pale, her eyes wide with terror. "They're coming... they won't let us leave now. Not without a fight."

Hayes turned, and her blood ran cold. The cats were advancing, their bodies moving as one, their eyes glinting with a predatory hunger. The gray tom stepped forward, his scarred face twisted in a snarl, his gaze fixed on her with a dark, burning hatred.

"Hayes," Eliza whispered, pressing something cold into her hand. "A hammer. Break the stone."

Hayes felt the weight of the hammer in her hand, a cold determination settling over her as she raised it, bringing it down on the stone with all her strength. The stone cracked, a loud, piercing sound echoing through the alley, and the cats hissed, recoiling as though struck by an invisible force.

The gray tom let out a guttural growl, its eyes flaring with an unnatural light as it leaped toward her, its claws outstretched. Hayes swung the hammer, knocking it aside, and brought the hammer down again, shattering the stone completely. A flash of light erupted from the broken rock, a wave of energy that sent the cats scrambling, their cries echoing through the alley as they fled, disappearing into the shadows.

And then, there was silence.

Hayes lowered the hammer, breathing heavily, her gaze fixed on the broken stone, the ancient binding shattered, the alley empty save for the faint, fading echoes of Isaac Gale's wrath.

"It's over," Eliza whispered, her face pale, her eyes wide with relief. "He's gone. The curse... it's broken."

Hayes nodded, the weight of exhaustion settling over her. But as they turned to leave, a single, cold whisper drifted through the empty alley, a sound that sent a final shiver down her spine.

"For now..."

They left the alley in silence, knowing that while the curse was broken, the city's shadows still held secrets, old and dark, waiting for the right moment to return.

The End

14

NIGHT LIGHTS

The clock struck 2:14 a.m., and the house was silent, wrapped in the deep quiet of the early hours. Hannah Blake lay awake in the master bedroom, staring at the ceiling, her husband David's soft breathing beside her. She had been restless all night, an uneasy feeling curling in her stomach that she couldn't explain. She rolled over to glance at the window, the dark forest visible beyond the edge of their backyard, when a sudden glow caught her eye.

At first, she thought it was a trick of the moonlight, or perhaps headlights from the road beyond the trees. But as she watched, the glow became brighter, taking on a strange, otherworldly hue. Her breath caught as she realized there wasn't just one light—there were seven, hovering in a perfect formation above the treetops, casting an eerie, bluish light that illuminated the tops of the trees.

"David," she whispered, nudging him, her voice filled with a quiet urgency.

He stirred, blinking groggily, but the moment his eyes met the lights outside, he was wide awake. They both sat up, staring out the window, transfixed by the strange, hovering lights. They were motionless, silent, suspended in the sky like stars that had strayed too close to the earth.

"What... what is that?" he murmured, his voice barely more than a whisper.

Hannah shook her head, unable to tear her gaze away. "I don't know... but it's not normal."

They sat there for a few minutes, watching the lights, their presence unsettling, almost hypnotic. And then, just as suddenly as they had appeared, the lights began to move, gliding silently across the sky in a slow, deliberate formation before vanishing over the horizon, leaving only darkness behind.

In the silence that followed, they turned to each other, their faces pale, their expressions mirroring the same unspoken thought.

The next morning, as they gathered in the kitchen for breakfast, their two children, Oliver and Emily, sat quietly, their usual chatter absent, their faces drawn and tense. Oliver, only eight, looked up at his mother with wide, frightened eyes.

"Mom... I saw the lights," he whispered, glancing nervously toward the window. "I tried to look away, but I couldn't. They were... calling me."

Hannah's heart clenched, and she glanced at David, who looked equally troubled. "It was probably nothing, honey," she said, trying to keep her voice calm. "Just something in the sky. Maybe even a weather balloon."

But Oliver shook his head, his small hands clutching his fork. "It wasn't just lights, Mom. It felt... wrong. Like they were looking for us."

Emily, who was six, hugged her knees to her chest, her voice barely audible. "I had a dream about them. They were here, inside the house."

Hannah and David exchanged a look, each of them feeling a chill settle over them. There was something deeply unsettling about the children's reactions, as though they understood something the adults couldn't see. It made Hannah's skin crawl, the unease from the previous night resurfacing with a force she couldn't ignore.

Later that morning, as Hannah sipped her coffee, scrolling through her phone, a news headline caught her eye:

"Strange Lights Spotted Over Local Forests: Officials Report Flare Testing"

She clicked on the article, her heart racing as she read the details. The lights had been seen all over town, reported by dozens of residents who had been as mystified as she and David had been. But according to the officials, the lights were simply part of a routine military flare test, nothing more than harmless, controlled activity.

Hannah frowned, a spark of doubt creeping into her mind. She knew what she'd seen. Those lights weren't flares—they had moved too deliberately, too controlled, hovering in perfect silence before disappearing without a trace. And the look in Oliver's eyes that morning... it hadn't been ordinary childhood fear. It was as if he'd sensed something more.

"What do you think?" David asked, glancing at the article over her shoulder, his expression wary.

She shook her head, her voice low. "I don't believe it. That was no military test. Those lights... they felt *wrong* somehow. Like they weren't just passing through."

David nodded slowly, his jaw tense. "We'll keep an eye out tonight. Just in case."

As the day wore on, Hannah couldn't shake the feeling that something was watching them, lurking just out of sight. She kept glancing out the window toward the forest, half-expecting to see the strange lights return, but the sky remained clear, the trees silent.

But that night, just as she was tucking the children into bed, Oliver's eyes filled with fear again.

"They're here, Mom," he whispered, gripping her arm. "I can feel them watching. They're waiting for something."

Hannah forced a smile, trying to reassure him. "There's nothing there, Ollie. Just trees and stars. You're safe."

But as she turned off the lights and closed the door to their room, she couldn't shake the feeling that Oliver was right—that something was indeed waiting for them, just beyond the edge of the forest.

And then, as she climbed into bed, she saw them again. The lights.

Hovering silently, just above the treetops.

This time, she could feel them reaching, as if drawn to her home, their strange, pulsing glow casting an eerie light over the trees.

Hannah froze, her heart pounding as the lights hovered above the forest, their bluish glow flickering like silent beacons. She glanced over at David, who was also staring, transfixed, his face pale in the dim light.

The lights were closer this time, no longer distant objects in the night sky but unmistakably near, right at the edge of their property. It was as though they'd drifted closer just to remind the family they hadn't gone anywhere, that they were watching.

"I can't stand it," David whispered, pulling himself from the trance. "I'm going out there."

"David, no!" Hannah grabbed his arm, her voice urgent. "It's not safe. We don't know what they are or who they belong to."

But David's jaw was set, and he shook his head. "I just need to see it up close. I'll be back in a few minutes, okay?"

Reluctantly, she let him go, her heart racing as she watched him throw on his coat, grab a flashlight, and step outside. She stayed by the window, watching as his figure disappeared into the dark yard, his flashlight a thin beam against the shadows. The lights remained, pulsing slowly, seemingly unfazed by his approach.

Seconds turned into minutes, and Hannah's anxiety grew. She strained to see him, her gaze locked on the spot where the trees met the yard. The lights seemed to shift, moving farther back, almost as if they were leading him deeper into the woods.

Then, just as her worry was reaching a fever pitch, she saw him—David's figure re-emerged, stumbling out of the trees, his face pale, his breath visible in short, panicked bursts.

Hannah ran to the door and pulled him inside, her voice frantic. "What did you see? Are you okay?"

David's eyes were wide, his face etched with disbelief. "There was... there was something moving out there. Not just lights. Shapes... shadows moving between the trees. They were tall, too tall to be people. And then... I heard them, Hannah."

She felt a chill settle over her. "Heard them? Heard what?"

He shook his head, his voice low, almost a whisper. "Voices. They were calling our names. Yours, mine, even the kids'."

The next morning, Hannah and David were shaken, but the rest of the world seemed blissfully unaware of the strangeness that had taken place just beyond the walls of their home. As Hannah sat at the kitchen table, her phone buzzed with an alert from the local news.

"*Authorities Reassure Residents: Lights Over Forest Due to Routine Training Exercises*"

Routine exercises. Her stomach twisted as she read the article, a now-familiar wave of unease washing over her. It was the same empty explanation, the same hollow attempt to put the public's mind at ease. But Hannah knew, deep down, that this was more than a simple training exercise. The lights, the shadows, the voices—they all pointed to something beyond explanation.

When she turned to David, he wore the same expression, a silent agreement that they couldn't let this go. Something was happening here, something the authorities were eager to keep hidden. And they were right in the middle of it.

Over the next few days, stories began trickling through the small town, whispered rumors spreading among neighbors and friends. A local woman claimed to have seen tall, faceless figures watching from the edge of her property, their heads cocked at an unnatural angle. Another resident reported waking up to find strange, circular imprints in his backyard, as though something massive had landed there in the night.

But it was when the children in town began to go missing that panic began to spread.

The first disappearance was a boy from the nearby neighborhood, eight-year-old Jonah Willis. His parents had put him to bed like any other night, only to wake up to an empty room, his window wide open, and the sheets pulled back as if he'd simply gotten up and walked out.

When the news broke, Hannah and David exchanged a look, the same unspoken fear mirrored in each other's eyes. They couldn't ignore the connection; the lights, the voices, the strange shadows moving through the forest—whatever was happening, it was escalating.

On the fifth night after the strange lights first appeared, Hannah was jolted awake by the sound of whispering—soft, insistent, just outside their bedroom window. She felt her heart leap into her throat, her body paralyzed by a fear so intense she could barely breathe.

She glanced at the clock. 3:12 a.m. The house was silent, the children asleep, but the whispering grew louder, more urgent, drifting through the walls as though it were coming from within the room itself.

"Hannah..."

She sat up, her gaze snapping to the window. And then she saw them—seven lights, hovering closer than ever before, directly outside, casting an unnatural glow across the backyard. The lights were bright, pulsating slowly, almost in sync with her heartbeat, and as she watched, she saw figures moving within the glow—tall, elongated shapes with impossibly long limbs and featureless faces.

She gasped, waking David, who sat up, his eyes widening as he took in the sight.

"My God," he breathed, his voice barely audible. "They're here."

The lights pulsed again, and the figures began to move toward the house, gliding soundlessly across the yard, their bodies flickering in and out of sight. The whispers grew louder, filling the room, a chilling chorus of voices that seemed to echo in their minds.

"Come outside, Hannah... come outside..."

David grabbed her hand, pulling her back. "Don't listen to them. Stay here."

But before they could process what was happening, a high-pitched, piercing noise filled the air, vibrating through the walls, setting every nerve on edge. The lights outside intensified, casting the room in an eerie, unnatural glow, and for a moment, it felt as though the walls themselves were dissolving, the room melting away into the blue light.

Then, just as suddenly as it began, the noise stopped, and the lights disappeared. The room fell silent, the only sound their own ragged breathing as they tried to process the impossible, chilling experience.

The next morning, a knock on the door jolted them back to reality. A tall man in a dark suit, flanked by two uniformed officers, stood on their doorstep, his face impassive, his eyes hidden behind dark sunglasses.

"Mr. and Mrs. Blake?" he asked, his tone smooth, practiced.

"Yes?" David replied cautiously, a protective hand on Hannah's shoulder.

The man held up a badge, his expression unreadable. "I'm Agent Foster with the Department of Defense. We understand you've reported seeing some... unusual lights near your home."

Hannah and David exchanged a look, their unease growing. "Yes," David said slowly. "But they were more than just lights. There were shapes, voices—"

Agent Foster held up a hand, silencing him. "I'm going to need you to forget what you think you saw. Those were government tests, classified training exercises that aren't open for public discussion. Any further speculation could be considered a breach of national security."

Hannah felt a surge of anger rise within her, the fear replaced by frustration. "Are you seriously trying to tell us that what we saw was just some routine test? We know what we saw. There were people—or... or *things*—in those lights. And we aren't the only ones who saw them."

Agent Foster's face remained impassive, but his tone hardened. "Let me make this clear, Mrs. Blake: I highly advise you to drop this line of questioning. The safety of you and your family depends on it."

With that, he turned and left, leaving Hannah and David standing in stunned silence, their minds racing with fear and anger.

That night, the lights returned, brighter and closer than ever. The whispers filled their minds again, but this time, they weren't calling from outside. They were inside the house, moving through the walls, whispering from the shadows.

The children woke up, their faces pale, their eyes wide with terror as they clung to Hannah and David. Oliver's voice trembled as he whispered, "Mom, they're inside. They're here."

Hannah hugged him close, her heart pounding as the lights grew brighter, the walls seeming to dissolve in the pulsing glow. And then, in the doorway of their room, a tall, shadowed figure appeared, its faceless head cocked to one side, as though watching them with silent curiosity.

The whispers grew louder, a cacophony of voices that seemed to fill every corner of the house, each one laced with a dark, insistent hunger.

"Come outside... come with us..."

And as the lights began to close in, Hannah realized with a cold, sickening certainty that this was no government test, no routine exercise. This was something far older, far more powerful, something that was not of this world.

And it wasn't going to leave until it had claimed them.

The Blakes could hardly sleep after the night of the terrifying visitation. The lights had vanished, but the air felt thick with something Hannah couldn't explain—like a residue of dread lingering over their house. Every creak in the floor, every flicker of light, made her heart race. But she knew they needed answers.

The following day, while David took the children to stay with a friend in town, Hannah set off alone. She couldn't ignore the feeling that whatever was happening to them was connected to the forest—and to something much older and darker than the so-called "government tests." Armed with a few local contacts and an instinct to dig deeper, she drove into the nearby town and found herself standing in front of the Alderwood County Historical Society, a modest building that held relics and records of the area's past.

Inside, Hannah met Mrs. Janine Cartwright, an elderly woman who had run the Historical Society for decades and knew the town's history better than anyone. When Hannah mentioned the lights, Mrs. Cartwright's face grew solemn, her eyes darkening.

"Oh, I know about the lights," she said softly. "But I doubt the story is what you'd call comforting."

"Please, I need to know," Hannah insisted. "My family's been seeing them every night, and something feels terribly wrong."

Mrs. Cartwright nodded, seeming to weigh her words carefully. "Those lights... they've been here for as long as Alderwood has been settled. The first records go back to the 1800s, when the original settlers wrote about *Wandering Orbs* appearing over the forest, luring people into the woods. But the story goes even further back—to the first people on this land, who spoke of beings they called the *Alunta*."

"Who... or what were the Alunta?" Hannah asked, a chill running down her spine.

Mrs. Cartwright's voice dropped to a whisper. "The Alunta were known as *the Forgotten Ones.* According to legend, they were ancient spirits, guardians of the land but also deeply resentful of anyone who disrupted the forest. When the settlers first arrived, they disturbed sacred sites, cut down trees, disrupted the natural balance. The lights began appearing, and shortly after, people vanished. The settlers would find bodies with signs of struggle, but no clear cause of death. Just an overwhelming expression of terror."

Hannah felt her throat tighten. "So... the lights are the Alunta?"

Mrs. Cartwright nodded. "It's believed that they draw power from the energy of the forest, feeding off of anyone foolish enough to look too long or to venture close. They lure people, filling their minds with illusions, tricking them with voices. Once someone has been marked by the lights, there's no going back. They'll keep coming for them."

Hannah shuddered, remembering the lights pulsing outside their house, the way they seemed to call her and David's names. "What do they want with people?"

The woman hesitated, her eyes filled with sadness. "They want company, but it's never as simple as that. Some say they're lonely, spirits that were forgotten or cast out. But they don't understand human life anymore, only the need to consume, to bind others to them. The Alunta want others to join them, to wander the forest as they do... eternally."

With Mrs. Cartwright's warnings echoing in her mind, Hannah hurried back to the house, her mind racing. She knew they needed some form of protection, something to break the link the lights had made with her family. But as she researched possible remedies, folklore offered few real answers. The legends only spoke of the danger of the Alunta, not how to keep them away.

David returned with the children as the day darkened, and Hannah shared what she'd learned, her voice tense with urgency. They agreed to keep the children away from the windows, forbidding them to look outside at night no matter what. But Hannah sensed it wouldn't be enough; the

Alunta had already made contact, already set their sights on the family.

As the sky turned to twilight, the air around the house grew still, thick, as if charged with an unseen energy. The children went to bed reluctantly, clutching their blankets, their small faces pale with fear. Hannah and David stayed by the window, the shades drawn, their breaths shallow, waiting.

And then, just as they feared, the lights returned.

The lights hovered outside, pulsing softly, casting a dim, ethereal glow across the yard. Hannah's pulse quickened as she and David watched through a small slit in the curtain. The lights were closer than ever, their glow brighter, more intense. And this time, they could see shapes within the lights—figures, tall and thin, their faces blurred, featureless, yet somehow undeniably watchful.

One of the lights moved closer to the window, and for a moment, Hannah felt a sharp, stinging sensation in her mind, as though a voice were pushing its way into her thoughts. She gripped David's hand, holding on tightly as the sensation grew stronger, filling her mind with a voice that was deep, ancient, and filled with a haunting sadness.

"We have wandered alone for centuries," the voice echoed in her mind, a whisper that chilled her to the bone. *"Join us, and we will be together. Forever."*

Hannah felt herself being drawn toward the window, her hand reaching out as if of its own accord. But David pulled her back, snapping her out of the trance, his face pale and filled with determination.

"We can't let them take us," he whispered, his voice shaking. "We have to fight them."

But as they turned to leave the room, a bright flash filled the house, a wave of cold air washing over them, and they realized the lights were inside.

The pulsing glow filled every corner, every shadow, as the Alunta surrounded them, their tall, shadowed forms gliding silently through the walls. The temperature plummeted, and a thick, oppressive feeling pressed down on them, making it hard to breathe, as if the house itself were being consumed by the presence of these ancient spirits.

The whispers grew louder, a chorus of voices filling the air, each one echoing with the same haunting message.

"We are the Forgotten Ones. Come with us, and you will be free from time... from sorrow... from pain."

Hannah gripped David's hand, her heart pounding, her mind racing as the lights moved closer, their glow suffocating, relentless.

But as she closed her eyes, a single memory surfaced—the words Mrs. Cartwright had spoken, something she hadn't understood until now.

"The Alunta were bound to the forest," she whispered, gripping David's hand. "They're spirits of the land, tied to what remains of their sacred places."

David's eyes widened as he understood. "If we get out of the forest... we might escape."

Without another word, they grabbed the children, hurrying down the stairs and out the back door, not daring to look back at the lights glowing behind them. The air outside was thick, as though pressing down on them, but Hannah focused only on putting one foot in front of the other, guiding her children through the dark woods, her heart pounding as the lights followed, moving silently through the trees, casting long shadows that seemed to stretch toward them.

The Alunta's whispers grew louder, filling the air, filling her mind, a haunting, insistent pull that made it harder to think, harder to remember why they were running. But as she pushed through the underbrush, she felt something change—the lights seemed to hesitate, their glow dimming, their shapes flickering like candles in the wind.

They had reached the edge of the forest.

Hannah felt a surge of hope as they stepped into the clearing beyond the trees, the lights growing weaker, fading, as though unable to follow. She turned to look back, seeing the Alunta hovering at the edge of the forest, their tall, shadowed forms watching them with an expression that was almost... mournful.

The lights pulsed once, then faded into the darkness, leaving only the silent forest behind.

As they staggered back toward their house, Hannah knew that while they had escaped the Alunta's pull for now, the spirits would remain in the forest, waiting for the next soul brave—or foolish—enough to cross their path.

The Forgotten Ones were bound to the land, but they were patient. And as long as the forest remained, they would wait.

In the days following their encounter with the Alunta, the Blakes were haunted not just by the experience but by the knowledge that the lights would always be there, waiting in the forest's shadowed depths. The whispers lingered in their minds, ghostly echoes that would resurface at night, making it difficult for them to sleep, leaving them tense and watchful.

Word of the strange lights spread quickly through the town, spurred by rumors and whispered warnings. Those who knew the history of the forest spoke in hushed tones of the Alunta, cautioning others to avoid the woods at night. But others, skeptics who scoffed at ghost stories and folklore, insisted the lights were nothing more than flares, weather phenomena, or reflections from the lake beyond the trees.

For the Blakes, however, the experience was all too real.

A week after their harrowing escape, Hannah received a visit from Mrs. Cartwright. The elderly woman moved with a quiet grace as she entered the Blakes' home, her expression serious, her eyes filled with a mixture of sympathy and caution.

"I heard what happened," Mrs. Cartwright said softly, sitting at the kitchen table. "You saw the Alunta more clearly than most do. Not many come close and live to tell the story."

Hannah nodded, her hands trembling slightly as she poured them both a cup of tea. "I can still feel them, Mrs. Cartwright. Like they're still watching. It's like they're waiting for us to come back."

Mrs. Cartwright placed a gentle hand on Hannah's. "You and your family escaped because you were wise enough to remember what they are: spirits bound to the land, cursed to wander the forest, forever searching. They wanted you to join them, to become one of them."

David, who had been listening quietly from across the room, spoke up. "Is there... is there any way to stop them? To break the connection?"

Mrs. Cartwright's face grew solemn. "The Alunta are bound by forces older than any of us, David. As long as there are those who disturb the forest, who cross into the sacred places, the Alunta will be drawn to them. They are protectors, but over time, they became something darker—hunters of those who invade their realm."

Hannah's heart sank. "So, we just have to live with this? Knowing they're always there, always waiting?"

The older woman nodded slowly. "Yes, but there is a way to protect yourselves. The Alunta may be spirits, but they respect boundaries. There are rituals, small wards, to protect your home. Salt, mirrors at the door, and symbols of protection placed at each entrance. These things hold power against them."

Mrs. Cartwright reached into her bag, pulling out a small amulet carved with ancient symbols. "Keep this in your home. It's been passed down for generations in my family, and it holds an old magic. It's not much, but it will make it harder for them to enter."

Hannah took the amulet, her fingers brushing over the cool, smooth stone, feeling a strange sense of calm settle over her. "Thank you, Mrs. Cartwright. I don't know how we can repay you."

The older woman smiled softly. "No need for thanks, dear. Just be cautious. The Alunta are not finished. They never are. But now, you have knowledge. Use it well, and you may just find peace."

News of the Blakes' encounter continued to circulate, stirring both fear and curiosity. Some neighbors shared stories of strange sightings, flickering lights in their own backyards, strange sounds at night. The local police received calls from frightened residents, but every official response ended with the same answer: "Nothing to be alarmed about."

But those who lived close to the forest knew better. Children were warned to stay indoors after dark, and even the most skeptical residents began to avoid the forest at night. Occasionally, someone would report seeing a flicker of blue light, a glimpse of a tall shadow standing at the forest's edge, watching with hollow eyes. The stories of the Alunta were kept alive, passed down like a warning, a reminder of the unseen forces that watched over the land.

For the Blakes, life slowly returned to normal, though they kept Mrs. Cartwright's amulet by the door and followed her advice to salt the windows and keep mirrors near the entrances. Though they never again saw the lights directly, they felt the weight of the forest nearby, a silent presence that seemed to hover just out of reach, waiting.

Months passed, the seasons changed, and the town began to settle back into its usual routines. But every so often, a flicker of light would appear in the trees, a faint blue glow that hovered silently before fading back into the shadows.

And the whispers would return, drifting through the night like an echo from another world.

The Alunta were still there, bound to the forest, guardians of a land they had never left. They waited in silence, patient and watchful, for the next soul to wander too close, for the next voice to answer their call.

And in the darkest hours of the night, when the town lay silent, they would gather in the forest, their lights flickering in the shadows, a silent, eternal reminder of the ancient spirits who watched over Alderwood—waiting for the day when they would no longer be *the Forgotten Ones.*

The End

15
THE HEAD HUNTERS

The Amazon River was alive. It pulsed and breathed with a rhythm as ancient as the jungle itself, a sprawling artery winding through miles of dense, humid greenery. For the group of university scientists, this trip was the expedition of a lifetime, a chance to explore one of the last truly wild places on earth and collect specimens for research. But the Amazon had its secrets, and as the group would soon learn, some of them were deadly.

The team had been assembled by Professor David Carter, an esteemed anthropologist with a reputation for his work in indigenous studies. He'd brought with him a mix of graduate students and researchers from the biology and anthropology departments, each of them eager to make a name for themselves by contributing to the field. Among them was Dr. Lila Reyes, a botanist with a particular interest in rare medicinal plants, and Jackson "Jack" Lowell, a graduate student specializing in ethnography.

They had been traveling up the Amazon for days, the dense forest pressing in on both sides of the river, its thick canopy casting everything in a greenish, filtered light. Their guide, a quiet, weathered man named Hector, had warned them about the dangers of the jungle—poisonous plants, deadly animals, and, of course, the intense heat and humidity. But nothing had prepared them for the eerie sense of isolation that settled over them as they ventured further from civilization, deeper into a world that seemed almost primeval.

By the fifth day, they had traveled far beyond the villages, deep into an area rarely visited by outsiders. The river narrowed, its murky water flowing slowly, thick with silt and rotting vegetation. It was here, in the heart of the jungle, that the true horror began.

It started innocently enough. Dr. Reyes had spotted an unusual vine hanging from a tree on the bank and asked Hector to bring the boat in closer so she could examine it.

As they neared the shoreline, Jack caught sight of something strange, swaying gently from a tree branch above them.

At first, he thought it was an animal carcass, maybe a monkey or a bird, but as the boat drew closer, his stomach twisted with a sickening realization. It was a body—a human body, suspended from the tree by its legs, its arms hanging limp, its skin pale and waxy.

But the most disturbing part was the head—or rather, the absence of it. The neck ended in a rough, jagged stump, blood long dried, the skin puckered around the cut as though the head had been roughly sawed off. Jack felt bile rise in his throat as he stared, unable to tear his gaze away from the horrific sight.

"Professor Carter," he managed to choke out, his voice barely more than a whisper. "Look..."

The rest of the team turned to see what had caught his attention, and a collective gasp filled the boat. Dr. Reyes covered her mouth, her face pale, her eyes wide with horror.

"What... what the hell happened to him?" she whispered, her voice trembling.

Hector, their guide, looked away, his face grim, his eyes filled with a mix of fear and resignation. "The Jivaro," he muttered, barely audible. "The head hunters."

The words sent a shiver down Jack's spine, a chill that cut through the humid air. He'd heard stories of the Jivaro, an indigenous tribe known for their practice of shrinking human heads, but he'd assumed they were exaggerated, the stuff of myths and legends. Surely such practices were long abandoned, remnants of a time when the jungle was ruled by rituals and spirits.

But the body hanging in the tree told a different story.

Professor Carter cleared his throat, forcing himself to remain calm, though his face was pale. "We need to document this," he said, his voice steady but strained. "Jack, take some photographs. Dr. Reyes, make note of our location. We need to record everything for the authorities back home."

As Jack raised his camera, Hector grabbed his arm, his face tense. "You don't understand," he said, his voice low, urgent. "This is a warning. The Jivaro don't want us here. If they've left this for us to see, it means we're trespassing... and we're in danger."

Professor Carter frowned, shaking his head. "We've come too far to turn back now, Hector. The university has invested in this expedition. This is just a scare tactic, meant to keep us from getting close to their territory. We'll be careful, stay by the river, and keep moving forward. We won't harm anything or anyone."

But Hector's expression was grim. "You may not intend harm, but to them, you are invaders. The Jivaro don't forgive... and they don't forget."

Despite his warning, Professor Carter remained resolute, and reluctantly, Hector guided the boat back into the main current, steering them further upriver. But as they moved away from the body, Jack couldn't shake the feeling that they were being watched, that a pair of unseen eyes followed their every movement from the shadows.

The jungle seemed darker, more oppressive, as though it, too, resented their presence. The air grew heavier, the silence punctuated only by the occasional call of a distant bird or the rustle of leaves as unseen creatures moved through the underbrush. And always, just beyond the edge of sight, was the faint, haunting sense that something was following them, moving silently through the trees, hidden but ever-present.

As night fell, they set up camp on a narrow stretch of shoreline, the air thick with the scent of damp earth and decaying vegetation. The team gathered around a small fire, their faces lit by the flickering flames, their expressions tense, uneasy.

They spoke little, each of them lost in their thoughts, their minds haunted by the image of the headless body hanging in the tree. Jack lay awake long after the others had fallen asleep, his mind racing, his nerves on edge. Every sound, every rustle of leaves, sent a fresh wave of fear through him, and he couldn't shake the feeling that they were not alone.

In the early hours of the morning, he heard a faint, shuffling sound coming from the edge of camp. Heart pounding, he sat up, straining his ears, peering into the darkness. The fire had burned low, casting only a dim glow across the campsite, and the jungle was alive with shadows, moving, shifting in the darkness.

And then he saw it.

Just beyond the edge of the firelight, hanging from a low branch, was another body. Like the first, it had been stripped of its head, the neck ending in a jagged stump, blood still fresh, trickling down its chest in dark, sticky rivulets. But this time, he recognized the clothes—the khaki shirt, the hiking boots. It was one of their own, a young researcher named Michael who had joined the team only a few months prior.

Jack's scream pierced the silence, waking the others, and within moments, the camp was alive with the sound of panicked voices, cries of horror as they took in the grisly sight before them.

Professor Carter staggered back, his face ashen, his eyes wide with terror. "We... we have to get out of here," he stammered, his voice barely more than a whisper. "This isn't... this isn't part of the expedition anymore. This is a nightmare."

But Hector shook his head, his face grim. "It's too late," he said, his voice filled with a quiet, resigned fear. "Once the Jivaro mark you, there's no going back. You've seen too much, trespassed too far. They will hunt you... until they have your heads."

The following day was a blur of panic and desperation. The team packed up camp, abandoning their equipment as they fled back downriver, their boat slicing through the water as they raced to put as much distance as possible between themselves and the jungle that seemed to close in around them.

But as they moved, they began to notice signs—strange symbols carved into the trees, small totems made from bone and feathers, marking their path like a twisted trail of breadcrumbs. It was as though the Jivaro were toying with them, allowing them to believe they were escaping, only to remind them, with each new sign, that they were never truly alone.

As night fell once more, they found themselves forced to stop, their exhaustion too great to continue. They set up a hasty camp, their nerves frayed, their faces pale and haunted. No one slept, each of them keeping a wary eye on the shadows, waiting for the inevitable.

And just before dawn, the silence was broken by a low, haunting chant, drifting through the jungle like a ghostly echo, filling the air with a sense of dread that sent shivers down their spines.

The Jivaro were coming.

One by one, they began to see them—dark figures moving through the trees, their bodies painted in red and black, their faces hidden behind masks carved from bone and wood, adorned with feathers and beads. They moved silently, slipping through the shadows like wraiths, their eyes fixed on their prey with a hunger that was both ancient and terrifying.

As the first of the Jivaro closed in on their camp, Jack realized, with a sickening sense of horror, that there was no escaping the head hunters. They had been marked, hunted, and now, one by one, they would fall.

And their heads, shrunk and preserved, would join the trophies hanging from the trees, a chilling testament to the jungle's unyielding, insatiable hunger.

The Jivaro tribe was more than a shadow in the jungle. They were a people bound by ancient rites, their history steeped in a complex system of beliefs and rituals, each one darker than the last. For centuries, they had lived deep within the Amazon, their territory shielded from the modern world by miles of dense forest and treacherous swamps. Outsiders knew them only by the stories that drifted out of the jungle, tales of fierce warriors and terrifying rites, of bodies without heads and trophies made from the shrunken skulls of their enemies.

As the group of scientists ventured further up the Amazon, they were stepping into a world that existed beyond time—a place where the Jivaro's dark traditions had gone untouched for centuries. It was here, within the depths of the jungle, that the tribe's legacy of headhunting and shrunken heads, or *tsantsa,* was born.

The practice of shrinking heads was not an act of mere brutality for the Jivaro; it was a profound ritual, deeply rooted in their spiritual beliefs. The Jivaro believed that every person possessed three souls, and among them was one known as the *muisak*, a soul that held the potential for vengeance and violence. According to Jivaro lore, when a person was killed, especially by violent means, the *muisak* would remain restless, its thirst for revenge unquenched.

In their view, an enemy's head was more than a trophy; it was a vessel containing the spirit of their foe, a spirit that, if left unchecked, would return to harm them. To prevent this, they developed the ritual of head-shrinking, a process that would trap the *muisak* within the head, rendering it powerless and allowing the spirit to remain under the control of the warrior who took it. Only then could they possess the strength, power, and knowledge of their enemy.

The shrinking process itself was gruesome, taking days to complete. The head was carefully removed, and the skull discarded. Then, the skin was boiled, treated with herbs, and painstakingly shaped, its features preserved in a grotesque mask that was sewn shut, locking the spirit inside. The head was worn or displayed, serving as both a trophy and a charm to protect the Jivaro warrior from the dangers of the jungle—and from the vengeful spirits of his enemies.

To the Jivaro, each tsantsa represented a battle won, a soul subdued, and an enemy defeated. And with every head claimed, the warrior grew stronger, his spirit infused with the power of his foes.

Centuries ago, before the arrival of European explorers, the Jivaro were locked in a fierce conflict with neighboring tribes. This "forgotten war," as Hector called it, was a brutal clash fought over territory, resources, and the right to control the sacred land that the tribes believed was favored by the spirits of the jungle.

The Jivaro were relentless warriors, fierce and unyielding, and they wielded the practice of headhunting as a weapon of psychological terror. Their enemies knew that to fall to a Jivaro warrior meant more than death—it meant a fate that would bind them to the jungle, their souls trapped in the twisted, shrunken heads that hung from the warriors' belts. Over time, the Jivaro's enemies began to fear them as demons rather than men, as something otherworldly and invincible.

According to legend, the war reached its peak during a season of drought and famine, when the rivers ran low and the jungle grew silent, as though mourning the blood spilled on its soil. The Jivaro priests, known as *uwishin*, called upon their gods for aid, performing rituals that invited spirits to possess their warriors, strengthening them, filling them with a rage that could not be tamed.

The priests chanted into the night, calling forth ancient forces, and under their guidance, the warriors hunted their enemies relentlessly, taking heads, binding souls, building a collection of tsantsa that became both a warning and a curse.

In the end, the Jivaro emerged victorious, their enemies scattered, their villages abandoned. But their victory came at a price. The priests warned that the spirits they had called upon were not easily appeased, that their power demanded blood, tribute, and respect. And so, the tradition of headhunting persisted, becoming an essential part of the tribe's existence—a dark legacy they could not escape, bound to them by blood and bone.

By the 20th century, many aspects of Jivaro life had remained unchanged for hundreds of years, but their isolation was slowly being eroded. Missionaries, explorers, and researchers had begun to make their way into the depths of the Amazon, bringing with them stories, technology, and diseases that threatened to disrupt the tribe's way of life. Most tribes had given up old practices, forced to assimilate in exchange for survival.

But the Jivaro resisted. They remained wary of outsiders, viewing them with suspicion and hostility. To them, these newcomers were intruders, disrespecting the land and the spirits that dwelled within it. The Jivaro believed that the spirits of their ancestors still roamed the jungle, watching over them, and that any disruption to the natural balance would awaken their anger.

For the Jivaro, the arrival of strangers meant one thing: danger. And to protect themselves, they turned once more to the ancient rite of headhunting, marking the borders of their territory with shrunken heads, a warning to all who dared to venture too close. To the Jivaro, this was not an act of violence but one of survival, a declaration that they would not surrender their land or their ways, no matter the cost.

Hector, who knew the jungle as well as any native, explained it to the scientists in hushed tones, his voice heavy with the weight of the tribe's history. "The Jivaro are not like us," he said, his face pale, his eyes dark with fear. "They do not see life and death as we do. They believe that to protect their people, they must preserve their enemies, keep their spirits bound to this world. It is a sacred duty—a curse, perhaps, but one they carry without hesitation."

The scientists began to realize that the Jivaro were more than just warriors; they were bound to the jungle by a pact as old as the trees themselves, a pact that demanded loyalty, blood, and reverence. They were guardians of a balance that was not easily understood, keepers of a darkness that lurked beneath the canopy, woven into the very fabric of the land.

But they also understood that, for the Jivaro, any outsider who trespassed on their land was a threat to this delicate balance. The scientists' presence in the jungle was an affront to the spirits, a reminder of the conflicts and losses that the Jivaro had endured over centuries. To the tribe, each of the scientists was an enemy, a soul to be subdued and bound to the land through the rite of the tsantsa.

As they moved deeper into the jungle, the scientists began to notice strange signs—small totems hanging from the trees, painted rocks arranged in peculiar patterns, symbols scratched into the bark. Hector recognized them as markers, warnings left by the Jivaro to mark the boundaries of their territory. But the scientists were undeterred, driven by a fascination that bordered on arrogance, unaware of the danger that lurked just beyond the edge of the light.

That night, as they huddled around the fire, Jack felt a cold wind brush against his neck, a chill that cut through the stifling humidity. He glanced around, the shadows flickering in the firelight, and for a brief moment, he thought he saw a figure standing just beyond the reach of the flames—a figure with dark, hollow eyes, its face twisted into an expression of rage.

He shook his head, telling himself it was a trick of the light, a product of exhaustion and fear. But deep down, he knew there was something watching them, something ancient and vengeful, drawn to their presence like a moth to flame.

The jungle was silent, too silent, as though it held its breath, waiting for the inevitable.

And as the night wore on, the chanting began again, low and haunting, drifting through the trees like the murmur of ghosts.

The Jivaro were coming.

And this time, there would be no escape.

The scientists had thought their greatest fear would be the Jivaro hunters, the shadowed figures moving silently through the jungle, their painted faces and piercing eyes peering from the dense foliage. But as the nights grew darker and their journey took them deeper into the Amazon, they began to feel another presence—a cold, oppressive force that seemed to permeate the very air around them, watching them from the shadows, filling their dreams with dark whispers and nightmarish visions.

Hector, their guide, had warned them of the spirits that haunted the jungle, souls trapped between worlds, bound to the land by centuries of blood and conflict. The Jivaro were feared by those who knew them, yes, but the spirits of the jungle were something else entirely. To the Jivaro, these spirits were guardians, protectors of the land, watching over their territory, taking revenge on any intruder who dared to disturb the balance. And now, as the scientists neared the heart of Jivaro territory, the spirits seemed to come alive, their whispers filling the air, their forms flickering in the corners of the scientists' vision.

The group set up camp on a narrow patch of dry ground, surrounded on all sides by dense jungle. They had decided to rest only for a few hours before continuing downstream, hoping to reach safer ground by dawn. The air was thick with tension, each of them painfully aware of the danger that lurked in the shadows. Jack, who hadn't slept in days, leaned against a tree, his flashlight flickering as he scanned the darkened canopy.

It was past midnight when he saw it—a faint, shimmering shape moving between the trees, drifting silently through the undergrowth. At first, he thought it was a trick of the light, a reflection on the leaves, but as he squinted, he realized the shape had a form, a pale, ghostly outline that took on the shape of a person. Its face was hollow, eyes dark and empty, a vacant, staring expression that seemed to pierce right through him.

Jack's breath caught in his throat, his heart pounding as he watched the figure. It moved slowly, gliding across the ground without sound, its gaze fixed on him. He couldn't move, couldn't speak; it was as though the very air had turned to ice, paralyzing him in place.

The figure raised an arm, pointing directly at him, its eyes dark and accusatory. And then, with a soundless scream, it vanished, leaving only the faint echo of a presence lingering in the air, a cold shiver that made his skin crawl.

When he finally found his voice, he stumbled over to Professor Carter, his face pale, his eyes wide with terror. "Professor... there's something out there," he stammered, his voice trembling. "I saw... I don't know what it was, but it wasn't human."

Carter frowned, shaking his head. "Jack, we're exhausted. This jungle plays tricks on the mind. Shadows, reflections—our imaginations can run wild out here."

But Jack shook his head, his voice barely a whisper. "It wasn't a trick. It was real."

As the night wore on, more of the group began to feel the strange, unexplainable presence in the jungle. Dr. Reyes awoke to the sensation of someone standing over her, watching her in the darkness. She opened her eyes, expecting to see one of her colleagues, but there was no one there—only the faint scent of decaying vegetation and the cold, still air. She tried to shake off the feeling, telling herself it was just nerves, but she couldn't escape the sense of being watched, the prickling sensation that crawled over her skin like an unseen hand.

Around the campfire, they began to hear faint whispers, voices that seemed to drift through the air, calling their names in low, mournful tones. The voices were soft, barely audible, but they grew louder as the night wore on, filling the silence with a chorus of whispers that seemed to come from everywhere and nowhere.

"Elise..."

"Jack..."

"David..."

Each voice was different, as though they were the echoes of lost souls, spirits calling out from the depths of the jungle, trapped in an eternal limbo. The scientists huddled closer to the fire, their faces pale, their eyes darting nervously into the shadows, but the whispers continued, relentless, filling the night with a dreadful, suffocating presence.

Professor Carter tried to calm them, his voice steady but strained. "They're just echoes," he said, though his own hands trembled. "The jungle is playing tricks on us."

But Hector, their guide, shook his head, his face grim. "They are the spirits of the lost," he said quietly. "The souls of those who died here, victims of the Jivaro, trapped in the jungle by the power of the tsantsa. They cannot leave... and they are angry."

On the third night, they found themselves surrounded by what seemed to be a collection of eerie totems—figures crafted from bones, feathers, and scraps of fabric, tied together and hung from the trees like grotesque ornaments. Each one had a small, hollowed-out head, painted with eyes that stared blankly ahead, watching over the path like silent sentinels.

But these weren't the only markers. Near the totems, they found a collection of shrunken heads, strung together like a necklace, each one shriveled and preserved, their faces twisted into expressions of agony. Dr. Reyes had to turn away, her stomach churning as she realized what they were looking at—these were the tsantsa, the shrunken heads of the Jivaro's enemies, bound to the trees to protect the tribe's territory.

As they stood there, frozen in horror, they began to feel a presence in the air, a heavy, oppressive force that pressed down on them, filling their lungs with the thick scent of decay. And then, slowly, one of the shrunken heads seemed to move, its hollow eyes turning toward them, its mouth opening in a silent scream.

Hector grabbed Jack's arm, pulling him back. "Don't look," he warned, his voice shaking. "The spirit of the tsantsa is bound to the jungle. It knows we're here... and it will come for us if we don't leave."

But as they tried to move away, the whispers returned, louder, angrier, filling the air with a haunting, disembodied chorus of voices, each one filled with rage and sorrow, a dark, echoing chant that seemed to rise from the very ground beneath them.

The voices grew louder, filling their minds with visions of the past—scenes of brutal conflict, of warriors tearing each other apart in a frenzy of violence, their bodies left to rot in the jungle, their heads taken as trophies. Each vision was more horrific than the last, each one driving them deeper into a terror they could not escape.

They ran, stumbling through the dense foliage, their hearts pounding, their breaths ragged, but the visions followed them, filling their minds with images of death and decay, each one more vivid, more terrifying, as though the spirits were forcing them to relive the horrors of the past.

As dawn broke, they found themselves on the edge of a clearing, their faces pale, their bodies trembling from exhaustion and fear. But even in the light of day, they could feel the presence of the spirits, watching them from the shadows, waiting for the night to return, for the chance to draw them back into the darkness.

Hector gathered them together, his face grim. "The spirits are bound to the jungle by the Jivaro. They cannot leave, cannot move on. They are trapped in the tsantsa, their souls bound to the heads that hang from the trees. And now, they believe we are part of that ancient debt, that we are here to disturb their rest."

Dr. Reyes shuddered, glancing back at the dense foliage behind them. "What... what do they want from us?"

Hector looked away, his voice low, heavy with a terrible knowledge. "They want what the Jivaro want. They want to bind us to this land, to add us to their collection. They want us to join them... in death."

The scientists stared at each other, their faces pale, their minds racing with the horror of what lay ahead. They knew now that their journey was no longer a simple expedition; it was a battle for survival, a desperate attempt to escape a jungle that seemed intent on consuming them, body and soul.

And as they gathered their things, preparing to move once more, they could feel the eyes of the spirits watching them, waiting, biding their time.

The jungle was alive, filled with the souls of the lost, and as night fell once more, they knew one thing for certain:

They would not leave without paying a terrible price.

With every step deeper into the jungle, the scientists felt the spirits' presence growing stronger, their whispers louder, more desperate. The air grew thick and heavy, as though the very atmosphere were charged with a malevolent energy that seeped into their skin, filling their lungs, clouding their minds. They were no longer just lost; they were trapped in a living nightmare, each turn in the dense foliage leading them further from the safety of the river and closer to the spirits that hunted them.

The team moved in silence, each one haunted by visions they couldn't explain. Jack kept seeing that hollow-eyed apparition from the night before, its empty stare following him, boring into his mind, forcing him to relive memories that weren't his own. And in every memory, he was an outsider, an intruder, glimpsing moments of violence, of ritual, of rage.

As the light began to fade, the jungle around them grew darker, the shadows longer, stretching like fingers eager to pull them into the depths. Hector urged them to keep moving, his voice taut with fear.

"We have to keep going," he whispered, his gaze darting around the trees. "The spirits don't like the daylight, but as night falls, they grow stronger. They'll feed on our fear, our despair. If we stop, we're as good as dead."

But the team was exhausted, their bodies and minds battered by days of fear and sleepless nights. Professor Carter, who had led them with unwavering determination, was pale and shaken, his eyes hollow, haunted. Dr. Reyes stumbled, clutching at a tree to steady herself, her face streaked with sweat and grime.

"We can't keep this up," she panted, her voice barely more than a whisper. "We're lost. They're driving us further in, like... like prey."

As the team staggered into a small clearing, they froze, their breaths caught in their throats. All around them, scattered across the ground and hanging from the trees, were dozens of shrunken heads, their faces twisted in expressions of horror, their mouths sewn shut, their eyes hollow and empty.

Jack felt a wave of nausea rise in his stomach as he realized these were no ordinary totems; they were the tsantsa, the spirits of those the Jivaro had claimed. Each head was bound to the jungle, forced to serve as an eternal guardian, a sentry to warn the living to stay away. But as Jack looked closer, he noticed something chilling—the heads weren't ancient artifacts. They were fresh.

Hector muttered a prayer under his breath, his voice shaking. "These are the ones who came before. Other expeditions, other travelers. They thought they could pass through, just like us. But the Jivaro took them... and now they guard this land forever."

A hush fell over the team as they looked around, each of them feeling the weight of the jungle pressing down on them, filling their minds with the inescapable sense of doom. It was then that they noticed a figure watching them from the shadows, a tall, gaunt form half-hidden by the foliage.

The figure stepped forward, revealing a face painted with dark stripes and white markings, his eyes cold, calculating. He held a long spear, its tip glinting in the fading light, and around his neck hung a necklace of small shrunken heads, each one an eerie, silent witness to the fate that awaited them.

One by one, more figures emerged from the jungle, surrounding the team, their faces expressionless, their eyes dark and unblinking. They moved in silence, their presence as ghostly as the spirits themselves, as though they were more shadow than flesh.

Hector's face turned ashen as he recognized the leader. "This is the shaman," he whispered. "He is the one who binds the souls to the land, the one who performs the ritual of the tsantsa. Once he marks you, there is no escape."

The shaman raised his spear, his gaze fixed on the team, and in that moment, Jack felt an overwhelming sense of despair. They were outnumbered, surrounded, and the jungle itself seemed to close in around them, cutting off any chance of escape.

But as the shaman stepped forward, Hector did something unexpected. He dropped to his knees, his head bowed, speaking in the Jivaro language, his voice low, pleading. The shaman paused, listening, his face impassive, and for a moment, the jungle was silent, the spirits watching, waiting.

Hector's voice grew louder, more desperate, and finally, the shaman responded, his tone harsh, commanding. Hector nodded, his face pale, his expression one of grim acceptance as he turned to the team.

"He says we can live," Hector translated, his voice shaking. "But only if we pay tribute. Only if we agree to let him take one of us."

A chill swept over the group, the realization of what Hector was saying sinking in. The shaman demanded a sacrifice—a life to appease the spirits, to allow the rest of them to escape. It was the only way to break the curse that held them, to release the spirits bound to the jungle.

Professor Carter stepped forward, his face set with determination. "No. I'll go," he said, his voice calm. "This was my expedition. I led us here. I'll stay."

But Hector shook his head, his eyes dark with fear. "He doesn't want you," he murmured, his voice barely audible. "He wants the one who saw the spirits. The one who heard their whispers."

Jack's heart sank as he realized Hector was looking at him.

The team fell silent, each of them grappling with the horror of what was being asked. Jack felt a wave of panic rise in his chest, but as he looked around, he saw the desperation in their faces, the terror that filled their eyes. They had been marked, hunted, and now, the only way out was to pay the ultimate price.

"I'll do it," he whispered, his voice shaking, his mind numb with fear. "If it means the rest of you can go... I'll do it."

The shaman gestured for Jack to follow, his expression unreadable, his eyes dark and unyielding. Jack glanced back at his friends, his heart heavy, knowing that this would be the last time he would see them. Dr. Reyes's face was streaked with tears, and Professor Carter's expression was one of quiet resignation, his shoulders slumped under the weight of guilt.

As he followed the shaman into the jungle, the sounds of the team's footsteps faded, leaving only the silence of the trees, the low hum of the spirits that filled the air. Jack could feel their presence all around him, a chorus of whispers that grew louder with each step, filling his mind with visions of the past, the horrors that had bound the Jivaro and the spirits together in a pact of blood and darkness.

The shaman led him to a small clearing, a circle of stones marking the ground, each one etched with symbols of protection, of binding. Jack knelt at the shaman's command, his heart pounding as the shaman began to chant, his voice rising in a haunting melody that seemed to call the spirits to him, drawing them closer, binding them to the ritual.

As the shaman continued, the air grew colder, the shadows deepening, and Jack felt a terrible weight settle over him, pressing down on his chest, filling his mind with a darkness that was all-consuming. The spirits had come, summoned by the shaman's chant, their forms flickering in the trees, their hollow eyes fixed on him, watching, waiting.

The shaman raised his hands, his voice rising to a crescendo, and as he spoke the final words of the ritual, Jack felt a sudden, sharp pain in his chest, a sensation of something being pulled from within him, tearing through his mind, his soul, leaving him hollow, empty.

His vision blurred, the world fading into darkness, and in his final moments, he saw the faces of the spirits around him, their expressions calm, peaceful, as though they were finally at rest.

And then, there was nothing.

The remaining members of the team stumbled back to the river, their faces pale, their bodies trembling, but they were alive. As they reached the edge of the jungle, they felt a strange lightness, a sense that the darkness that had followed them was gone, lifted by the sacrifice they had left behind.

They knew they would never forget Jack's final act, the price he had paid to release the spirits from their torment, to free them from the curse that had bound them to the jungle. But as they looked back at the dense, silent trees, they knew one thing for certain:

The jungle had claimed its due.

And as they boarded the boat, drifting away from the haunted land that had nearly taken them all, they could feel the spirits watching, lingering, their whispers carried on the wind—a reminder of the darkness that lay hidden in the heart of the Amazon, waiting for the next unwitting soul to wander too close.

The End

16

DARKNESS

It started on an ordinary summer day. The kind of day where the air shimmered with heat and sunlight poured down relentlessly, casting long shadows over the small town of Eldermoor. People went about their routines, enjoying the warmth, savoring the late summer's simple pleasures. Children played in sprinklers, families gathered for picnics in the park, and couples walked the shaded trails under trees heavy with green leaves.

But by mid-afternoon, a peculiar shift began in the sky. The blue began to deepen, the sunlight dimming just slightly as a blanket of thick clouds crept in from the horizon, casting a shadow over the town. A few people glanced up, curious but unalarmed; an overcast day was rare in summer but not unheard of. By evening, however, a sense of unease had settled over Eldermoor.

The clouds seemed darker than usual, heavier, more like ink than vapor. Streetlights flickered on earlier than normal as shadows stretched across the roads and sidewalks, long fingers of darkness swallowing the familiar shapes of houses and trees. That night, there were no stars, no glimmer of the moon; the sky was pitch black, an impenetrable darkness that seemed to press down on the town like a weighted blanket.

For days, the darkness remained. Eldermoor was trapped beneath the thick veil, which blocked out even the faintest hint of sunlight. Daytime felt like dusk, a strange, dim twilight that left people feeling off-kilter, disoriented. Panic crept through conversations at the grocery store, in hushed voices over coffee cups. Phones buzzed with messages from loved ones, rumors of a strange phenomenon spreading to nearby towns, a strange eclipse that hadn't been forecasted.

But the strange, unnerving lack of light was only the beginning.

On the fourth night, a teenager named Brian Wilkes reported seeing something while taking out the garbage. It was nearly midnight, the streets silent and empty. He had just set the trash bag by the curb when he heard a soft rustling, like someone—or something—moving in the bushes at the edge of his yard. He turned, peering into the shadows, his heartbeat quickening. The air was thick, the darkness nearly suffocating.

And then he saw it.

A shape, tall and slender, standing perfectly still just beyond the glow of his porch light. It was unlike anything he had ever seen—a thin, spindly creature with long, sinewy limbs that clung to the ground, almost like a spider. Its skin was slick, black and wet, reflecting the dim light like oil on water. The creature's body was elongated, its head cocked to one side, as if studying him, though he could see no eyes, only a smooth, featureless face.

Brian's breath caught in his throat as the creature shifted, lowering itself on all fours, its body tensed, as if ready to pounce. Before he could scream, it turned, moving with unnatural speed, skittering into the darkness on its long, jointed limbs, disappearing into the night.

The next morning, Brian told his parents about the encounter, but they dismissed it as a nightmare, a trick of his imagination brought on by the oppressive darkness. Yet, he couldn't shake the memory of the creature's strange, glossy skin, the way it had moved, fluid and silent, as though it were a part of the darkness itself.

Within days, rumors of the creatures spread through town. Eldermoor residents reported glimpses of them lurking in alleyways, slipping between shadows, moving just out of sight. Some claimed they had seen them watching from the woods, their tall, thin forms silhouetted against the darkened trees. Others reported hearing strange, guttural sounds in the night—low, chittering noises that sent chills down their spines.

Then, the disappearances began.

It started with small things: pets left outside at night that never returned, birds that fell silent, leaving the trees and rooftops empty. But soon, people started vanishing too.

The first to disappear was Mr. Grayson, an older man who lived alone on the edge of town. He'd been known for his late-night walks, despite his neighbors warning him of the strange sightings. One evening, he left his house for a stroll and was never seen again. His front door was found wide open, a flashlight lying on the ground, its beam flickering into the endless dark.

Panic spread. People kept to their homes, locking their doors and windows, pulling curtains tight against the strange, all-consuming darkness outside. Families gathered together, huddling in dimly lit rooms, their only company the quiet crackle of emergency broadcasts warning them to stay indoors.

But the creatures grew bolder.

On the sixth night, a family was attacked. The Harpers had been up late, talking in their living room, the uneasy atmosphere making sleep impossible. They heard a soft scratching sound at their back door, faint at first but growing louder, more insistent. Mr. Harper approached cautiously, pressing his ear to the door, his breath shallow.

The scratching stopped.

For a moment, there was only silence. Then, with a force that rattled the entire house, something slammed into the door, shaking it in its frame. The family screamed, pulling back, as the door splintered, the lock giving way, and the thing forced its way inside.

It was one of the creatures, but up close, it was far more terrifying than anyone could have imagined. Its skin glistened, black and wet, dripping onto the floor, a thick, viscous slime pooling at its feet. Its body was thin, almost skeletal, with long, spindly arms and legs that stretched unnaturally, bending at strange angles. Its head was smooth, featureless, its face devoid of eyes or mouth, yet somehow it seemed to sense them, tilting its head as if listening.

The creature let out a low, rattling hiss, dropping to all fours, its body twitching, every movement a strange, jerky shuffle. Then, with a sudden burst of speed, it lunged forward, its limbs moving in a blur, its slick, wet skin leaving a dark trail as it crossed the floor.

The Harpers barely escaped, fleeing out the front door as the creature gave chase, its guttural, inhuman sounds echoing behind them. They ran through the darkness, the creature close on their heels, its slick, clawed hands reaching out, barely missing them as they stumbled down the street, desperate for help.

By dawn, they were gone. No sign of the Harpers remained, only dark smears on their floors, and a silence that settled over the town like a shroud.

As the days passed, Eldermoor was transformed into a place of fear, held captive by an unyielding darkness and a sense of impending doom. The creatures moved freely at night, their strange forms glimpsed in the brief flashes of light from windows or street lamps. People locked themselves in their homes as soon as the dim twilight fell, daring not to venture outside, terrified of the things lurking in the shadows.

By the end of the second week, the darkness had grown thicker, almost physical, pressing against windows and doors like a living thing. The few who remained in Eldermoor were trapped, isolated, surrounded by an endless night and a fear that grew with each passing hour.

In whispers, people spoke of the creatures as if they were shadows brought to life, a darkness given form. They began to call them *Night Crawlers*, beings born of the strange, oppressive blackness that had swallowed their town whole. No one knew where they came from, or what had brought them, but one thing was clear: they were hunting, claiming the town one soul at a time.

And as the third week began, the townspeople held their breath, wondering who would be next.

Eldermoor had turned into a ghost town. Houses stood dark and silent, their windows covered, doors barricaded. Those who were left moved in whispers, their faces pale, their eyes hollow from sleepless nights. It was as if the town itself had fallen under a spell, frozen in a perpetual twilight where no light could penetrate.

The Night Crawlers, as people had come to call them, grew bolder, their sightings more frequent. Every night, their slick, inky forms would appear on the streets, slipping between the shadows, moving silently along fences, peering into windows. Each sighting brought a fresh wave of terror, leaving people afraid to sleep, afraid to even close their eyes. But staying awake only intensified their despair, the endless darkness pressing in on their minds, making it hard to tell reality from nightmare.

The town organized what little they had left into survival strategies. Some clustered in groups, gathering in homes fortified with furniture and makeshift barricades. They rationed food, took turns keeping watch, their eyes scanning the windows for any sign of movement. Others, however, opted for solitude, convinced that the creatures were drawn to large groups, that their best hope for survival lay in isolation.

One night, as the darkness grew thicker, and the low, guttural sounds of the Night Crawlers echoed in the streets, the town's emergency radio system crackled to life. Sheriff Dean Blackburn's voice, rough and steady, filled the airwaves, a lifeline for the frightened people of Eldermoor.

"This is Sheriff Blackburn," he said, his voice echoing through the static. "I know you're scared. I know it feels like there's no way out. But we're going to get through this. We don't know what these things are, but we know they don't like light. If you have flashlights, candles, anything, use them. Keep them close."

He paused, and there was a hint of desperation in his voice. "We're working on a plan to drive them out. Some folks have managed to make it to the high school—it's well-lit and fortified. If you can make it there safely, we'll be there. We'll protect each other."

But his voice trembled as he added, "If you can't make it, don't open your doors for anyone after dark. Stay silent.

They... they seem to be able to hear us. They're drawn to sound, to movement."

The broadcast ended, and Eldermoor fell silent once more. For those still able to move, the high school became a beacon of hope, a place to flee in the rare hours of daylight, though getting there meant crossing blocks of open, unprotected streets.

The next morning, a group of survivors from the neighborhood near the town's edge decided to attempt the journey to the high school. Among them was Claire Rivers, a mother of two, her face gaunt, her eyes rimmed with exhaustion. She carried her youngest child in her arms, her older son clutching her hand, his face pale with fear.

They moved quickly, sticking to the narrow streets, skirting the darkened alleyways where they'd seen shadows moving the night before. A few others joined them—Mr. Carver, the elderly man who'd refused to leave his home but now wore a look of grim determination; Lisa Moreno, a young woman who hadn't slept in days, her gaze haunted.

Every creak of wood, every rustling leaf, made them freeze, their breaths held, their hearts pounding. They could feel the creatures nearby, watching from the shadows, as if deciding whether to let them pass or drag them into the darkness.

Halfway to the school, they heard it—a low, chittering sound, followed by the soft thud of claws against pavement. Claire tightened her grip on her children, her heart racing as she saw one of the Night Crawlers slip from the shadows, its oily, black body slinking toward them, its limbs bending at unnatural angles.

"Don't run," Mr. Carver whispered, his voice shaking. "They're faster than us. Stay still. Maybe it'll leave."

The creature moved closer, its slick, featureless face pointed directly at them, its body swaying, as if listening. Then, with a sudden, jerking motion, it dropped to all fours, its long limbs spreading wide, crouching, ready to pounce.

In a desperate moment, Claire reached into her bag and pulled out a flashlight, clicking it on and pointing it directly at the creature. The beam cut through the darkness, illuminating the creature's slimy skin, which glistened in the light like tar. The Night Crawler shrieked, its body writhing as it recoiled from the light, its limbs folding inward as though trying to shield itself.

The group didn't wait to see if it would recover. They ran, the flashlight casting a shaky beam ahead of them as they bolted through the streets, fear driving them toward the high school. Behind them, they heard the Night Crawler's enraged hissing, but it didn't follow, retreating instead into the shadows.

When they finally reached the high school, they found it fortified with floodlights, their beams cutting through the darkness, casting a protective circle around the building. Sheriff Blackburn and a handful of volunteers had set up barriers at the entrances, armed with flashlights and other makeshift defenses. Inside, families huddled together, their faces pale, their eyes hollow with fear and exhaustion.

Claire and her children were quickly ushered inside, joining the other survivors in the dimly lit gymnasium where rows of cots had been set up. The room was tense, every creak of the building setting nerves on edge, every shadow a potential threat. But in the safety of the light, they found a fragile sense of hope.

The sheriff spoke quietly to the group, his voice steady but grim. "We're doing what we can. We're safe as long as the lights stay on, but we can't stay here forever. The generators are running low, and the longer this darkness holds, the more dangerous it'll get. We need to find a way to get supplies—and maybe a way out."

A heavy silence settled over the group as they realized the dire reality of their situation. The darkness was spreading, consuming everything in its path, and they were running out of time.

That night, as the survivors huddled in the dim light, Sheriff Blackburn and a few volunteers ventured out to find fuel and food. They kept to the main roads, staying close to the light, their flashlights cutting narrow beams through the blackness. The town was silent, deserted, but as they moved deeper into the residential area, they came upon a grisly scene.

Dozens of people, taken in the night, their bodies half-hidden in the darkness, their faces twisted in expressions of terror. The sheriff's flashlight revealed long, clawed marks on the walls, dark stains on the ground, signs of struggle and despair. The Night Crawlers had claimed the town, leaving only the high school as the final sanctuary.

Sheriff Blackburn's face hardened, and he turned to his group, his voice low and filled with resolve. "We're outnumbered, and we're running out of options. If we stay, we die. Tomorrow, we move. We head for the next town and hope to find help. No matter what we hear, no matter what we see, we don't stop until we're clear of this place."

They returned to the high school, their grim expressions alerting the others to the horror that awaited them outside. But there was no time for despair—only the fight for survival.

At dawn, as the dim light of another sunless day struggled to break through the darkness, the survivors prepared to leave. Armed with flashlights, makeshift weapons, and sheer determination, they formed a tight group, ready to make the journey to the next town. Sheriff Blackburn led the way, his face set with grim purpose, his eyes scanning the shadows for any sign of movement.

The journey was brutal. The Night Crawlers were everywhere, slipping between shadows, their inky forms skittering along the ground, lunging at anyone who strayed too close. But the survivors held their ground, their flashlights keeping the creatures at bay, pushing through the darkness with nothing but each other and the light they carried.

By the time they reached the edge of town, many were injured, their numbers fewer than when they had started. But they were alive, and as they left Eldermoor behind, they felt the weight of the darkness lifting, the sky growing lighter, the oppressive silence giving way to the sounds of the world beyond.

As they looked back, they could see the Night Crawlers standing at the town's edge, watching them with hollow faces, waiting, as though bound to the darkness that had consumed Eldermoor. And the survivors knew that as long as the darkness remained, the Night Crawlers would continue to haunt the empty streets, claiming any soul that dared to return.

They left with heavy hearts, knowing that Eldermoor was lost, swallowed by a darkness that would never release it.

Days after the survivors' escape from Eldermoor, the nearby town of Ashgrove had become a place of refuge and rumor. Word of the strange darkness that had consumed Eldermoor spread quickly, capturing the attention of locals and outsiders alike. Some called it a hoax, a wild story born of panic, while others whispered of ancient curses and otherworldly forces.

But for Sheriff Blackburn and the others who had witnessed the horrors firsthand, the darkness and its creatures were terrifyingly real. Determined to find answers, Blackburn reached out to a professor of ancient cultures and mythology, Dr. Evelyn Harper, hoping she could help unravel the mystery of the darkness and the creatures haunting Eldermoor.

Dr. Harper was a distinguished researcher specializing in obscure legends and ancient rituals. She listened intently as Blackburn recounted the events that had unfolded in Eldermoor, her face growing more serious with each word. After a long silence, she produced an old, leather-bound journal, its pages yellowed with age, covered in handwritten notes and sketches.

"This journal belonged to my grandfather," she explained, her voice low. "He was an archaeologist who studied lost civilizations and ancient curses. Decades ago, he led an expedition into an isolated area of the Amazon rainforest, where he encountered a tribe that had legends of a 'Dark Veil'—a phenomenon where night fell without end, bringing with it creatures that hunted in the shadows."

Blackburn leaned in, his pulse quickening. "You think that darkness in Eldermoor is related?"

Dr. Harper nodded. "There are disturbing similarities. According to the tribe's legend, the Dark Veil was a punishment—a curse meant to trap wandering souls in a never-ending night, a boundary between the living and the dead. The creatures, which they called *Kar'karun,* were once human, souls who had become bound to the darkness, twisted into hunting shadows, doomed to prey upon anything living within the Veil."

As Blackburn scanned the journal, he saw sketches of thin, elongated figures—creatures with slick, featureless faces, just like the Night Crawlers. Scribbled notes described their inky black skin, their animalistic movement, and a warning: *Beware the Whispering Dark; it devours all light.*

Digging deeper into the journal, they found accounts of a ritual used by the tribe to protect themselves from the Dark Veil. The ritual, performed only by the most revered shamans, was said to ward off the darkness by creating a barrier of light. According to the notes, the ritual was difficult and dangerous, as it required gathering several specific elements from sacred places.

The final page held a faded drawing of a stone altar, surrounded by symbols and torches. Beneath it, a scrawled note read, *To release the Veil is to release the curse. To awaken the forgotten is to become their prey.*

Dr. Harper looked up, her face grave. "The tribe believed the Veil could be summoned by accident, that disturbing certain places or rituals could unleash the darkness and awaken the Kar'karun. It's possible that someone, or something, triggered the Veil over Eldermoor."

Blackburn's mind raced. "So if someone disrupted this... ancient boundary, they could have unintentionally released the darkness?"

Dr. Harper nodded. "It's possible. And once the Veil is opened, it consumes everything within its reach, trapping anything it touches in a realm between worlds. The creatures—the Night Crawlers—are the guardians of that darkness. They hunt to maintain the Veil, to keep the living from escaping its grasp."

Determined to find the source of the darkness and put an end to it, Blackburn and Dr. Harper made plans to return to Eldermoor. They gathered a small team, equipped with powerful lights and a portable generator, hoping the intense light would hold the creatures at bay long enough for them to investigate the town and search for the disrupted boundary.

As they approached the town, the darkness grew thicker, almost physical, as if pressing against them, resisting their intrusion. The town was silent, every building deserted, the streets empty. Their flashlights cut narrow beams through the blackness, illuminating glimpses of claw marks on walls, windows shattered from the inside, remnants of lives interrupted by terror.

They followed Dr. Harper's map to a small clearing just outside the town, where an old stone structure lay half-buried in the earth. It was overgrown with weeds, obscured by time and shadow, yet unmistakably similar to the altar depicted in her grandfather's journal.

"This is it," Dr. Harper whispered, her voice tense. "The boundary marker."

As they began to examine the stones, they found markings scratched into the earth around the altar, symbols that appeared recent, as though someone had disturbed the ground. There were candle stubs, remnants of ash, and small bones scattered around—a hastily performed ritual, one that had likely gone horribly wrong.

"It must have been a local or someone who knew of the legend," Blackburn said, his voice filled with dread. "Someone tried to summon something without understanding what they were releasing."

Dr. Harper nodded grimly. "They opened the Veil, inviting the darkness in. Now it's here, and the Kar'karun are bound to it, hunting until there's nothing left to consume."

Realizing that they had one chance to close the Veil, Dr. Harper and Blackburn prepared to perform the ancient ritual. They set up a ring of powerful floodlights around the altar, hoping to recreate the barrier of light described in the journal. With a shaky hand, Dr. Harper lit torches and placed them at each corner of the altar, chanting in the old language transcribed in her grandfather's notes.

As the light intensified, the darkness seemed to retreat, pulling back from the town's edge. But as Dr. Harper continued, the air grew colder, and the low, guttural sounds of the Kar'karun filled the clearing. Figures began to emerge from the shadows—dozens of Night Crawlers, their slick black bodies skittering toward the edge of the light, their faces featureless, blank, yet somehow filled with a terrible hunger.

The creatures moved closer, testing the boundary of light, their limbs stretching, claws reaching for any weakness in the circle. Dr. Harper's voice wavered, but she continued, her chants rising in intensity as the light pulsed, pushing the creatures back, their shrieks echoing in the night.

The Veil seemed to waver, the darkness pulsing, flickering, as though trying to cling to the town, to the world. And then, with one final, desperate burst of light, the barrier held, and the darkness shattered.

The Kar'karun shrieked, their bodies dissolving into the shadows, their forms disintegrating as the darkness lifted, releasing Eldermoor from its grip. The sky brightened, the oppressive weight lifted, and the town was bathed in the soft, golden light of dawn for the first time in weeks.

As the first rays of sunlight touched the town, Blackburn and Dr. Harper stood in silence, their faces pale, their minds numb with the memory of what they had witnessed. Eldermoor lay in ruins, its streets empty, its buildings scarred by the darkness. But the town was free, the Veil lifted, the Kar'karun gone—at least for now.

Dr. Harper looked to Blackburn, her expression somber. "The Veil is fragile. It could be reopened, even by accident. The darkness will always be there, waiting."

Blackburn nodded, understanding the gravity of her words. "We'll warn others. Make sure no one disturbs this place again."

Together, they left Eldermoor behind, knowing they had encountered forces beyond comprehension, an ancient darkness that lingered in the hidden places of the world, waiting for the unwary, the curious, to open the door once more.

And as they drove away, they couldn't shake the feeling that, somewhere in the shadows, the Kar'karun were still watching, waiting patiently for the night to return.

The survivors of Eldermoor settled uneasily in Ashgrove, struggling to rebuild their lives in the aftermath of the darkness. The memories of the Night Crawlers haunted them, the terror they had experienced etched into their minds like scars. Each night, the darkness felt heavier, the shadows deeper, as though remnants of the Veil lingered around them, watching from the edges of the light.

Claire Rivers, who had fled Eldermoor with her children, tried to create a sense of normalcy, enrolling them in a new school, filling their days with routines. But each night, she found herself double-checking the locks, positioning flashlights by the door, her nerves on edge. Her children were plagued by nightmares, visions of slick, black shapes moving through their rooms, silent whispers calling them into the night.

Dr. Evelyn Harper and Sheriff Dean Blackburn continued their research, combing through the journals and any records they could find, hoping to uncover more about the Veil and its dark guardians. They knew the Kar'karun were bound to the darkness, part of an ancient curse that could resurface if the Veil was disturbed again. The Veil was fragile, a boundary between worlds that required only a single mistake to unleash chaos.

Months later, a peculiar package arrived at the Ashgrove Historical Society, addressed to Dr. Harper. Inside was a small, polished stone covered in strange, ancient symbols, a relic she hadn't seen in any of her studies. With it was a note scrawled in shaky handwriting:

The darkness waits for those who seek it. Beware the whispers; they know the way back.

Dr. Harper's hand trembled as she read the note, her mind racing. She didn't know who had sent it, but the message was clear—the Veil was far from gone, and the Kar'karun were only a shadow away.

Blackburn and Dr. Harper shared a grim understanding: while Eldermoor might have been freed, the darkness was never truly vanquished. It was part of something older, waiting in the spaces between worlds, drawn to those who dared to search too deeply, to those who ignored the warnings etched into the bones of forgotten places.

They kept the relic locked in a glass case, a warning to anyone who visited the Historical Society. But every so often, Evelyn would catch a glimpse of something in its reflection, a shadowed figure standing behind her, watching, waiting. She felt the same cold, silent dread each time—a reminder that the Kar'karun were patient, timeless.

And as long as the Veil endured, so too would the darkness, lurking in the corners of the world, waiting to consume the next soul who dared to open the door to the other side.

The End

17
THE WRECK

The dense summer foliage made the woods feel like a tunnel, and each snap of a twig or rustle in the underbrush made the boys jump, though none would admit it. Jared, Owen, and Liam were three sixteen-year-olds with little fear of the ordinary things—steep trails, thorny bushes, even the deep, dark ravines—but as they ventured further down the wooded path that afternoon, the air grew thick with something they couldn't quite explain.

"Come on, it's just around here," Jared urged, his voice barely a whisper, though he wasn't sure why he was keeping it down.

Owen rolled his eyes but picked up his pace. "You keep saying that, but where are you taking us, dude? We've been hiking for hours."

Liam, bringing up the rear, was starting to feel uneasy. The woods seemed darker than usual, the light filtering through the trees casting strange shadows over the ground. But he kept his mouth shut, not wanting to be the one to ruin the adventure.

Then they saw it—a glint of metal, half-hidden in the overgrowth, down at the bottom of a steep ravine. It looked like an old car, but one that had been abandoned for years, its metal frame rusted and bent, as though it had taken a hard hit.

Jared's eyes gleamed with excitement. "I told you it was here. Look at that thing. Must've been sitting there for ages."

The three of them scrambled down the rocky slope, curiosity overtaking any hesitation they might have felt. The car was old, a model they couldn't recognize, its once-bright paint now faded and chipped, leaving only traces of color beneath a layer of rust and dirt. The windows were shattered, the doors dented and warped, as though it had been in some kind of violent accident.

"Who do you think drove this?" Owen asked, running a hand along the broken window, peering inside.

"No idea," Jared replied, but his tone betrayed a hint of reverence. "But whoever they were... they didn't get out of here."

Liam was quiet, his gaze locked on the car's interior. There were strange things inside, items that didn't seem to fit—a child's shoe, an old purse, a broken watch glinting in the dusty beam of light from above. And in the back seat, propped up in the corner, was an old, faded doll. Its glassy eyes stared out, chipped in places, its face twisted into an eerie smile. The boys exchanged glances, a chill settling over them despite the humid air.

"What's with the doll?" Liam muttered, reaching a tentative hand toward it.

Owen shrugged, but Jared nudged him, grinning. "Go ahead, bring it home. Maybe it'll tell you who left it here."

But as Liam lifted the doll, a scrap of paper slipped from beneath it, landing at his feet. He bent down, picking it up, his eyes narrowing as he read the words scrawled hastily across the page.

Help Us!

The three boys stared at each other, their earlier excitement melting into nervous glances.

"What... what does it mean?" Owen stammered, his voice barely audible.

Liam folded the paper, shoving it into his pocket. "Maybe someone left it here for a reason. Maybe they were... trapped or something."

Jared forced a laugh, his voice shaky. "Come on, let's not go ghost hunting or anything. It's just an old car. But yeah... maybe we should go."

They climbed out of the ravine, their footsteps quickening, a silence settling over them that hadn't been there before. Each of them kept looking over their shoulder, feeling a prickle of unease that they couldn't shake, as though something—or someone—was watching them from the shadows.

That night, Liam tossed and turned, unable to sleep. Every time he closed his eyes, he saw the wrecked car, the broken doll, and the desperate plea scrawled across the paper. He finally drifted off, but only briefly, awoken by the sound of soft scratching against his bedroom window.

Groggy and unsettled, he sat up, peering out into the dark yard. Nothing was there. He sighed, lying back down, but as soon as he closed his eyes again, the sound returned, louder this time—a persistent, rhythmic scraping.

He turned on his bedside lamp, his heart pounding, but the room was empty, save for the faint sound of the scratching. Trying to calm himself, he walked over to the window, lifting the shade—and froze.

There, on the outside ledge, was the doll from the car, its face pressed against the glass, staring straight at him, its expression seeming more sinister in the dim light.

Liam stumbled back, his hand flying to his mouth to stifle a scream. His heart thundered as he stared at the doll, its head tilted, those glassy eyes catching the light, as though it were alive.

And then, just as he blinked, it was gone.

He backed away, his skin prickling with fear, but as he turned to return to bed, he heard a faint whisper in his ear, so soft he almost didn't hear it.

Help us...

Liam bolted from his room, his heart racing, his mind reeling. He knew, without a doubt, that something had followed them home from the wreck. Something that was far from human, and very, very angry.

The next morning, Liam tried to brush off the events of the night as a bad dream. He convinced himself that he must have imagined the doll at his window, that the whispers were nothing more than his mind playing tricks. But as he walked to school, he couldn't shake the lingering feeling of dread. He kept glancing over his shoulder, his nerves on edge, as though something was following him, hidden in plain sight.

At lunch, he found Owen and Jared waiting for him, their expressions troubled.

"You guys feel... off today?" Owen asked, glancing nervously at Liam. "I didn't sleep a wink last night. I kept hearing these weird noises in my room, like... footsteps, but no one was there."

Jared nodded, his face pale. "Same. I even checked my whole house, just to be sure. Thought maybe someone had broken in, but... nothing. And it got weirder."

Liam looked between them, heart pounding. "What happened?"

Jared swallowed, then reached into his backpack, pulling out a crumpled scrap of paper. He unfolded it, revealing words written in shaky, smeared ink.

Help Us!

Owen's face drained of color. "Wait... how did you get that?"

"I found it on my dresser this morning," Jared whispered. "It wasn't there last night. And look at this."

He turned the paper over, revealing a single name scrawled in large, bold letters: *Sarah.* The ink looked fresh, almost wet, and Liam could feel an icy chill settle over them.

"Sarah..." Liam repeated. "Do you think... she was in the car?"

Owen looked around, his voice barely a whisper. "This is freaky. Maybe she was... one of the people in the wreck. And maybe she's not... gone."

The boys decided they couldn't let it go. Something about the wrecked car was haunting them, literally and figuratively, and if they wanted any peace, they needed answers. After school, they headed back to the ravine, retracing their steps with heavy reluctance.

The woods felt different this time, as though the trees themselves were watching, waiting. A heavy silence hung in the air, broken only by the occasional rustle of leaves. They made their way down the ravine, their steps slow, cautious, until the wrecked car came into view, looking even more ominous in the dim afternoon light.

The doll was gone from the back seat.

"Where... where did it go?" Owen stammered, his voice tight with fear. "It was here yesterday."

Liam felt a surge of dread, but he pushed forward, moving to the driver's side. He tried to open the door, but it wouldn't budge, rusted shut. Through the cracked window, he could make out the front seat—a mess of old, decaying objects: faded photos, broken jewelry, and a torn piece of fabric that looked suspiciously like part of a child's dress.

Then, as he leaned closer, he saw another scrap of paper wedged between the seat and the console. He pulled it out, his heart hammering as he read the words scrawled in the same panicked handwriting:

We can't leave.

The note was short, but it filled him with a sense of dread that made his skin crawl. He could almost feel the desperation in each word, a plea from someone who had been trapped, unable to escape whatever nightmare had taken place here.

"Guys," he said, his voice trembling. "They're... they're still here."

As they searched the car further, Owen found an old Polaroid camera half-buried beneath a pile of decaying clothes in the back seat. He pulled it out, wiping the dust from its lens.

"Maybe... maybe there are some photos left," he said, more to himself than to the others. He turned the camera on, his thumb hovering over the button, unsure if he wanted to capture whatever image might appear.

He snapped a photo, the flash illuminating the car's interior. The camera whirred, and a moment later, the Polaroid developed, the image slowly forming in front of their eyes.

The three boys leaned in, staring as the image took shape.

It was the inside of the car, just as they saw it now—except in the back seat, barely visible, was the faint outline of a person. A young woman with dark hair, her face twisted in terror, staring straight at the camera with wide, empty eyes.

Owen dropped the photo, his hands shaking. "Did... did you guys see that?"

Liam picked up the photo, his heart pounding. The image was unmistakable, and the longer he stared at it, the colder he felt, as though he were staring into the eyes of something that shouldn't be there.

"I think... I think we found Sarah," he whispered.

Jared shuddered, his gaze shifting back to the car. "We have to get out of here. I don't know what we're messing with, but... it's not safe."

They scrambled up the ravine, each of them too scared to look back, the feeling of being watched pressing down on them. But as they neared the edge, a faint whisper echoed through the trees, a voice carried on the wind, soft but insistent.

Help us... don't leave us here...

They bolted, running through the woods until they were safely back on the road, hearts pounding, breaths labored. They didn't speak, each of them gripped by the same overwhelming fear—that whatever was haunting the wrecked car had now latched onto them.

That night, each of them was plagued by nightmares. Liam dreamed of the car, but this time it was pristine, whole, as if no accident had ever touched it. He was sitting in the passenger seat, looking over at the driver—a woman with long, dark hair, her face familiar from the photograph.

She turned to him, her eyes wide and pleading.

"We're trapped," she whispered, her voice hollow. "Please... help us leave."

He tried to respond, but his mouth wouldn't move, his body paralyzed. The woman's face twisted in despair, her form flickering, shifting, as though she were caught between two worlds, unable to fully exist in either.

Then he heard it—a soft, high-pitched laughter from the back seat. He turned, his heart racing, and there was the doll, sitting upright, its chipped smile wider, its glassy eyes fixed on him.

He jolted awake, drenched in sweat, his heart hammering. The room was dark, silent, but as he lay there, trying to steady his breathing, he felt a strange sensation—a presence, watching him from the corner of the room.

He turned on the light, his gaze darting around, but the room was empty. Yet the feeling remained, a chilling reminder that whatever had happened in that car, whatever tragic accident had taken place, had left behind more than just memories.

It had left behind restless spirits, bound to the wreck, trapped in a nightmare they couldn't escape. And now, it seemed, they had brought that nightmare with them.

The following day, Jared, Owen, and Liam met at the edge of the woods, each one visibly shaken, dark circles under their eyes. None of them had slept well, haunted by nightmares that blurred the line between dreams and reality. They shared their stories, each boy recounting chilling visions of the woman in the car, the doll's sinister grin, and the desperate whispers that lingered even after they'd woken up.

"We need to know what happened to that car," Jared said finally, his voice trembling. "If we don't, I feel like... like we'll never get rid of her. Or that doll."

Owen shuddered, casting a wary glance toward the woods. "Yeah, well, how are we supposed to find out? This happened years ago. No one will remember it."

Liam's gaze drifted to his backpack, where he'd stashed the photograph they'd taken inside the car. "Maybe we can find something in town. Newspapers, old records, anything that could give us a clue."

The others agreed, their curiosity mingling with fear. If they could find out who Sarah was—and why she was calling for help from beyond the grave—maybe they'd finally be free of whatever curse had followed them home.

The boys made their way to the town library, a quiet, dusty place that rarely saw visitors. The librarian, Mrs. Marston, looked at them with surprise when they approached her desk, asking for old newspaper archives. She didn't ask questions, merely pointing them toward a back room filled with rows of ancient, yellowed newspapers and clippings.

They spent hours sifting through the stacks, flipping through brittle pages filled with stories from the town's history. At first, they found nothing, only mundane reports on county fairs, high school graduations, and town council meetings. But then, Jared's voice broke the silence.

"Guys... I think I found it."

The others gathered around as Jared carefully laid out a clipping dated fifteen years ago. The headline read:

"Family of Four Perishes in Tragic Accident: Mystery Surrounds Abandoned Vehicle in Eldridge Ravine."

Liam's throat tightened as he read the article, his heart sinking with each word. The story described a young family—a mother, father, and their two small children—who had gone missing on a drive to visit relatives. Their car had somehow veered off the road, tumbling down the ravine where the boys had found it. Search parties combed the area for days, but the family was never found, only the wrecked car, abandoned and empty. No bodies, no clues—only the faintest signs of a struggle inside.

The mother's name was Sarah.

"That's her," Liam whispered, the weight of the revelation pressing down on him. "She's the one in the car. She's the one who wrote that note."

Owen looked around, a shiver running down his spine. "But... where are they now? Why didn't they find the bodies?"

Jared shook his head, his voice low. "I don't think they ever left. I think they're... still there. Somehow."

The boys agreed to return to the wreck that afternoon, hoping that confronting the spirits would bring them some peace—or at least answers. They gathered flashlights, salt, and whatever they thought might protect them from whatever haunted the wreck. As the sun began to dip below the horizon, casting an eerie twilight over the woods, they retraced their steps down the familiar path, hearts pounding, nerves frayed.

As they reached the edge of the ravine, the car came into view, looking even more ominous in the dim light. The shadows seemed thicker around it, as though it were a portal to somewhere darker, more sinister.

Slowly, they approached the wreck, their flashlights casting beams across the car's rusted frame, the broken glass glittering faintly in the failing light. They steeled themselves, stepping closer, peering into the car's interior.

And then they heard it.

A faint, muffled cry, coming from the depths of the car, the sound barely audible but filled with despair.

"Help us..."

The voice sent chills down their spines, freezing them in place. It was a woman's voice, weak and distant, as though she were calling from somewhere just beyond reach. Liam felt a surge of dread, but he forced himself to step forward, his flashlight illuminating the back seat.

The doll was back, sitting upright in the seat, its head tilted at an unnatural angle, its glassy eyes staring directly at him.

And next to it was another scrap of paper, resting on the torn fabric of the seat. Liam reached out with trembling hands, picking it up and reading the words scrawled in the same desperate handwriting:

They took us.

Owen's voice was barely a whisper. "Who... who took them?"

As if in response, a soft, high-pitched giggle echoed through the ravine, chilling them to the bone. The shadows seemed to shift, twisting and coalescing, forming shapes that flickered just beyond the edge of their vision. They could feel eyes watching them, a presence that was both cold and oppressive, as though the very air around them were filled with malice.

Then, from the trees above, they heard it—a rustling sound, as though something large and heavy were moving among the branches, creeping closer. The boys' flashlights flickered, their beams trembling as they pointed them toward the sound.

And there, hanging from the branches just above them, were three shadowed figures—thin, twisted shapes with hollow, empty eyes and expressions frozen in horror. Their limbs were long and twisted, their bodies hanging limply, like puppets on invisible strings.

One of them—a woman with dark hair—opened her mouth, her face contorted in terror, her voice a hoarse whisper.

"Help us... please..."

The boys stumbled back, their hearts pounding, but as they turned to run, the shadows seemed to close in around them, shifting and twisting, blocking their path. The woman's face faded, replaced by something darker, more sinister, as though a malevolent force had taken over her form, watching them with a cruel, unblinking gaze.

Owen screamed, breaking the trance, and they bolted up the ravine, their breaths ragged, the shadows clawing at their heels. They didn't stop running until they were clear of the woods, the town lights flickering in the distance, a beacon of safety in the encroaching darkness.

In the days that followed, the boys struggled to shake the fear that gripped them. They no longer doubted that they had disturbed something beyond understanding, something that had been waiting in the wreck for years, bound to the twisted fate of those who had perished in the crash.

They tried to go about their lives, but the memories haunted them—the twisted faces in the trees, the doll's sinister smile, the desperate whispers that filled their dreams. And each night, when the world grew dark and silent, they could feel it—the pull of the ravine, as though something were calling them back, beckoning them to return.

The haunting spread beyond them. Stories began to circulate around town—children whispering about strange shadows in the woods, parents warning their kids to stay away from the ravine. The legend of the wrecked car grew, passed down as a warning, a tale of caution for anyone who dared to venture too close.

For the boys, the memory of that day in the woods remained a dark, unspoken bond. They never spoke of it again, each of them silently vowing to stay far away from the ravine. But no matter how much time passed, they knew one thing for certain:

The shadows in Eldridge Ravine were waiting.

And they would never stop calling for help.

Months passed, and though Jared, Owen, and Liam tried to move on, the events of that summer haunted them relentlessly. They hadn't returned to the ravine, each boy too frightened to even venture into the woods. But the memories refused to fade, replaying every night in their dreams—the doll's grin, the pleading whispers, the hollow eyes staring at them from the trees.

One evening, after yet another restless night, Liam made a decision. He couldn't live like this, trapped in fear, haunted by something he couldn't understand. The others deserved peace too, but there was only one way to find it: they had to go back.

He gathered Jared and Owen that afternoon, explaining his plan, his voice steady despite the terror that flickered in his eyes. At first, the others resisted, their expressions mirroring the fear he felt, but in the end, they all agreed. It was time to face whatever lurked in the ravine.

They met at dusk, flashlights in hand, and made their way to the edge of the forest. The sun was setting, casting a dim, orange glow over the trees, the shadows stretching long and thin across the ground.

The air felt heavier as they neared the ravine, the silence more oppressive, broken only by the occasional rustle of leaves or the distant hoot of an owl. And as they reached the spot where the wrecked car lay hidden in the shadows, the oppressive feeling deepened, a cold, eerie stillness that prickled at their skin.

They approached the wreck cautiously, their flashlights casting beams of light across the twisted metal. Everything was as they had left it—the broken windows, the rusty frame, the scattered debris. But as they moved closer, Liam noticed something he hadn't seen before.

There, scrawled across the side of the car in dark, smeared letters, was a message:

They won't let us go.

Liam's blood ran cold, his hand tightening around his flashlight as he took in the words, feeling the weight of them settle over him. He glanced at the others, their faces pale, their eyes wide with fear.

"What... what does that mean?" Owen whispered, his voice barely audible.

Before anyone could answer, they heard it—a faint, muffled sobbing coming from somewhere nearby. The sound sent chills down their spines, and they scanned the area, their flashlights casting eerie shadows across the ground.

Then, they saw her.

A figure stood at the edge of the clearing, barely visible in the dim light—a woman with dark hair, her face twisted in anguish, her eyes hollow and filled with despair. She looked at them, her gaze piercing, as though pleading for help.

"Please..." she whispered, her voice echoing through the stillness. "They won't let us leave."

The boys froze, their hearts pounding, but Liam stepped forward, his voice trembling as he spoke.

"Sarah... is that you?"

The woman nodded, her form flickering, as though she were struggling to remain visible. She took a step forward, her gaze desperate.

"We're trapped here," she murmured, her voice thick with sorrow. "Bound to this place... to this darkness. They took us... and they won't let us go."

Owen's hands shook as he raised his flashlight, casting it over the trees, searching for any sign of movement. "Who took you, Sarah? Who's keeping you here?"

But before she could answer, a shadowed figure emerged from the darkness, moving with unnatural speed. It was tall, its limbs twisted and elongated, its face hidden in shadow. The figure moved silently, its body swaying as it approached, and the air grew colder, a chill that seeped into their bones.

Sarah's face twisted in terror as she glanced at the figure, backing away. "They're coming... you have to leave. They won't let you go either."

The boys turned to run, but the shadows closed in around them, the air growing heavy, suffocating. They stumbled, their breaths coming in shallow gasps as the darkness pressed against them, the whispering voices growing louder, more insistent.

Stay with us... don't leave...

They broke free of the shadows, stumbling up the ravine, their hearts pounding as they raced through the woods. But the voices followed them, echoing through the trees, filling their minds with whispers and pleas. Every shadow seemed to move, every branch a claw reaching for them, pulling them back toward the wreck, toward the darkness that refused to release them.

When they finally burst out of the woods, gasping for breath, they turned to look back, half-expecting to see the shadowed figures lurking at the edge of the trees. But there was nothing—only the silent, still forest, as though nothing had ever been there.

The boys didn't speak, too shaken to put their experiences into words. They walked home in silence, the weight of what they had seen pressing down on them, each of them haunted by the same terrible realization:

The spirits were trapped. And now, having returned to the ravine, they, too, were bound to it, marked by the darkness that had claimed the wreck. It wouldn't end here. The whispers would follow them, the shadows waiting for the moment they let down their guard.

The boys parted ways, each one retreating to the safety of their homes, but the sense of dread lingered, a shadow that clung to them, a reminder that the darkness was never far behind.

Days turned into weeks, and the boys found themselves slipping deeper into fear, unable to escape the nightmares that haunted their nights, the whispers that lingered in the silence. Each of them began to see things—shadows shifting in their rooms, faces appearing in mirrors, and always, always, the doll with the sinister grin, watching from the corners.

Liam was the first to break, returning to the ravine alone one evening, desperate to confront the spirits, to find some way to end the curse that had been placed on them. But he never returned. The next morning, the townspeople found his flashlight lying at the edge of the ravine, its beam still on, casting a faint, flickering light over the darkness below.

Jared and Owen knew the truth, though they refused to speak of it. Liam had joined the others, trapped in the ravine, bound to the wreck that had claimed so many before him. And as the days passed, they began to feel the pull of the ravine once more, the whispers calling them back, drawing them toward the darkness that awaited them.

They tried to resist, to ignore the voices, but each night the pull grew stronger, the shadows growing darker, the whispers louder.

And soon, like the others before them, they, too, would return to the wreck, drawn by the promise of an escape that would never come, bound to the endless darkness that lay in wait, deep in the heart of Eldridge Ravine.

The town of Millfield had always been quiet, a place where people knew each other and dark secrets rarely saw the light. But after the strange events in Eldridge Ravine and the mysterious disappearance of the three boys, whispers spread like wildfire.

In the weeks that followed, townsfolk began to notice strange occurrences. Residents living near the ravine reported hearing voices in the dead of night—soft, desperate whispers carried on the wind, calling for help, echoing through the silent woods. Shadows flitted at the edge of their vision, fleeting figures that vanished as soon as one looked directly at them. Dogs barked endlessly, unwilling to stray near the tree line, their hackles raised, their eyes fixed on something unseen.

The parents of Jared, Owen, and Liam held out hope that the boys had run away, that maybe they would turn up in a nearby town. But as days turned into weeks, it became clear that something sinister had happened. Search parties were organized, scouring the ravine, but every expedition ended the same: with a haunting sense of dread and the unmistakable feeling of being watched.

Not long after, people began to avoid the ravine altogether, especially after dusk. Those who dared to go near it spoke of strange, lingering figures among the trees—long-limbed shadows that seemed to pulse with darkness, bodies contorted in unnatural shapes, their heads cocked to one side, watching with hollow, empty eyes. The rumors spread of seeing *three* specific shadows among them, slightly smaller than the others, standing just outside the ravine, waiting.

These figures were often accompanied by a chilling laugh that echoed through the trees, high-pitched and childlike. Many claimed to have seen a doll propped against a tree near the ravine's edge, its face cracked, its glassy eyes fixed in an unsettling gaze, as though it were watching anyone who came close.

And then, there were the new reports of disappearances.

One day, a group of urban explorers from a nearby town heard about the mysterious car wreck and the haunting rumors surrounding it. Determined to document something paranormal, they ventured into the ravine with cameras, flashlights, and a sense of invincibility.

The town tried to warn them, but they brushed off the local tales as superstition. They set out on a foggy evening, their voices fading as they disappeared into the trees. Hours passed with no word. The next morning, only their cameras were found, left scattered in the mud near the edge of the ravine, their batteries drained, the last few seconds of footage showing nothing but static and the faint sound of laughter.

After that, the sheriff placed a fence around the ravine and posted signs warning against trespassing, hoping it would deter thrill-seekers and curiosity-driven wanderers.

But it wasn't enough. The whispers, the shadows, and the calls for help persisted, bleeding into the everyday lives of the townspeople, an insidious reminder of the darkness that lay at the heart of their town.

Years passed, and the memories of Jared, Owen, and Liam faded, but the ravine remained, a constant, eerie presence on the edge of town. On cold, misty mornings, people would catch glimpses of the boys' faces in the windows of the abandoned houses nearby, their expressions twisted in a mixture of fear and sadness.

At one point, the townsfolk erected a small memorial near the ravine, a stone plaque engraved with the boys' names, surrounded by flowers and candles. But over time, the memorial was neglected, left to weather and decay, the candles melted, the flowers wilted. People became uneasy around it, unwilling to linger, feeling an unseen presence hovering just out of sight.

The ravine, it seemed, wanted to be forgotten. And anyone who attempted to memorialize or remember the lost souls would eventually fall silent, leaving the site abandoned once more.

The haunting of Eldridge Ravine became a cautionary tale, whispered in hushed tones among the townspeople. Parents warned their children to stay away from the woods, to avoid the ravine at all costs. But children are naturally curious, and as the years passed, new generations were drawn to the forbidden place, their imaginations fueled by stories of ghosts and restless spirits.

Some children claimed to see faces in the shadows, to hear soft, pleading whispers that seemed to come from the ground itself. Others spoke of a doll that would appear in different places, watching, waiting, its chipped smile as unsettling as the stories that surrounded it.

As the town grew older, Eldridge Ravine became a place of legends, a shadowed scar on the town's memory, a reminder of the dangers lurking just out of sight. But the warnings persisted, passed down through generations, an unspoken promise that the darkness in the ravine would never fully leave.

And at night, when the town lay silent and the shadows grew long, the people of Millfield could still hear it—the faint, distant sound of laughter and the soft, chilling whispers that echoed through the trees, calling out to anyone willing to listen:

Help us... we can't leave...

And with each passing year, the darkness waited, patient and unyielding, for the next curious soul who would venture too close, drawn in by the promise of a mystery, unaware that some secrets were never meant to be uncovered.

The End

18
THE SEA WHISPERER

The *Sea Whisperer* was an old, creaking ship that spent most of its time moored along the lonely coast of Blackwater Bay. The vessel was an odd sight—a rusted iron hull, thick ropes coiled like sleeping serpents, sails that flapped in the salty breeze like ghostly flags. Despite its worn appearance, it drew visitors from towns all along the coast, tourists eager for the advertised "journey of a lifetime" and a glimpse of the wide-open sea.

The ship's captain, Arlen Kane, was a tall, stoic man with piercing blue eyes and a voice as rough as the ocean itself. Captain Kane had been taking tourists out into the bay for years. He had a reputation for charm and seafaring knowledge, his face weathered from decades spent under the sun and spray. His crew—a handful of silent, gaunt men—moved with practiced precision, barely saying a word, their expressions blank and unreadable.

The townspeople who lived near Blackwater Bay warned tourists to avoid the *Sea Whisperer*. There were tales, whispered in quiet conversations, about people who boarded the ship and never returned. The local newspaper had even published an article detailing disappearances linked to the boat, but Captain Kane dismissed it all as superstition.

"People lose track of time on the open water," he'd say with a wry smile. "Get a taste of the sea, and sometimes they don't want to come back."

But there were always a few tourists willing to ignore the warnings, their curiosity outweighing caution. They flocked to the dock, enchanted by the old ship and the promise of adventure. And once they'd paid their fare, Captain Kane would smile, welcome them aboard, and promise them an experience they'd never forget.

On the day that would mark the ship's final voyage, four passengers stood on the dock, gazing up at the looming ship with a mixture of excitement and unease. Each of them had been drawn to the *Sea Whisperer* by different means—

fascination, a sense of danger, a desire to escape. But all of them shared a thrill at the prospect of leaving land behind, of letting the ocean swallow their worries.

There was Mark, a photographer eager to capture the raw beauty of the open water; Julia, a writer struggling with a creative block and searching for inspiration; Dean, a retired fisherman who missed the sea and felt restless in his quiet life on land; and Sophia, a travel blogger documenting her journey along the coast, hoping to uncover hidden places no one else had seen.

Captain Kane greeted them warmly, his eyes gleaming as he shook each of their hands, welcoming them aboard with a deep, rumbling voice. Behind him, his crew moved like shadows, silent and efficient, loading supplies, securing ropes, and casting furtive glances at the new passengers. There was something off about the crew—a stiffness to their movements, a hollowness in their eyes—but none of the passengers seemed to notice, caught up in the thrill of their upcoming journey.

"Welcome to the *Sea Whisperer*," Kane said, his voice carrying a strange, soothing quality. "You're in for a real treat today. We'll be taking you further out than most ever go. This will be a journey... well, unlike any other."

The words held an edge, a subtle warning disguised as hospitality, but the passengers were too excited to notice. They boarded eagerly, watching as the shoreline receded, replaced by the wide, open expanse of the sea.

Once the ship was well beyond the sight of land, Captain Kane turned his attention to the passengers, his eyes colder, darker, as though a mask had slipped. He guided the ship deeper into the ocean, far past the usual routes, to where the water was a dark, endless blue, the depths unknowable.

For the first few hours, everything seemed normal. The passengers were given free rein to explore the ship, taking in the creaking wood, the salt-sprayed decks, the sun glinting off the water. Mark snapped photos, eager to capture the ship's charm, while Julia and Sophia wandered along the deck, marveling at the vastness of the sea. Dean chatted with one of the crew members, a grizzled old sailor named Harker, though Harker seemed distracted, his eyes darting toward the horizon as though watching for something unseen.

As the sun began to set, casting long shadows across the deck, a strange tension settled over the ship. The air grew cold, the water darker, almost black, swallowing the light like ink. The crew grew quieter, their movements more deliberate, each one casting furtive glances toward Captain Kane, as though waiting for some unspoken signal.

Then, without warning, Kane gave a nod to his men, and they sprang into action. The passengers watched, confused, as the crew began closing off sections of the ship, locking doors and sealing hatches with heavy chains. The friendly demeanor that had marked the start of the journey was gone, replaced by an air of grim purpose.

Dean approached one of the crew members, his voice laced with concern. "What's going on? Why are you locking everything up?"

The sailor looked at him with blank, hollow eyes, his face devoid of expression. "You'll understand soon enough. Best you stay calm."

The other passengers grew uneasy, exchanging worried glances. They had no idea what was happening, but the feeling of danger was unmistakable. Captain Kane approached them, his face cast in shadow as he looked each of them over, his expression unreadable.

"We're heading into deeper waters now," he said softly, his voice carrying an edge that sent a chill down their spines. "It's best you follow instructions. Things can... change out here."

As night fell, the ship took on a sinister quality, the shadows stretching longer, swallowing the light. The passengers felt the weight of the darkness around them, the endless sea below, pressing in on them, making the deck feel smaller, confining. The usual sounds of the ship—the creak of the wood, the soft slosh of the waves—faded, replaced by an eerie silence, as though they had entered a different realm, a place where sound had no power.

Then, from the depths of the water, came a low, echoing hum, a sound that vibrated through the hull of the ship, filling the air with a deep, primal resonance. It was a sound that seemed to come from below, from something vast and ancient lurking in the blackness beneath them.

The crew members stood motionless, their faces pale, their eyes distant, as though entranced by the sound. Captain Kane's expression softened, taking on a look of reverence, of almost fanatical devotion. He turned to the passengers, his eyes gleaming with a strange, unsettling light.

"This is where it begins," he murmured, his voice low and reverent. "The sea has its own secrets... its own demands. To cross into its depths, you must pay a price."

The passengers felt a surge of terror as the captain's words sank in, their unease shifting into full-blown fear. They glanced at each other, their expressions mirroring the same silent question: what had they stepped into?

Mark, his voice shaking, took a step back. "What... what do you mean, a price?"

Kane smiled, a slow, sinister grin that didn't reach his eyes. "The sea is a hungry thing. It demands tribute—a soul for every voyage. That's the only way the *Sea Whisperer* continues its journey."

Sophia backed away, her hand flying to her mouth, her eyes wide with horror. "You... you take people out here to feed them to the sea?"

Captain Kane nodded, his expression unreadable. "It's how we survive. The sea is our master. To deny it... would be to invite a far worse fate."

As the passengers processed his words, the crew moved in, their faces expressionless, their eyes empty, as though they were no longer themselves, their bodies mere puppets moving to the ocean's silent command.

A sense of cold dread gripped the passengers as they realized there was no escape. They were too far from shore, too deep in the heart of the ocean, surrounded by darkness. The *Sea Whisperer* was no vessel of adventure; it was a trap, a means to feed something ancient and terrible that lurked beneath the waves.

And as the ship drifted deeper into the night, the ocean seemed to pulse around them, alive with a hunger that would not be denied.

Captain Kane's eyes glimmered with a strange light as he watched the passengers, their faces pale with terror. To him, this was no act of cruelty—it was necessity. The *Sea Whisperer* had been his life for decades, and the sea, his true master, demanded more than devotion; it demanded obedience.

He walked toward the edge of the deck, peering into the darkness that lay just beyond the ship's hull, and let his thoughts drift back to the beginning.

The pact had been made almost thirty years ago, on a night just like this one, under a pitch-black sky, with the sea stretching endlessly around them, vast and hungry. Kane had been younger then, a man driven by the thrill of the ocean and an insatiable need for freedom. But he'd made a critical mistake, pushing the *Sea Whisperer* beyond its limits in search of uncharted waters.

Caught in a brutal storm, the ship had been battered, nearly torn apart by the fury of the waves. Lightning flashed, illuminating the terrified faces of his crew as they struggled to keep the vessel afloat, and in a moment of despair, Kane had felt the looming inevitability of death. He was staring into the abyss, knowing it was only a matter of time before the sea would take them.

Then, through the storm, he'd heard a voice.

It had been deep and resonant, almost a vibration in the air, a presence as ancient as the ocean itself. The voice had filled his mind, offering him a deal, a way to save his ship, his life, and the lives of his crew. But there was a price. In exchange for safe passage, he would serve the sea, becoming its hand, its vessel. And the *Sea Whisperer* would require offerings—souls that would sink into the ocean's depths, feeding the dark force that lay below.

Kane had no choice. He'd accepted the deal, and in that moment, he felt the weight of the pact settle over him, a heavy, cold presence that filled him with dread. The sea calmed, the storm dissipated, and the ship sailed on, undamaged, with the whisper of the ocean echoing in his mind: *You are mine now.*

Kane's crew, bound to him by loyalty and fear, had been pulled into the pact as well. The transformation had been gradual, almost imperceptible at first—small things, like their eyes growing darker, their skin paler, their voices hollow. But over time, they became something else, their humanity slowly leached away by the sea's dark power, turning them into something closer to shadows than men.

Now, they were bound to the *Sea Whisperer*, ageless, existing in a liminal state between life and death. They could feel the call of the ocean within them, an insatiable pull that bound them to the ship and to the pact. Their minds had become hazy, as though wrapped in fog, their memories distant and fragmented. They no longer felt fear, or hunger, or warmth; all they felt was the relentless drive to obey the sea's command.

They had become servants, guardians of the ship, and enforcers of the pact, and any trace of their former lives had been washed away by the sea. They lived only to fulfill the pact, carrying out their duty with emotionless precision, their movements as mechanical and inevitable as the tides.

Every voyage required a ritual, a tribute to appease the ocean's endless hunger. The offerings—the passengers, chosen unwittingly—were lulled by the beauty of the sea, drawn to the vastness of the water, never realizing they were being led to their doom.

As the *Sea Whisperer* drifted out into deeper waters, the ritual began. The crew moved in silence, their faces expressionless as they prepared for what was to come. They tied thick ropes along the edge of the ship, creating a makeshift altar. Buckets of salt water were drawn up from the depths and poured onto the deck in an intricate pattern, forming symbols that seemed to pulse and glow under the moonlight.

Captain Kane stood at the center of the deck, his gaze fixed on the water, his mind attuned to the ocean's demands. He could feel the presence lurking just below the surface, waiting, watching, its hunger growing with each passing moment. The dark power of the sea surged within him, filling him with a cold, merciless purpose.

The crew joined him, their hands clasped as they murmured a low chant, their voices blending into a haunting melody that echoed across the water, filling the air with an eerie, unnatural energy. The chant was ancient, its words older than language, a call to the depths that awakened the sleeping force below.

One by one, the passengers would be taken, their lives given to the sea, their souls drawn down into the cold, black depths, becoming part of the endless tide. And in return, the *Sea Whisperer* would sail on, safe from the sea's wrath, its journey eternal.

Kane opened his eyes, his gaze settling on the terrified faces of the passengers. Mark, Julia, Dean, and Sophia stood huddled together, their expressions a mix of confusion and horror as they realized the nature of the trap they'd stepped into.

"Please," Julia whispered, her voice trembling. "This isn't happening... it can't be."

Captain Kane's face softened for a moment, a brief flicker of regret crossing his features. But the sea's power surged within him, cold and unyielding, banishing any trace of sympathy. He was bound to the ocean's will, and he could no more disobey than he could stop the tides.

"It's already begun," he said, his voice low, heavy with resignation. "The sea claims what it wants, and we are merely its instruments."

Sophia backed away, her eyes wide with terror. "You don't have to do this. You can let us go."

Kane shook his head, his expression grim. "If I break the pact, the sea will take us all. I've seen its wrath, felt its power. I'd rather die a thousand times than face the sea's fury."

Dean clenched his fists, his face set with determination. "Then we'll fight. We'll jump overboard if we have to."

The captain's gaze hardened. "There's no escape. The sea will find you, no matter where you go. And you... will become part of it."

As he spoke, the water around the ship began to churn, black tendrils rising from the depths, winding up along the sides of the hull like fingers of dark smoke. The passengers stared, frozen with fear, as the tendrils took shape, forming twisted, spectral figures that hovered above the water, their hollow eyes fixed on the ship, on the passengers, their mouths open in silent screams.

These were the souls of the previous passengers, the ones who had been claimed by the sea, forever bound to the depths, serving as a reminder of the pact's dark price. Their ghostly forms drifted toward the ship, reaching out, beckoning, their expressions twisted in agony.

The sea's call grew louder, filling the air with a dark, resonant hum that vibrated through the ship, urging Kane and his crew to complete the ritual, to deliver the offerings that the ocean demanded.

And as the passengers stood trembling on the deck, they realized the full horror of their fate.

The sea was alive, hungry, and it would not be denied.

The *Sea Whisperer* creaked and groaned as the dark tendrils of mist curled around it, spectral figures drifting over the waves. Mark, Julia, Dean, and Sophia felt the weight of their fates settling over them, an unshakable sense of doom pressing down like a suffocating fog. The figures hovering above the water drew closer, their hollow eyes fixed on the passengers, their mouths twisted in silent, eternal screams.

But even with death approaching, instinct kicked in, and the four of them found strength in desperation. Dean, the retired fisherman, had been on boats his whole life, and if this was going to be his last voyage, he was going to fight.

"Listen, we're not out of options," he whispered fiercely, grabbing Mark's arm. "We don't have to let them take us without a fight."

Captain Kane watched them, his face impassive, as though their struggle meant nothing, as though they were already lost. But the flash of defiance in Dean's eyes caught his attention. He tilted his head, almost curious, a grim smile tugging at the corner of his mouth.

"Fight if you wish," he said softly, his voice carrying an eerie calm. "But the sea always claims what it's owed."

Dean rallied the others, keeping his voice low. "The crew might be loyal to Kane, but they're human, just like us. If we can get them off balance, we can break through, maybe even take control of the ship."

Sophia's eyes darted around the deck, her mind racing. "But the captain... he's not just human, is he? There's something... wrong about him. And those things in the water—they're coming for us."

Julia nodded, her face pale but resolute. "We might not get out of this alive, but I'd rather go down fighting than just... be taken."

Dean, Mark, and Sophia shared a glance, and then they nodded in silent agreement. They were in this together, and they'd take whatever chance they could find.

The four of them split up, moving quickly across the deck, taking stock of what little they had. Dean managed to pry a metal rod from the ship's railing, Mark found a length of rope, and Sophia spotted a small knife discarded near the galley entrance. Armed with makeshift weapons, they approached the nearest crew member—a grizzled sailor with sunken eyes and an empty stare.

Dean struck first, the metal rod crashing against the sailor's head. But to his horror, the man didn't react. He simply turned, his eyes devoid of life, as though he were nothing more than a shell. He lunged at Dean, his hands cold as ice as they closed around Dean's wrist, holding him with a strength that felt inhuman.

The others jumped in, each of them striking the sailor, their blows desperate. It took all four of them to pry him off, pushing him back with a strength born of pure terror. The sailor stumbled, his expression unchanged, his body moving with a jerking, mechanical motion as he stepped back into the shadows.

The other crew members turned, watching with hollow, unseeing eyes. It was as if the ship itself were alive, aware of their defiance, and the passengers realized they were surrounded.

"They're not alive!" Sophia gasped, her voice filled with horror. "They're bound to this ship... like ghosts."

Kane's voice cut through the silence, calm and mocking. "They are my crew, and they belong to the sea. Just as you soon will."

But there was a glimmer of something in his eyes—a flicker of something almost human, a reminder of the man he had once been. He looked away, his gaze drifting toward the water, as though he were listening to a silent command.

With the captain distracted, Dean seized the opportunity, grabbing the wheel and steering the ship away from the spectral figures that loomed over the waves. The vessel lurched, the deck tilting as it changed course, throwing the crew off balance.

For a brief moment, they thought they'd succeeded. The ghosts faded into the mist, their hollow eyes losing focus as the ship veered off its cursed path. But the relief was short-lived.

Captain Kane's face darkened, his eyes narrowing as he looked at the passengers with a cold fury. "You think you can escape? You don't understand the power of the sea. It has marked you—it will claim you, no matter where you go."

He raised his hand, and the water around the ship began to churn violently, dark tendrils of mist rising from the depths, reaching for the deck. The sea roared, a low, malevolent hum filling the air, and the passengers could feel the darkness closing in, pressing down on them with an ancient, insatiable hunger.

But Julia, her heart pounding, stepped forward, desperation giving her courage. "You made a choice, Captain Kane! You chose to serve the sea, to become its puppet. But we didn't make that choice—we're still human."

Her words seemed to strike something deep within him, and for the briefest moment, a shadow of regret crossed his face. His grip on the ship's railing tightened, his eyes flickering with a mixture of anger and pain. He looked at Julia, his expression shifting, as though he were caught between loyalty to the sea and a sliver of his own lost humanity.

"You don't understand," he whispered, his voice heavy. "The sea doesn't bargain. It takes what it's owed."

But Julia didn't back down. She held his gaze, refusing to look away, and in that moment, the other passengers rallied around her, their eyes filled with defiance. They weren't about to give in, not without a fight.

Kane hesitated, the force of the passengers' will shaking him. In his decades of service to the sea, he had never encountered such resistance. He had always thought the sea was inevitable, that its power was absolute. But these people—these defiant souls—were showing him a strength he hadn't seen in years.

He took a step back, glancing at the churning waters, the dark tendrils that pulsed and writhed, waiting for him to complete the ritual. He was caught between the pull of the ocean and the flicker of humanity that still lingered within him, a shred of the man he'd once been.

The passengers moved toward him, their eyes hard, their determination unyielding.

"End this," Julia said, her voice low but firm. "You don't have to be a slave to this curse. Let us go, and end this cycle."

The captain's gaze shifted to the ocean, and in that moment, he made a decision. He took a deep breath, steeling himself, and turned back to his crew, his voice rising above the roar of the sea.

"The pact is broken," he declared, his voice trembling. "No more souls will be given to the sea."

The crew members froze, their hollow eyes flickering with confusion, as though the words had broken some ancient spell. The spectral figures on the water let out a collective wail, their faces twisting in agony as they began to dissolve, their forms breaking apart and sinking into the depths.

The dark mist receded, the sea calming, as though the ocean itself were recoiling from Kane's defiance. For the first time in years, the passengers felt a sense of relief, a sense of freedom from the weight of the pact that had bound the *Sea Whisperer*.

Kane turned back to them, his face drawn, his eyes heavy with the knowledge of what he had just done. "I've broken the pact," he said softly. "The ship is no longer bound... but I am. The sea will have its due, one way or another."

He stepped to the edge of the deck, his gaze fixed on the water below. The passengers watched in silence, understanding what he was about to do. The sea demanded a life, a tribute, and Kane had chosen to give himself in exchange for their freedom.

With one last look at the crew, the passengers, and the ship he had served for so many years, Captain Kane leapt from the deck, vanishing into the dark, churning waters below.

The sea calmed, the waters smoothing as though in acceptance of the sacrifice. The remaining crew members, free of the sea's hold, began moving like men awoken from a long, dreamless sleep. They looked around, dazed, as if seeing the ship and each other for the first time in years.

In silence, the passengers and crew worked together to turn the ship back toward land, the sense of freedom finally sinking in. As they neared the shore, they looked back at the endless sea, the memory of Kane's final sacrifice weighing heavy on their minds.

The sea had claimed its due, but the *Sea Whisperer* was free at last, the dark pact broken, the cycle ended.

For now, the sea was quiet, its hunger appeased.

The End

19

FOOTSTEPS

The clock read 2:47 a.m., and the only sounds in the house were the soft breaths of Peter and Emily, lost in sleep, and the occasional hum of the heater as it struggled against the chill of the night. The wind outside rattled branches against the window, a sound that usually blended into the quiet stillness of their home.

But tonight, something different broke the silence.

A faint creak echoed from the attic, barely loud enough to disturb Peter and Emily. Emily opened her eyes, disoriented, her heart beating faster as she strained to listen. Another sound followed—a soft, steady patter, like footsteps crossing the floor above them. She held her breath, waiting for Peter to wake up, but he only shifted, lost in his dreams. The footsteps paused, then continued, a slow, deliberate rhythm that set her nerves on edge.

Peter stirred beside her, blinking into the darkness, his voice groggy. "Did you hear that?"

Emily nodded, her hand clutching the blanket. "It sounded like... footsteps. Upstairs."

They lay there in silence, listening, but after a moment, the sounds stopped, leaving only the faint hum of the heater and the tick of the clock. Peter gave her a reassuring squeeze. "Probably just the house settling. Old beams creak sometimes."

Emily forced a nod, but unease tugged at her as she lay back down. She closed her eyes, willing herself to fall asleep, but it was hours before she did, her mind racing with unsettling possibilities.

The next few nights passed in silence, but each evening, Emily found herself lying awake, waiting, straining to hear the slightest creak or shuffle from above. Peter told her she was just imagining things, that it was easy to hear things that weren't there in a quiet house at night. But the doubt festered, and she couldn't shake the feeling that something wasn't right.

Then, on the fifth night, the footsteps returned.

This time, they were louder. The steps were slow, almost measured, moving across the length of the attic above their bedroom. Peter woke up again, sitting up in bed, his brow furrowed as he listened. The footsteps stopped once more, just as they had before, fading into the silence of the night. He sighed, rubbing his face.

"Probably a raccoon," he muttered, though his voice lacked conviction. "We'll check it out in the morning."

But when morning came, they both found reasons to avoid the attic—Peter with work, Emily with errands. By the time night fell, they'd managed to convince themselves it was nothing, just an animal or the sound of an old house settling.

Until the footsteps started again.

The sounds became a pattern. Each night, the footsteps returned, the rhythmic shuffle louder, clearer. One night, the creaking started closer, as though whatever was making the sound had moved down from the attic, descending the narrow staircase to the second floor. Emily lay frozen, gripping Peter's hand, her breath shallow, as they listened to the sounds of something—or someone—moving through their home.

And then, just as quickly as they'd started, the footsteps stopped, the house falling back into silence.

When they turned on the lights and searched, the house looked as it always did—empty, undisturbed. But there was something different in the air, a feeling of watchfulness, as though an invisible presence lingered in the corners, slipping back into the shadows the moment they looked.

On the seventh night, the footsteps moved again, this time closer, the sound of floorboards creaking in the hallway outside their bedroom. Emily bolted upright, her heart hammering as she stared at the door, half-expecting it to swing open. Peter sat beside her, his face pale, his expression one of barely contained fear.

"Maybe we're just... hearing things," he whispered, but even as he said it, his voice shook, and they both knew it was a lie.

The footsteps continued, louder now, echoing through the quiet house, coming from places where no one should be—around the corner, near the stairwell, sometimes right outside their door. And then, one night, just as they lay in bed, too afraid to move, the footsteps stopped, replaced by a soft, chilling sound—a whisper, low and unintelligible, coming from just beyond the bedroom wall.

Emily felt a chill crawl down her spine as the whisper grew louder, repeating the same words in a raspy, broken voice.

"We're here... we're here..."

Peter's hand closed over hers, his grip tight as they sat, frozen in fear, the words echoing through their minds. They weren't alone. Something else had moved in, something that lived in the spaces of their home, creeping closer each night.

And this time, there was no denying it.

The following morning, Peter and Emily sat at the kitchen table, bleary-eyed and tense. Neither had slept. The whispers from the previous night still echoed in their minds, each word laced with a cold dread that refused to fade.

"We can't ignore this anymore," Emily said, her voice firm. "We need to find out what's up there."

Peter nodded reluctantly. "We'll check the attic. Maybe there's... something that explains all of this."

They climbed the narrow staircase, each step heavier than the last, the weight of the unknown pressing down on them. When they reached the attic door, Peter hesitated, his hand on the knob, glancing back at Emily, who nodded, her face pale but determined. He turned the knob, the door creaking open, and they were hit with a wave of stale, cold air that sent a shiver through them.

The attic was dim, shadows pooling in the corners, dust motes swirling in the slant of morning light. Boxes and old furniture sat haphazardly, a forgotten collection of objects from previous decades, but something about the space felt... wrong. A sense of unease permeated the air, a heaviness that made the room feel far colder than the rest of the house.

They began searching, moving boxes and sifting through old belongings, but found nothing unusual—until Emily noticed something odd about the floorboards in the far corner.

"Peter... look," she whispered, pointing to a small, square section of the floor that didn't match the rest. The wood looked newer, as though it had been replaced recently, and it sat slightly higher than the surrounding boards.

Peter crouched down, carefully prying at the edge of the board until it lifted, revealing a small, hollow compartment underneath. Inside was a stack of faded papers, a worn leather-bound journal, and, tucked beneath it all, a single, crumbling photograph.

Emily took the photograph, her hands trembling as she held it up. The image was of a family—a man, woman, and young girl, standing in front of what looked like their house, though it was far older, more dilapidated. The family's expressions were grim, almost hollow, their eyes dark and sunken. And in the background, behind them, was the attic window of the house... the same window that now stood at the end of the hall just outside their bedroom.

"What is this?" Emily whispered, her voice barely audible.

Peter opened the journal, flipping through the brittle pages, skimming the scrawled handwriting. The entries were sporadic, filled with fragmented thoughts, disjointed words that painted a dark picture.

The journal belonged to a man named Thomas Greaves, the former owner of the house. He had lived here with his wife, Marianne, and their young daughter, Lillian, nearly seventy years ago. As Peter read through the entries, he noticed a shift in the tone of the writing—what began as a normal account of family life turned darker, more frantic.

November 3rd, 1953

"They won't leave. I hear them in the walls, creeping through the floors, breathing in the night. Marianne says it's just the house, that it's settling, but I know better. I've seen them... shadows moving in the corners, watching, waiting."

November 27th, 1953

"Lillian hasn't been herself. She talks to the empty air, calls out to things I can't see. At night, she whispers, tells me they're here, that they're waiting for us. Last night, I heard footsteps coming from her room, but when I checked, she was asleep, her hands cold as ice."

December 10th, 1953

"We are not alone. I don't know what I did, what brought this upon us, but they are here. They are in our home, and they will not leave until they take what they want."

The final entry was barely legible, the words scrawled in a shaky hand, as though written in a frenzy.

December 18th, 1953

"They have taken Marianne. She was here, and then she was gone, her voice echoing through the house, fading into the walls. Lillian says she can see her in the shadows, but I don't believe it. I won't believe it. I am all that's left, and I know they're coming for me too. They live here now, and we are only guests...*

The entry ended abruptly, the rest of the pages blank. Peter's hands shook as he closed the journal, his mind reeling with the realization that something terrible had happened in their home, something that left a mark, a lingering presence that had seeped into the walls, the floors, the very air.

Emily clutched the photograph tightly, her face pale as she processed what they'd read. "Do you think... do you think they're still here? Thomas, Marianne, Lillian... whatever's left of them?"

Peter swallowed, his throat dry. "Maybe. But it sounds like there's something else too. Something that took them."

They left the attic in a hurry, closing the door tightly behind them, as though it could keep the darkness contained. But the silence that followed was thick with tension, as if the house itself was listening, aware of their discovery.

That night, they went to bed early, lying side by side in the dark, each of them haunted by the secrets they had uncovered. Sleep eluded them, and as the hours crept by, they lay there, waiting, listening, their minds replaying the words from Thomas's journal, the footsteps, the whispers, the horror that had unfolded so many years ago.

Then, just after 3 a.m., the footsteps began again, louder than before, moving from the attic to the second floor, the creaks growing closer, more insistent. The footsteps stopped outside their door, a low, rasping breath filling the silence.

And then came the whisper, low and chilling, echoing from the other side of the door.

"We're here... don't let us in..."

Emily clung to Peter, her heart racing, as they lay motionless, too terrified to respond. But the whisper grew louder, the words seeping into their minds, filling the room with a sense of dread that felt almost tangible, pressing down on them, tightening around their throats.

And then, as quickly as it began, the sound stopped. The house fell silent once more, leaving only the soft tick of the clock and the fading echo of footsteps in the darkness.

They didn't sleep for the rest of the night, their minds reeling with the knowledge that whatever haunted their home was far from finished with them. It was still there, lurking in the shadows, waiting, growing bolder with each passing night.

The house was colder than usual, a chill settling into every corner, creeping up from the floorboards and settling into Emily and Peter's bones. After the sleepless night, they moved through their morning in a daze, speaking in hushed tones, casting wary glances at every shadowed corner.

They both knew that they could no longer ignore it. The footsteps, the whispers, the journal—the entity wasn't going to leave them alone. They needed to confront whatever was haunting their home, face the darkness that had lingered in the house for over seventy years.

That evening, as the sun dipped below the horizon, they gathered candles, flashlights, and a thick bundle of sage, hoping it might help ward off whatever presence lingered. Peter pulled the journal from the attic, gripping it tightly, as though the scrawled words of Thomas Greaves could somehow protect them.

As they waited for midnight, a silence settled over the house, heavier than usual, as though the walls themselves were holding their breath. They took their place in the living room, candles flickering, the journal lying open on the coffee table, its faded ink stark against the aged paper.

At the stroke of midnight, the temperature in the room dropped sharply, and a deep, oppressive feeling filled the air. The house seemed to come alive, the floor creaking, the walls groaning, as though something immense and unseen were pressing against it, trying to break through.

Then, the footsteps began.

They were louder this time, unmistakable, slow and deliberate, moving down from the attic, one creak at a time, making their way toward the second floor.

Peter and Emily held hands, gripping each other tightly, their eyes fixed on the staircase as the footsteps grew louder, descending toward them. Shadows stretched and twisted along the walls, dark shapes flickering at the edges of the candlelight, shifting as though they had a life of their own.

The footsteps stopped at the foot of the stairs, and then a whisper echoed through the room, chilling them to the bone.

"We're here..."

Emily's grip on Peter's hand tightened, her heart pounding in her chest. "What... what do you want from us?" she called out, her voice trembling.

The silence that followed was heavy, suffocating, and for a moment, they thought they'd imagined the response that followed—a faint, broken voice, filled with sorrow.

"We were taken... trapped... we can't leave."

The air grew colder, and the shadows darkened, pooling near the edges of the room, as though gathering strength. Peter took a deep breath, steadying himself, and raised the journal.

"Thomas Greaves," he said loudly, hoping to reach the spirit he sensed was near. "We found your journal. We know what happened to you, to your family. But we need to know what's keeping you here. Is there something we can do to set you free?"

The silence deepened, and for a moment, they thought they'd lost whatever tenuous connection they'd made. But then, a figure materialized in the doorway, faint and flickering, barely visible in the candlelight.

It was Thomas.

He stood there, his face pale and hollow, his eyes dark and filled with a sadness that seemed to stretch beyond the confines of the room. He raised a hand, pointing toward the attic, his voice barely more than a whisper.

"It's... her. She is still here."

Emily felt a chill crawl down her spine, dread pooling in her stomach. "Her? Who do you mean?"

Thomas's face twisted, his expression one of terror. "She's... the one who took us. She bound us here, feeding off our fear, our pain. She hides in the shadows, waiting... always waiting."

Peter's hand shook as he looked at Thomas. "How can we make her leave? How can we break her hold?"

Thomas's figure flickered, his voice fading. "She fears the light... but she cannot be banished. She can only be driven back... kept at bay. As long as she's bound to the house, we are all trapped with her."

The shadows in the room darkened, coalescing, forming a figure that was tall and thin, its face hidden in shadow, its form shifting like smoke. The oppressive feeling intensified, filling the room with a sense of dread so deep it felt almost physical, pressing down on them, stealing the breath from their lungs.

The figure took a step forward, and Emily felt a cold hand brush against her shoulder, an icy chill that sank deep into her bones. She gasped, stumbling back, her heart pounding as she looked into the empty, hollow eyes of the figure looming over them.

"Go," it hissed, its voice a low, guttural whisper. "This is... my home..."

Peter grabbed the sage, lighting it with shaking hands, letting the smoke fill the room. The figure recoiled, hissing, its form flickering, twisting in pain as the sage smoke surrounded it. The shadows shifted, retreating, but the figure's hollow gaze remained fixed on them, filled with a hate so intense it seemed to burn.

But as it retreated, Thomas's figure faded as well, his form dissolving into the darkness, his expression one of sorrow and resignation. Emily felt a pang of despair, realizing that as long as the entity remained, Thomas and his family would be trapped, their spirits bound to the darkness that had claimed them.

With one last, desperate glance, Thomas's voice echoed in the room, a final plea.

"Don't let her take you... don't let her in..."

The figure vanished, taking the shadows with it, leaving the house in silence once more. The oppressive feeling lifted, and for a moment, they felt relief.

But then, from somewhere deep within the house, they heard it—the faint sound of footsteps, moving through the attic, descending the stairs, coming ever closer.

And they knew, with a chilling certainty, that this was far from over.

The days that followed their encounter with Thomas and the malevolent entity left Emily and Peter on edge, their nerves frayed, every creak and rustle in the house a reminder of the darkness that lurked within. They needed answers, some way to understand what was haunting them—and why it wouldn't let go.

Emily turned to the town's small historical society, hoping that the house's history might provide some clues. She spent hours combing through dusty records, yellowed papers, and faded photographs. The house itself was nearly a century old, but it was only in the records from the 1950s that she found something unsettling.

A name kept appearing: Margaret Leland.

According to the records, Margaret had once owned the house. She had moved in shortly after the death of her husband, but her stay had been short. Within months of moving in, she had vanished under mysterious circumstances, leaving behind a trail of rumors and whispers that had haunted the town for years.

Locals claimed that Margaret had been a strange woman, deeply involved in occult practices, someone who dabbled in séances and dark rituals. Some of the older townspeople remembered seeing her late at night, standing by her attic window, her silhouette framed in the moonlight as she stared out over the town. Children avoided the house, saying that Margaret would call to them from her window, whispering promises and warnings in a low, raspy voice.

But then, one night, Margaret was simply gone.

Her absence was noticed immediately. A neighbor, disturbed by the eerie silence coming from the house, had gone inside only to find the attic door wide open, strange symbols scratched into the floor. They found no sign of Margaret, no trace of where she might have gone.

After her disappearance, the house was put up for sale, and Thomas Greaves had moved in shortly after with his family, unaware of the house's dark history. But it seemed that Margaret hadn't left completely. In the weeks that followed, Thomas and his family began experiencing strange phenomena, the sounds of footsteps, voices, and the feeling of being watched.

Emily's heart raced as she pieced together the story, realizing with a sickening dread that Margaret had never truly left. She had become part of the house, bound to it by whatever dark forces she had summoned in life.

But it wasn't until she found an old, faded newspaper clipping that the full horror of the haunting became clear.

The article described Margaret Leland as a woman obsessed with the idea of immortality, someone who believed she could transcend death itself. She had been a fixture in local folklore, a woman who invited others into her home for "ceremonies" that left them feeling shaken, sometimes ill. Neighbors reported seeing strange lights emanating from her attic, shadows moving in the dead of night, figures that appeared and vanished in the blink of an eye.

Margaret's diary, recovered years later by a distant relative, had contained entries detailing her attempts to make contact with "those beyond the veil," spirits that she believed could grant her eternal life. Her writings grew darker as she documented her attempts to invoke these spirits, to summon them, to bind them to her.

One entry in particular sent chills down Emily's spine:

July 18, 1952

"The veil between the living and the dead grows thin. Tonight, I will complete the ritual. I have seen them in the shadows, waiting, watching, whispering my name. They promise freedom from death, a life beyond life... if I prove myself worthy."

The last entry was a single, scrawled sentence, written in shaky, almost illegible handwriting:

I will live forever.

Emily showed the records to Peter, her hands trembling as she recounted the story. Margaret's ritual had not granted her immortality—it had bound her spirit to the house, trapping her in a twisted existence somewhere between life and death. And worse, she wasn't alone. She had drawn other spirits into the house, trapping them in the same darkness, forcing them to feed her power.

"Thomas and his family... they were victims," Peter murmured, his face pale. "She took them, bound them here to sustain herself. And now she's trying to do the same with us."

They realized that the dark presence lurking in the attic was not merely a spirit, but something much more sinister—a soul that had rejected death, one that had chosen to haunt the living, to pull others into its grasp in a twisted attempt at immortality. The footsteps, the whispers, the shadowed figure—they were all pieces of Margaret's presence, fragments of her essence that she used to keep her grip on the world of the living.

Desperate for freedom, Peter and Emily devised a plan. They couldn't simply wait for her to consume them, couldn't ignore the darkness that grew more oppressive each night. They needed to weaken her hold on the house, to break the bindings that had anchored her there.

They gathered candles, salt, and a small mirror, items that they had read could disrupt a spirit's hold, and that night, they returned to the attic. The air was thick, cold, as though the house itself were resisting their presence. The shadows seemed to ripple, the dim light barely penetrating the darkness that clung to the walls.

Peter held the mirror in his hand, his face pale but determined, while Emily sprinkled salt along the edges of the attic floor, forming a barrier that they hoped would prevent Margaret from moving beyond the room. The silence was suffocating, pressing down on them as they worked, their every movement echoing in the empty space.

Then, from the shadows, they heard it—the soft, familiar sound of footsteps, coming closer, circling them. The figure began to materialize, a twisted silhouette emerging from the darkness, her form barely visible in the flickering candlelight.

Margaret.

Her face was hollow, her eyes dark and endless, filled with a malice that sent a chill through them both. She stepped forward, her voice a low, rasping whisper that seemed to echo from every corner of the attic.

"You think you can drive me out?" she hissed, her eyes narrowing. "This is my home. I built this. You... are nothing but guests."

Peter held the mirror up, angling it toward her, and Margaret recoiled, her form flickering, distorting as though the reflection was disrupting her presence. She let out a guttural scream, her figure contorting, the shadows swirling around her as she tried to retreat.

Emily stepped forward, her voice steady. "You don't belong here, Margaret. You've taken enough. It's time to let go."

Margaret's form flickered, twisting, her face a mask of rage and desperation. "I cannot leave. I *will not leave.* I... will live forever!"

But as the words left her mouth, her form began to dissolve, breaking apart as the mirror's reflection fractured her image. The shadows shifted, the room filling with a howling wind that seemed to come from within the walls, rattling the floorboards, shaking the house to its foundation.

The wind died down, and Margaret's form faded, dissolving into the air, leaving behind only a faint, lingering whisper that echoed through the empty attic.

"Forever..."

When the last trace of Margaret's presence vanished, the house fell silent, the oppressive weight lifting, replaced by a calm that felt almost surreal. Emily and Peter stood in the attic, their breaths coming in shallow gasps, the realization slowly sinking in.

The house was finally still.

They returned to the first floor, the sense of dread that had filled the house replaced by a quiet, almost peaceful silence. They knew that Margaret's presence had been broken, her grip on the house severed, her spirit finally forced to release its hold on the living.

In the days that followed, they felt a lightness return to the house, a warmth that hadn't been there before. They had reclaimed their home, freed it from the dark legacy that had haunted it for decades.

But sometimes, in the quiet hours of the night, when the wind brushed against the windows and shadows gathered in the corners, they could still hear it—a faint, echoing whisper, a reminder of the woman who had refused to leave, who had chosen to linger in the darkness, desperate to escape the one thing even she could not outrun.

Death.

The End

20
THE TROPHY HUNTER

David Warren sat in his grand study, a room dimly lit by the fading evening light that crept in through the bay window. The walls around him were lined with his most prized possessions—mounted heads and lifelike figures of creatures from every corner of the globe. A lion's fierce snarl was forever frozen under a glass case to his left, while a massive elephant's head loomed above the fireplace, its tusks gleaming in the low light. Each trophy represented a conquest, a memory of adrenaline, dominance, and a thrill he hadn't felt in years.

David had always been drawn to hunting. The thrill of the chase, the sense of power that coursed through him as he stalked his prey, had fueled his entire life. Wealth, prestige, and accomplishment—all had come as natural byproducts of his relentless ambition. Hunting was no mere sport for him; it was an art form, a way to express his control over the natural world. But lately, he'd felt a gnawing emptiness. He'd hunted and conquered everything there was, from the Big Five in Africa to the rarest creatures he could legally track. Each new hunt had left him with a more fleeting satisfaction than the last.

But tonight, as he stared into the dimly lit eyes of his trophies, he felt nothing.

He had poured himself a glass of aged scotch, savoring its warmth, his thoughts dark and unshakable. What more was there? He'd exhausted the limits of what the world could offer, he thought, swirling the amber liquid in his glass. His heart, once electrified by the thrill of danger and death, now beat sluggishly, dulled by the repetition of past hunts. He needed a challenge, something that would make his blood race again, make his hands steady with purpose.

It was then that a thought, dark and unbidden, crossed his mind.

He let it linger, turning the idea over in his mind, feeling a rush of excitement bloom within him for the first time in years. He wanted the ultimate trophy, something that would be unlike anything in his collection. His mind raced, his pulse quickening as the thought solidified, becoming a tantalizing notion that he couldn't ignore. The answer was simple yet horrifyingly clear: *He would hunt a human.*

Once the seed of the idea was planted, it was impossible to shake. David's every thought revolved around it, growing more detailed, more intoxicating. This would be his masterpiece. The most dangerous, the most rewarding hunt of his life. But he knew that, unlike his previous hunts, this one would need to be handled with the utmost precision and secrecy. There would be no taxidermy shop, no brash displays of his work—this would be his private triumph, a secret only he would savor.

David's life of wealth and status afforded him luxuries that the average man couldn't dream of, and he had connections in dark corners around the world. Through subtle inquiries and anonymous messages, he reached out to underground networks, searching for anyone who might be able to assist him in such a unique pursuit. The logistics would be critical—he couldn't simply choose any random target. He needed someone who would be both a challenge and a worthy addition to his private collection.

After weeks of planning and waiting, a lead emerged. A contact from an exclusive, off-the-grid hunting club responded to his request. They specialized in "unique game," the man said in the message. David's pulse raced as he read it, his hands shaking with excitement as he followed the instructions to an encrypted chat.

"I hear you're looking for the ultimate prey," the message began. "We can arrange that, for the right price. Are you ready to pay?"

David didn't hesitate. "Money is no object," he replied. "I want this to be done right. I want the prey to be chosen carefully, and I want to be assured that this will be worth my time."

There was a pause before the next message arrived. "Understood. Meet us at the coordinates provided. Bring no one, and do not leave a trace of your travel. We'll take it from there."

David felt a thrill he hadn't experienced since his early hunting days, when he'd been new to the game, driven by pure ambition. He committed the coordinates to memory, the location remote and unfamiliar, and deleted the message without a second thought. This hunt, he told himself, would be the pinnacle of his life's work.

A week later, David found himself in a secluded lodge deep in the mountains. Snow dusted the surrounding landscape, and an eerie silence hung in the air as he waited for his contact. The lodge was rustic but well-kept, with the smell of aged wood and the flicker of a fire casting shadows over the walls. His heart beat steadily, his senses on high alert.

Finally, the door opened, and a tall man with piercing eyes and an aura of dangerous calm entered the room. He was dressed in dark, unmarked clothing, his expression cool and calculated as he extended a hand.

"Mr. Warren," he said, his voice low and measured. "You may call me Alastair. I understand you're looking for something... extraordinary."

David nodded, trying to conceal his anticipation. "Yes. I want a hunt that will test my skills to the limit. I want a prey that will fight back."

Alastair smiled, a chilling smile that hinted at a lifetime of secrets and a willingness to cross any line. "You're in the right place. We have a network of clients like you—people who appreciate the ultimate hunt, the thrill of pursuing the most challenging game of all. We can arrange a human hunt, but I must warn you—this will be unlike anything you've ever experienced. Once we start, there's no turning back."

David felt his pulse quicken, the thrill flooding his veins. "I'm ready."

Alastair gestured for him to sit, and as they settled into their seats, he laid out the rules of the hunt.

"Our hunts are carefully curated, Mr. Warren. We select candidates who are physically capable, individuals who will provide a challenge. They're taken discreetly, no one to miss them, and we give them a chance—a small one, but a chance—to survive."

David's eyes gleamed. "And if they survive?"

"They're allowed to live, free of charge," Alastair said, his gaze steady. "But let's just say... that outcome is exceedingly rare. Most can't handle the pressure. They break, they flee, they make mistakes. That's where you come in. You're free to hunt them, to do what you wish. The only rule is that the trophy remains your secret. No one outside our circle must ever know."

The thrill of the chase, the ultimate challenge, a trophy no one else could ever claim. It was exactly what David wanted.

"When does the hunt begin?" he asked, his voice barely more than a whisper.

Alastair's smile widened. "Tonight. Our prey is already in the forest, a mile from here. The only question is whether you're ready, Mr. Warren."

David didn't hesitate. He stood, adrenaline coursing through him. "I was born ready."

Dressed in his hunting gear, David moved silently through the dense forest, the only sound his steady breathing and the faint crunch of snow beneath his boots. The moon was high, casting an eerie glow over the landscape, and his rifle was loaded, primed for the kill.

Every nerve in his body was electrified, his senses heightened as he scanned the shadows, listening for any sound, any movement that might give away his prey. This was what he lived for—the thrill of the hunt, the pursuit of something dangerous, something that could turn the tables at any moment.

He moved deeper into the trees, feeling the weight of the silence, the tension mounting with each step. And then, he heard it—a faint rustling, the snap of a branch, followed by hurried footsteps.

He froze, his pulse pounding as he raised his rifle, his eyes narrowing as he searched for the source of the sound. There, just beyond the reach of the moonlight, he caught a glimpse of his prey—a young man, dressed in simple, tattered clothes, his eyes wide with fear as he darted between the trees, glancing back with a look of pure terror.

David's heart raced, a thrill surging through him as he watched the man stumble, struggle to regain his footing, his face etched with desperation. This was it—the ultimate hunt, the moment he had been waiting for. He took aim, his finger hovering over the trigger, savoring the anticipation, the power, the control.

But as he steadied himself, something strange happened. The man turned, his gaze locking onto David's, and for a brief moment, their eyes met. There was something haunting, almost pleading, in the man's expression, a raw humanity that pierced through the thrill, filling David with a flicker of doubt.

For the first time, he felt the weight of what he was about to do, the reality of taking a life—not an animal, not a beast, but a human being. The thrill faded, replaced by a chilling awareness of the man's terror, his helplessness.

But the moment passed as quickly as it had come. David took a deep breath, steadying himself, dismissing the doubt that lingered in the back of his mind.

This was what he had wanted, the ultimate test, the greatest trophy.

He pulled the trigger.

The forest echoed with the sound of the shot, a sharp crack that shattered the silence, and David felt a twisted satisfaction as he watched his prey fall, his body crumpling to the ground, lifeless.

The thrill returned, colder and sharper than ever, as he approached the fallen man, a sense of triumph flooding him as he realized that he had finally claimed his ultimate trophy.

But as he stood over the lifeless body, the man's haunting gaze seemed to linger, a shadow in the night, a reminder that this hunt had come at a cost, a darkness that would follow him long after the thrill had faded.

The adrenaline from the hunt lingered in David's veins long after he returned to his estate. He felt alive, rejuvenated, more invigorated than he had in years. The man's lifeless body, now stored away in a hidden, climate-controlled room in his basement, was proof of his prowess, a testament to his dominance. This was what he had wanted—a trophy unlike any other. And yet, a strange unease gnawed at him, a haunting echo that filled the stillness of his grand mansion.

David brushed it off at first, attributing it to the novelty of this particular kill. But as the days passed, the unease grew, festering in the back of his mind. He found himself returning to the basement, standing over the lifeless body, the man's face frozen in that final moment of fear. In the dim light, the man's eyes seemed to watch him, accusing, as if challenging him from beyond the grave. David could feel a chill creeping over him each time he entered the room, a cold that seeped into his bones and left him unsettled.

He had always been meticulous in preserving his trophies. But this one—this human—was different. He had his taxidermist friend, Tom, take care of the body, offering a hefty sum to ensure discretion. Tom had worked with him for years, stuffing and mounting the most exotic of David's kills. But when David revealed the nature of this newest acquisition, even Tom, who had seen it all, looked at him with a mixture of shock and discomfort.

"You really want to go through with this?" Tom had asked, his eyes narrowing as he examined David.

David had simply nodded, his tone sharp. "Just do what I asked. And keep your mouth shut."

Yet, despite his initial confidence, doubt crept in like a shadow, slowly consuming his thoughts. He couldn't shake the image of the man's pleading gaze, couldn't ignore the lingering feeling that he had crossed a line from which he could never return.

It started with whispers. Soft, unintelligible murmurs that seemed to echo through the halls of his mansion, drifting up from the basement late at night. David would lie in bed, his mind restless, his body tense, as the whispers grew louder, filling his room with a low, constant hum. He tried to tell himself it was his imagination, a trick of his guilty conscience, but the whispers persisted, growing clearer with each passing night.

One night, as he lay in the darkness, he heard his name.

"David..."

The voice was faint, barely more than a whisper, but it sent a chill through him, a prickling sensation that crawled down his spine. He sat up, his heart racing, his eyes scanning the shadows that filled his room. The house was silent, but the voice lingered, an echo that seemed to emanate from the walls themselves.

He tried to ignore it, dismissing it as a product of his mind, the inevitable result of pushing boundaries no one was meant to cross. But the next night, it happened again.

And this time, the voice was clearer, louder, as if someone were standing right beside him.

"David... why?"

The question hung in the air, each syllable a chilling accusation that seemed to burrow into his mind. He could feel the weight of the man's gaze in the darkness, a suffocating presence that filled the room, leaving him cold and trembling.

The voice was relentless, filling his nights with accusations, questions, and the haunting echo of his own name. Sleep became elusive, and David found himself haunted by memories of the man's last moments, the look in his eyes as he pulled the trigger. The thrill that had once consumed him was gone, replaced by a growing sense of dread, a feeling that he had awakened something dark and unforgiving.

Days turned to weeks, and the darkness within David grew. The whispers were no longer confined to the night; he heard them in the silence of his study, in the echoing halls of his mansion, in the creak of the floorboards beneath his feet. They were everywhere, a constant reminder of the life he had taken, the line he had crossed.

Desperation drove him back to the basement, to the room where his "trophy" now stood, fully preserved and mounted, displayed as though it were a masterpiece. But what had once filled him with pride now filled him with dread. The man's eyes, lifeless yet hauntingly expressive, seemed to follow him, accusing, condemning.

David found himself speaking to it, trying to justify his actions, to explain the thrill, the need for a challenge, for a hunt that would truly test him.

"You were... you were meant to be a masterpiece," he whispered, his voice cracking as he stared into the vacant eyes. "You were... you were the ultimate trophy."

But the words sounded hollow, empty, and he could feel the darkness creeping in, filling the room with a cold that left him shivering.

The whispers grew louder, more insistent, until they were no longer whispers but voices—angry, pleading, filled with pain and accusation. They echoed through the mansion, a cacophony of voices that left him clutching his head, desperate for silence, for escape.

He tried to drown them out, drinking himself into a stupor each night, but the voices persisted, filling his mind with images of his past hunts, each kill flashing before his eyes, each animal's gaze searing into him, a reminder of his relentless pursuit of dominance, of power.

But now, he was the one hunted, haunted by the lives he had claimed, by the ultimate trophy that had become his ultimate nightmare.

One night, as he stumbled through the mansion, his mind clouded by alcohol and fear, he heard a new sound—a slow, deliberate knock coming from the basement door. The sound echoed through the silent mansion, each knock a heavy, measured beat that filled him with a terror he couldn't explain.

"David..." the voice whispered, the sound echoing up from the basement, filling the halls with a cold, haunting presence. "Come down..."

He felt compelled, drawn to the door, his feet moving of their own accord as he made his way down the dimly lit stairs. The air grew colder with each step, the darkness thickening, pressing down on him, suffocating.

When he reached the basement, he found himself standing before his trophy, the man's figure looming in the shadows, his eyes seeming to glow in the faint light. David's breath caught, his heart pounding as he stared into the face of the man he had hunted, the man whose life he had claimed for the sake of a thrill.

And then, in the silence, the man's mouth moved, his lifeless lips forming a single word, a final, damning question.

"Why?"

The word filled the room, a haunting echo that reverberated through the darkness, leaving David frozen, his mind unraveling, his sanity slipping away.

He stumbled back, his hands clutching his head, his thoughts consumed by the voices, the accusations, the guilt that clawed at his mind. The darkness closed in, filling his vision, swallowing him whole as the voices grew louder, drowning out his thoughts, his memories, his very sense of self.

In the weeks that followed, David's mansion grew silent, its halls empty, its rooms cold and untouched. No one saw him again, and rumors began to circulate—a man who had finally become the prey, haunted by the darkness he had unleashed.

The mansion stood as a silent testament to his descent, a monument to the thrill that had driven him, and the darkness that had claimed him in the end.

And in the basement, in the dim light, the ultimate trophy waited, a reminder of a man's ambition turned nightmare, a warning to those who dared seek the thrill of the forbidden.

The townspeople began whispering about the strange happenings at Hollowcrest Manor. David Warren's mansion, once a symbol of wealth and success, had turned into an ominous relic, shrouded in mystery. Servants no longer came and went; visitors were turned away. No lights ever flickered from the windows at night, yet there was a constant, chilling presence that seemed to loom over the estate.

Neighbors reported hearing faint noises from the manor's direction—echoing knocks, low murmurs, and sometimes, the blood-curdling sound of a man crying out in the night. The groundskeeper, one of the last to maintain the estate, spoke of shadows moving within, though he never saw David himself.

In the following weeks, rumors spread that David had gone mad. The few people who dared approach the estate claimed they'd seen him pacing the windows late at night, his face gaunt and hollow, muttering to himself. He had aged visibly, the lines on his face deepening, his skin taking on an ashen hue as though he were decaying from the inside out.

Inside the mansion, David was locked in his own personal hell. The voices had grown louder, more insistent, filling every corner of his mind, leaving him no escape. He couldn't sleep, couldn't eat, couldn't find a moment of peace. Every time he closed his eyes, he saw the faces of those he'd hunted—the lion, the rhino, the hippo, the elephant—each one transformed, twisting into something darker, their expressions a mixture of fear and accusation.

And always, at the center of it all, was the man—the ultimate trophy, the face that haunted him with unending scrutiny, his eyes hollow, his mouth twisted in silent reproach.

David had begun keeping a journal, the only outlet he had left for the spiraling chaos within his mind. At first, his entries were brief, disjointed ramblings about his sleepless nights and the growing unease that seemed to grip him tighter with each passing day.

January 15: I can still hear him. Even in the silence, he is there. Watching. Waiting.

January 23: The voices won't stop. The man... he's here. I feel him. I tried moving the trophy, but it changes nothing. The eyes... they follow me.

The entries grew darker, more frantic, and by early February, his writing was barely legible, scrawled in uneven lines across the pages. He wrote of seeing the man's figure standing at the foot of his bed, of hearing footsteps echoing through the halls, of whispers filling his ears like a swarm of insects.

February 3: He's in the walls. I hear him. Every room. I can't escape him.

February 6: Tried locking the door. It doesn't matter. He's here... he is everywhere. I am his prey.

Desperate for answers, David turned to the occult, scouring ancient texts and summoning rituals that promised protection against restless spirits. He ordered talismans, amulets, anything that claimed to ward off the dead. But none of it worked. If anything, the haunting only intensified, the voices growing louder, more visceral, filling his mind with the haunting refrain of a single word:

Why?

The question was relentless, echoing through his thoughts, gnawing at his sanity. He had no answer, nothing to give the tortured soul he had claimed. He had taken a life for the thrill of it, for a fleeting moment of satisfaction. But now, that satisfaction had soured, leaving him hollow, consumed by the very darkness he had unleashed.

One night, in a fit of madness, David tore through the mansion, ripping down portraits, shattering glass, anything to drown out the voices. He stumbled into his study, panting, his hands shaking as he clutched the edge of his desk. The moonlight cast an eerie glow across the room, illuminating his trophies—the animals he had hunted and displayed with pride.

But now, their faces seemed twisted, grotesque, their once-fierce expressions now filled with a sinister mockery, as if they were watching him, relishing his torment.

He turned toward a full-length mirror in the corner, catching a glimpse of his own reflection. What he saw made him stumble back in horror. His face was pale, his eyes sunken, haunted by a madness that had transformed him into something almost unrecognizable. He looked like the man he had hunted—hollow, drained of life, a ghostly figure trapped in his own skin.

And then, as he stared, his reflection began to change. The man appeared beside him in the mirror, his eyes lifeless, his face frozen in that final, accusing expression. David screamed, stumbling backward, his heart racing as the reflection watched him with a calm, unyielding gaze.

"Why?" the reflection whispered, its voice filling the room.

David's knees buckled, his hands clutching his head as the voices grew louder, each one echoing the same question, a relentless chorus that filled his mind with the weight of his guilt.

"I... I don't know!" he screamed, his voice raw, desperate. "I did it because... because I wanted to! Because I needed... something more!"

But his answer only seemed to fuel the voices, their anger intensifying, their accusations growing louder, filling every corner of his mind.

Days turned into nights, and David lost track of time, his existence reduced to a blur of darkness and despair. He wandered the mansion, muttering to himself, his mind fractured, consumed by the spirits that haunted him. His body grew weak, his eyes hollow, his hands trembling as he clung to the walls, his mind slipping further into madness.

One night, he found himself drawn to the basement, the room where he had kept the man's body, his ultimate trophy. The air was thick with the stench of decay, the darkness pressing down on him as he stumbled forward, his eyes wild, his breath shallow.

The room was empty now, the trophy gone, but he could still feel the man's presence, a lingering shadow that filled the space, a weight that left him gasping for breath.

And then he heard it—the sound of footsteps, soft, deliberate, moving closer.

David turned, his eyes wide with terror as he saw the man standing in the doorway, his figure silhouetted against the darkness, his gaze filled with a cold, unyielding fury.

"Why?" the man whispered, his voice low, filled with a sorrow and anger that pierced David's heart.

David fell to his knees, his hands clutching his head, his mind unraveling as he tried to answer, tried to find some justification, some meaning for what he had done.

But there was none.

The man stepped closer, his eyes locking onto David's, a haunting, unbreakable gaze that filled him with a terror he had never known. David felt the darkness closing in, felt the weight of his actions pressing down on him, crushing him, consuming him.

And in that final moment, as the man reached out, his hand cold and unforgiving, David understood.

He was the trophy now.

The hunted had become the hunter, and David, trapped in his own darkness, was left with nothing but the echo of his own guilt, the relentless question that would haunt him for eternity.

"Why?"

The townspeople noticed the mansion had grown silent. The whispers of strange noises and lights had ceased, and the once-imposing estate now stood as a cold, hollow shell. When a local servant finally braved the front door, she found the house empty, dust settling over the once-grand halls, the air thick with an unshakable chill.

David Warren was never seen again.

The only trace of him was a single, haunting portrait in his study—a painting of a man with lifeless eyes, staring into an empty void, his expression a mixture of fear and regret.

And beneath it, scrawled in fading ink, was a single word:

Why.

The End

21
THE WITCHING HOUR

The town of Eldergrove was quiet that night, nestled under a thick layer of fog that clung to the streets and pressed against windows, as though trying to seep into the homes themselves. Midnight had come and gone, and most of the townspeople were asleep, their breaths falling in sync with the rhythm of the clock tower, its hands inching closer to three in the morning.

But not everyone was sleeping.

At exactly 2:57 a.m., every light in Eldergrove flickered, plunging the town into a moment of darkness so complete that even the moon seemed to disappear. Street lamps blinked, porch lights faded, and for three seconds, the only sound was the faint, electric hum of things that should have stayed quiet.

Then, at 2:58, the lights returned, casting an eerie glow over the silent streets. But something had changed, an almost imperceptible shift that pressed down on the town with a cold, malevolent presence. It was a feeling the townspeople never spoke of, a fear that lingered just at the edge of their minds—a fear of *the Witching Hour*, when darkness ruled, and the veil between the living and the dead grew thin.

That night, one house at the edge of town remained awake. In the parlor, beneath the dim light of a single lamp, sat a newcomer, a young woman named Mara Caldwell. She'd moved to Eldergrove just a week ago, eager for the quiet life that the small, secluded town promised. But since her arrival, she hadn't felt the peace she'd sought. Something about Eldergrove unnerved her—its deserted streets, the way the locals averted their eyes when they saw her, how they refused to speak about anything that happened after dark.

Mara sat in her armchair, sipping tea, her gaze fixed on the old grandfather clock in the corner. Its rhythmic tick-tock was her only companion, filling the room with a steady, pulsing beat that kept her grounded.

But as the clock struck 2:59, the ticking seemed to slow, dragging out the seconds, stretching time like a rubber band about to snap. Mara blinked, wondering if she was imagining it. The air grew thick, a chill creeping up her spine as the final second ticked toward three.

At precisely 3:00 a.m., a sharp knock echoed through the house.

She froze, her heartbeat quickening as the knock came again, louder, more insistent, each rap heavy and measured, like a call from something that waited in the dark.

It was an odd hour for visitors, but something compelled her to answer. She crossed the room, each step hesitant, as though some part of her knew this was no ordinary guest. She opened the door, the chill from outside hitting her like a slap.

On her doorstep stood a woman, tall and thin, dressed in a dark cloak that flowed around her like shadows. Her face was partially hidden beneath a hood, but Mara could see her eyes—dark, piercing, filled with an intensity that made her stomach twist.

"Good evening," the stranger said, her voice low, almost musical. "Or rather... good morning."

Mara shivered, unable to find her voice, her hand gripping the doorknob tightly.

"May I come in?" the woman asked, her lips curving into a faint smile that didn't reach her eyes.

Every instinct in Mara's body screamed at her to say no, to shut the door and lock it, to put as much distance as she could between herself and this woman. But her mouth moved of its own accord, the words slipping out in a whisper.

"Please... come in."

The woman stepped over the threshold, her movements fluid, graceful, as though she were gliding rather than walking. She looked around the room with a curious gaze, her fingers trailing along the edges of furniture, lingering on the old grandfather clock, which seemed to tick slower and slower with each second.

"You have a lovely home," she said, her tone polite, but there was something in her voice, a dark undercurrent that sent a shiver down Mara's spine.

"Thank you," Mara replied, her voice barely above a whisper. "But... I don't think I know you."

The woman's smile widened, and for a brief moment, her eyes seemed to flash, reflecting the dim light in a way that was almost inhuman.

"Oh, you know me," she said, her voice a soft, lilting whisper. "Everyone does, though most would rather forget. I am here only in the quietest hours, when the world is silent, when the barriers grow thin... and when I am invited."

Mara felt her breath catch, a strange pressure settling in her chest, her heart pounding as the woman stepped closer, her eyes never leaving Mara's face.

"Tell me, Mara," the woman continued, her voice barely more than a whisper, "do you know what happens during the Witching Hour?"

Mara swallowed, her throat dry, the fear clawing at her mind. She had heard stories, whispers in town about strange things that happened in Eldergrove. Disappearances, sightings of figures drifting through the fog, strange sounds that echoed through the empty streets. But none of the townspeople would give her a straight answer, and over the days, she'd brushed it off as superstitious nonsense.

"No... I don't know," she whispered, her voice trembling.

The woman tilted her head, a glint of amusement in her eyes. "They didn't tell you, did they?" she asked softly. "They never do. And yet they know, all of them. They know that Eldergrove is a place of secrets, a place where the Witching Hour holds sway."

She reached out, her fingers brushing Mara's cheek, the touch cold as ice. Mara shivered, feeling an energy seep into her, filling her with a fear that went beyond anything she'd ever known.

"Tonight, you will see," the woman whispered, her voice soft, almost tender. "Tonight, the veil will lift, and you will understand."

As the clock struck 3:01, a deep, resounding chime echoed through the house, the sound vibrating in Mara's bones, filling her mind with a sense of dread so intense she could barely breathe. She felt the room darken, shadows thickening, the walls seeming to close in around her.

The woman's face twisted, her eyes darkening as she leaned close, her breath cold against Mara's skin.

"Tonight, you will learn the truth of the Witching Hour," she said, her voice barely more than a hiss. "You will see what lies beyond, what waits in the shadows, what hungers for the living..."

The air grew thick with darkness, the woman's features blurring, becoming indistinct, a shadow that seemed to seep into the walls, filling every corner, every crevice, every shadowed part of the room. Mara felt a weight pressing down on her, her body growing cold, her vision fading, and in that moment, she understood that this woman was no ordinary visitor.

She was something else, something ancient, something that had existed long before the town, before the houses, before the lives of those who had come to inhabit Eldergrove.

Mara's eyes fluttered, her vision blurring as the shadows swallowed her, and she felt herself slipping into darkness, her thoughts fading, her mind overwhelmed by the terror that had filled her heart.

As the Witching Hour continued, the town lay silent, each house steeped in shadows, each inhabitant lost in dreams that were not their own. And in the quiet, in the darkness, something old and malevolent moved, watching, waiting, as the clock ticked on, its hands marking the final seconds of the Witching Hour.

And for Mara, the darkness would hold her, keeping her secrets, as the veil between worlds slowly lowered, leaving only the faintest whisper lingering in the air, a warning to all who dared to listen:

Beware the Witching Hour.

The next morning, Eldergrove seemed almost peaceful, its streets bathed in the soft light of dawn. But for Mara, peace was a distant memory. The events of the night had left her shaken, her mind filled with fragmented memories of shadows that twisted and whispered, of the cold touch of the stranger's hand, and the weight of darkness pressing down on her soul.

Despite her fear, an inexplicable compulsion drove her to learn more, to uncover the truth behind the stranger's words, behind the Witching Hour. She needed answers, and there was only one place to find them.

Eldergrove's library was an old building nestled at the edge of town, a relic of a time long past. Its walls were covered in ivy, the bricks weathered and cracked, and inside, the smell of dust and old paper hung thick in the air. Mara spent hours combing through records, reading every history book, every scrap of folklore she could find on the town. But Eldergrove's history was carefully curated, each record merely hinting at the darker truths hidden beneath its quaint exterior.

Finally, tucked away in a forgotten corner of the library, she found it—a leather-bound journal covered in layers of dust, its pages yellowed with age. The handwriting was cramped and hurried, as though the writer had been too afraid to linger on the words for long.

The author was a man named Walter Hawthorne, one of Eldergrove's earliest settlers, and his entries were filled with a strange mix of fascination and terror.

The journal's entries grew more frantic as Walter described his first encounters with the strange phenomena that seemed to settle over Eldergrove each night at three a.m.—the Witching Hour. He wrote of a shadowy presence that prowled the streets, a force that appeared only at the edges of vision, slipping through the darkness, silent yet palpable. According to Walter, the presence was something ancient, something that had existed long before the settlers had built their homes, a force that had claimed Eldergrove as its own.

"This thing," Walter wrote, *"isn't human, nor has it ever been. It wears a form, a cloak of flesh and shadow, but it is no more human than a nightmare. I have seen it, heard its whispers, felt its eyes upon me. It lingers in the shadows, moving between worlds, waiting for the Witching Hour to draw thin the veil between the living and the dead."*

Mara felt a chill as she read, her eyes scanning the entries, each one more disturbing than the last. Walter had documented the townspeople's superstitions, their fears, and the strange rituals they performed in secret, leaving offerings of herbs and charms at their doorsteps, hoping to ward off the entity that walked their streets in the dark.

But it was a later entry that made her breath catch.

"The people of Eldergrove know it by many names—the Shadow, the Hunger, the Watcher—but the one they whisper most is 'the Veiled One.' It wears a face only when invited, slipping through the cracks, weaving itself into the lives of those who dare open the door when it knocks."

Mara's mind raced, recalling the face of the woman who had appeared at her door, the intense gaze, the words that seemed to chill the air itself. The Veiled One, the ancient force that haunted Eldergrove, had knocked on her door, drawn to her as though it knew her, as though it had waited for her.

She turned the page, her hands trembling, her eyes skimming over the words. Walter had written of people who had gone missing, of disappearances that had gone unexplained, people who had last been seen speaking to a stranger in the dead of night, their faces twisted in fear.

"Those who answer the knock," Walter wrote, *"do not return the same. They come back hollow, as though something of themselves has been taken, leaving them a shadow of who they once were. Others are never seen again, vanishing as though swallowed by the darkness itself."*

As she read, a sense of dread filled her, memories of the previous night returning with renewed clarity—the strange feeling of compulsion, the way her mouth had moved on its own, inviting the stranger inside. Mara realized with a sickening certainty that the Veiled One had chosen her, had marked her, and that it was far from finished.

Walter's final entry was brief, his handwriting shaky and erratic.

"The Veiled One grows bolder with each passing night, as though feeding on those who vanish, growing stronger, darker. I hear it knocking on my door now, its voice whispering my name, promising secrets I dare not learn. I can resist it no longer. Perhaps if I answer, it will take me and leave the town in peace."

Mara closed the journal, her heart racing, her mind racing with the implications of what she had read. Walter had answered the knock, had invited the Veiled One inside, and he had never been seen again. She felt a chill settle over her, the realization dawning that she had done the same, that she had invited this ancient force into her life, bound herself to it by some dark, unbreakable pact.

The library seemed to close in around her, the shadows darkening, pressing down, filling the room with an oppressive weight. She hurried out, her mind filled with the horrific knowledge that the Veiled One would return, drawn by her invitation, bound to her by a power she couldn't understand.

That night, Mara sat alone in her darkened home, her heart pounding as the clock ticked closer to three. She had lit every lamp, filled every corner with light, but she knew it would do no good. The Veiled One would come for her, drawn to the pact they had made, its presence slipping through the shadows, moving through the quiet streets of Eldergrove.

The clock struck 3:00 a.m., and once more, the lights flickered, plunging her into darkness. She heard the faint sound of footsteps outside, slow, measured, the weight of them filling the silence, echoing through her home. And then, just as it had the night before, a sharp knock echoed through the room, a sound that seemed to reverberate through her very bones.

Mara took a shaky breath, her hand clutching the edge of the table, her mind racing with fear. She could feel it now—the presence waiting just outside her door, an ancient force that lingered at the edge of reality, drawn to the thin veil that separated their worlds.

And then, through the silence, she heard it—a voice, low and soft, filled with a dark, malevolent amusement.

"Open the door, Mara," it whispered, the sound drifting through the walls, filling the room with a chill that stole her breath. "Let me in, and I will show you secrets beyond your understanding. I will grant you knowledge, power... all you need to do is open the door."

She froze, her heart pounding, her mind filled with the memory of Walter's journal, the warning he had left behind. But the voice grew more insistent, filling her mind, weaving through her thoughts like a dark spell, a promise that seemed to seep into her very soul.

"You invited me once," the Veiled One whispered, its tone coaxing, inviting. "Now, open the door, and let us complete the pact. Let me in, and I will make you one of mine."

Mara clutched her head, the words filling her mind, drowning out her fear, her thoughts blurring, her resolve crumbling as the darkness pressed in, the voice winding through her, binding her to its call. She took a step toward the door, her hand reaching out, her body moving of its own accord, the compulsion too strong to resist.

And then, just as her hand brushed the doorknob, she heard another sound—a faint, almost imperceptible whisper, a voice from within herself, a warning that broke through the fog in her mind.

"Don't let it in..."

She froze, the reality of the horror that awaited her cutting through the Veiled One's whispers, filling her with a renewed sense of fear. She backed away, her eyes fixed on the door, her heart pounding as the voice on the other side grew darker, more insistent.

"You cannot hide from me, Mara," the Veiled One hissed, its voice filled with a venom that sent chills through her. "I am bound to you now. And when the next Witching Hour arrives, I will return."

The shadows seemed to recede, the room growing still, the weight of the Veiled One's presence lifting, leaving behind only the lingering chill of its promise.

As dawn broke, Mara sat alone in her darkened home, her mind filled with the knowledge that the Veiled One was bound to her, that it would return, and that her only hope was to find a way to break the pact before the next Witching Hour.

Mara's sleep was haunted by whispers, shadows pressing in around her, promises of knowledge and power from a voice she knew all too well. The Veiled One's words lingered in her mind even as dawn broke, and when she awoke, she was driven by a single, urgent purpose: to understand how Eldergrove had come to harbor this dark entity—and how to break the bond before the next Witching Hour.

Returning to the library, Mara made her way to the deepest shelves, searching for anything that might shed light on Eldergrove's past. The library held an array of old texts on local history, forgotten legends, even rumors of occult practices whispered about the town's founders. Tucked away in a dusty corner, she found a brittle, leather-bound book entitled *The Hidden Histories of Eldergrove*. Its pages were yellowed, crumbling at the edges, as though the knowledge inside had been kept hidden for a reason.

She sat down, flipping carefully through the pages, her heart racing as the story of Eldergrove's origins began to unfold.

The book detailed the town's founding in the early 1700s, when a group of settlers fleeing persecution had arrived, seeking a place to practice their beliefs without fear. These settlers were not like others—they were devout practitioners of mysticism and occult practices, those who had sought communion with the forces of nature and, more dangerously, with the entities that existed beyond the veil.

They had chosen Eldergrove for its remoteness, the thickness of its forests, and the way the mist clung to the land like a protective shroud. But the settlers quickly learned that they were not alone in Eldergrove. Strange happenings began soon after they arrived: flickering lights that danced through the trees, shadows that seemed to move of their own accord, and whispers that filled the air during the dark hours of the night.

As Mara read on, a chilling realization dawned on her—the settlers hadn't fled to Eldergrove by chance. They had been drawn to it, compelled to settle on ground where they believed an ancient, powerful entity slumbered. They referred to this entity as "the Veiled One," an ageless force that watched over the land and had existed long before the first settlers had arrived.

"It is neither living nor dead," an early passage read, *"but something between, a guardian of the unseen. We are its keepers, and in return, it will protect us, granting us knowledge, power, and a life beyond the limitations of flesh."*

Eldergrove's founding settlers, desperate to survive in the isolated, hostile land, struck a bargain with the Veiled One. They would honor it with ritual offerings, their souls and devotion, in exchange for protection and prosperity. Each year, they would leave gifts at the edge of the forest—herbs, rare stones, and even blood sacrifices, feeding the Veiled One with small fragments of their lives, keeping its hunger at bay.

But the settlers were ambitious, and their thirst for knowledge grew. Within a decade, the rituals intensified, and they sought ways to commune directly with the Veiled One, to bind themselves to its power in life and in death. They held ceremonies under the cloak of night, entering trances to connect with the spirit world, pulling back the veil and allowing the Veiled One to slip into their lives, to merge with their existence.

An entry in the book caught Mara's attention, its tone more frantic than the others:

"To live beyond life is to be bound, neither dead nor living. We have given ourselves, but the Veiled One is never satisfied. It demands more with each passing generation, its hunger growing insatiable, a darkness that cannot be filled."

The Veiled One's pact became a curse, and Eldergrove's settlers soon realized they had invited something far darker than they had understood. The entity's visits, once restricted to annual offerings, grew more frequent, each appearance marked by a thick fog and a chill that seeped into their bones.

Eventually, the settlers noticed a pattern: each night, precisely at 3:00 a.m., the Veiled One would appear, stepping out from the shadows, moving among them, watching, waiting. They called it the Witching Hour, a time when the Veiled One's power was at its peak, when it could reach through the veil and pull the townspeople into its grasp.

Mara felt a cold shiver as she read, the words ringing eerily close to her own experience. The settlers had done everything to appease the Veiled One, to contain its power, but they had learned too late that their pact was unbreakable, binding them and their descendants to its whims.

The later entries in *The Hidden Histories of Eldergrove* took on a darker, desperate tone, detailing the settlers' attempts to undo the pact, to seal the Veiled One back into the void from which it had come. They had consulted ancient texts, performed grueling rituals, but nothing worked. They could only lessen its power, diminish its influence by warning others, passing down the rituals, and keeping the town isolated from outsiders.

One final entry caught Mara's eye, dated in the late 1750s, written by one of the last surviving elders of the original settlers:

"We are bound to it, we and all who come after us. No barrier can hold it back, no ritual can weaken it. We have tried, and still, it returns each night. It will take what it desires, claim those it chooses, until Eldergrove itself has withered to dust. Only when the last of us has fallen will it finally be free."

The Veiled One had turned Eldergrove into its hunting ground, feeding off the fear, the lives, the very essence of those who dared to invite it in. Mara understood, with a sickening dread, that her own invitation had marked her as its next prey. The knowledge she had gained only confirmed her worst fear—the Veiled One would return at the next Witching Hour, drawn by the bond they now shared.

As she closed the book, she noticed something tucked into its back cover—a small, folded piece of parchment, faded and worn. Carefully unfolding it, Mara saw it was a map, scrawled in ink, marking a path through the forest to a clearing at Eldergrove's edge. In the center of the clearing was a symbol—a dark spiral, surrounded by runes.

Her pulse quickened as she realized that the settlers had left behind one final ritual, a last-ditch attempt to sever the Veiled One's hold, hidden deep within the forest. The ritual was described in notes scrawled along the edges of the map, instructing the bearer to bring a piece of the Veiled One's essence, to draw the runes in blood, to set fire to herbs that would thin the veil enough to cast it back into the shadows.

But the warning was clear: the ritual was a dangerous one, a last resort meant to be used only by those who could withstand the darkness that would surely follow.

With the map clutched in her hand, Mara felt a glimmer of hope. Perhaps she could use this ritual, find a way to end the pact that had bound Eldergrove to the Veiled One for centuries.

As she left the library, Mara's resolve hardened, her mind set on the forest and the ritual that lay within. She knew the Veiled One would come for her that night, hungry, vengeful, ready to claim the soul she had promised it. But she would be waiting, armed with the knowledge of Eldergrove's dark past, and with a determination to end the curse that had haunted the town for generations.

The next Witching Hour would come, and this time, Mara would face the Veiled One on her own terms.

As dusk settled over Eldergrove, Mara gathered what she needed—a piece of the Veiled One's essence, the ingredients specified in the ancient notes, and the map she'd found. She had a few hours until the next Witching Hour, and she knew she would need every minute. Her heart raced with a mix of fear and determination. If the ritual worked, she might finally break Eldergrove's centuries-old pact with the Veiled One, freeing herself and the town from its grasp.

The map led her deep into the forest surrounding Eldergrove, the trees closing in as she followed the faint trail, their gnarled branches reaching overhead like skeletal hands. The only sounds were her own footsteps, crunching over leaves, and the occasional hoot of an owl, as though the forest itself was watching her, aware of the ritual she was about to attempt.

Finally, she reached the clearing marked on the map. The ground was bare, the trees forming a perfect circle around a dark, moss-covered stone slab at the center. Runes were etched into its surface, symbols of protection and binding, worn with age but still pulsing with a faint, eerie energy. This place had been untouched for centuries, preserved by the settlers as a place of last resort—a final attempt to contain the Veiled One should it ever grow too powerful.

Mara knelt by the stone, arranging her materials: herbs gathered from the forest, stones marked with the runes from the map, and the faint, twisted piece of the Veiled

One's essence she had taken from her own home—a single strand of dark, fine hair she had found in her room after its first visit, as though it had left a part of itself behind as a promise.

As she began to set up the ritual, the sky grew darker, the air around her growing cold, and she felt the familiar, oppressive weight of the Veiled One's presence creeping into the clearing. She knew she was running out of time—the Witching Hour was approaching, and the entity would soon be strong enough to reach her again.

Mara took a deep breath, centering herself, and began to chant the words scrawled in the margins of the map, each syllable heavy with the power of the settlers' ancient pact. She could feel the weight of the ritual pressing down on her, a dark energy that pulsed through the forest, making her skin prickle, her breath grow shallow.

As she spoke, the runes on the stone began to glow, a faint, blue light illuminating the clearing. She sprinkled the herbs around the edges of the slab, the scent filling the air, mingling with the cold, damp smell of the forest. Her voice grew louder, her hands moving in a rhythm that felt both foreign and familiar, as though she were channeling the spirits of those who had come before her.

Suddenly, a gust of wind swept through the clearing, extinguishing her lantern, plunging her into darkness. But the stone continued to glow, casting an eerie light over the clearing. Mara felt the Veiled One's presence intensify, a dark shape forming at the edge of her vision, its figure barely distinguishable from the shadows around it.

"Mara..." the voice whispered, low and mocking, filled with a dark amusement. "You think you can break what has bound us for centuries? You think a few words can undo our pact?"

She ignored it, focusing on the ritual, her voice steady, her words ringing out into the night. But the Veiled One's voice grew louder, filling her mind with whispers, promises, threats, memories that weren't her own.

"I have been here longer than your bloodline, longer than your ancestors dared to dream," it hissed. "I am the shadows, the hunger, the guardian of this land. And you... you are mine."

Mara felt a wave of nausea wash over her, her hands trembling as she struggled to keep her focus. But she knew that if she faltered, if she allowed her fear to overtake her, the ritual would fail, and the Veiled One would claim her as it had claimed so many others.

With a final, trembling breath, Mara raised the strand of hair, holding it over the glowing runes as she chanted the words that would sever her bond with the Veiled One. She could feel the energy building, the forest around her growing darker, colder, as though the very ground beneath her was rebelling against her actions.

The Veiled One shrieked, a sound that pierced the night, filling the clearing with a rage so intense it made the air vibrate, the trees tremble, the earth itself seem to shift beneath her feet. But Mara held her ground, her voice strong, her words steady, each one a nail in the entity's coffin.

And then, in a blinding flash of light, the Veiled One's figure began to unravel, the shadows peeling away, revealing a shape that was neither human nor animal, a twisted mass of darkness that pulsed with an unnatural light. It writhed, twisting, shifting, its form flickering as it fought against the ritual's power, its screams filling the air with a desperation that sent a chill through her.

Mara focused on the final words, her voice rising above the creature's screams, filling the clearing with the settlers' ancient incantation. The runes on the stone glowed brighter, their light growing until it filled the entire clearing, forcing the Veiled One to retreat, its figure dissolving, shrinking, collapsing under the weight of the ritual.

With a final, shuddering breath, the Veiled One let out a scream that echoed through the forest, a sound filled with a rage, a hunger that would never be satisfied. And then, in a burst of darkness, it vanished, the shadows receding, the air growing still, leaving Mara alone in the silence of the night.

As dawn broke over Eldergrove, the townspeople awoke to a quiet that felt strange, almost foreign. The usual fog that clung to the streets was gone, the air lighter, fresher, as though a weight that had lingered for centuries had finally been lifted.

Mara returned to the town in the early morning light, her body exhausted, her mind filled with the weight of what she had done. She knew the Veiled One was gone, its presence severed, its hunger silenced, and the town of Eldergrove finally freed from its shadow.

But as she passed through the streets, she felt a strange emptiness, a quiet that was almost too silent, too still, as though the town itself was adjusting to a new reality, a life without the constant presence of the Witching Hour.

In the days that followed, Eldergrove's residents noticed a change. The air felt cleaner, the nights less oppressive, and for the first time in generations, they could walk the streets without fear, the specter of the Witching Hour nothing more than a memory. But while most of the townspeople were content to leave the past behind, a few noticed something strange—a faint whisper that lingered on the edges of their minds, a voice that called out from the shadows, promising secrets and power.

And Mara, the girl who had lifted the veil, knew better than anyone that the Witching Hour might return, that shadows had a way of slipping back through cracks, of finding their way home.

But for now, Eldergrove rested, the pact broken, its dark history hidden in the silence of the forest, waiting to be uncovered once more.

The End

22
THE DOLL

It was just past 8:00 p.m., and the house was quiet. Olivia tucked the blankets around her daughter, Lily, pulling them snug as the child's eyes began to droop. The bedtime ritual had become Olivia's favorite part of the day, a peaceful close to the chaos of work, errands, and life's never-ending responsibilities. She leaned over, planting a gentle kiss on Lily's forehead.

"Mommy, where's my doll?" Lily murmured, her tiny fingers reaching for the plush toy she loved to sleep with every night.

"Oh! I almost forgot," Olivia said, crossing the room to the dresser. She picked up the doll—a new one she'd gotten just days earlier, a gift she hadn't been able to resist because of how much it reminded her of Danielle, her coworker. The resemblance was almost funny, really: the doll had the same reddish-brown hair, the same freckles, even a hint of the same friendly but serious expression that Danielle always wore. Olivia had felt a twinge of guilt when she first saw the doll in the store, thinking she was somehow laughing at her coworker's expense, but it was all in good fun. And besides, Lily adored the doll.

"Here you go, sweetheart," Olivia said, handing the doll to Lily, who hugged it close. But as she started to turn away, she heard a soft thud, followed by a tiny, disappointed sigh.

"Mommy, I dropped her," Lily said, reaching down over the edge of the bed.

Olivia crouched to retrieve the doll, but as she picked it up, her stomach sank. One of the doll's arms lay on the floor beside it, torn loose, the threads where it had been attached frayed and uneven. She examined it, surprised by how sudden the damage had been. The doll was brand new.

"Don't worry, sweetie," she whispered, setting the doll beside Lily and tucking the severed arm into her pocket. "I'll sew it back on tomorrow, and she'll be good as new. Just try to sleep."

Lily nodded, curling up with the doll's one remaining arm clutched to her chest, drifting off almost immediately. Olivia watched her for a moment, the tiny doll tucked under her daughter's chin, looking just as peaceful. But something about the situation left her uneasy, though she couldn't quite place why. She brushed the thought away, chalking it up to a long day, and went back downstairs.

The next day was just as chaotic as usual. Olivia barely managed to get Lily off to school before rushing into work. Her office was already buzzing with activity as she settled in at her desk, coffee in hand, and glanced over her schedule. Meetings, project deadlines, and a company-wide presentation loomed ahead. But just as she was about to start her work, she overheard a whisper from the desk behind her.

"Did you hear about Danielle?" one of her colleagues murmured.

Olivia turned, her heart skipping a beat. "What happened to Danielle?"

Her coworker, looking both shocked and subdued, leaned in. "She was in an accident. Lost her arm, they said. She was getting out of her car, and somehow the door slammed on it. They couldn't save it."

Olivia felt her blood run cold. Danielle, her bright, warm-hearted colleague, was missing an arm—the very arm that had come loose from Lily's doll the night before. She tried to tell herself it was just a coincidence, but the resemblance between the doll and Danielle seemed more than an eerie twist of fate. She kept herself together, putting on a brave face, but the thought haunted her all morning, lurking just behind her every attempt to focus.

When she got home that evening, Olivia pulled the doll out of Lily's room and inspected it again, her fingers trembling as she examined the stitches where the arm had come loose. A thin, pale thread hung from the doll's shoulder, frayed and uneven, but there was something odd about the spot, something she hadn't noticed before. A faint stain, barely visible, marked the place where the arm had been torn away. It looked almost... like blood.

She stared, her heart pounding, and dropped the doll as if it had burned her, taking a step back. The doll lay still on the floor, its one remaining arm outstretched, as though reaching for something just beyond its grasp.

The next few days were filled with a mounting sense of dread that Olivia couldn't shake. Every time she looked at the doll, it seemed to mock her, its remaining arm and reddish-brown hair taunting her with the memory of Danielle's accident. She tried to tell herself it was nothing, just her imagination running wild, but deep down, she felt that the doll was somehow connected, as absurd as it seemed.

And then, just as she began to push the thought aside, it happened again.

It was Saturday afternoon, and Lily was playing in the living room, the doll perched on the sofa beside her. Olivia had taken her eyes off her daughter for only a moment, but when she glanced back, she saw that Lily had dropped the doll again, its leg now lying several inches away on the carpet.

"Mommy, her leg fell off!" Lily said, looking up at her with wide, curious eyes. She didn't seem upset, more curious than anything, as though this were all part of some game she didn't fully understand.

Olivia's stomach twisted as she picked up the doll, her hands trembling. The fabric around the doll's leg joint was torn, the stuffing poking through, and as she turned it over, she noticed another faint stain, this one just below the hip, darker, almost rust-colored.

That night, she went to bed with a pit of dread in her stomach, the doll's broken body lingering in her mind. She had nearly convinced herself to throw it away, to put an end to the growing feeling of unease. But she hadn't gotten around to it before Monday morning arrived.

When she arrived at work, she found the office somber, her coworkers gathered in small, hushed groups, exchanging looks of shock and disbelief. She braced herself, her hands clenching at her sides as she approached the nearest group.

"It's James," one of them said quietly. "He... he was in an accident. He lost his leg."

The world spun around Olivia, her heart pounding as the realization sank in. James, the manager who'd just been promoted, had lost his leg in a construction accident. The detail was almost too much to bear, too coincidental to dismiss. First Danielle, now James. And each time, the doll had mirrored their injuries, the severed parts matching perfectly.

Over the next week, Olivia tried to rationalize what was happening, but the pattern was undeniable. Each time the doll broke, each time a part tore away, someone at her office was injured in the exact same way. It was as if the doll were connected to them, somehow influencing their fates, drawing them into its strange, horrific game.

Desperation gnawed at her, but she couldn't bring herself to throw the doll away, afraid of what might happen if she did. She couldn't explain it, but she felt a twisted sense of responsibility, as though the doll had some power over her, binding her to it.

Then, late one night, as she sat alone in the living room, the doll lying on the table in front of her, she noticed something strange—a small, faint movement, so subtle she almost thought she'd imagined it. The doll's one remaining arm twitched, its fingers curling as though reaching for something unseen.

Olivia's breath caught, her heart racing, as the doll's head turned ever so slightly, its gaze fixing on her with an intensity that felt almost human.

And then, in a voice so faint it was barely more than a whisper, she heard it speak.

"Mommy..."

Her blood ran cold, her mind racing with fear and confusion as the doll continued to stare at her, its face twisted into a dark, mocking smile.

"Mommy," it repeated, its voice hollow, filled with an echo of malice. "Let's play..."

As the words lingered in the air, Olivia felt a chill settle over her, a darkness that crept into every corner of the room, filling her mind with a terror she couldn't escape. She knew, with a sickening certainty, that the doll wasn't just a toy—it was something far darker, something that wanted her, that had claimed her.

And as the Witching Hour approached, she understood that this was only the beginning.

The next morning, Olivia couldn't shake the horror of the night before. The doll's whisper had echoed through her mind, chilling her with its hollow voice, a sound that seemed to linger in the corners of her home, following her every step. She knew she had to find out more. There was something unnatural about the doll, a darkness woven into its very fabric, and she couldn't ignore it any longer.

That afternoon, after dropping Lily at her grandmother's house, Olivia returned home and searched through the box where she'd first found the doll. She'd bought it from a small, dusty antique store on the edge of town—a place she'd wandered into on a whim after work. She remembered feeling drawn to it, the way the doll's lifelike appearance had caught her eye. She hadn't thought twice about its origins or why it bore such an uncanny resemblance to Danielle.

But now, as she held it in her hands again, her mind raced. She needed answers. A quick search online led her to the store's address, and she left immediately, the doll wrapped tightly in her bag, her heart pounding as she drove.

The antique store was as eerie as she remembered, its windows lined with dusty trinkets and forgotten objects. A small bell jingled as she stepped inside, and the shopkeeper, a thin, elderly man with sharp eyes, looked up from behind the counter.

"Back so soon?" he said, his voice low, his gaze drifting to the bag clutched in her hands.

Olivia nodded, trying to hide her unease. "I... I bought a doll here a few weeks ago," she began, pulling the doll from her bag and placing it on the counter. "I need to know where it came from."

The shopkeeper's expression darkened, his eyes narrowing as he took in the doll's twisted, one-armed form. He glanced at her, his face a mask of suspicion. "Most people don't come back asking questions about that doll," he said quietly, his fingers tracing the edges of the doll's frayed sleeve. "Once they take it, they usually don't bring it back."

"Please," Olivia insisted, her voice trembling. "There's something wrong with it. My daughter's been playing with it, and every time it... breaks, someone I know is injured. It's like it's... connected to them somehow."

The shopkeeper let out a sigh, nodding as though he had heard similar stories before. He turned, pulling a dusty, leather-bound book from a shelf behind the counter, flipping through its fragile pages until he found what he was looking for.

"This doll," he said, pointing to a faded illustration that looked remarkably similar to the doll on the counter, "is what some call a *muraikusa*—a cursed vessel, crafted to bind misfortune to those who possess it. It's said to be a rare form of sympathetic magic, a curse cast on a person by embedding pieces of them within an object, creating a tether to their life force."

Olivia stared at him, her blood running cold. "How is that possible? Who would create something like that?"

The shopkeeper glanced down at the doll, a shadow crossing his face. "The legend goes that these dolls were made by witches, those skilled in the dark arts. A witch would craft the doll in the likeness of someone they sought to control or harm, using bits of fabric, strands of hair, anything that connected the doll to its intended victim."

He gestured to the doll's torn fabric and frayed threads. "Over time, the doll gains power by drawing upon its victim's essence, like blood, hair, or in some cases, more intimate items tied to the victim's life force. If the doll's limbs or parts are damaged, the injuries are reflected in the victim's life. Every injury, every wound, draws the doll closer to the person, creating a bond that is nearly impossible to break."

A chill ran down Olivia's spine as she listened. "And the person... they have no control over it?"

The shopkeeper shook his head. "No. The curse is nearly unbreakable. The doll's creator—the one who crafted it—holds the power to control it. Unless you find the person who bound this curse and destroy its connection, it will continue to spread its influence, marking everyone who comes into contact with it."

Olivia's heart sank, her mind racing as she pieced together the implications. Her coworker Danielle was the first connection, the one the doll most resembled, and somehow, others had become entangled in its reach. But what she couldn't understand was who would craft such a thing—and why it would end up in a store, sold to her of all people.

"Where did you get this doll?" she asked, her voice a shaky whisper.

The shopkeeper's gaze dropped, his face unreadable. "It came in with a collection from a house outside of town—a woman named Iris Montgomery. She was... well, people say she was a witch, someone who dabbled in curses and binding spells. Her family has lived in this town for generations, and some say she left pieces of herself in the objects she created, making them vessels of her will."

A cold realization settled over Olivia. The name Montgomery wasn't new to her; it was the same last name as her friend Danielle's. Danielle had always mentioned a distant, eccentric aunt, someone her family rarely spoke about, an old woman who lived alone and was rumored to have a "gift" that nobody understood.

"So... this doll," Olivia whispered, "it was crafted by her aunt?"

The shopkeeper nodded, his expression grave. "If Danielle's aunt made it, then it's likely connected to her bloodline—anyone tied to her life force would be vulnerable to its influence."

Olivia's mind raced, her thoughts consumed by the doll's dark origins, the malevolent intent that lay within its stitches. It was more than a toy—it was a weapon, crafted by someone who had long passed but whose influence lingered on, woven into the very fabric of the doll.

The shopkeeper leaned closer, his eyes narrowing. "If you truly want to stop this, there may be a way. But it's dangerous. The doll must be destroyed, but not by conventional means. Burning it, tearing it apart—it won't work. A cursed vessel like this must be taken to the place of its creation and dismantled in a ritual that severs the bonds holding it together."

Olivia's throat tightened. "And that place...?"

The shopkeeper sighed, his expression dark. "Danielle's aunt lived on the outskirts of town, in the old Montgomery estate. That house is where the doll was crafted, and it's likely the only place you'll be able to break the curse. But be warned—objects like this rarely go down without a fight. The curse will resist, doing everything it can to remain whole."

Olivia took a deep breath, her mind made up. She couldn't risk anyone else's safety, not Lily's, not her coworkers'. She had to end this, once and for all.

That night, Olivia drove to the Montgomery estate, the doll clutched tightly in her hands. The house was a crumbling, dilapidated structure hidden behind overgrown trees, its windows dark, its presence looming in the night like a specter. She forced herself to walk up the steps, her hand trembling as she pushed open the creaking door.

Inside, the air was thick, cold, as though the house itself were alive, breathing, watching her every move. The floors groaned beneath her weight, the walls lined with faded portraits of faces she didn't recognize, but that somehow felt familiar. She followed the sense of dread that pulled her forward, leading her to a small room at the back of the house.

There, on an old wooden table, sat a collection of jars, bundles of herbs, and scraps of cloth, remnants of Iris Montgomery's spells, each one a piece of a life long gone but far from forgotten. She placed the doll in the center, taking a deep breath, and began the ritual the shopkeeper had instructed her to perform.

With each word she spoke, the air grew colder, the shadows darker, and she could feel the doll fighting back, its threads tightening, its fabric twisting, as though it were alive, struggling to stay whole. She pressed on, her voice steady, reciting the words that would sever its connection, breaking the power that bound it to the lives it had claimed.

As she spoke the final words, the doll's fabric split, its stitches unraveling, the dark stain at its shoulder spreading, soaking into the fabric as though releasing years of pent-up rage and malice. The doll shuddered, its limbs falling limp, its head lolling to one side as the last traces of the curse faded, leaving only silence in its wake.

Olivia staggered back, the weight lifting, the darkness receding. She looked down at the now-lifeless doll, its twisted smile gone, its presence nothing more than a faded memory.

She had broken the curse. The doll's dark legacy was over, its power severed, its influence silenced.

But as she turned to leave, she felt a faint, lingering chill, as though something in the house was watching, waiting, a dark echo of Iris Montgomery's will, bound to the shadows of the home she had left behind.

The Montgomery estate lingered in Olivia's mind long after she left, its dark, decaying rooms still imprinted with the scent of dust, herbs, and something far more sinister. She had thought destroying the doll would bring her peace, but the oppressive feeling of being watched followed her back home, an invisible weight that pressed against her.

The shopkeeper had warned her that cursed objects, especially those crafted by a skilled hand, left behind echoes—a shadow of the curse that often clung to its surroundings. Now, she wondered if the Montgomery estate itself was cursed, if it held a piece of Iris Montgomery's malevolence, waiting, watching, bound to the decaying walls. The doll had been destroyed, but her relief was short-lived. She couldn't shake the feeling that Iris's influence had not entirely vanished.

The next day, Olivia received a call from Danielle, her coworker who had lost her arm in the strange accident. It was the first time they'd spoken since the accident, and Olivia could sense a weariness in her voice.

"Olivia," Danielle began, her voice trembling. "I don't know how to explain this, but I've been feeling... different. Ever since the accident, I've had these strange dreams. And last night, I saw her. I saw my aunt Iris."

Olivia's heart skipped a beat. "What... what did she look like?"

Danielle's voice grew quieter, as though speaking the words was painful. "It was her, but she looked older, thinner, like a shadow of herself. And her eyes... they were full of anger, like she was trying to reach me, to speak to me from... somewhere else."

A chill ran down Olivia's spine. She had hoped that breaking the doll's curse would sever any connection with Iris, but it seemed that the old witch's influence lingered in ways she hadn't anticipated.

"Danielle," Olivia began cautiously, "I think there might be something left of her, something that didn't leave with the doll. You mentioned she practiced strange rituals. Do you remember anything else about her? Any stories your family told about her life or her... powers?"

Danielle hesitated before replying. "There were rumors," she said, her voice barely more than a whisper. "When I was a kid, my family would say she was 'touched by darkness,' that she could make things happen just by thinking them. But there was one story that always frightened me the most. My mother told me Iris had been a respected healer once, but something changed her. She lost someone close to her, and that's when the curses began. She started binding pieces of herself to objects, creating cursed vessels that would hold her anger, her resentment."

Olivia shuddered as Danielle continued, her voice soft and fearful. "They said her most powerful curse was bound to her last creation—a doll crafted in the likeness of a young woman she'd lost, someone she was trying to protect... or maybe control. My family always said that as long as that doll remained intact, a part of Iris would live on."

A dark realization washed over Olivia. The doll had been destroyed, yes, but Iris's spirit, her essence, could still be attached to the land, woven into the very soil of Eldergrove. Destroying the doll might have only released her spirit, unleashing her rage upon the town itself.

The following night, Olivia lay in bed, unable to sleep. Shadows seemed to dance on the walls, and every creak, every faint sound made her tense. She could feel something lingering just beyond her senses, an oppressive presence that grew stronger as the hours wore on. She realized that if Iris's spirit truly was bound to Eldergrove, she had to find a way to release it. Otherwise, it would continue to haunt the town, and her family, with its anger and pain.

Determined to put an end to Iris's hold on her life, Olivia went back to the antique shop, hoping the shopkeeper could offer guidance one last time. The man was waiting, as though expecting her, his gaze grave as he listened to her story.

"Ah," he said, nodding slowly. "You did well to destroy the doll, but if her spirit has taken root in the land, there is only one way to set it free. You'll need to perform a ritual of release. It's risky, but it's the only way to sever the final connection and lay her spirit to rest."

He explained the process in hushed tones, drawing symbols on a piece of parchment, his eyes dark and wary. She would need to gather specific herbs and perform the ritual at midnight, under a waning moon, in the heart of the Montgomery estate. She had to call Iris's spirit forth, confront it, and sever the last threads that bound it to the land. Only then could Iris's spirit be freed from her curse.

Armed with the shopkeeper's instructions, Olivia returned to the Montgomery estate once more. The house loomed before her, its windows dark and empty, its walls seeming to pulse with an energy that filled the night air with dread. The moon was high, casting long shadows across the ground, and a chill crept through her bones as she stepped inside, the darkness swallowing her as the door swung shut behind her.

She followed the shopkeeper's instructions, drawing a circle in the center of the living room, placing the herbs at each point, lighting the candles in a steady, rhythmic pattern. She could feel the air growing heavy, a pressure building around her, as though the house itself were holding its breath, waiting for what was to come.

As midnight approached, Olivia knelt within the circle, her voice steady as she began the incantation. The words were ancient, foreign, each syllable carrying a weight that seemed to pull at her mind, filling the room with a resonance that made the walls tremble.

Then, slowly, the shadows began to shift, pooling together, forming a dark figure at the edge of the room. The figure took shape, becoming a woman, her features twisted, her eyes hollow, filled with an anger that burned brighter than any flame. It was Iris—her presence cold, unyielding, a force of pure rage and resentment.

"You dare summon me here?" Iris's voice echoed through the room, low and haunting, filled with an authority that made Olivia's skin crawl. "You thought you could destroy my work, rid yourself of me?"

Olivia forced herself to remain calm, her gaze locked on Iris's, her voice steady. "I know what you've done, Iris. You've bound yourself to this town, to the people who live here, and your anger is spreading, claiming lives that were never meant to suffer. I've come to set you free, to end this curse."

A dark, mocking laugh filled the air, the shadows twisting around Iris, her figure growing taller, her eyes blazing. "Free me?" she sneered. "I don't wish to be free. I have become one with this land, my anger rooted in its soil, my pain flowing through its people. Why would I abandon the power I have gained?"

Olivia's heart raced, but she held her ground, her voice unwavering. "Because you lost the person you loved most, and that pain has only grown, twisted into something that's consuming you. You have to let go, Iris. Holding on to this curse, this hatred—it will destroy you."

For a brief moment, a flicker of something almost human appeared in Iris's eyes, a glimmer of sorrow, of regret. But it was quickly replaced by fury, her expression twisting into a mask of rage.

"I am bound to this land," Iris hissed. "My pain is my power, my curse my legacy. You cannot break what has become part of Eldergrove itself."

Olivia felt a surge of strength, her determination hardening. She held up the final symbol, a piece of the doll's torn fabric she'd taken from her home. "You may be part of this land, but you're not invincible. This ritual will end your hold. You will rest, or you will be destroyed."

With a final, trembling breath, Olivia completed the incantation, the last words echoing through the house like a drumbeat. The candles flickered, the shadows swirling around Iris, her figure beginning to disintegrate, the darkness peeling away, her form unraveling as the spell took hold.

Iris's scream filled the room, a sound filled with rage and sorrow, a final echo of the curse that had bound her to Eldergrove for centuries. The shadows collapsed, the energy in the room dissipating as Iris's spirit was finally released, fading into the night, leaving behind only silence.

The weight lifted, the air clearing, as though a dark fog had been lifted from the estate. Olivia collapsed to her knees, exhaustion washing over her, a deep sense of relief filling her as she realized that Iris was truly gone. The curse had been broken, and the town of Eldergrove would finally know peace.

In the days that followed, Olivia felt the change in the air, the lightness that had returned to Eldergrove, as though the land itself had been freed from its dark grip. The Montgomery estate remained empty, its walls quiet, its rooms free from the haunting shadows that had plagued them for so long.

And as for Olivia, she knew that Iris's curse would linger in her memory, a reminder of the darkness that had once claimed her life. But she could move forward now, her heart lighter, knowing she had ended a legacy of pain, bringing peace to herself and to Eldergrove.

With the curse broken, Eldergrove was finally at peace. The fog that had lingered over the town for generations was gone, and the oppressive weight that had held the town in a grip of fear seemed to lift with each passing day. The townspeople noticed the difference immediately: birds returned to the trees, the air felt fresher, and an unfamiliar lightness filled the streets, as though Eldergrove was taking its first deep breath in centuries.

For many, this new peace was a welcome relief, but for others, it stirred curiosity and questions. The curse's end brought about a shift in the town's history, one that had always been spoken of only in whispers. Families who had been in Eldergrove for generations began sharing stories once hidden—rumors of hauntings, strange encounters, and the silent terror they had all learned to live with.

Over the next year, as life slowly returned to normal, Eldergrove found itself at a crossroads. Some of the younger residents, eager to leave the past behind, saw the change as a chance to revitalize the town, to invite new growth, new businesses, even tourists to enjoy Eldergrove's quaint charm. But the older families, those who had grown up under the shadow of Iris Montgomery's curse, were hesitant, fearing that delving too deeply into Eldergrove's past could awaken whatever darkness had once resided there.

Word of Eldergrove's mysterious transformation spread, drawing the attention of paranormal investigators, historians, and enthusiasts intrigued by the town's history. An article in a regional magazine sparked the interest of a small but growing number of tourists who wanted to experience "the town that banished its curse."

Some of these visitors claimed to feel a "residual energy" in places like the old Montgomery estate, though none could definitively say what that energy was. A local historian, fascinated by Iris's life, began digging into town records, piecing together stories from the Montgomery family and the rituals that had kept Eldergrove under Iris's shadow. But even with the curse broken, the house remained a place that held a certain eerie mystique, its rooms empty, its walls silent, as though waiting.

It wasn't long before the town council began to see the estate as a potential attraction, something that might bring in revenue while allowing Eldergrove to acknowledge its past. They toyed with the idea of restoring the estate, turning it into a historic landmark, even a museum of sorts. But the older residents resisted. Some things, they argued, were better left undisturbed.

For Olivia, life had moved on in the most ordinary ways. Lily had outgrown her fear of the doll, now just a memory of a strange story her mother rarely mentioned. But every so often, Olivia would feel a faint chill, a prickle on the back of her neck, as though the shadows in her own home had yet to settle. In quiet moments, she would catch herself glancing over her shoulder, half-expecting to see a figure in the corner of her eye, though she always found nothing but empty air.

It wasn't fear she felt, but a reminder—a subtle, lingering presence, as though Iris's influence would always be woven into the very fabric of Eldergrove. She could feel it in the whispers of the townspeople, in the unease that filled the air whenever the Montgomery estate was mentioned, in the stories of "The Doll" that became part of local folklore.

Occasionally, Olivia would walk past the estate, its windows dark, its walls quiet, but she couldn't shake the feeling that something of Iris remained—a memory imprinted into the house itself, watching from the empty rooms, unwilling to fully let go.

As Eldergrove moved forward, Olivia found herself invited to speak at town gatherings, her experience woven into the town's story of resilience. She spoke cautiously, never giving away too many details, but sharing enough to remind people of the strength it took to free Eldergrove from its shadowed past. The children in town grew up hearing her story, passing it on with a mixture of fear and fascination, each retelling adding its own twist, until Iris Montgomery became more legend than fact.

The town's local library eventually compiled a collection of old records, accounts from families who had lived through the curse, photographs of the Montgomery estate in its earlier days. Eldergrove found itself proud of its mysterious past, a town once haunted but now strong enough to withstand its own history. For the first time, the townspeople felt safe in sharing their stories, their encounters with the supernatural—a testament to what they had endured and overcome.

And yet, deep in the woods, the Montgomery estate stood as a reminder, a silent monument to a power once wielded by a woman who had chosen revenge over peace. The land, while freed of Iris's immediate curse, retained a subtle energy, an echo of the dark rituals that had been performed there. Locals still avoided it at night, glancing warily at the shadows, unwilling to tempt fate by venturing too close.

As time passed, Eldergrove embraced a new identity, a town steeped in mystery but no longer defined by fear. Iris Montgomery's curse was gone, but her legacy lingered in the minds of those who walked the streets, a reminder of the thin line between past and present, between peace and the forces that, for a time, had bound the town in shadows.

And whenever a chill passed through the air, or the fog returned on quiet nights, Eldergrove's residents would pull their children close, whispering the cautionary tales, and reminding themselves that peace in a town like Eldergrove was hard-won—a delicate balance, forever aware of what had once lurked in the shadows.

The End

23

JACK OF ALL TRADES

The city's heartbeat pulsed through the streets, a steady rhythm of headlights and sirens, of voices blending together in the crowded hum of life. In the heart of this metropolis, tucked away in an unassuming neighborhood, was a small mechanic's shop where Jack Lawson spent his afternoons. With grease-streaked hands and an easy smile, Jack was known as a reliable, laid-back guy—the kind of man people went to when they needed something fixed. In his old, worn jumpsuit, he looked like any other mechanic, blending into the background of oil and metal.

People liked Jack. He was charming without trying, confident without the arrogance that came with it. He could swap a carburetor with his eyes closed, fix a busted transmission by dinner, and still have time to clean up and head to his night job. At O'Malley's Pub, where he worked as a bartender, he kept up a steady flow of drinks, jokes, and effortless charm. He knew everyone's name, everyone's favorite drink. And he was a good listener, always leaning in just a little closer when someone had a story to tell.

By day, he was a man people depended on. But by night, as he poured drinks under dim lights and low music, his mind drifted to darker places. Jack was no stranger to the shadows of the city, nor to the thrill of secrets. With practiced ease, he kept a dual life hidden from those around him, a life most people would never imagine.

Tonight was no different. He clocked out from the shop, took a quick shower, and slipped into his bartender's uniform—a clean white shirt, sleeves rolled up, an apron tied around his waist. He arrived at O'Malley's, nodding to the regulars, flashing a charming grin at anyone who looked his way. As he wiped down the counter, he scanned the room, his eyes drifting over the crowd until they landed on a new face, a young woman sitting at the far end of the bar.

Her name was Jessica, he'd learned after she'd ordered her first drink—a vodka tonic with a twist. She was new to the city, she'd said, looking to make friends, settle into a new job. Jack had nodded, flashing that easy smile as he slid her drink across the counter. She seemed like the friendly type, a little shy, perhaps, but open to conversation.

Throughout the night, Jack played the part perfectly: the attentive bartender, the harmless listener. He made sure her glass was never empty, asking questions that were innocent enough, keeping her comfortable, relaxed. Little by little, he gathered information, each piece fitting into his mental puzzle, every word telling him what he needed to know.

It was only when the pub was nearly empty, the music turned low and the lights dimmed, that he made his move. He leaned closer, lowering his voice just enough to make it sound private, conspiratorial.

"You know," he said, his tone casual, friendly, "if you ever need someone to show you around the city, I'd be happy to help. It can be tough being new here."

Jessica smiled, her cheeks flushing slightly. "Thanks, Jack. That would be nice."

Jack's smile widened, his eyes catching hers for a lingering moment. "Great. Let's plan something soon."

The hook was in.

Jack's apartment was a short walk from O'Malley's, a tidy space that was as unassuming as the man himself. He kept things organized, minimal, nothing that would give anyone cause to look twice. But for all its simplicity, it wasn't where Jack kept his secrets. That honor belonged to a storage unit on the far side of town, hidden away in a sprawling complex where hundreds of identical units stretched in neat, narrow rows.

No one knew about the storage unit, and no one would have thought to ask. It was just one more thing in Jack's life that blended in, unnoticed. By day, he was a man of trades—a mechanic, a bartender, a friendly face. But by night, as he sat alone in the cold metal box of his storage unit, he was something else entirely.

The unit was stark and uninviting, its concrete walls and dim lighting casting harsh shadows across the room. Shelves lined the walls, filled with tools, supplies, and personal mementos. But at the center of the unit, hidden under heavy tarps and blankets, were things far darker than most could imagine: the bodies of his victims, carefully wrapped and preserved, their faces frozen in silent horror.

Jack moved through the space with practiced ease, checking each tarp, making sure everything was as it should be. He knew every inch of the unit, every detail of the dark collection he had built over time. He didn't linger, didn't let himself feel anything as he surveyed his work. Each body represented a carefully chosen moment, a thrill, a hidden part of himself he couldn't reveal to the world. And when he was here, alone with his collection, he felt a twisted satisfaction—a sense of control, a mastery over life and death that filled him with a sick, quiet joy.

Tonight, as he left the storage unit, locking the heavy door behind him, he felt the familiar rush of excitement, the thrill of a secret kept hidden, a life lived in shadows. He knew he had to be careful, that his double life depended on his ability to blend in, to disappear when necessary. But that was part of the thrill, part of what kept him coming back, night after night, to O'Malley's, to his hidden unit, to the game he played with his unwitting prey.

Jessica's face drifted into his mind as he walked back to his apartment, a slow smile spreading across his lips. He had a new project now, a new addition to his collection. And as he lay in bed, staring up at the ceiling, he felt the excitement of the hunt settle over him, filling him with a dark satisfaction that was as familiar as it was intoxicating.

The following day, Jack went through his routine as usual, moving from the mechanic's shop to O'Malley's without a hitch. No one suspected a thing. He was the same charming, dependable Jack, always there with a friendly smile and a steady hand.

But that evening, as he was preparing drinks, he noticed a shift in the atmosphere. A group of people had gathered at the far end of the bar, their voices hushed, their expressions tense. One of the regulars, a woman named Dana, glanced up and met his eyes, her face pale.

"Hey, Jack," she called, her voice a bit shaky. "Did you hear? That girl—Jessica, I think? The one who was in here last night?"

Jack felt a flicker of unease, but he kept his expression neutral, his smile easy. "Jessica? The new girl?" He poured her drink, sliding it across the bar.

Dana nodded, leaning in as if sharing a secret. "Yeah, she went missing. Just... vanished. Her friends are freaking out. She was supposed to meet them this morning, but no one's heard from her. They found her phone in an alley nearby, but that's it."

Jack's stomach twisted, a feeling he couldn't quite place filling him as he processed her words. This wasn't part of his plan. He had intended to take his time, to wait until the perfect moment. But it seemed Jessica had slipped through his fingers, leaving him with a loose end, a risk that could unravel everything he'd worked so hard to keep hidden.

He forced a sympathetic frown, nodding in understanding. "That's awful. She seemed really nice. I hope they find her soon."

Dana sighed, taking a long sip of her drink. "Yeah… it's scary, though. People don't just disappear. Not in this city."

As Jack continued working, the weight of her words settled over him, pressing down with a force that made him uneasy. He knew he couldn't afford to let his guard down, not now, not with people starting to ask questions.

But the thrill of the hunt was intoxicating, the thrill of secrecy, of the shadows he lived in, too strong to resist. He would have to be careful, to keep his game going without leaving any traces, any signs of the darker life he led.

And as he poured drinks, his mind drifted to his storage unit, to the quiet space where his secrets were kept hidden, a silent collection that bore witness to the man he truly was.

For Jack, life was about more than fixing cars or serving drinks. It was about mastering every skill, every craft, every thrill. And as long as he could keep his secrets buried, he would remain the perfect handyman—the Jack of all trades.

The city buzzed with hushed murmurs after Jessica's disappearance. O'Malley's was no different. People came in with worried faces, voices low as they traded theories and speculated on her last movements. Jack could feel the tension, the way eyes glanced around, nervous and suspicious. And as a regular fixture at the bar, he knew he had to keep up his usual charm, blend into the background, play the part of the helpful, concerned bartender.

But as the days passed, he sensed the growing scrutiny. Whispers traveled through the bar—rumors, speculation, pieces of conversations he couldn't ignore. It was as if a net were tightening around him, each thread pulling him closer to unwanted attention.

Then one evening, just after his shift began, the door opened, and a woman entered, her gaze sharp and unyielding. Jack had never seen her before, but her serious expression and tailored blazer told him she wasn't here for a drink. She approached the bar with a purposeful stride and took a seat directly across from him, her eyes fixing on him in a way that made his skin prickle.

"Evening," Jack greeted, offering her a nod as he reached for a glass. "What can I get you?"

The woman tilted her head, her lips curving into a faint, humorless smile. "Just a club soda," she replied, her voice calm but pointed.

Jack poured the drink, sliding it across the bar. "First time here?" he asked, keeping his tone casual.

She held his gaze, the intensity in her eyes unbroken. "Detective Lauren Price," she said, pulling a badge from her jacket and setting it on the bar. "I'm looking into Jessica Monroe's disappearance."

Jack felt a chill creep down his spine, but he masked it with an easy smile. “Yes, I remember her. A sweet girl. I was working the night she was here.”

Detective Price nodded, her expression unreadable. “We’re retracing her steps, talking to anyone who might have seen her before she disappeared.” She leaned forward slightly, as though trying to catch even the smallest flicker of emotion. “Some patrons said they saw the two of you talking quite a bit.”

Jack shrugged, keeping his tone light. “Just making her feel welcome. She was new in town and looked a little lost. It’s what I do—talk to customers, make them feel at home.”

The detective watched him, her gaze searching, as if peeling back layers he hadn’t even known were there. “Did she mention anything about where she was headed? Anyone she was planning to meet up with?”

Jack shook his head. “No, she didn’t say. Just seemed like she was here to unwind.” He made sure to keep his expression neutral, his voice steady. “Wish I could help more.”

Detective Price’s eyes narrowed slightly, her expression hinting at doubt. “You seem pretty good at making people comfortable, Jack,” she said, almost offhandedly. “A lot of people here say you’re the kind of guy they trust, that you’re always there when they need something.”

Jack nodded, smiling modestly. “Just doing my job.”

She reached into her pocket and pulled out a card, sliding it across the bar toward him. “If you remember anything, or if anything else about that night comes back to you, give me a call.”

Jack took the card, his fingers brushing against it as he kept his face calm, friendly. "Of course, Detective. Hope you find her safe."

She lingered a moment longer, her gaze piercing, before finally standing. "Goodnight, Jack."

As she walked away, Jack felt a chill linger in the air. He pocketed the card, watching her silhouette disappear through the bar's doorway, his mind racing. He had done his best to deflect her questions, to keep his answers vague, but her presence left him uneasy. She was sharper than most—too perceptive, too keen on the details. It was a reminder that he'd have to be extra careful, that every move from here on had to be flawless.

As he returned to his work, Jack noticed the conversations had quieted, and the bar felt darker, heavier. He tried to ignore the prickling feeling at the back of his neck, the sense that everyone's eyes were on him, that each of his actions was being weighed and measured.

And then came a surprise: Dana, a bar regular who had been there the night Jessica vanished, approached him as he was wiping down a glass.

"You okay, Jack?" she asked, her voice hesitant. "It's been a weird few days."

Jack smiled, keeping his voice light. "Yeah, it's been strange. I just hope they find Jessica. People don't just... disappear."

Dana's eyes lingered on him, her gaze troubled. "You know... Detective Price asked me some questions too. She's not like the other cops—they were in and out, but this one...

she's sticking around. Asking about people who come and go, what they talk about, who they're with."

Jack felt his grip tighten on the glass, but he forced a calm smile. "Just being thorough, I guess."

Dana shrugged, fidgeting with her drink. "I guess. But it's kind of eerie, right? Makes you wonder who you can trust."

Her words, though casual, carried an unintended weight. Jack could feel the walls of his double life closing in, the space he'd kept so carefully hidden suddenly shrinking. He nodded, offering a sympathetic smile, even as his mind spun with plans and precautions. He would have to watch his every step, keep his mask in place, remain the unassuming, dependable man everyone thought they knew.

As he finished his shift and left the bar, he could feel the detective's card in his pocket, a constant reminder that eyes were on him now, watching, waiting for any crack in his facade.

In the dead of night, Jack made his way to the storage unit, his mind still replaying his encounter with Detective Price. He had used this unit for years, a hidden space where his secrets were kept under lock and key. But as he reached the metal door, a cold dread settled over him, the certainty that every trip here was another risk, a fresh chance to be discovered.

He unlocked the door and stepped inside, the familiar smell of metal and chemicals filling his lungs. The bodies, wrapped and concealed, lay under tarps along one side of the room, each one a reminder of his carefully orchestrated hobby. He moved through the space methodically, checking each tarp, ensuring that everything was exactly where it should be. This was his ritual, a routine that gave him control over the chaos he hid from the world.

But tonight, as he moved through the unit, he couldn't shake the feeling that something was wrong. He felt a presence lingering, as if the weight of his actions had finally taken shape, as if Detective Price's questions had somehow seeped into this space, leaving him exposed, vulnerable.

He stood there, in the center of his grim collection, letting the silence press down on him, feeling the tension coil in his chest. The detective's visit had rattled him, shaken the confidence he'd held for so long. He realized, with a sick sense of clarity, that his secrets were no longer safe, that the game he'd been playing had taken on a life of its own.

And as he closed the door to the storage unit, locking it with a metallic click, he understood one thing with chilling certainty: he was being watched. Detective Price would be back, and she wouldn't stop until she uncovered the truth.

He had played his part perfectly, hiding in plain sight as the friendly, dependable handyman. But now, the mask was slipping, and he would have to be more careful than ever.

For Jack, there was no turning back. The net was closing in, and he would either have to escape its grasp or face the consequences of the dark life he had so carefully concealed.

Jack could feel the weight of Detective Price's presence looming over him even after she had left O'Malley's. She had planted a seed of doubt in the bar regulars, each of them now second-guessing their familiarity with him. He knew that every friendly smile, every glance, every conversation was now tinged with a hint of suspicion. It was a subtle shift, but Jack was sharp enough to notice.

His days took on a new edge. The ease with which he moved through his routines at the mechanic shop and the bar was gone, replaced by a hypervigilance, a relentless need to appear even more average, more trustworthy. But at night, his thoughts were plagued by an unsettling question: how much did Detective Price already suspect?

Lauren Price had been in the business long enough to recognize when something didn't add up. She'd watched Jack carefully, noting every subtle flicker of unease that crossed his face. She had questioned countless bartenders, but Jack had left her feeling that there was something more—a mask he wore too perfectly, hiding something just below the surface.

In the days following her visit to O'Malley's, Price did what she did best. She dug. She combed through Jack's background, looking for any signs of trouble, any hint of a crack in his unassuming facade. Nothing in his file suggested he was anything more than a hardworking, solitary man who had moved to the city several years prior, working his way up from job to job. But to Price, he seemed too clean, too flawless in his efforts to stay out of the spotlight.

With each passing day, she became more convinced that Jack knew more about Jessica's disappearance than he let on. There was a distance in his demeanor, a practiced detachment that set off alarm bells in her mind. And so, she began to haunt O'Malley's, becoming a regular presence, her eyes always watching him, taking note of his interactions, studying the way he navigated the crowd.

As the days wore on, Jack felt the strain of Price's scrutiny. She came into the bar nearly every night now, watching him with a gaze that was too intent, too focused. Each time she ordered a drink, she'd make small talk with him, her questions innocent on the surface but designed to catch him off guard.

"So, Jack," she said one evening, swirling her drink thoughtfully. "Been working here long?"

"Few years now," Jack replied smoothly, though he could feel the tension in his voice. "Good place. Keeps me busy."

"Must get to know a lot of people," she mused, her gaze steady. "I imagine you see all kinds coming through here."

Jack nodded, his smile strained. "Yeah, all kinds. Keeps the job interesting."

She leaned in slightly, her voice dropping. "You ever notice anyone acting... unusual? Someone who stands out?"

Jack forced a chuckle. "In this city? Everyone's a little unusual."

But her questions gnawed at him, picking away at his carefully built mask. He began noticing little things around him, things he had dismissed before but now saw in a new light: the way a few of his regulars looked at him, the occasional glances exchanged by patrons who once had been friendly but now seemed cautious, wary. It was as if Detective Price had sown a subtle distrust in the air, and Jack knew that he needed to be vigilant, to keep his secrets buried at all costs.

One evening, after closing up at O'Malley's, Jack took a detour to the storage unit. It was time to check on his collection, to ensure that every piece was exactly where he had left it. The storage unit had always been his sanctuary, a place where he could let down his mask and revel in the shadows he'd hidden so well from the world.

But when he arrived, something felt... off.

He unlocked the heavy door, pushing it open and stepping inside, his eyes scanning the familiar rows of shelves, the carefully wrapped tarps, the tools and keepsakes meticulously organized along the walls. Everything seemed in place, but an unease prickled at the back of his mind, a sense that something had changed.

He stepped deeper into the room, his gaze sweeping over his collection, until he spotted it—a small, folded scrap of paper wedged under one of the tarp-covered bodies. His pulse quickened as he reached for it, unfolding it slowly, his mind racing with possibilities.

"I know what you're hiding. Don't get too comfortable."

The note was unsigned, the handwriting neat but unfamiliar. Jack felt his breath catch, a cold dread settling in his stomach. Someone knew. Someone had been in his unit, had seen the things he had hidden there. The thought sent a jolt of fear through him, his mind spinning with questions. Who could have done this? And, more importantly, how much did they know?

He crumpled the note, shoving it into his pocket, his heart racing as he scanned the room again. Everything else seemed untouched, but he knew that whoever had left the note had crossed a line. His sanctuary, his hiding place, had been breached. The only question now was who it could be.

As he left the storage unit, locking it behind him, Jack's mind raced with possibilities. Detective Price? Some anonymous onlooker? He realized that his game had taken on a new, dangerous edge, and that he would have to play smarter, more carefully than ever before.

The next night, Jack arrived at O'Malley's, his mind still reeling from the discovery in his storage unit. He moved through his routine mechanically, forcing himself to smile, to greet his regulars as usual, but his thoughts were consumed by the note, by the realization that he was no longer in control.

Detective Price was there again, her eyes following his every move, her presence a reminder of the mounting pressure around him. Tonight, she didn't approach him with questions. Instead, she sat at the far end of the bar, watching him in silence, her gaze steady, unyielding.

He knew he had to regain control, to put an end to the scrutiny before it was too late. But how? He couldn't afford any more slip-ups, any more eyes on his secrets.

Then, in a moment of resolve, he decided on his next move. He would draw Detective Price closer, lure her into his confidence, let her think she was gaining ground. He would befriend her, play the role of the willing, innocent witness, until she felt she knew him, trusted him. And then, when the moment was right, he would remove her from the equation, just as he had done with those who had come too close before.

As he prepared another round of drinks, Jack felt a calm settle over him. It was a twisted sort of clarity, a sense of purpose that filled him with dark satisfaction. He had always been a man of many trades, capable of adapting, of perfecting every skill he set his mind to.

And now, he would add one more skill to his repertoire: eliminating the one person who threatened to unravel his life.

Jack knew he had to act fast. The note in his storage unit was a chilling reminder that his life was slipping out of his control, that someone out there knew his darkest secret. Detective Price's relentless presence only added to the urgency. She had unsettled his world, casting a subtle but undeniable web of suspicion around him, and Jack understood that he needed to dismantle her interest in him piece by piece.

Over the next few days, Jack adjusted his approach, laying low, appearing as the epitome of a calm, cooperative citizen. He made a point to show concern over Jessica's disappearance, asking his regulars if they had heard anything and feigning frustration at the ongoing mystery. It was all calculated, carefully designed to keep the heat off him.

Detective Price, meanwhile, continued to haunt O'Malley's. Each night she returned, observing him with quiet intensity, watching for any crack in his perfectly composed mask. But tonight, Jack had a plan to finally unsettle her.

As Price settled in at her usual spot, Jack approached her with a sympathetic smile, wiping down the counter before setting her usual club soda in front of her.

"Detective," he began, leaning in slightly, "I just wanted to say... I appreciate how hard you're working to find Jessica.

People around here are on edge, you know? It's nice to know you're watching out for all of us."

Price lifted an eyebrow, studying him. "Just doing my job, Jack. People deserve answers."

Jack nodded, keeping his expression earnest. "It's just that... I haven't been able to stop thinking about that night. I keep replaying it, wondering if there was anything I missed, anything I could have said that would have helped her."

Detective Price's gaze softened, just a little, her sharp expression melting into something that hinted at empathy. She held her glass but didn't drink, her eyes trained on him. "It's tough," she said finally. "Cases like this... they're never easy. But we all try to do what we can."

Jack seized the moment, nodding thoughtfully. "I know it sounds strange, but I feel like maybe I should have paid more attention, you know? Maybe been more protective. The city can be a dangerous place."

He saw it, the faintest flicker of understanding in her eyes. By showing vulnerability, he was drawing her in, letting her feel as if he, too, was haunted by Jessica's disappearance. It was a subtle dance, a way to cloud her instincts and steer her away from the truth.

Detective Price sipped her soda, studying him over the rim of the glass. "A lot of people here say you're dependable, Jack. That you're the kind of guy people go to when they need help."

Jack smiled, leaning back slightly, sensing that his gamble was working. "I try to be. Life's tough enough without people looking out for each other, right?"

She nodded, but her eyes were still assessing him, as if searching for something beneath the surface. "You know, Jack, in this line of work, you learn that people often hide their pain under a smile. You ever feel like you're carrying more than you let on?"

Jack's stomach twisted, but he kept his expression calm, feigning thoughtfulness. "Maybe," he replied softly. "I guess we all have our secrets."

Price leaned back, her gaze shifting as if she were weighing her next words carefully. But just as she opened her mouth to speak, the door to the bar swung open, and a pair of police officers stepped inside, one of them looking directly at her. Price glanced at Jack, a faint hint of regret in her eyes, before standing to join her colleagues.

"Another time, Jack," she said, her tone almost cordial. "We'll pick up where we left off."

Jack watched her leave, a chill settling over him. He knew he'd planted the seed of doubt in her mind, but he also realized something else—she was getting close, close enough that she was prying into his past, his weaknesses. He had achieved his goal, yet he felt anything but relieved.

That night, Jack returned to his storage unit, desperate to regain control over his situation. The dark interior greeted him, the cold, stale air filling his lungs as he stepped inside and locked the door behind him. He turned on a small flashlight, illuminating the tarped forms of his victims, carefully arranged in the space he had so meticulously hidden from the world.

He moved through the unit, checking each tarp, each shelf, making sure everything was exactly as he had left it.

But as he reached the center of the room, his flashlight caught a glint of something metallic near one of the tarps—a small, black device with a flashing red light.

A recording device.

Jack's heart pounded, a flood of anger and fear crashing over him. Someone had been here again, and this time, they had left a piece of themselves behind—a trap meant to catch him in the act, to turn his sanctuary into a weapon against him.

He clenched his jaw, forcing himself to breathe, to think. He couldn't afford to lose control, not now. With a swift, practiced movement, he picked up the device, disabling it before slipping it into his pocket. He would need to find out who had placed it here, and he had a sinking feeling that Price might be behind it.

The walls were closing in on him. He was running out of time, and he knew it.

The next night at O'Malley's, Jack was prepared. He had gone over his plan a dozen times in his head, perfecting every word, every expression. He had made his decision. Detective Price had to be eliminated.

When she entered, he greeted her as usual, keeping his tone casual, his movements relaxed. But tonight, he planned to plant seeds of doubt that would buy him enough time to cover his tracks and make a final move.

"Detective," he said, leaning across the bar with a somber look, "I don't want to sound paranoid, but... I think someone's been following me."

Price raised an eyebrow, her expression sharpening. "Following you? What makes you say that?"

Jack sighed, glancing around as if nervous, then lowered his voice. "It's little things—footsteps behind me on my way home, feeling watched. I thought maybe it was just the stress, but... well, I found something odd in my storage unit the other day. A recording device."

The detective's expression barely changed, but Jack caught the faint flicker of recognition in her eyes.

"You found a recording device?" she asked, her voice carefully neutral.

Jack nodded, his expression one of unease. "Yeah. It felt... invasive, you know? Like someone's trying to set me up or something."

Price's gaze was unyielding, but Jack saw a hint of hesitation there, a moment of calculation. He knew he had her attention, knew she would be weighing her options carefully.

"Well, Jack," she said slowly, "if someone is trying to intimidate you, it's best to bring it to the police."

Jack forced a small smile. "Thanks, Detective. Just... strange times, I guess."

As she left the bar that night, Jack knew he had planted a small wedge of distrust. He had bought himself precious time to cover his tracks, to ensure that whatever she was looking for, she wouldn't find. But he also knew this was his last chance. He would have to deal with her directly, eliminate the threat she posed once and for all.

In the darkness of his apartment, Jack began planning. Detective Price's keen instincts and relentless nature had made her a threat he couldn't ignore, and the only solution was to remove her before she got too close. He would make it look accidental, a run-in with a "dangerous stranger," something that would throw her off his trail for good.

He ran through his options, calculating each step with the same precision he used in his mechanic work, the same care he took with every victim he lured. He would arrange a final meeting, a place secluded enough to ensure she wouldn't make it out.

As he finalized his plan, a thrill ran through him, a rush of exhilaration mixed with the dark satisfaction of his trade. He was about to confront his most dangerous prey yet.

But as he stared into the dim reflection in his window, he couldn't shake the feeling that this time, he was playing a game that had spiraled beyond his control, a game where even he couldn't be sure he would come out on top.

And as he prepared for his final move, he knew that this encounter would either secure his secrets... or expose him for the monster he truly was.

Jack spent the next few days meticulously preparing for his final move. He knew that this time, everything had to be flawless. Detective Price was no ordinary mark; she was shrewd, perceptive, and relentless. But Jack was confident in his plan, a dark calm settling over him as he rehearsed every detail in his mind.

He chose a secluded location: an abandoned warehouse on the outskirts of the city, a place where no one would come, where any noise would be swallowed by the empty, desolate surroundings. He would lure her there under the pretense of discussing the recent "harassment" he had mentioned, setting the stage for a final, decisive encounter.

On the night of the confrontation, he left his apartment just after midnight, navigating the streets with a practiced ease that belied his intentions. By the time he reached the warehouse, he had cleared his mind, reducing his emotions to a razor-sharp focus. He was ready.

At O'Malley's, Jack had been careful to make his encounter with Detective Price seem natural. Earlier that evening, he had mentioned to her that he was meeting a potential witness who had information about Jessica's last night. He played the part perfectly, letting his voice waver with nerves, his gaze darting around as though afraid of being overheard.

"Meet me at the old warehouse on Glenview at midnight," he had said, his voice barely a whisper. "This guy wants to meet somewhere out of the way. Said he'd only talk if it's just the two of us. Figured you'd want to be there, Detective."

Price had looked at him carefully, her expression guarded but intrigued. "Fine. But if this guy's jerking us around, you'll be the first to answer for it."

Jack had nodded, masking the satisfaction that simmered beneath the surface. "Understood, Detective. I just want to help."

And now, as he stood in the shadows of the warehouse, he watched as Price arrived, her dark silhouette visible in the glow of the streetlamp outside. She stepped out of her car, her movements cautious, her hand resting on her hip, where her service weapon lay concealed. Jack felt a flicker of respect. She was sharp—almost too sharp—but tonight, she had underestimated him.

The door creaked open as she entered, her footsteps echoing in the vast, empty space. Jack kept to the shadows, his heart steady, his breath controlled. He waited, watching her eyes scan the room, searching for him.

"Jack?" she called out, her voice firm but tinged with suspicion. "Where is this 'witness' you told me about?"

Jack stepped forward, letting her see him just beyond the reach of the dim light filtering through the broken windows. "He'll be here soon, Detective. I just thought... maybe we could talk first. Away from prying eyes."

Price's eyes narrowed, her hand inching closer to her weapon. "Talk about what, exactly?"

Jack took a step closer, keeping his movements slow, unthreatening. "About Jessica. About you. About how you've been watching me."

Price's jaw tightened, her gaze never leaving his face. "It's my job to watch, Jack. To look for answers. People don't just disappear without leaving a trace."

A small smile curled at the edge of his lips, a faint glimmer of the darkness he kept hidden. "And what if there was no trace to leave, Detective? What if the person responsible was... careful?"

Price's eyes sharpened, her body tensing. "What are you getting at, Jack?"

Another step. "I think you know, Detective. You've known for a while, haven't you? You just needed proof."

Her hand moved to her weapon, her voice dropping to a low warning. "Don't come any closer, Jack."

But Jack held his hands up, a calculated gesture of innocence. “I only want to talk, Lauren. You came here for answers, and I think you’ve already found them.”

She hesitated, her fingers tightening around her weapon as she tried to assess his intentions. But Jack could see it—the flicker of doubt, the split-second uncertainty that was all he needed. In a swift motion, he lunged forward, grabbing her arm before she could react, twisting it behind her back and pinning her against the wall.

Price struggled, her movements fierce, her voice a low snarl. “Let go of me, Jack. You’re making a mistake.”

Jack leaned in close, his voice calm, almost serene. “The only mistake I made was letting you get this close, Detective. You see, I’ve always been good at fixing things, at handling problems that others can’t. And tonight, you’re just another problem to be solved.”

She gritted her teeth, a fierce determination blazing in her eyes. “People know where I am, Jack. If I don’t check in, they’ll come looking.”

Jack laughed softly, a dark edge to his voice. “Oh, I’ve planned for that too, Lauren. I’m very thorough.”

In a final, desperate move, Price twisted in his grip, her elbow connecting with his ribs in a sharp jab that forced him to loosen his hold. She spun around, drawing her weapon and pointing it directly at him, her breathing labored, her eyes burning with fury.

“Put your hands where I can see them, Jack,” she ordered, her voice steady. “It’s over.”

Jack held up his hands, a look of amused resignation on his face. “You think it’s that easy, don’t you, Detective? That you can just walk out of here, call for backup, and make everything right?"

Price took a step back, her gaze unwavering. "I know enough about you to make sure you never see the light of day again. This is where it ends, Jack."

Jack's smile faded, his eyes turning cold, calculating. "For you, maybe."

In a flash, he lunged at her again, his movements swift and calculated. She fired a shot, the sound echoing through the warehouse, but Jack twisted, dodging just enough for the bullet to graze his shoulder. The pain flared, sharp and hot, but he ignored it, grappling for the weapon as they struggled, each of them fighting for control.

They moved in a deadly dance, their movements a blur of violence and desperation. Price was skilled, her training evident in every calculated strike, but Jack had the advantage of raw, ruthless force. He managed to knock the gun from her grip, sending it skittering across the floor as they collided with a metal beam, the impact forcing the air from her lungs.

Price tried to push him away, but Jack tightened his grip, pressing her back against the cold metal. His face was close to hers, his expression twisted with a dark satisfaction.

"You were right about me, Detective," he whispered, his voice low and chilling. "But it won't matter now. No one's coming for you."

With a final, brutal movement, he pinned her arms, his strength overwhelming hers. Price's eyes flashed with defiance, even as she struggled, even as she realized the grim reality of her situation. She refused to beg, refused to give him the satisfaction.

"You think this makes you invincible?" she hissed, her voice strained but fierce. "Someone will figure it out. Someone will bring you down."

Jack's smile returned, cold and predatory. "They can try."

With one swift, decisive motion, he silenced her, his grip firm as he watched the light fade from her eyes, his own expression one of cold detachment. When it was over, he stepped back, breathing heavily, the weight of what he had done settling over him.

He took a moment to collect himself, adjusting his shirt, wiping the smear of blood from his hands. The warehouse was silent now, the echoes of their struggle fading into the dark, empty space. He glanced at Detective Price's still form, a sense of finality settling over him.

He had won. He had removed the last obstacle in his path, the one person who had dared to look beyond his mask, to see the darkness he kept hidden. And now, as he turned to leave, he knew that his secrets were safe once more.

But as he stepped into the night, a faint unease lingered at the edges of his mind, a whisper that told him he would never truly be free. For in a city as vast as this, there were always eyes, always people who watched, who questioned. And though he had silenced Detective Price, he knew that others might come, that the shadows he hid in would never be entirely safe.

But for now, Jack of All Trades walked free, his secrets buried in the darkness, his life once more under his control.

The days following Detective Price's disappearance were some of the most tense in Jack's life. He returned to his routines, meticulously performing each step with the same care he had always practiced, but he felt the weight of her absence looming over him. At O'Malley's, whispers filled the air once again, talk of another person gone missing—a detective, no less—and Jack could sense the growing unease among the regulars.

He knew he had covered his tracks well. The warehouse had been scrubbed of any trace, and Detective Price's vehicle had been left miles away, at the edge of a riverbank, creating the perfect illusion of her leaving town abruptly, perhaps for a lead she never mentioned. But he also knew that people would eventually connect her disappearance to Jessica's. After all, Price's investigation had drawn attention to both herself and those she questioned.

Jack was prepared for the scrutiny; he had practiced this patience for years. But he wasn't prepared for the lingering feeling that something was wrong, that despite his best efforts, something had slipped. And he would have to work hard to control it, to ensure he stayed one step ahead.

A week after Price's disappearance, Jack was in the middle of a slow night at O'Malley's, the bar quieter than usual. He was polishing glasses behind the counter when the door creaked open, and a tall, older man in a rumpled suit walked in. The man had a stern, tired expression, his eyes sharp and searching as they settled on Jack.

"Evening," Jack greeted, his voice steady as he continued his work.

The man nodded, taking a seat at the bar. "I'll have a whiskey, neat."

Jack poured the drink and set it in front of him, offering a polite smile. "Anything else I can get you?"

The man studied him for a moment, then shook his head. "No, just the whiskey, thanks." He sipped it slowly, his gaze fixed on Jack, watching him with a quiet intensity that reminded Jack of Price's initial visits.

Jack forced himself to remain calm, his expression neutral. "Passing through town?"

The man gave a faint smile. "Not exactly. Name's Detective Mason. I'm a friend of Lauren Price."

Jack's heart skipped a beat, but he kept his reaction in check, nodding with a sympathetic expression. "Oh, Detective Price. I heard she's been missing. You here to help with the investigation?"

Mason tilted his head, his gaze unblinking. "Something like that. I'm here to follow up on her last case, retrace her steps. Seems she was focused on a missing girl named Jessica. Thought I'd ask a few questions, see if anyone remembers anything."

Jack nodded, leaning in slightly. "Yeah, it's been rough around here. People are on edge. Jessica was here the night she disappeared, and Detective Price came by a few times to ask questions."

Mason watched him carefully, taking another sip of his whiskey. "And you? Did you talk to her about Jessica?"

Jack shrugged, keeping his voice even. "Sure, we talked. Just small things. I didn't know Jessica well, but I was one of the last people to see her that night. Detective Price wanted to know if I noticed anything unusual."

Mason nodded slowly, setting his glass down. "I'm sure she did. She was very thorough, Lauren was. Liked to leave no stone unturned. It's odd, though," he added, his gaze sharp. "She didn't mention anything unusual in her notes about you. Said you were helpful. Thought that was strange, considering she was so good at noticing details."

Jack smiled faintly. "Guess she didn't find anything out of the ordinary."

The detective's gaze lingered, a hint of suspicion in his eyes. "Maybe. But tell me, Jack, did Lauren seem... concerned about anything? Like she had uncovered something she wasn't sharing?"

Jack shook his head, keeping his expression calm. "No, nothing like that. She seemed focused on Jessica's case. That was all."

Mason stared at him for a long moment, then nodded, finishing his whiskey. "Alright. Well, if you think of anything she might have mentioned—anything at all—give me a call." He set a card on the counter, his eyes still fixed on Jack. "You never know what detail might help."

Jack picked up the card, nodding politely. "Of course, Detective. I'll be sure to reach out if I remember anything."

As Mason left, Jack felt the familiar prickling unease settle over him. Detective Price had been thorough, but she had also been cautious, careful not to reveal her suspicions. Yet she must have left clues behind, traces of her investigation that Mason was now picking up, drawing him closer to Jack's carefully guarded secrets.

He knew he would have to be careful. Mason was watching him, and he was clearly willing to go to great lengths to find out what had happened to Price. But Jack had outmaneuvered people before, and he knew that he could do it again.

Over the following days, Detective Mason returned to O'Malley's several times, each visit unannounced and increasingly scrutinizing. He asked questions, speaking with the regulars, his approach more direct and intrusive than Price's had been. Jack had anticipated this, and he made sure to remain as unremarkable as possible, his answers consistent and calm, his demeanor always friendly and helpful.

But Mason's attention was relentless, his gaze unyielding, and Jack knew he was searching for something, looking for any crack in Jack's mask. It was a silent, tense game between them, each of them watching, each of them waiting for the other to slip.

One evening, after the bar had closed, Mason lingered outside, catching Jack as he locked up. The air was thick with tension, the streetlights casting long shadows across the empty sidewalk.

"Jack," Mason began, his tone conversational but his eyes cold, "I can't shake the feeling that Lauren was on to something here. She was a damn good detective, and she wouldn't just walk away from a case without reason."

Jack met his gaze, his expression carefully neutral. "I'm sorry she's missing, Detective. I really am. But I don't know what you want from me. I've told you everything I know."

Mason nodded slowly, his eyes narrowing. "You're right. Maybe you don't know anything. But I'll be around, Jack. Just in case you remember something."

Jack nodded, watching as Mason turned and disappeared into the night, his figure swallowed by the shadows. The tension in Jack's chest tightened, the weight of Mason's gaze lingering long after he'd gone. It was clear that Mason wasn't going anywhere, that he would keep digging until he found answers.

That night, Jack returned to his apartment, his mind racing with possibilities, with plans and contingencies. He had one option left, one final move that could put an end to Mason's investigation before it uncovered his hidden life. He would have to remove Mason, to silence the detective just as he had silenced Price.

He began crafting a plan, carefully piecing together every detail, every alibi. He would make it look accidental, like a robbery gone wrong, a routine case of a detective in the wrong place at the wrong time. It would be swift, clean, and untraceable.

The next night, Jack waited, watching from a distance as Mason left the precinct and headed down an empty side street. Jack had rehearsed this moment in his mind, prepared himself for the final confrontation. But as he moved closer, he felt a flicker of doubt, a shadow of something he couldn't quite place.

Mason paused, his body tensing as he sensed a presence behind him. He turned, his eyes narrowing as he met Jack's gaze, the recognition dawning on his face.

"Jack," he said quietly, his voice steady. "I should have known."

Jack took a step forward, his voice calm, almost regretful. "You shouldn't have come looking, Detective. Some things are best left buried."

Mason squared his shoulders, his gaze unwavering. "You can try to silence me, Jack, but you won't stop the truth. Someone else will come after me, someone else will ask questions. It's only a matter of time."

Jack's face hardened, a cold resolve settling over him. "Then I'll deal with them, just as I'm dealing with you."

With a final surge, Jack lunged, his movements swift and precise. But Mason was ready, his body moving with practiced ease, and the two of them clashed in a fierce struggle, each of them fighting with everything they had.

In the end, it was Jack who gained the upper hand, his years of experience, his ruthlessness overpowering Mason's determination. As Mason fell, his final words echoed in the silent street, a chilling warning that lingered in Jack's mind.

"They'll come for you, Jack. You can't hide forever."

And as Jack disappeared into the night, he felt the weight of those words settle over him, a reminder that his secrets would never truly be safe, that no matter how well he hid, the shadows he walked in would eventually turn against him.

For now, Jack of All Trades was free. But he knew, deep down, that his freedom came with a price—a price he would continue to pay, one life at a time.

After silencing Detective Mason, Jack expected a reprieve, a return to the peace he once found in the shadows. But the fallout was immediate and relentless. Mason's disappearance sent shockwaves through the precinct, and the city's newspapers buzzed with headlines about the missing detectives. The police intensified their efforts, combing through every detail of Jessica's and Price's cases, dredging up threads that had previously gone unnoticed. Jack knew they were getting closer, and his every step felt heavier, laden with the dread that his perfect life was beginning to fracture.

At O'Malley's, the air was thick with suspicion. Regulars he once called friends seemed guarded, distant, as if they, too, sensed that something dark lurked beneath his calm exterior. Jack had been careful, calculating. But even he couldn't ignore that he had entered a new phase, a point of no return, and the sensation of eyes on him felt constant and oppressive.

One night, after closing the bar, Jack decided to stop by his storage unit. He felt the need to check on his collection, a twisted habit he had developed over the years, a ritual that grounded him. But as he stepped inside, he was met with a horrifying sight.

The tarps, which he had so meticulously arranged, had been disturbed. A corner of one lay peeled back, exposing the contorted, lifeless face of his most recent victim. His heart hammered in his chest as he realized the implications—someone had been here, someone knew.

He moved deeper into the unit, his flashlight trembling in his grip. Tucked into a corner, taped to the wall, was another note. He ripped it down, unfolding it with a sense of dread.

"The walls are closing in, Jack. They know."

Jack's mind raced, his thoughts spiraling as he tried to piece together what was happening. This wasn't just someone stumbling upon his unit by accident. This was a message, a direct challenge. Someone was playing with him, taunting him, and they were getting dangerously close.

He thought of Price, of Mason. Had either of them left clues he hadn't found, breadcrumbs leading back to him? He realized he might have underestimated the reach of his hunters. This time, he wasn't in control; he was the one being cornered.

The following day, Jack returned to his mechanic job, keeping his head down, trying to blend in. But he couldn't shake the feeling of being watched. Everywhere he went, he sensed eyes on him—co-workers who glanced his way, customers who lingered a bit too long, police cars that seemed to pass his shop more often. The paranoia gnawed at him, a constant reminder that his secrets were unravelling.

That evening, as he tended the bar at O'Malley's, he noticed new faces among the patrons—undercover officers, no doubt, sent to observe him, to catch any slip. He remained calm, serving drinks, making small talk, pretending to be oblivious. But his mind was racing, calculating his next move.

A woman at the end of the bar caught his attention. She was dressed plainly, her expression calm, but there was something in her gaze—a quiet intensity that made him uneasy. She watched him with the same curiosity he had seen in Price's eyes, an unwavering gaze that felt both familiar and deeply unsettling.

When he approached her, she offered a polite smile, her voice casual as she ordered a drink. But as he handed it to her, she leaned in, her words barely audible over the noise of the bar.

"You're good at what you do, Jack," she murmured, her gaze piercing. "But everyone makes mistakes."

Jack's blood ran cold, though he forced a smile. "I'm sorry, do I know you?"

She shrugged, taking a sip of her drink. "Not yet. But you might know me soon enough."

With that, she stood, leaving a twenty on the bar, and walked out without another word. Jack watched her go, his pulse pounding as he realized he had been warned. Whoever was after him was close, watching his every move, waiting for him to falter.

Over the next few days, Jack's life became a waking nightmare. The police presence around him grew, and the sense of isolation thickened as those he once relied on drifted away, wary and distant. He had always believed he could outsmart anyone who came too close, that he was untouchable. But now, he was losing his grip, his confidence cracking under the relentless pressure.

One evening, he returned to his apartment to find his door slightly ajar. He froze, the hairs on his neck standing on end. Every instinct told him to turn and leave, to run. But he forced himself inside, his heart hammering in his chest.

The apartment was dark, the silence oppressive. He moved cautiously, his mind racing as he searched for any signs of intrusion. In the center of his coffee table, he found it—a plain manila envelope. He opened it, pulling out a single sheet of paper.

"You've made a career out of hiding, but your time is running out."

He staggered back, the room spinning as he realized the extent of his predicament. Someone was inside his life, leaving breadcrumbs he couldn't ignore, showing him just how thoroughly they knew him.

Jack understood he had no choice but to abandon everything. His apartment, his jobs, his collection—all of it would have to go. He would disappear, slip into the shadows, start fresh somewhere far away. But he couldn't shake the feeling that even if he ran, they would follow. They would find him.

That night, he emptied his apartment, packing only the essentials, abandoning the remnants of his old life. He took one last trip to his storage unit, clearing out what he could, erasing every trace. By dawn, he was on the road, his mind set on disappearing for good, on leaving behind the relentless chase that had consumed him.

But as he drove through the empty streets, a dark car appeared in his rearview mirror, keeping pace with him, its headlights casting an ominous glow. He turned onto side streets, weaving through back roads, but the car followed, unwavering, relentless.

Panic gripped him, his heart pounding as he realized he couldn't escape. They had him, and he was out of moves, out of options.

Desperation took hold, and he pulled over in a secluded area, stepping out of the car, his breaths coming in shallow gasps. The dark car stopped a short distance behind him, its engine rumbling in the quiet night. The woman from the bar stepped out, her expression calm, her eyes locked onto his.

"You didn't think you'd get away, did you, Jack?" she asked, her tone cold, unfeeling.

Jack's voice was strained, a mixture of fear and defiance. "You think you're so smart? You think you can judge me?"

The woman's gaze was steady, her expression unreadable. "No, Jack. I'm just here to bring justice. The justice you've evaded for so long."

He lunged at her in a final act of desperation, but she sidestepped, moving with practiced ease. In moments, he was on the ground, her foot pressed against his back as she called for backup. The sirens echoed through the night, a symphony of his defeat, of the life he had built crumbling around him.

As the police closed in, Jack felt a hollow emptiness settle in his chest, a chilling realization that he had become the prey in his own game, the hunted instead of the hunter. His life as a master of secrets, of darkness, had finally caught up to him, and there would be no escaping this time.

As he was led away in handcuffs, the woman's words echoed in his mind, a final reminder of the life he had lost, of the price he would pay.

"Everyone makes mistakes, Jack. And you just made yours."

The End

24
STONE COLD

Evelyn Thorne was a fixture of the city's aging high-rise, the type of person you'd glance at once and dismiss as part of the scenery. She was quiet, solitary, with a guarded face that revealed nothing. She lived on the eleventh floor, in a small apartment with a dim view of the sprawling, indifferent city. Most days, her neighbors barely noticed her—until they did.

As she moved through the hallways, a faint chill seemed to follow her, an unsettling, inexplicable sensation that lingered like a faint fog. People often brushed it off as the hum of the outdated heating system or the wind slipping through the cracks in the old building. But Evelyn knew better. It was her presence, her secret, something she carried in her dark, unblinking eyes.

Evelyn's secret was one she had learned to conceal over the years. It was not something she could speak of to anyone, nor was it something anyone would believe. To Evelyn, eye contact was not a fleeting gesture; it was a weapon, a power that bound others in place, trapping them in the silent depths of her gaze.

No one knew where it came from or why it had happened to her, least of all Evelyn herself. She had discovered it by accident, years ago, when she had locked eyes with a man who had grabbed her arm outside a late-night grocery store. His face had twisted with anger, but the moment his eyes met hers, a terror unlike any she'd ever seen flickered across his face. His body froze, rooted to the spot, his eyes wide with fear, unblinking and paralyzed. She had simply stepped back, watching him as he stood there, shaking, unable to break free. She had walked away, leaving him frozen in place, the echoes of his panicked breaths fading as she disappeared into the night.

Since then, she had avoided looking directly at anyone. She kept her gaze low, guarded, even as she maneuvered through the crowded city streets, slipping through unnoticed. But on the rare occasion when someone dared to confront her, they would feel the weight of her gaze, a pull that left them trapped, vulnerable, unable to look away.

On this particular evening, Evelyn returned to her apartment carrying a small bag of groceries, her coat buttoned tightly against the autumn chill. She was almost to her door when she heard a voice behind her.

"Excuse me, ma'am?"

Evelyn turned slowly, her eyes meeting those of a man in his mid-30s. He was holding a clipboard, dressed in the standard blue uniform of a utility worker. She knew that gaze—the feigned politeness, the expectation of compliance. A routine visit, or so he thought.

"We're just doing some inspections on the heating system," he said, his tone clipped. "If you don't mind, I'd like to take a quick look inside your apartment."

Evelyn's face remained impassive as she studied him. She noticed the faint unease in his eyes, the way his fingers tightened around the clipboard, as if some part of him sensed that there was something unusual about her, something that didn't fit. But he brushed it off, forcing a professional smile.

"Do you have an appointment?" she asked, her voice low and calm.

He shifted uncomfortably, a flicker of impatience crossing his face. "It's just a quick inspection. Won't take long."

She sighed, glancing down, careful to avoid his gaze. "I'd prefer if you came back another time."

He took a step closer, his voice firm. "Look, ma'am, it's mandatory. Just open the door, and I'll be in and out in five minutes."

It was then that Evelyn made the decision. She lifted her eyes, meeting his.

The man's expression shifted, his smile faltering as he stared back at her, his body tensing, his breathing shallow. He opened his mouth to speak, but no words came. His face drained of color, his eyes widening with terror as he felt himself trapped, immobilized, unable to look away. Evelyn held his gaze, feeling the familiar pulse of power, the cold tendrils of her ability wrapping around him like a vice.

"Leave," she said softly, her voice barely more than a whisper.

He remained frozen, his mouth half-open, his eyes locked on hers, the clipboard slipping from his hand and clattering to the floor. She watched him, noting the sheen of sweat that had broken out on his forehead, the way his shoulders shook, his body unable to obey the simplest command to move.

After what felt like an eternity, she released him, stepping back and breaking eye contact. The man stumbled, gasping, his hand flying to his chest as he backed away, his eyes darting around the hallway as though seeking an escape.

"I—I'm sorry," he stammered, his voice barely a whisper. "I'll come back later."

Without waiting for a response, he turned and fled down the hallway, his footsteps echoing through the silence, fading into the distance.

Evelyn watched him go, her expression unreadable. She knew he wouldn't be back. He wouldn't even remember her apartment number. He would only remember the feeling of her gaze, the paralyzing fear that would haunt his thoughts for days, maybe weeks, until it blurred into an incomprehensible nightmare.

She turned back to her door, unlocking it and stepping inside, the comforting darkness wrapping around her like a cloak. She set the groceries on the counter, her mind already slipping back into the solitude she had come to cherish.

But as she settled into her apartment, a nagging thought surfaced in her mind, a realization that brought with it an unfamiliar dread.

In a city this crowded, it was only a matter of time before someone would return, someone with a stronger will, someone unwilling to look away.

And Evelyn, the woman who had mastered the art of remaining unseen, knew that the city she had once moved through so freely was becoming smaller, its shadows growing colder, as her secret threatened to come to light.

Evelyn's life returned to its usual routine, but the encounter with the utility worker lingered in her mind like a shadow. For years, she had perfected the art of solitude, moving through the world unseen, unnoticed. But now, she sensed a shift, a ripple that spread through her quiet existence, warning her that things were beginning to change.

Days passed in a blur of mundane tasks, yet the atmosphere in the building felt different. People's eyes lingered on her a moment too long, their gazes filled with something she couldn't quite place—curiosity, suspicion, perhaps even fear. She kept her own gaze low, careful to avoid making eye contact, but she knew that her control was slipping, that the delicate balance she'd maintained was starting to unravel.

One afternoon, Evelyn returned from the grocery store to find a moving van parked outside the building. A few cardboard boxes sat stacked by the elevator, and as she stepped inside, she heard footsteps approaching.

"Hold the door!" a voice called out, breathless and friendly.

Evelyn turned, her fingers tensing on the elevator button, but she couldn't avoid it—the sight of a young woman hurrying toward her, a wide smile on her face, a coffee cup balanced precariously on top of the last of her boxes.

"Thanks," the woman said, stepping into the elevator. "I'm Mira, by the way. Just moved in—apartment 11B."

Evelyn nodded, her face expressionless. "Welcome."

Mira looked her over, her eyes bright and curious. "Do you live here on the eleventh floor too?"

"Yes," Evelyn replied, her voice curt.

"Well, that's nice. I was hoping I'd meet someone up here—get the lay of the land, you know?" Mira chuckled, completely oblivious to Evelyn's discomfort.

Evelyn's grip on her grocery bag tightened. This woman was friendly, talkative—a stark contrast to the quiet, unassuming neighbors she had been able to ignore for years. She forced herself to remain calm, to keep her gaze on the wall, anywhere but Mira's face.

As the elevator reached their floor and the doors opened, Evelyn stepped out without a word. But Mira followed, walking beside her as they moved down the hall.

"So, I guess we're neighbors," Mira continued. "Funny coincidence. I don't know many people here, but you seem nice."

Evelyn's pace quickened. "Yes. Have a nice day."

She reached her door and unlocked it, stepping inside before Mira could say another word. As she closed the door, she heard Mira's footsteps retreat down the hall, her cheerful humming fading as she disappeared into her own apartment.

Evelyn leaned against the door, her pulse racing. It was a minor encounter, but she knew the type: a neighbor who would want to stop and chat, who would knock on her door at odd hours, who would keep her from her isolation. Evelyn had spent years mastering the art of invisibility, but people like Mira were dangerous—they saw too much, asked too many questions.

Over the following weeks, Mira's presence became a constant irritant, a disruption to Evelyn's carefully controlled life. Every time she stepped out of her apartment, Mira was there with a smile and a friendly wave. She asked Evelyn about her day, her hobbies, her life. Evelyn offered little in return, keeping her responses short, evasive. But Mira's persistence only grew, and Evelyn could sense the curiosity simmering behind her questions.

One evening, as Evelyn was returning home, she found Mira waiting for her in the hallway, her expression thoughtful.

"Evelyn," Mira began, her tone softer than usual, "I don't mean to pry, but... you seem so... alone. I mean, you never have visitors. I was just wondering if everything's alright."

Evelyn felt a chill creep down her spine, her defenses rising. "I'm fine. I prefer it this way."

Mira hesitated, a look of genuine concern in her eyes. "I get that. I just... I thought you might like some company. I know what it's like to feel isolated, and I don't want you to feel that way if you don't have to."

Evelyn's gaze drifted toward Mira, and for a split second, her control wavered. She met Mira's eyes, a flash of annoyance breaking through her otherwise calm demeanor.

Instantly, Mira's face paled, her eyes widening in shock as she froze, her body locking in place. Evelyn's stomach twisted as she felt the familiar pulse of her power take hold, an invisible weight pressing down on Mira, filling her with terror. For a long moment, Mira stood there, her face blank with horror, her breathing shallow.

Evelyn looked away, breaking the connection. Mira gasped, stumbling backward, her expression one of confusion and fear as she struggled to regain her composure.

"I'm sorry," Mira stammered, her voice barely a whisper. "I don't know what came over me. I just... I felt..."

Evelyn's face remained impassive. "Goodnight, Mira."

Without another word, she turned and walked into her apartment, closing the door firmly behind her. She could hear Mira's footsteps fading down the hall, faster this time, as though she were fleeing.

The next morning, Evelyn could feel the shift. She sensed the glances from her neighbors, the way conversations dropped to a hush as she passed. Mira had spoken to someone; she had spread the unease she had felt, even if she couldn't fully explain it. The building's residents were now eyeing her with suspicion, their gazes wary, nervous.

She knew she couldn't afford to let this escalate. In a city where people valued their privacy, she had always managed to stay hidden, her presence a mere shadow in the background. But now, her anonymity was slipping, and the walls around her were closing in.

Her gaze fell on her reflection in the hallway mirror as she made her way down to the lobby. Her eyes, dark and unreadable, stared back at her. She saw the depth of her power there, the quiet but terrible ability that had set her apart. And she knew, in that moment, that if anyone else dared to pry into her life, she would have no choice but to use it again.

The city was beginning to close in on her, the subtle discomfort of others inching closer to outright fear. And Evelyn Thorne, the woman who had spent years hiding from the world, now understood that she might have to become something darker, something colder, to protect the life she had so carefully constructed.

As she stepped out into the bustling street, she could feel the weight of her secret pressing down on her, a reminder that she was never truly alone, that someone would always be watching, always questioning.

But this time, she wouldn't allow it. She would do whatever it took to remain in the shadows, to keep her secret buried.

Evelyn kept to herself even more rigidly, retreating deeper into her isolation as she sensed the shift in the building's atmosphere. She could feel the suspicion intensify with each passing day, the weight of wary glances pressing down on her as neighbors passed in the hallways, their voices lowering to whispers when they thought she wasn't listening. Her solitude, once a comfortable refuge, was now a cage, growing smaller with each questioning look, each moment of silence that followed her presence.

Despite her efforts to stay invisible, Mira was relentless. She continued her casual, cheerful attempts at conversation, as if nothing had happened, as if that moment in the hallway—Evelyn's slip, her accidental gaze—hadn't happened at all. But Evelyn could see the faint, lingering fear in Mira's eyes, the way her hands tensed whenever they crossed paths.

But then, one evening, everything changed.

It was late, and Evelyn was returning from her weekly grocery run. She preferred going out late at night when the streets were quieter, the city's buzz fading into a dull hum. As she approached her building, she saw a small group of residents gathered near the entrance. Mira was among them, her voice low and urgent, her expression serious.

Evelyn hesitated, but she couldn't avoid the group. She walked past them, her gaze fixed ahead, hoping to slip by unnoticed. But Mira called out to her.

"Evelyn," she said, her tone cautious but resolute. "We were just... talking. About some things we've all noticed."

Evelyn stopped, her hand tightening around her grocery bag. She turned slowly, meeting Mira's gaze with a look that bordered on cold detachment.

"What things?" she asked, her voice calm but carrying an edge.

The others shifted uncomfortably, avoiding her eyes. Mira took a step closer, her hands wringing together. "It's just... well, there's something about you. Something that doesn't feel right. I mean, every time we try to talk to you, it's like... there's this wall. Like you're hiding something."

Evelyn's heart pounded, but she kept her face expressionless. "I prefer to keep to myself. I don't see how that's any of your concern."

Mira hesitated, glancing at the others before speaking again. "It's not just that. I... I don't know how to explain it, but there's something about the way you look at people. I felt it the other night. It's like you... like you can see through people. Like you're looking into them."

A ripple of discomfort passed through the group. Evelyn could see the unease in their faces, the way they shifted back, as if her very presence was enough to unnerve them.

"I'm not sure what you're implying, Mira," Evelyn replied, her voice calm and cool. "But perhaps you're letting your imagination get the better of you."

Mira's eyes flashed with a mix of fear and determination. "Maybe. But I know what I felt. And others have felt it too."

Evelyn's patience wore thin, a flicker of irritation crossing her face. "Is there a point to all of this?"

Mira took a step back, her resolve faltering. "I just... I think we have a right to know if something's wrong."

Evelyn's gaze hardened, her voice dropping to a near whisper. "Be careful, Mira. Curiosity can lead to dangerous places."

With that, she turned and walked away, her footsteps echoing down the hallway. She could feel their eyes on her back, the tension thickening in the air, but she refused to let it bother her. She had lived in the shadows for years, and she would continue to do so, no matter what.

But as she closed her door behind her, she couldn't shake the feeling that her secret was slipping from her control, that the delicate walls she had built around her life were beginning to crumble.

Two days later, Evelyn's worst fears came to fruition.

It was early evening, and Evelyn was alone in her apartment, savoring the quiet that had become her only sanctuary. But her solitude was shattered by a sharp, insistent knock at her door. She froze, the sound jarring in the stillness of her apartment.

Another knock. Louder this time.

Reluctantly, she moved to the door, peering through the peephole. Mira stood on the other side, looking tense, her arms folded tightly over her chest.

Evelyn opened the door just a crack, her expression neutral. "Yes?"

Mira hesitated, glancing around as though making sure they were alone. "I know you told me to be careful, Evelyn.

But I can't ignore this... this feeling that something is wrong. And I'm not the only one."

Evelyn's patience was thin. "We've already discussed this. If you can't accept my desire for privacy, that's your problem."

Mira's voice dropped, her face tight with fear and frustration. "I saw you, Evelyn. The way you looked at that man in the hallway, the way he froze, like he was paralyzed. I don't know what you're capable of, but it's not... normal."

Evelyn's gaze sharpened, a flash of cold warning in her eyes. "Be careful what you say, Mira. I don't take kindly to accusations."

Mira took a step back, visibly shaken, but she held her ground. "Fine. You want to keep secrets, go ahead. But I'm not the only one watching you. Everyone is."

Without another word, Mira turned and hurried down the hall, her footsteps fading as she disappeared around the corner.

Evelyn closed her door, her heart pounding. She had always known that her secret would be hard to keep, but she had underestimated the tenacity of someone like Mira. She could feel the walls closing in, the faintest crack forming in the carefully constructed life she had built.

That night, Evelyn sat in the darkness of her apartment, her mind racing. She had managed to keep her ability hidden for years, but now it was slipping through her fingers, the facade of normalcy crumbling under the weight of suspicion. She knew that Mira wouldn't stop, that the others wouldn't stop. They would keep pushing, digging, until they uncovered the truth.

And that was something Evelyn couldn't allow.

For years, she had restrained herself, avoided using her power unless absolutely necessary. But now, as she stared into the shadows, she realized that restraint was no longer an option. If Mira and the others continued to pry, they would eventually find out what she was hiding, and her quiet life would be shattered beyond repair.

With a deep breath, Evelyn rose from her chair, her gaze cold and resolute. She would take control of the situation, once and for all. Mira had left her no choice. She had forced Evelyn's hand, driven her to a point she could no longer turn back from.

The next time Mira came knocking, Evelyn would be ready.

And this time, she wouldn't hold back.

Evelyn spent the following days preparing herself for what she knew was coming. She could feel the shift in the building's atmosphere, the way the walls seemed to close in around her, trapping her. The quiet whispers, the sidelong glances from her neighbors—every interaction felt charged, as though the entire building were holding its breath, waiting for something to break.

Her mind raced with memories of her first encounters with her power. The fear in her victims' eyes, the paralyzing horror that gripped them, rooting them in place, unable to escape her gaze. She had spent years keeping that side of herself locked away, hidden from the world. But now, she could feel it creeping back, a dark force stirring within her, urging her to take control.

And the first step was Mira.

It was a rainy evening when Mira returned, her presence heralded by an insistent knock on Evelyn's door. This time, Evelyn didn't hesitate. She opened the door wide, letting Mira step inside.

Mira's expression was determined but wary, a look of guarded resolution in her eyes. She glanced around the dimly lit apartment, her gaze lingering on the shadows cast by the sparse furniture and the heavy drapes.

"We need to talk, Evelyn," Mira said, her voice steady but strained. "I can't keep pretending that everything's normal. People are scared of you. They've seen things... strange things."

Evelyn closed the door softly, turning to face Mira. "Have they now?" she murmured, her voice cold and detached. "And what have they seen, exactly?"

Mira swallowed, but she held her ground. "They've seen the way people react to you. The way they freeze, like they're trapped... terrified. They don't know what it is, but they know it's not normal."

Evelyn took a slow, measured step closer, her gaze fixed on Mira's face. "And what do you think it is, Mira?"

Mira hesitated, glancing down as if searching for the right words. When she looked up, Evelyn saw a flash of fear in her eyes. "I don't know. But whatever it is... you're hurting people. I've tried to understand, tried to give you the benefit of the doubt, but I can't ignore this anymore. People deserve to feel safe in their own building."

Evelyn's lips curled into a faint, humorless smile. "Safe? What a convenient excuse to pry into someone else's life.

Tell me, Mira, why do you care so much about other people's safety?"

Mira faltered, her expression uncertain. "Because it's the right thing to do," she replied, though her voice lacked conviction.

Evelyn took another step closer, and Mira instinctively backed away, her eyes widening as she felt the familiar pull of Evelyn's gaze. But this time, Evelyn didn't hold back. She allowed the full force of her power to reach Mira, the cold, paralyzing fear that seeped into her, trapping her in place.

"Right and wrong are subjective, Mira," Evelyn whispered, her voice low and icy. "You wanted to see what I was hiding, didn't you? You wanted to uncover the truth."

Mira's face drained of color, her body locked in place as Evelyn's gaze held her captive. She struggled to breathe, her eyes wide with terror as she felt the weight of Evelyn's power pressing down on her, rooting her to the spot.

"Now you know," Evelyn continued, her voice a soft, menacing whisper. "This is the truth you were so desperate to find."

Mira's mouth opened in a silent scream, her eyes glistening with tears as the horror overtook her, filling every inch of her mind. Evelyn watched, cold and detached, as Mira trembled, her body rigid, helpless against the force holding her in place.

And then, just as suddenly, Evelyn released her.

Mira stumbled backward, gasping for breath, her face pale and slick with sweat. She looked at Evelyn, her eyes wide with a mixture of fear and disbelief.

"Leave," Evelyn said softly, her voice a chilling command. "And don't come back."

Without another word, Mira turned and fled, her footsteps echoing down the hallway as she disappeared into the night. Evelyn closed the door, a strange sense of calm settling over her as the silence filled the room.

The next day, the building was abuzz with whispers. Evelyn could feel the change, the way people avoided her, their faces a mixture of fear and suspicion. Mira had spread the word, though Evelyn doubted she had told them the full extent of what she had experienced. Fear had a way of clouding memory, distorting reality, and Evelyn knew that Mira's recollection of their encounter would be fragmented, warped by the terror she had felt.

But it didn't matter. The seeds had been planted, and the residents were now wary, their unease a palpable force that seemed to follow her wherever she went. She saw it in their eyes, the way they glanced at her, their gazes skittering away whenever she looked in their direction.

She relished the silence, the way the air grew thick with tension whenever she entered a room. It was a new kind of power, one she had not fully realized before—a power that extended beyond her gaze, that reached into the hearts and minds of those around her.

Yet she knew it wouldn't be enough. People like Mira would always dig, would always press, would always try to uncover the secrets that others kept hidden. And Evelyn couldn't allow that. She couldn't allow anyone to threaten the solitude she had built, the life she had carefully constructed.

That evening, Evelyn's doorbell rang, its shrill tone cutting through the quiet. She opened the door to find two uniformed officers standing outside, their expressions neutral but wary.

"Ms. Thorne?" one of them asked, his tone polite but cautious.

Evelyn nodded, her face expressionless. "Yes?"

"We're here to follow up on some complaints," he continued, his gaze flicking over her face. "A few residents have expressed concerns about... unusual behavior in the building."

Evelyn raised an eyebrow, her gaze cool and detached. "Unusual behavior? I'm not sure what you mean."

The officer hesitated, glancing at his partner before continuing. "Several residents have mentioned feeling uncomfortable around you. They've described... episodes of fear, of feeling frozen in place when you look at them."

Evelyn's expression remained calm, but she felt a flicker of anger beneath the surface. "That sounds like superstition, officer. Perhaps they're letting their imaginations get the better of them."

The officer shifted uncomfortably, clearly unsettled by her steady gaze. "Be that as it may, Ms. Thorne, we're obligated to follow up on these complaints. We just want to ensure that everyone feels safe in this building."

Evelyn forced a smile, though it didn't reach her eyes. "Of course. I understand. If there's anything I can do to alleviate their concerns, please let me know."

The officer nodded, but Evelyn could see the doubt in his eyes, the way his gaze flickered with unease. She could feel his fear, subtle but present, like a faint pulse beneath the surface.

"Thank you for your cooperation, Ms. Thorne," he said finally. "We'll be in touch if we need any further information."

Evelyn watched as they turned and left, their footsteps echoing down the hallway. She knew this was only the beginning, that the residents' fear had now reached beyond the walls of her building, drawing the attention of others.

And she knew what she had to do.

That night, Evelyn sat alone in her apartment, the city lights casting faint shadows across the room. She had tried to avoid this moment, tried to live a quiet life, to keep her power hidden. But now, she understood that her solitude was a fragile illusion, one that could be shattered by the prying eyes and whispered fears of those around her.

She couldn't leave; this place was the only home she had known for years. But she couldn't allow the fear to spread, to draw more attention, to bring more outsiders into her life.

The building was quiet, the night settling over it like a blanket. She rose from her chair, her movements slow and deliberate, her gaze cold and focused. She would take back her control, one way or another. She would ensure that her secret remained buried, that her life continued undisturbed.

And if that meant confronting those who threatened her peace, silencing the voices that sought to expose her, then so be it.

Evelyn Thorne, the woman who had lived in silence and shadow for so long, was ready to show her neighbors the true extent of her power.

They wanted to know her secret. She would give them more than they had bargained for.

Evelyn moved through the building with an eerie calm, her footsteps light and purposeful as she crossed the dim hallways. She could feel the weight of her decision pressing down on her, but her resolve was unwavering. For too long, she had hidden in the shadows, allowing the quiet existence she cherished to be threatened by prying eyes and curious whispers. Tonight, that would end.

Her first stop was Mira's apartment.

The hallway was silent as she approached, the only sound her own measured breathing. She paused outside Mira's door, her hand resting lightly on the frame. She knew Mira would be inside, hiding from the fear she herself had unleashed. Evelyn's fingers closed into a fist, and she rapped sharply on the door.

After a long moment, she heard shuffling footsteps on the other side. The door opened a crack, revealing Mira's pale face, her eyes wide with surprise—and something else, a glint of dread.

"Evelyn..." Mira's voice was barely a whisper. "What... what are you doing here?"

Evelyn's gaze was calm, unreadable, but her eyes held a glint of something dark. "You spread the fear, Mira. You wanted everyone to see me, to know me. Isn't that right?"

Mira swallowed, her face blanching as she backed away. "I... I didn't mean to— I was just—"

"Curious," Evelyn finished for her, her voice soft, almost gentle. She stepped inside, closing the door behind her with a quiet click.

Mira backed up against the wall, her breaths coming in shallow, panicked gasps. "Please, Evelyn... I don't want any trouble."

Evelyn met her gaze, and Mira's body went rigid, her eyes widening in terror as she felt the familiar, paralyzing force take hold. Evelyn allowed her power to wash over Mira, cold and unyielding, filling her with a fear that reached down to her bones, freezing her in place.

"This is what happens, Mira," Evelyn whispered, her voice barely more than a murmur. "This is what happens when you look too closely."

Mira's eyes filled with tears, but she couldn't look away, couldn't move. She was trapped, suspended in Evelyn's gaze, her mind spiraling into a state of pure, unfiltered terror. Evelyn held her there for a long, agonizing moment, letting the fear take root, burrowing deep into Mira's psyche.

Finally, Evelyn broke eye contact, releasing her from the grip of her power. Mira collapsed to the floor, gasping, her body shaking as she clutched at her chest, her face pale and hollow with fear.

Evelyn leaned down, her voice soft but laced with warning. "Tell them it was a mistake, Mira. Tell them to stop asking questions. Or next time, I won't let go."

Mira nodded frantically, too terrified to speak. Evelyn watched her for a moment, her face impassive, then turned and left, closing the door behind her.

As Evelyn made her way back down the hallway, she could feel the shift in the air, the weight of her actions settling over her like a shroud. She had taken control, but she knew it wouldn't be enough. The residents were scared, yes, but fear was a volatile thing. Left unchecked, it would only grow, spreading through the building like a slow-burning fire.

She needed to make her message clear. This wasn't just a warning—it was a promise.

She descended to the lobby, her footsteps echoing through the empty halls. She could feel the eyes of the night security guard on her, the man's gaze tracking her as she crossed the room. She turned to meet his eyes, allowing him to feel the full force of her stare, the cold, unrelenting power that lay within her.

The man froze, his face blanching as he felt the weight of her gaze settle over him. Evelyn watched him, her expression calm and unyielding.

"Tell them," she said quietly, her voice carrying through the stillness. "Tell them to stop watching, to leave me in peace. I won't be kind again."

The man nodded, his movements stiff and robotic, his face pale with fear. Evelyn held his gaze for another moment, then turned and left, her footsteps fading into the silence.

For the next few days, the building was silent. The residents avoided her, their gazes skittering away whenever she passed. The whispers had stopped, replaced by a tense, uncomfortable silence that filled the air like a thick fog. No one dared to approach her, to ask questions or offer even a polite greeting. They had seen her, understood the force of her power, and they were afraid.

Evelyn relished the quiet. For the first time in years, she felt at peace, the fear she had instilled in others creating a protective barrier around her, a shield that kept prying eyes and intrusive whispers at bay. She moved through her days in a state of calm detachment, her presence casting a long, unspoken shadow over the building.

But as the days passed, a new kind of dread crept into her mind, a gnawing realization that she couldn't quite shake. Her secret had been exposed, yes, but in a way that would only fuel the curiosity, the need to understand. She had wielded her power as a weapon, but it had come at a cost, drawing attention that she could never fully erase.

She knew the residents would never truly forget, that the fear she had instilled would remain, simmering beneath the surface, waiting for the right moment to erupt. And when it did, she would be ready. She would protect the life she had built, the quiet solitude she had fought so hard to maintain, even if it meant embracing the darkness within her.

As Evelyn gazed out her window, watching the city lights flicker in the distance, she felt a strange sense of acceptance settle over her. She was no longer hiding. She was no longer the shadow in the background, the woman who moved unseen. She was something else entirely—a force to be reckoned with, a figure of fear and mystery that no one dared to confront.

And in that final, bone-chilling realization, Evelyn understood the full extent of her power. She was no longer merely a person living in the shadows; she had become the shadows, a presence that loomed over the building, cold and unyielding, a figure that would forever haunt the minds of those who had once tried to understand her.

The residents would learn to live with the fear, to coexist with the darkness she embodied. And Evelyn would be there, watching, waiting, a silent guardian of the solitude she cherished.

For she was stone cold—a being who held the power of fear itself, a creature who commanded silence, and she was finally free.

The End

25
VILLAGE OF THE DAMNED

The road stretched out ahead of them, winding through dense woods that seemed to press in from all sides, shrouded in mist and shadow. It had been hours since the last town, and now, as twilight settled over the landscape, the air grew colder, the trees casting long, twisting shadows across the road.

Rachel gripped the steering wheel, her eyes fixed on the narrow road, her mind filled with a growing sense of dread. She and her husband, Mark, hadn't planned on taking such a remote route, but their GPS had rerouted them due to a massive road closure on the main highway. They'd been following the winding backroads for hours, feeling more and more lost with each turn. Rachel glanced over at Mark, who was frowning as he tried to pull up the map on his phone.

"No signal?" she asked, her voice tense.

Mark shook his head, his brow furrowed. "Nothing. I can't even get a GPS signal out here."

Rachel sighed, gripping the wheel tighter as the road grew narrower, the trees seeming to close in around them, the shadows thickening, turning the landscape into a dark, looming wall. "This isn't right," she muttered, glancing at the rapidly darkening sky. "We should have hit a town or at least another road by now."

Mark was about to reply when they saw it—a sign looming out of the mist, its letters faded but legible:

Welcome to Ashbourne

The name struck an odd note in Rachel's mind. She had never heard of it, nor had she seen it on any maps. The village seemed tucked away, hidden from the world, its presence barely more than a whisper in the surrounding woods. She slowed the car as they entered the village, the streetlights casting a dim, yellowish glow over the deserted streets.

The village itself was eerily quiet. The houses, quaint and old-fashioned, lined the street in neat rows, their windows dark, their doors shut tight, as though the place had been abandoned for years. Rachel's stomach twisted as they drove deeper into the heart of Ashbourne, her instincts screaming that something was wrong.

"Where is everyone?" Mark murmured, his eyes scanning the empty sidewalks. "It's not that late, but there's no one out here."

They pulled up beside an old inn, its faded sign barely visible in the dim light: **The Ashbourne Rest**. A single light flickered in the window, casting a weak glow across the cobblestone street. Rachel and Mark exchanged a glance, a silent agreement that this was the only place that might offer them shelter for the night. The woods were too dark, too dangerous to navigate in the dead of night, and staying in the car didn't seem like a wise choice.

They stepped out of the car, the night air biting into their skin, filling their lungs with a chill that seemed to seep into their bones. The village was silent, the only sound the soft crunch of their footsteps on the cobblestones, echoing eerily in the stillness.

As they approached the inn, the door creaked open, and a figure stepped out, silhouetted against the weak light. The man was tall, his face shadowed, his eyes watching them with a strange, unsettling intensity. He looked as though he'd been expecting them.

"Travelers, are you?" he asked, his voice a low, gravelly murmur that filled the silence.

Rachel forced a polite smile, though her skin prickled with unease. "Yes, we, uh... we took a wrong turn somewhere and ended up here. Is there a room we could rent for the night?"

The man nodded, his gaze lingering on them, his expression unreadable. "We don't get many visitors. Ashbourne isn't on most maps." He stepped aside, gesturing for them to enter. "But I have a room. You'll be safe here."

The last sentence struck an odd note in Rachel's mind, an unsettling emphasis on the word "safe." She glanced at Mark, who shrugged, his expression uncertain, and together they stepped into the inn.

The interior was dimly lit, the walls lined with faded wallpaper and antique furniture that looked as though it hadn't been touched in years. The air was thick, musty, filled with the scent of damp wood and something else, something she couldn't quite place—a faint metallic tang that set her teeth on edge.

"Your room is upstairs," the man said, his voice breaking the silence. "End of the hall."

They followed him up the narrow staircase, the floorboards creaking beneath their feet, each step filling Rachel with a growing sense of dread. She couldn't shake the feeling that they were being watched, that unseen eyes followed their every move, lurking in the shadows, waiting.

As they reached the top of the stairs, the man stopped, turning to face them. His eyes were dark, hollow, filled with a quiet malice that made Rachel's skin crawl.

"One rule," he said, his voice a whisper. "Do not leave your room after midnight."

Rachel felt a chill settle over her, her mind racing with questions she didn't dare ask. She forced a nod, trying to ignore the sinking feeling in her stomach as the man handed them a key, his fingers lingering just a little too long.

"Sleep well," he murmured, his gaze lingering on them as he turned and disappeared down the stairs, leaving them alone in the dimly lit hallway.

Their room was small and sparse, with a single bed, a small dresser, and a window that overlooked the dark, empty street. The walls were covered in peeling wallpaper, faded and stained, and the floorboards creaked with every step. Rachel shivered as she looked around, feeling as though the walls themselves were closing in, watching her, waiting.

Mark dropped their bags by the bed, his face pale, his gaze fixed on the window. "Did you notice how he looked at us? Like he... expected us to show up here."

Rachel nodded, her voice barely more than a whisper. "I don't like this place, Mark. There's something... wrong here."

He wrapped his arm around her shoulders, pulling her close, his voice soft but steady. "We'll be fine. Just one night, and we'll leave first thing in the morning."

But as the night wore on, the feeling of unease only grew. Outside, the village was silent, its streets dark and empty, as though the world beyond their window had ceased to exist. Rachel lay awake, listening to the silence, her mind racing with questions, her heart pounding with a fear she couldn't explain.

And then, just past midnight, she heard it—a faint sound, barely more than a whisper, drifting through the walls.

A soft, rhythmic tapping, coming from somewhere down the hall.

She held her breath, listening as the sound grew louder, more insistent, filling the silence with a hollow, unending beat. It was slow, deliberate, like footsteps, each tap echoing through the walls, filling her with a creeping dread.

"Mark," she whispered, nudging him, her voice trembling. "Do you hear that?"

Mark stirred, his eyes widening as he listened, his face pale, his gaze fixed on the door. The tapping grew louder, closer, as though someone were walking down the hall, each step deliberate, filled with a quiet, malevolent intent.

Rachel felt her heart race, her mind filling with a terrible certainty. She remembered the innkeeper's words, his warning not to leave their room after midnight, and a chill settled over her, a dread so deep it was almost paralyzing.

Then, the tapping stopped, leaving only silence, thick and suffocating, pressing down on them, filling the room with a sense of foreboding. They held their breaths, waiting, their eyes fixed on the door, their minds racing with questions they didn't dare ask.

And then, from the hallway, a faint, chilling whisper drifted through the air.

"Welcome... to Ashbourne."

They lay frozen, listening to the silence, their minds filled with a creeping dread. Rachel clutched Mark's hand, her fingers trembling, her heart pounding as the whisper faded, leaving only the heavy, oppressive quiet. She wanted to open the door, to look out into the hallway, to see if anyone was there. But the innkeeper's warning echoed in her mind, a command she couldn't ignore.

The hours passed slowly, each second dragging by, filling the room with a tension that was almost unbearable. Outside, the darkness deepened, pressing against the windows, as though the village itself were alive, watching, waiting.

And as dawn finally broke, casting a weak light across the street, they both knew that Ashbourne was not the quiet village it appeared to be.

For this was a place filled with shadows, a village with secrets buried in the darkness, a place where something ancient, something malevolent, lingered just beyond the edge of sight.

And they were not the first to find themselves trapped here, drawn into the heart of the village of the damned.

The morning brought little comfort to Rachel and Mark. They packed their things in silence, the events of the previous night hanging over them like a dark cloud. The inn was quiet, the only sounds the faint creaks of the old building settling and the distant hum of wind outside. The sense of dread that had filled the room during the night seemed to linger, the walls themselves thick with an eerie silence.

As they made their way down the narrow staircase, they found the innkeeper waiting for them in the lobby. He stood by the front desk, his expression unreadable, his eyes fixed on them with an intensity that made Rachel's skin crawl.

"Leaving so soon?" he asked, his voice a low murmur that echoed through the empty room.

Mark forced a polite smile, his hand tightening around Rachel's. "Yes, we need to get back on the road. Thank you for the room."

The innkeeper's gaze lingered on them, his lips curving into a faint, almost mocking smile. "You'll find it hard to leave Ashbourne. The road out of here isn't always... easy to find."

Rachel's heart skipped a beat, a chill settling over her. "What do you mean?"

He shrugged, his expression unreadable. "People who come here don't tend to leave. Ashbourne has a way of keeping its visitors."

Mark bristled, pulling Rachel closer as he led her toward the door. "We'll be fine. Thanks for your hospitality."

But as they stepped out into the pale morning light, Rachel couldn't shake the innkeeper's words, the way he'd watched them with that strange, knowing look. She glanced around the empty street, the sense of isolation more intense than ever. The village was silent, its streets deserted, the houses dark and lifeless, as though the town itself were holding its breath.

They made their way down the main street, hoping to find any sign of life, anyone who could point them toward the way out. But Ashbourne seemed empty, its buildings looming over them like silent sentinels, each one filled with an air of decay and abandonment. The few shops they passed were shuttered, their windows dusty and cracked, their signs faded and worn.

“Where is everyone?” Rachel murmured, her voice barely more than a whisper.

Mark shook his head, his gaze scanning the empty streets. “Maybe the town is just... emptying out. Rural towns do that sometimes.”

But Rachel wasn’t convinced. There was something about Ashbourne, something hidden beneath its quiet, forgotten surface, a darkness that seemed to pulse just beneath the skin, waiting for the right moment to reveal itself.

As they continued walking, they noticed something strange—a faint fog rolling in from the edges of the village, thick and low, curling around the buildings, swallowing the streets. It seemed to creep closer with each step, filling the air with a chill that settled over them like a shroud.

Mark stopped, his gaze fixed on the fog. “This is strange. The weather was clear when we arrived, and now this... it doesn’t feel right.”

Rachel shivered, her eyes darting around, searching for any sign of movement, of life. But the fog thickened, wrapping around the village, pressing in from all sides, turning the world into a silent, gray void. She felt the weight of the silence pressing down on her, filling her lungs with a cold, suffocating dread.

As they turned a corner, they saw a figure standing in the distance, shrouded in the mist, barely visible against the gray landscape. The figure was motionless, watching them with an intensity that made Rachel’s heart pound, a sense of danger prickling at the back of her neck.

Mark raised his hand, waving cautiously. "Hello? We're trying to find the way out of town. Can you help us?"

The figure didn't respond, didn't move. It simply stood there, watching them, its silhouette dark and indistinct, as though it were part of the fog itself. Rachel felt her stomach twist, a growing certainty that something was terribly wrong, that the figure was not... natural.

"Mark," she whispered, tugging at his arm. "We need to go. Now."

But before they could turn, the figure began to move, drifting toward them with a slow, deliberate pace, its movements silent, unsettling, as though it were gliding over the ground. Rachel backed away, her heart racing, her mind filled with images of shadowed faces, hollow eyes, things that belonged to the dark, things that were never meant to be seen.

They turned and ran, their footsteps echoing through the empty streets, the fog pressing in around them, filling the air with a chill that bit into their skin, seeping into their bones. But no matter how far they ran, they couldn't shake the feeling that the figure was following, drifting silently through the mist, closing in with every step.

They rounded a corner, their breaths coming in ragged gasps, only to find themselves facing a dead end. The street narrowed to an alley, lined with crumbling brick walls, the fog thickening around them, filling the air with a heavy, oppressive silence.

Mark turned, his face pale, his eyes wide with fear. "We have to find another way out."

But as they backed away from the alley, the fog parted, revealing the figure standing at the entrance, blocking their path. It was closer now, close enough for them to see the faint outline of a face—a face that was wrong, twisted, filled with a quiet, unending malice.

"Who... who are you?" Rachel managed, her voice trembling.

The figure tilted its head, its eyes hollow, empty, filled with a darkness that seemed to reach out, wrapping around them, pulling them down into a place of shadows and silence.

"Welcome to Ashbourne," it murmured, its voice soft, chilling, echoing in the silence.

Rachel felt a wave of nausea wash over her, a cold dread filling her mind. She could feel the figure's gaze piercing into her, its presence pressing down on her, filling her with a sense of despair that was almost suffocating. She took a step back, her hand clutching Mark's, her mind racing, desperate to escape.

But there was no way out.

The figure began to fade, its form dissolving into the fog, leaving only the echo of its voice lingering in the air, a faint whisper that seemed to seep into their minds, filling them with images of things they couldn't understand—faces, shadows, places filled with a darkness that felt endless.

They stumbled out of the alley, their minds reeling, their bodies trembling as the fog closed in around them, swallowing the streets, turning the village into a silent, empty maze. The buildings seemed to loom over them, filled with a quiet, malevolent energy, as though the village itself were alive, watching, waiting.

As they wandered the empty streets, searching for any sign of an exit, they began to notice other things—small, unsettling details that seemed to deepen their sense of dread. Windows with curtains that twitched as they passed, doors that creaked open on their own, shadows that shifted in the corner of their vision, gone before they could fully see them.

The village was empty, and yet it wasn't. There was something here, something hiding just beneath the surface, watching them, following them, filling the silence with a quiet, unending malice.

"Rachel," Mark whispered, his voice filled with a quiet terror. "I don't think we're alone."

She nodded, her heart pounding, her mind filled with a growing certainty that they were not meant to be here, that Ashbourne was not a place for the living. They had stumbled into something ancient, something dark, a village bound by shadows and secrets, a place that had been waiting for them, calling to them, drawing them in.

As night began to fall, casting long shadows over the streets, they realized with a chilling certainty that there was no escape, that the village would not let them go, that they were bound to Ashbourne, just as those who had come before them.

And as the fog thickened, wrapping around the village, filling the air with a cold, silent dread, they understood that they were not the first to be trapped here, that they had entered a place where the living became the lost, where shadows ruled and silence reigned.

They were in the village of the damned.

As night descended over Ashbourne, the fog grew thicker, swallowing the village in a dense, oppressive silence. Rachel and Mark huddled in their room at the inn, their hearts racing, their minds filled with the unsettling encounters from earlier. The figure in the fog, the shifting shadows, the dead-eyed villagers who watched them from darkened windows—Ashbourne was alive with something unseen, something ancient and twisted.

The innkeeper's warning echoed in Rachel's mind: *Do not leave your room after midnight.*

She glanced at the door, the thin crack of light beneath it flickering as though something were moving on the other side. She reached for Mark's hand, squeezing it tightly, her voice barely a whisper. "Mark, there's something horribly wrong with this place. We need to leave first thing in the morning."

Mark nodded, but his expression was tense, his gaze fixed on the shadows pooling beneath the door. "I don't think it's going to be that easy. I have this feeling..." He trailed off, his face pale. "It's like this village doesn't want us to leave."

A faint sound drifted through the walls, a soft, hollow tapping that seemed to echo from somewhere deep within the building. The sound was slow, rhythmic, filling the silence with a beat that grew louder with each passing second.

Tap. Tap. Tap.

They held their breath, listening, as the tapping continued, moving through the walls, filling the air with a cold, unyielding dread. Rachel's mind raced with questions, images of the strange figure in the fog filling her mind, a chill settling over her as she realized the tapping wasn't random. It was coming closer, moving toward their room.

"What... what is that?" she whispered, her voice trembling.

Mark shook his head, his gaze fixed on the door. "I don't know, but I don't think we should open the door."

The tapping stopped, leaving only silence, thick and heavy, pressing down on them. They held their breath, their eyes locked on the door, waiting, listening. And then, in the quiet, a faint whisper drifted through the air, soft and chilling.

"Welcome... to Ashbourne."

The next morning, Rachel and Mark left the inn at dawn, determined to find answers. The innkeeper was nowhere to be seen, and the lobby was empty, its shadows stretching across the floor in the weak morning light. They stepped outside, shivering in the cold, their eyes scanning the empty streets for any sign of life.

"We need to find someone," Rachel murmured. "Someone who knows what's happening here."

They wandered through the village, the silence heavy, oppressive, filling the streets with a sense of abandonment. The houses loomed over them, their windows dark, lifeless, as though watching their every move. The fog had dissipated with the sunrise, but the air was thick, charged with an energy that made Rachel's skin prickle.

As they walked, they noticed something strange: scattered across the ground were faded pieces of paper, crumpled and weathered, the ink smudged and barely legible. Rachel picked one up, her brow furrowing as she tried to read the faded text.

It was a newspaper clipping, dated decades ago. The headline sent a chill down her spine: *Mysterious Disappearances Plague Ashbourne: Village Residents Vanish Without a Trace.*

"Mark, look at this," she whispered, handing him the paper.

Mark's eyes widened as he read the article, his face growing pale. "It says people have been disappearing from this village for years. Entire families... gone without a trace."

Rachel nodded, her mind racing. "But if so many people disappeared, why does no one outside the village know about it? Why didn't anyone come to investigate?"

Mark looked around, his gaze troubled. "Maybe they did. But if Ashbourne didn't want them to leave..."

They continued through the village, searching for more clues. They found old posters tacked to walls, faded photographs left in the dirt, personal belongings scattered as though the residents had left in a hurry, never to return. The village felt like a place frozen in time, a ghost town where the past lingered, haunting every corner, every shadow.

Their search led them to the village library, a small, weathered building tucked away at the end of a narrow street. The windows were dark, the door slightly ajar, creaking as they pushed it open. Inside, the air was heavy, filled with the scent of old paper and dust, the shelves lined with rows of faded books, their covers worn and frayed.

Rachel scanned the shelves, her eyes catching titles that seemed out of place—*Ashbourne's Secrets*, *Legends of the Lost*, *The Haunting of Black Hollow.* She pulled one down, opening it to a random page, her eyes widening as she read the words:

"The village of Ashbourne has always been a place of mystery, a town shrouded in shadows, hidden from the world. It is said that Ashbourne was founded on cursed ground, that its inhabitants are bound to the land, unable to leave, forever tied to the darkness that lies beneath..."

Her stomach twisted as she read on, the words filling her with a growing sense of dread. According to the book, Ashbourne had been cursed since its founding, its residents bound to the village by an ancient ritual, a pact made with something dark, something unholy. The curse, the book said, demanded sacrifices—souls to feed the darkness, to keep the village hidden from the outside world.

"This is why people disappear," she murmured, her voice barely more than a whisper. "The village demands them. It takes them."

Mark's face was pale as he looked at her, his voice filled with quiet terror. "Rachel, do you think... do you think we're next?"

As they left the library, the sky darkened, heavy clouds rolling in, casting the village in shadow. The streets were empty, silent, the air thick with a sense of foreboding, as though the village itself were watching, waiting.

They decided to head back to the inn, hoping to find the innkeeper, to demand answers. But as they approached, they saw a figure standing in the doorway, watching them with hollow, empty eyes. It was the innkeeper, his face twisted into a strange, unreadable expression, his gaze fixed on them with a quiet malice.

"You shouldn't have stayed," he murmured, his voice barely audible over the rising wind. "Once Ashbourne has you... it doesn't let go."

Rachel felt a chill settle over her, her mind racing. "What do you mean? We didn't ask to be here!"

The innkeeper's gaze darkened, his expression unreadable. "Ashbourne chooses who it wants. It calls to you, draws you in. And once you're here, you're part of it. Bound to it."

Mark took a step forward, his voice filled with defiance. "There has to be a way out. We're not staying here."

The innkeeper's lips curved into a faint, mocking smile. "You think you can escape?" He shook his head, his voice a low, haunting whisper. "You're part of the village now. Part of its shadows."

With that, he turned and disappeared into the inn, leaving them standing in the doorway, their minds reeling, their hearts pounding with a terror they couldn't shake.

Rachel and Mark knew they couldn't stay. They had to find a way out before nightfall, before the village's shadows closed in around them, trapping them forever. They rushed back to their car, but as they approached, they saw it: their tires were slashed, the metal twisted and broken, as though something had clawed at the car, tearing it apart with inhuman strength.

Panic set in, filling Rachel's mind with a sense of helplessness, a certainty that they were trapped, that Ashbourne had them in its grasp, and there was no escape.

"We have to try to get to the edge of the village," she whispered, her voice trembling. "There has to be a way out."

They set off on foot, their hearts racing, their minds filled with images of the figure in the fog, the shifting shadows, the empty eyes of the innkeeper. The village seemed to twist and change as they walked, the streets narrowing, turning into a maze of darkened alleys, each path leading them deeper into the heart of Ashbourne, into the very soul of the village of the damned.

As night fell, they felt it—a presence, dark and unyielding, pressing in around them, filling the air with a chill that seeped into their bones. Shadows stretched across the streets, reaching for them, filling the silence with a soft, whispering chant that echoed in their minds, filling them with a terror they couldn't escape.

"Stay with us... join us... become one of us..."

The village was alive, filled with voices, shadows, a darkness that reached into their minds, binding them, claiming them. And as the last light faded, they understood the truth: Ashbourne was not just a village.

It was a trap, a prison for lost souls, a place where shadows ruled, where the living became the lost, where the damned would linger, forever bound to the darkness.

And they had become part of it.

The village had transformed around them as night settled, twisting into a maze of darkness and shadow. Every street seemed to lead them back to the heart of Ashbourne, as if the village itself were pulling them deeper, wrapping them in a web from which there was no escape.

Rachel and Mark moved in silence, their breaths shallow, their minds racing. They clung to each other, their eyes darting to every shadow, every flicker of movement in the fog that clung to the ground. The village was silent, save for the soft rustling of unseen figures moving in the dark, following them, watching.

"Rachel," Mark whispered, his voice filled with a quiet desperation, "we have to find a way out. There has to be a path that leads to the edge of the village."

Rachel nodded, her heart pounding. She could feel the weight of unseen eyes, a presence that grew stronger with each step. It felt as though the village were alive, pulsing with a dark, unrelenting energy that seeped into her bones, filling her with a dread that was almost unbearable.

They turned down an alley, hoping to find an exit, but the walls seemed to close in, the path narrowing, twisting until it led them to a dead end. Rachel felt a chill settle over her, a certainty that they were being corralled, led into a trap.

And then, from the shadows, a voice drifted through the air, soft and chilling.

"Why do you resist?"

They turned, their backs pressed against the wall, their eyes wide as a figure stepped out of the fog. It was the innkeeper, his face twisted into a strange, unreadable expression, his eyes dark, hollow, filled with a quiet, unending malice.

"You're part of Ashbourne now," he murmured, his voice a soft, mocking whisper. "There's no escape. The village... it claims those who wander into its embrace."

Mark took a step forward, his voice filled with defiance. "Why? Why are we here? What does this place want with us?"

The innkeeper's lips curved into a faint smile, his gaze fixed on them with a look that sent a chill down Rachel's spine. "Ashbourne was born from darkness. Long ago, a pact was made—a promise to something ancient, something that exists beyond the edge of this world. The village requires souls to sustain it, to feed the darkness, to keep it hidden from the world beyond."

Rachel's stomach twisted, her mind racing. "So... we're just sacrifices? People for this place to consume?"

The innkeeper nodded, his face expressionless. "Those who come to Ashbourne are chosen. Called. And once they're here, they belong to the village, to the shadows that rule it."

Mark clenched his fists, his jaw tight. "We're not staying here. We're not going to be part of your curse."

The innkeeper's smile faded, his eyes darkening. "You don't have a choice. Ashbourne doesn't let go."

As they turned to flee, the village seemed to change around them, the streets twisting and warping, turning into a maze of narrow alleys and dead ends. They ran, their breaths coming in ragged gasps, their footsteps echoing through the darkness, but every path led them back to the center of the village, to the heart of the shadows that watched them, followed them, bound them.

The fog thickened, pressing in from all sides, filling the air with a chill that seeped into their skin, numbing their senses, wrapping them in a suffocating embrace. Rachel felt her mind spinning, the edges of her vision blurring, as though the village itself were pulling her into its depths, binding her to the darkness that lay at its core.

They stumbled into the village square, the buildings looming over them, their windows dark, empty, watching. The fog swirled around them, thick and heavy, filling the air with a cold, metallic scent that made Rachel's stomach twist. She could feel the presence of something ancient, something malevolent, pressing down on her, filling her mind with a quiet, unending terror.

"Rachel," Mark whispered, his voice trembling, "I don't think we're going to get out of here."

She shook her head, refusing to accept it, her mind racing, desperate to find a way to escape. But as she looked around, she saw them—figures emerging from the shadows, their faces pale, hollow, their eyes empty, filled with a darkness that seemed to reach out, wrapping around her, pulling her down into a place of silence and despair.

These were the lost souls, she realized, the ones who had come before, drawn into Ashbourne's grasp, bound to the village, forever part of its curse. They moved slowly, silently, their eyes fixed on her and Mark, as though waiting, watching, preparing to welcome them into the fold.

Rachel backed away, her heart pounding, her mind filled with images of shadows, of hollow faces, of endless darkness.

"We can't stay here," she whispered, her voice trembling. "We have to find a way out."

But as the lost souls moved closer, their forms blending with the fog, filling the air with a quiet, unyielding malice, she realized with a chilling certainty that they were out of time, that the village had claimed them, that they were bound to Ashbourne, forever part of its shadows.

In a final act of desperation, Rachel called out, her voice breaking the heavy silence, filling the air with a plea that echoed through the darkness.

"Whoever or whatever is here, please... let us go. We didn't choose this!"

Her voice faded, swallowed by the fog, leaving only silence, the heavy, suffocating silence of Ashbourne. But then, from the shadows, a faint whisper filled the air, a voice that was both soft and cold, filled with a quiet, ancient sorrow.

"Leave... if you can."

Rachel's eyes widened, her heart racing as the words sank in. She turned to Mark, a spark of hope igniting in her mind. "Mark, did you hear that?"

He nodded, his face pale, his gaze fixed on the shadows. "But how? Where do we go?"

Before she could answer, the fog parted, revealing a narrow path that led out of the village, a thin, winding trail that cut through the darkness, disappearing into the forest beyond. It was barely visible, almost hidden, as though it existed only for those who were desperate enough to take it.

They didn't hesitate. Hand in hand, they took off down the path, their footsteps silent, their breaths shallow as they followed the trail, their minds filled with a growing sense of dread. The path was lined with shadows, figures that watched them with hollow eyes, whispering soft, chilling words as they passed.

"Come back... stay with us... join us..."

The voices filled the air, echoing in their minds, filling them with a quiet, unyielding terror. But they pressed on, their eyes fixed on the edge of the forest, on the faint glimmer of light that waited beyond the darkness.

As they reached the edge of the village, the air grew colder, thicker, filling their lungs with a chill that felt almost alive. They could feel the weight of the village's presence pressing down on them, filling their minds with a sense of despair that was almost paralyzing, as though the village itself were reaching out, pulling them back into its grasp.

They took a step forward, crossing the invisible line that marked the edge of Ashbourne, and felt a surge of resistance, a force that seemed to hold them in place, filling the air with a tension that was almost unbearable.

Rachel gritted her teeth, her mind filled with a fierce determination, a refusal to let the village claim her, to become one of its lost souls. She took another step, forcing herself forward, feeling the resistance weaken, the darkness lifting, as though she were breaking through the village's hold.

Mark followed, his face pale, his gaze fixed on the path ahead, his mind filled with the same determination. And together, they crossed the boundary, stepping out of Ashbourne, leaving the village and its shadows behind.

They didn't stop until they reached the main road, the village a distant memory, a shadow that lingered at the edges of their minds, a place that felt both real and unreal, as though it had been a nightmare, a twisted dream from which they had barely escaped.

As they stood by the roadside, catching their breath, they looked back, their minds filled with a quiet, haunting fear. But Ashbourne was gone, the village hidden behind the trees, its presence a shadow that lingered, a memory that would forever be etched into their minds.

They knew that they had been given a second chance, a rare gift from a place that rarely let anyone go. And as they walked away, their footsteps echoing in the silence, they carried with them the memory of Ashbourne, the village of the damned, a place bound by shadows, by darkness, a place that would forever haunt their dreams.

And somewhere in the village, hidden in the depths of the fog, the shadows watched, waiting, knowing that one day, Ashbourne would call again, drawing new souls into its depths, binding them to the darkness, forever part of the village of the damned.

The End

26

THE GRAVE ROBBERS

The rain fell in a steady drizzle over St. Sebastian's Cemetery, the air thick with the scent of wet earth and decaying leaves. Dark clouds covered the moon, casting the graveyard in shadows that seemed to stretch and move, giving life to the cold stone statues and ancient headstones that lined the path.

Lucas gripped his flashlight tighter, the beam slicing through the darkness as he scanned the rows of graves. Beside him, Alex moved with quiet determination, his eyes focused on a specific spot farther down the hill. They had been planning this night for weeks, ever since they'd overheard an old bartender spinning stories of the Devereux family tomb, hidden deep in the cemetery's oldest section. The Devereux family, he'd said, had been one of the wealthiest in the region, known for hoarding ancient, priceless artifacts buried with them in elaborate coffins.

"Think about it," Alex had whispered to Lucas in the back of the bar, his eyes glinting with excitement. "The jewelry alone could be worth a fortune. Enough to set us up for life."

Lucas had been reluctant at first, but the thought of treasure, of escaping his dead-end job and endless debt, had gnawed at him until his curiosity and desperation outweighed his sense of dread. And now, here they were, shivering in the cold night air, their minds filled with visions of gold, jewels, and relics buried beneath centuries of dust.

"Are you sure this is the right way?" Lucas whispered, glancing around the empty cemetery, the eerie silence broken only by the patter of rain on stone.

Alex nodded, his face lit by the pale glow of his phone. "According to the map, it's up ahead, right beneath the old sycamore tree. Just stay close and keep quiet."

They moved carefully, their footsteps muffled by the wet grass and fallen leaves. The darkness seemed to press in around them, thick and unyielding, as though the cemetery itself were watching, waiting. Lucas felt a chill run down his spine, his mind racing with images of skeletal hands reaching up from the earth, of hollow-eyed ghosts watching from the shadows.

They reached the sycamore, its twisted branches reaching out like skeletal fingers, casting long shadows across the nearby graves. In the faint glow of the flashlight, Lucas saw the Devereux family crest carved into the largest headstone, a symbol worn down by years of rain and wind, but still unmistakable—a skull surrounded by thorny vines.

"This is it," Alex whispered, dropping to his knees as he pulled a crowbar from his backpack, his hands trembling with anticipation. "We just have to break open the door to the vault. The old man said it hadn't been touched in years. Who knows what we'll find in there?"

Lucas swallowed, his heart pounding as he watched Alex wedge the crowbar into the heavy stone door, the sound of metal against stone echoing through the cemetery. The rain grew heavier, the wind picking up, filling the air with a chill that seemed to seep into his bones. He glanced around, his eyes scanning the darkened graves, the shadows shifting and moving, as though something unseen were watching, waiting.

"Hurry up," he whispered, his voice barely audible. "This place... it doesn't feel right."

Alex grunted, his muscles straining as he pried open the door, the heavy stone groaning as it gave way, revealing a narrow staircase that descended into the earth. A wave of cold, stale air rushed out, filling their lungs with the scent of damp stone and ancient decay.

"After you," Alex said with a grin, gesturing toward the dark stairway.

Lucas hesitated, a knot of dread twisting in his stomach as he stared down into the darkness. But the thought of treasure, of freedom from his financial burdens, urged him on. He took a deep breath, stepping carefully onto the first stone step, his flashlight casting an eerie glow on the narrow walls as he descended.

The staircase was steep, winding down into the earth, the air growing colder with each step. The walls were lined with moss, their surfaces slick and damp, the silence thick, pressing down on them, filling the air with a weight that made it hard to breathe. Lucas felt his heart pounding, his mind racing as he imagined the riches that lay just beyond, hidden in the shadows of the tomb.

Finally, they reached the bottom, the narrow stairway opening into a small, dimly lit chamber. The walls were lined with ancient stone coffins, each one adorned with faded carvings and symbols that seemed to pulse with a quiet, sinister energy. The air was thick, heavy, filled with the scent of old wood and dust, a silence that felt alive, watching.

Alex's face lit up as he approached the nearest coffin, his eyes glinting with excitement. "This is it. Look at these carvings—this has to be the Devereux family vault."

Lucas nodded, his hands trembling as he held the flashlight steady, his mind racing with visions of gold, of jewels, of treasures hidden within the ancient coffins. But as he took a step closer, he felt a strange sensation, a chill that seeped into his bones, filling him with a quiet, unyielding dread.

"Are you sure we should be doing this?" he whispered, his voice barely audible. "What if... what if we're disturbing something we shouldn't?"

Alex scoffed, rolling his eyes as he pried open the lid of the nearest coffin, revealing a skeleton adorned with jewelry that sparkled in the dim light. "Don't go soft on me now, Lucas. Look at this! It's worth a fortune. We just need to grab what we can and get out of here."

But as he reached for a gold necklace draped around the skeleton's neck, a faint sound echoed through the chamber—a soft, whispering voice that seemed to drift from the shadows, filling the air with a quiet, chilling murmur.

"Leave..."

They froze, their hearts pounding, their minds racing as the voice grew louder, echoing through the chamber, filling the silence with a soft, haunting chant.

"Leave this place... leave... before it's too late..."

Lucas's hands trembled, his flashlight shaking as he scanned the room, his mind filled with images of restless spirits, of ancient curses that lingered in the darkness, waiting for those foolish enough to disturb their slumber.

"Did you hear that?" he whispered, his voice filled with a quiet, unyielding terror.

Alex smirked, dismissing the voice as nothing more than their imagination. "It's just the wind, Lucas. Don't let an old graveyard spook you."

But as he pulled the necklace from the skeleton's neck, the ground beneath them seemed to shudder, a faint, rumbling sound filling the air, as though something deep within the earth had stirred, awakened by their presence.

Lucas took a step back, his heart racing, his mind filled with a growing sense of dread. "Alex... I don't think we're alone."

Before Alex could respond, the chamber grew colder, the air filling with a thick, oppressive darkness that seemed to close in around them, pressing down on them, filling their minds with a terror they couldn't explain.

And then, from the shadows, figures began to emerge—dark, twisted shapes that moved with a slow, deliberate grace, their hollow eyes fixed on Lucas and Alex, their forms barely more than shadows, filled with a quiet, unending malice.

The whispering grew louder, filling the chamber with a chilling, unearthly chant that echoed through the walls, filling their minds with images of death, of decay, of lives stolen and bound to the earth.

"Return... what is ours..."

The shadows closed in, their forms shifting and writhing, their eyes filled with a darkness that seemed to reach into Lucas's mind, filling him with a sense of despair, of unending sorrow. He felt his knees weaken, his breath shallow, his mind racing with images of graves, of bones, of lives lost and forgotten.

"Alex, we need to leave," he whispered, his voice trembling, his hands clutching the flashlight as though it were his last link to sanity.

But Alex seemed frozen, his eyes wide, his face pale, as the shadows drew closer, filling the air with a cold, metallic scent that made Lucas's stomach twist.

And as the shadows reached for them, their voices filling the chamber with a chant that echoed through the silence, Lucas realized with a chilling certainty that they had made a terrible mistake, that they had disturbed something ancient, something malevolent, something that would not let them leave.

For they had entered the domain of the dead, and the dead would not let them go.

The shadows circled around Lucas and Alex, their hollow eyes filled with an ancient malice, their voices a haunting chant that reverberated through the tomb, filling the air with a weight that was almost suffocating.

"Return... what is ours..."

The cold seeped into Lucas's bones, chilling him to the core as he clutched his flashlight, his hands trembling. He glanced at Alex, whose face had gone pale, his mouth open in shock, the gold necklace still clutched in his hand.

"Alex," Lucas whispered, his voice barely more than a breath, "we need to put it back."

But Alex didn't respond. His gaze was fixed on the shadows, his eyes wide with fear, his body frozen as though caught in the spell of the spirits that surrounded them. The shadows moved closer, their forms twisting, shifting, their hollow eyes locked on Alex with an intensity that made Lucas's skin crawl.

"Alex, listen to me!" Lucas reached out, gripping Alex's arm, trying to shake him from his trance. "Put it back! Whatever these things are, they're angry—we have to leave!"

Alex blinked, his gaze snapping to Lucas, a flash of desperation in his eyes. "But the treasure... we can't just leave it. This is our chance—our only chance to get out of this miserable life!"

Lucas's stomach twisted, a cold dread filling him as he watched Alex clutch the necklace even tighter, his greed overtaking his sense of reason. The shadows grew closer, their whispers filling the air, their forms stretching toward Alex, reaching out with hands made of mist and darkness, as though drawn to the relic he held.

"Return... what is ours..." The chant grew louder, more insistent, filling the chamber with an unearthly echo that rattled Lucas's mind, sending waves of fear through him.

"Alex, please," he begged, his voice trembling. "Look around! We're in over our heads. This isn't just some old grave—there's something... alive here. Something that wants us gone."

But Alex shook his head, his expression stubborn, defiant. "It's just an illusion, Lucas. Old ghost stories to keep people away from treasure like this. They can't hurt us."

As if in response to his words, the ground beneath them shuddered, a low, rumbling sound filling the air, growing louder, more intense, as though something deep within the earth were waking, disturbed by their presence, by Alex's refusal to heed its warning.

The shadows surged forward, their forms twisting, filling the air with a thick, metallic scent that made Lucas's stomach turn. He stumbled back, his heart racing, his mind filled with images of bones, of ancient curses, of restless spirits that had waited centuries for revenge.

And then, before he could stop him, Alex turned toward one of the other coffins, his eyes wild, his hands reaching out to pry it open. "If there's more treasure here, I'm not leaving without it. This is our chance, Lucas!"

"Alex, no!" Lucas's voice echoed through the chamber, but his words were lost as Alex forced open the lid, revealing another skeleton, its bones adorned with rings, bracelets, and a gold crown that glinted in the dim light.

But as Alex reached for the crown, a hand—cold and bony, with flesh stretched tight over ancient bones—rose from the coffin, gripping Alex's wrist with an unearthly strength. Alex gasped, his eyes widening in horror as the skeleton pulled him closer, its hollow eye sockets fixed on him, its jaw opening in a silent scream.

The shadows closed in, their voices rising into a haunting wail that filled the chamber, a sound that seemed to shake the very walls, filling Lucas's mind with a terror he couldn't escape. He watched, paralyzed, as Alex struggled, his face twisted in fear, his body writhing as the skeletal hand held him in an unbreakable grip.

"Lucas!" Alex's voice was a desperate, terrified scream, his eyes pleading. "Help me!"

Lucas's mind raced, his heart pounding as he took a step forward, his hand reaching out. But as he approached, the shadows swarmed around Alex, their forms twisting, filling the air with a cold, suffocating darkness that wrapped around him, binding him, dragging him down into the depths of the tomb.

"Return... what is ours..." The chant grew louder, filling Lucas's ears, drowning out Alex's screams, until all that remained was silence, thick and heavy, pressing down on him, filling the chamber with a sense of finality.

And then, as suddenly as they had appeared, the shadows vanished, retreating back into the darkness, leaving only Lucas standing alone, his flashlight flickering, his mind reeling, his body trembling with a fear that left him paralyzed.

The room was empty, silent, the air thick with the lingering scent of decay, of death, of something ancient and malevolent that had claimed its prize.

Alex was gone.

Lucas stumbled back, his mind racing, his heart pounding as he tried to make sense of what had just happened. The chamber was silent, the shadows gone, but the weight of the curse, of the ancient spirits that lingered in the tomb, hung in the air, filling him with a dread that felt unbreakable.

He turned, his flashlight casting a dim glow over the stone coffins, the faded carvings, the symbols that seemed to pulse with a quiet, unending malice. He could feel the presence of the spirits, a weight that pressed down on him, filling his mind with images of the dead, of lives stolen and bound to the earth, of curses that had been waiting for centuries to be broken.

He took a shaky breath, his hands trembling as he tried to steady himself, to push down the terror that gnawed at him, filling his mind with visions of shadows, of bones, of things that waited in the dark.

"I have to get out of here," he whispered, his voice trembling, the words barely more than a breath.

But as he turned to leave, he felt it—a cold, bony hand brushing against his shoulder, a whisper filling his ear, soft and chilling.

“Return... what is ours...”

He spun around, his flashlight casting a beam of light over the empty tomb, his mind racing, his heart pounding as he searched the shadows, his breath shallow, his mind filled with a terror that was almost paralyzing.

But the room was empty, silent, save for the faint echo of the voice, lingering in the air like a ghostly breath.

He stumbled up the stairs, his footsteps echoing through the silence, his mind filled with images of the shadows, of the spirits that had claimed Alex, of the curse that had bound them to the tomb, waiting for those foolish enough to disturb their rest.

Lucas emerged from the tomb, the rain falling in a steady downpour, filling the air with the scent of wet earth and decay. The cemetery was silent, the shadows thick, pressing in from all sides, as though the very land itself were alive, watching, waiting.

He staggered down the path, his mind racing, his heart pounding, his body trembling as he tried to make sense of what had happened, to push down the terror that filled him, a dread that felt unbreakable.

But as he reached the gate, he stopped, his breath catching, his heart skipping a beat as he saw it—a figure standing at the edge of the cemetery, shrouded in darkness, its hollow eyes fixed on him with a quiet, unending malice.

It was Alex.

Or, at least, what was left of him.

His face was pale, his eyes hollow, his body wrapped in shadows, his form twisted, filled with a darkness that seemed to reach out, wrapping around him, binding him to the cemetery, to the curse that had claimed him.

Lucas backed away, his heart pounding, his mind filled with images of bones, of shadows, of things that waited in the dark, of curses that could not be broken.

And as he turned to flee, he heard it—a faint, chilling whisper that filled the air, soft and haunting, echoing through the cemetery.

"Return... what is ours..."

Lucas ran, his footsteps echoing through the silence, his mind racing, his heart pounding as he fled the cemetery, his mind filled with a terror that he knew he would never escape.

For the curse had claimed him, bound him to the shadows, to the voices that lingered in the dark, waiting, watching, whispering their ancient song.

And as he disappeared into the night, the shadows watched, knowing that one day, he would return to the cemetery, drawn by the curse, bound to the darkness, forever part of the grave robbers' fate.

Days passed since Lucas had fled St. Sebastian's Cemetery, yet he could not shake the feeling of being watched. Every shadow seemed to hide unseen eyes, every whisper of wind carried faint voices, and every flicker in the darkness made his heart race. His dreams, when he managed to sleep, were filled with hollow-eyed figures, shadowed faces, and Alex—his lifeless gaze haunting Lucas as if pleading for release.

He tried to return to normal, to forget the night in the cemetery, but the memory lingered, clinging to him like a dark cloud. He felt cursed, bound to the graveyard, as though the spirits had marked him, tethered him to the same fate that had claimed Alex.

On the fourth night, he heard it.

He was lying in bed, tossing and turning, the clock ticking in the silence, when a faint, hollow tapping echoed through his room. He froze, his heart pounding, his mind racing with memories of the graveyard, of shadows and curses that lingered in the dark.

Tap. Tap. Tap.

It was a sound he couldn't ignore, a sound that filled him with a dread so deep it made his hands shake, his breath catch. He slowly sat up, his eyes scanning the room, his heart racing as the tapping grew louder, more insistent, filling the silence with a rhythm that was almost familiar.

He knew that sound.

It was the sound of the coffin lids in St. Sebastian's, creaking open in the darkness.

"Return... what is ours..."

The whisper filled the air, soft and chilling, the same words he'd heard in the tomb, the same voices that had called to him and Alex from the shadows. He clutched his head, squeezing his eyes shut, his mind racing as the voices grew louder, filling his thoughts, pressing down on him, pulling him back to that cursed night.

He couldn't stay here. He needed to leave, to find a way to escape the curse, to silence the voices that haunted him.

The next day, Lucas found himself standing before an old bookstore on the edge of town, a place known for its collection of rare, arcane texts. The windows were covered in dust, the sign faded, and the door creaked as he pushed it open, stepping into the dimly lit interior. The scent of old paper and leather filled the air, a silence that seemed to swallow every sound, as though the walls themselves held secrets.

He approached the counter, where a stooped, elderly man was paging through a thick, yellowed book, his glasses perched on the edge of his nose. The man looked up, his gaze sharp, assessing, as though he saw straight through Lucas's exterior and into the terror that lay beneath.

"I need... I need help," Lucas stammered, his voice barely more than a whisper. "With a curse."

The old man's eyes narrowed, his expression serious. "A curse, you say? Not the usual reason people come here. Curses are ancient, powerful things. Once you're marked, it's not easy to escape."

Lucas swallowed, his mind racing. "There has to be a way. Something that can free me, break the connection."

The man nodded, his gaze thoughtful. "Tell me what happened."

Lucas recounted the events of that night—the tomb, the shadows, Alex's disappearance, the whispers that had haunted him ever since. The man listened in silence, his expression growing darker, his fingers tracing patterns over the worn cover of his book.

"You encountered a grave curse," he said finally, his voice barely more than a murmur. "A spirit bound to the earth, one that clings to the living, feeding off their life, their energy, until they are dragged back to the place of its origin."

Lucas felt a chill settle over him. "Is there a way to end it? To put the spirit to rest?"

The man studied him for a moment, his gaze unyielding. "There is only one way to free yourself from such a curse. You must return to the place where it began, to the tomb, and appease the spirits. They require restitution—a return of what was taken, an acknowledgment of their power. Only then might they release you."

The thought of returning to the graveyard, of facing the spirits that had claimed Alex, filled Lucas with a dread that was almost paralyzing. But he knew he had no choice. If he didn't end this, the curse would consume him, drag him back to the cemetery, just as it had dragged Alex into the shadows.

That night, Lucas found himself once again standing before the gates of St. Sebastian's Cemetery. The air was thick with mist, the faint scent of decay filling his lungs, the silence heavy, oppressive, pressing down on him, filling his mind with images of shadows, of hollow eyes watching him from the darkness.

He took a deep breath, steadying himself, and stepped forward, his flashlight cutting through the mist as he made his way down the path, his footsteps echoing through the silence, his heart pounding with each step. The cemetery felt different this time—colder, darker, as though the very ground were alive, pulsing with a quiet, unending malice.

The sycamore tree loomed ahead, its twisted branches casting long, skeletal shadows across the tombstones, the

Devereux family crest barely visible in the dim light. He hesitated, his mind racing with memories of that night, of Alex's screams, of the shadows that had claimed him, of the curse that lingered in the air, waiting for him.

Taking a deep breath, he stepped forward, making his way down the stone steps into the Devereux vault, his flashlight casting long shadows across the narrow walls, illuminating the ancient carvings that seemed to pulse with a quiet, sinister energy.

As he reached the bottom, he felt it—a presence, cold and unyielding, filling the air with a chill that made his skin prickle, his mind race. The coffins were exactly as he remembered, the lids slightly ajar, the symbols carved into the stone glowing faintly, as though alive with a dark, unearthly power.

"Return... what is ours..."

The whisper filled the air, soft and chilling, the shadows gathering around him, filling the chamber with a darkness that seemed to pulse, to breathe, pressing down on him, filling his mind with a terror he couldn't escape.

He held up his hands, his voice trembling. "I... I'm here to return what was taken. Please, let this end."

A faint, hollow voice drifted through the air, filled with a quiet, unending malice. "It is not enough. You disturbed our rest, desecrated our tomb. Only sacrifice can appease us."

Lucas felt his stomach twist, his heart pounding as the shadows closed in, their hollow eyes fixed on him, their forms shifting, writhing, filling the air with a suffocating darkness. He stumbled back, his mind racing, his heart filled with a terror that left him paralyzed.

"What... what do you want?" he whispered, his voice barely audible.

The shadows moved closer, their voices filling the air, soft and haunting. "Your life... your spirit... bound to us, forever."

He backed away, his heart racing, his mind filled with images of shadows, of darkness, of things that waited in the depths, things that could not be appeased. He knew, with a chilling certainty, that the spirits would not let him leave, that they would claim him, drag him down into the darkness, bind him to the curse that lingered in the tomb.

In a final, desperate attempt, he pulled a small vial of holy water from his pocket—a last-minute gift from the old man at the bookstore. He held it up, his hand trembling, his mind filled with a quiet, desperate prayer.

"Let me go," he whispered, his voice filled with a defiance he didn't feel. "You can't have me."

The shadows recoiled, their forms twisting, shifting, as though repelled by the light, the holy water radiating a faint glow that pushed them back, filling the chamber with a dim, unearthly light.

But the voices only grew louder, filling the air with a haunting, unyielding chant that echoed through the tomb, a curse that wrapped around him, bound him, filling his mind with a terror that he couldn't escape.

And as the shadows closed in, their hands reaching for him, he knew, with a final, chilling certainty, that he was bound to the curse, forever part of the grave robbers' fate, forever haunted by the spirits that lingered in the darkness, waiting, watching.

As he disappeared into the shadows, his final scream echoing through the tomb, the Devereux vault fell silent once more, the curse renewed, waiting for the next soul foolish enough to disturb its slumber.

The End

27
SURVEILLANCE

Darren Connors sat alone in his dimly lit apartment, flipping through the channels on his television with a restless energy. Outside, the city hummed with life—people walking the streets, cars rumbling past, the faint sound of laughter and conversation drifting up from the sidewalks below. Yet, something in the air felt strange, like a static charge pressing against his skin, an invisible weight that had been creeping into his life for the past few days.

Darren couldn't explain it, but he felt... watched. It was an uneasy, itching feeling at the back of his mind, a prickling awareness that had made him increasingly paranoid. And it wasn't just the nagging thought that someone had broken into his email or hacked his social media accounts. This was deeper, darker, as if something far more sinister was studying him, cataloging every move he made.

As he stood to make a cup of coffee, his eyes drifted to the small spider in the corner of his kitchen window, its thin legs stretched out as it perched, unmoving, in the shadows. He frowned, shivering slightly as he stared at it. The spider had been there for days, watching—always watching. It seemed to follow him with its tiny, unblinking eyes, never retreating, never looking away. Darren had even tried to get rid of it once, brushing it outside with a piece of paper, but the next morning, it was back.

A low chuckle escaped his lips, though it felt forced. "Come on, Darren. It's a spider, for God's sake," he muttered to himself, shaking his head. But the feeling didn't go away. In fact, it was growing stronger.

The kettle whistled, snapping him out of his thoughts. He poured the water over his coffee grounds and took a slow sip, the warmth doing little to ease his nerves. He tried to focus on the warmth, on the familiar smell, but his mind drifted back to the spider in the corner, the one that seemed to be... observing him.

"Alright," he said, setting down his coffee. "Enough with the paranoia."

But as he reached for his phone, he noticed something strange: a blackbird sitting on the windowsill outside, its head tilted, beady eyes fixed on him. It was silent, unmoving, and as Darren watched, his heart began to race. The bird didn't flinch, didn't chirp, didn't peck at the glass. It just sat there, like a statue, staring at him through the window with an unsettling intensity.

The feeling was back, stronger than ever, a suffocating certainty that the world was filled with eyes, all of them turned toward him.

Trying to shake the feeling, Darren grabbed his jacket and left his apartment, stepping out into the cold, crisp night. The street was empty, the buildings looming over him like silent sentries. But as he walked, he noticed the same blackbird perched on the next building over, its gaze fixed on him as it followed his steps. He quickened his pace, glancing over his shoulder, but everywhere he looked, there it was—perched on a lamppost, on a parked car, in the branches of a nearby tree.

His breathing grew shallow, his mind racing with questions he couldn't answer. *How could it be everywhere? How could it be... watching him?*

He took a deep breath, forcing himself to look away, to dismiss it as coincidence. But the tension gnawed at him, an unshakable sense of being under constant surveillance, an awareness that every step he took, every glance he made, was being recorded, analyzed, watched.

He turned the corner, stepping onto a quieter street, and there it was again—a black cat, its eyes glinting in the shadows, watching him from a nearby fence. It sat perfectly still, its tail flicking slowly, its gaze intense, unwavering. As he passed, its head turned, following his every movement.

A shiver ran down his spine, the familiar prickle of fear creeping over his skin. But this wasn't just paranoia anymore; it was something tangible, something real. He could feel their eyes, sense their presence, like an invisible network surrounding him, following his every move. He broke into a jog, then a sprint, his footsteps echoing through the empty street, his mind racing.

When he finally made it back to his apartment, he slammed the door shut, locking it, double-checking it, his heart pounding in his chest. He stood in the entryway, catching his breath, his mind still filled with images of those unblinking eyes, those silent, watching creatures.

He went to the bathroom, splashing his face with cold water, trying to ground himself, to shake the fear that had taken hold of him. He looked up, meeting his own reflection in the mirror, trying to laugh off the absurdity of it all.

But as he stared into his own eyes, he noticed something he hadn't seen before—a glint, a faint flash of light deep within his pupil. It was barely visible, a tiny point of red light, but it was there, faintly blinking, like the recording light on a camera.

He stumbled back, his breath caught in his throat, his mind reeling as the truth began to dawn on him.

They weren't just watching from the outside.

They were watching from within.

In the days that followed, Darren became a man possessed, desperate to uncover the truth behind the surveillance he knew was consuming him. He scoured the internet, finding obscure forums and articles, conspiracy theories about hidden cameras, about animals embedded with recording devices, about the possibility that every living creature was nothing more than a vessel for observation.

He was met with ridicule, with laughter, with people calling him crazy. But every night, as he lay in bed, he would hear it—the faint buzzing, the clicking, as though his own thoughts were being recorded, as though something were scanning his every memory, his every movement, tracking his every action.

And every day, more creatures appeared—birds perched outside his windows, stray cats lingering in alleyways, even insects that seemed to gather in clusters around his apartment, their eyes dark and unblinking, watching him with a cold, alien intelligence.

His paranoia grew, a gnawing dread that consumed his every thought. He began taking apart electronics, smashing devices, searching for the cameras he was certain were hidden within. But the more he searched, the more he destroyed, the deeper he spiraled, until his apartment was littered with broken devices, shattered screens, remnants of his desperate search for freedom from the invisible eyes that surrounded him.

Then, one night, as he sat alone in his darkened apartment, the power cut out, plunging the room into silence. He froze, his breath catching, his heart pounding as he felt the weight of the silence press down on him.

And then, through the darkness, he saw them—tiny, faintly glowing eyes, dozens of them, clustered in the corners of the room, lining the walls, filling the space with a quiet, unyielding presence.

They were everywhere—on the ceiling, on the floor, in the walls, all staring at him, watching, waiting.

"Why...?" he whispered, his voice trembling, his mind racing with terror.

In response, a faint, mechanical voice echoed through the room, a voice filled with a cold, detached malice.

"We observe. We record. You are... a specimen."

The words sent a chill down his spine, his mind reeling as the truth sank in. Every creature, every living thing he had ever encountered had been part of it—a network, a system of surveillance, watching him, tracking him, studying him.

His life was not his own. He was nothing more than a subject, an experiment, his every thought, every action cataloged, recorded, controlled.

And as he stood there, surrounded by those countless eyes, he knew with a chilling certainty that he would never be alone again, that every moment, every breath, would be watched, recorded, analyzed by forces beyond his understanding.

In the silence, he could feel them—the unseen, alien eyes, studying him from somewhere beyond the stars, their intentions cold, unfeeling, as they observed the lives of humanity, one creature at a time.

And Darren knew, in that final moment, that there was no escape from their gaze.

Darren spent the next few days in a constant state of terror, barely sleeping, his mind a battleground between logic and an unrelenting paranoia. He avoided the windows, knowing those creatures were outside, staring through the glass, their eyes unblinking and fixed on him. He even avoided his own reflection, afraid of seeing that glint in his eyes again—the faint red flash that had shattered any sense of normalcy left in his life.

But the true horror was the revelation that every animal, every insect, every living thing around him was a part of it. They were all watching, connected by a network of surveillance, their every move a means to observe and record his life.

The creatures seemed to multiply around him, more animals gathering each day, drawn to him like a magnet. Every time he stepped outside, he felt the weight of their eyes on him, creatures he had once dismissed as part of the natural world now exposed as spies. Stray dogs watched him from alleyways, pigeons followed him across streets, even flies seemed to linger in his apartment longer than before.

Darren tried to blend in, hoping he could somehow throw them off, but everywhere he went, he could feel their presence, hear the faint clicking and whirring as if his every move was being documented, cataloged.

One evening, at his wit's end, Darren found himself once again online, scrolling through obscure message boards and conspiracy websites. He read post after post, each filled with strange tales of surveillance and invisible eyes, his mind reeling as he connected his own experiences to the scattered reports he'd found.

Then, buried deep within a thread, he found it: a post by someone named *WatcherZero*, detailing his own experiences with "The Surveillance Network." The user described a world where humanity was under constant observation, where every creature acted as a camera, a recording device, feeding information back to a network controlled by an unseen intelligence.

"They see through everything," the post read. *"It's not just technology. It's life itself. Every creature, every insect, even the eyes of other humans—they're all part of the network. And once you've been marked, there's no escape."*

Darren's pulse quickened as he read, his heart pounding with a mix of terror and recognition. This *WatcherZero* described everything he'd been experiencing, everything he had been trying to ignore or rationalize. He reached out, his hands shaking, typing a message to the user, desperate for any response, any hope that he wasn't alone in his nightmare.

But his message was met with silence. WatcherZero's last post had been over a year ago, and Darren couldn't shake the feeling that he might have met a dark fate—another victim of the network, silenced, erased.

With no other options, Darren decided he had to take matters into his own hands. If he couldn't get answers online, he'd confront the creatures head-on, force them to reveal the truth.

Late that night, armed with nothing but a flashlight and his phone, Darren ventured outside. He felt the prickling sensation on the back of his neck, an awareness that he was being watched, followed. He turned his flashlight toward the street, the beam illuminating a row of blackbirds perched on the power line, their eyes glinting as they stared down at him in silence.

He pointed the light at them, his voice trembling with a mixture of fear and anger. “Who are you? Why are you watching me?”

The birds didn’t move, their beady eyes unblinking, their heads tilted slightly as though mocking him. Then, slowly, they began to caw, a sound that sent a chill down his spine, filling the air with a rhythm that seemed almost mechanical, calculated.

He clenched his fists, fighting the urge to turn and run. “Tell me why you’re doing this! Who are you working for?”

But there was only silence, a silence filled with a sense of deep, unyielding malice. He could feel the weight of their gaze, a presence pressing down on him, filling his mind with a terror he couldn’t escape.

He backed away, his heart racing, his mind filled with a sense of helplessness. But then, as he turned to leave, he heard a faint, metallic voice echo through the air, as if speaking from within the flock of birds, a voice devoid of emotion, cold, calculating.

“We are... observing.”

The words sent a chill down his spine, his mind racing as he tried to process the meaning, the implications. He stumbled back, his heart pounding, as he realized the truth: they weren’t just observing his actions—they were studying him, cataloging his every reaction, his every fear.

"Why?" he whispered, his voice barely audible.

The silence stretched, the only sound the faint rustling of feathers as the birds continued to watch him, their eyes filled with a dark, unyielding malice.

"Human behavior... is of interest," the voice replied, echoing through the night, filling the air with a sense of finality, as though the words were both an answer and a warning.

Darren felt a wave of nausea wash over him, his mind reeling with the implications. He was a subject, a specimen, an experiment in some vast, unknowable study. His every movement, every thought, was being recorded, analyzed, fed back to something far beyond his comprehension.

And he knew, with a chilling certainty, that there was no way to escape their gaze.

As the days passed, Darren's paranoia grew, consuming him, driving him to the brink of madness. He took to staying inside, keeping the blinds drawn, refusing to answer his phone, isolating himself from the world. But the feeling of being watched persisted, the knowledge that every insect, every animal, every person he encountered was a part of the network, a tool in the hands of an unseen intelligence.

One night, unable to sleep, he heard a faint buzzing in his apartment. He followed the sound, his heart racing, until he found its source—a fly perched on his windowsill, its wings vibrating in the stillness. He approached slowly, his mind filled with a mix of terror and fascination as he reached out, his fingers trembling as he touched the fly, feeling the faint hum of electricity beneath its tiny body.

The fly didn't move, didn't flee, its eyes fixed on him with an unblinking stare. And as he watched, he saw it—a faint red light, blinking within its compound eyes, a light that pulsed in time with his own heartbeat.

He backed away, his mind racing, his heart pounding as he realized the truth: it wasn't just animals. The network extended to every living creature, every part of the world around him. He was surrounded by eyes, a network that spanned the globe, an invisible web of surveillance that stretched beyond anything he could comprehend.

In a final act of desperation, he smashed the fly, watching as its body disintegrated into fragments of metal and circuitry, a mechanical husk where once he had seen life.

And then, in the silence that followed, he heard it—a voice, cold and distant, echoing through the room, filling the air with a sense of finality.

"You cannot stop the observation. You are... ours."

The words hung in the air, a declaration, a reminder that he was nothing more than a subject, a piece of data in a vast, alien network that spanned the universe.

And as he stood there, surrounded by silence, he knew that he would never be free, that his every movement, every thought, would forever be watched, recorded, cataloged.

For he was part of the surveillance, a specimen in a world where privacy was an illusion, where every living thing was an eye, a recorder, a piece of a system that would never release him from its grasp.

The revelation of the surveillance network consumed Darren, a truth so vast and terrifying that it shattered any sense of normalcy he had left. Days blurred into nights, his reality twisted by the inescapable awareness that he was never alone, that his life was little more than a series of data points in a massive, otherworldly study.

He stopped answering calls from friends, ignoring the knocks at his door, convinced that everyone in his life was part of it. Even the rare times he ventured out, every person he encountered seemed to wear an unsettlingly blank expression, their eyes unblinking, observing him with that familiar, cold detachment.

Paranoia bled into his thoughts, unraveling his sense of self. He could feel their presence everywhere: in the birds outside his window, in the hum of the streetlights, even in the insects that gathered in dark corners of his apartment. But what unnerved him most was the knowledge that they could be hiding within any living thing, that their eyes were embedded in the fabric of the world around him.

In the depths of his isolation, Darren found himself searching for any glimmer of hope. He scoured the dark corners of the internet for mentions of the surveillance network, for anyone who might have shared his experience and lived to tell the tale. Most of what he found were dead ends, dismissed as paranoia, conspiracy, or delusion. But then, late one night, he stumbled across a website buried deep in the search results, titled *Eyes Unveiled.*

The website was an ancient-looking forum, almost empty, but the posts that were there felt hauntingly familiar. Threads with titles like *"I Am Never Alone"* and *"Living in a World of Watchers."* One post, however, stood out. It was from someone who called themselves *The Last Observer,* and it described, in painful detail, the exact experiences Darren had gone through.

"Once you've been marked," the post read, *"you can never be free. But there are ways to fight back, if only for a little while. They fear certain things, things they can't control. The network relies on connectivity, on unbroken links... disrupt the links, disrupt their reach."*

Darren's heart pounded as he read the post, a strange hope filling him. If there was a way to disrupt the network, even temporarily, maybe he could break free, maybe he could escape their gaze.

But he knew he couldn't trust just anyone, not even the faceless stranger online. He needed a real, tangible lead—someone he could speak to, something he could physically hold, a way to escape the invisible prison that had ensnared him.

Then, as he scrolled to the bottom of the page, he found an address—no name, just a city and street number, along with a time: *Tuesday at midnight.* It was less than an hour away, deep in the industrial outskirts of town. Every instinct told him this could be another trap, another extension of the network's reach, but he was desperate. And if there was even a chance this was real, he had to try.

Darren arrived at the address just after midnight, his body tense, his mind racing with fear and anticipation. The building was dark, a dilapidated warehouse surrounded by broken glass and graffiti. He checked his phone; there was no signal, a complete dead zone. He took a deep breath, steeling himself, and walked toward the entrance.

As he stepped inside, he was greeted by a low, flickering light at the end of a narrow hallway. Every instinct screamed for him to turn back, but he forced himself to move forward, his mind racing with images of hidden cameras, of unblinking eyes recording his every move.

At the end of the hallway, a figure stood in the shadows—a man, tall and thin, his face obscured by the hood of a worn, dark jacket. He glanced up as Darren approached, his eyes glinting in the dim light, studying him with a piercing intensity.

"You came," the man said, his voice low, filled with a quiet understanding that made Darren's skin crawl.

Darren nodded, his throat dry. "Are you... are you The Last Observer?"

The man smiled faintly, his eyes never leaving Darren's. "Names don't matter anymore. But yes, I've been where you are now. Watched, followed, unable to escape their eyes." He gestured for Darren to sit, pulling out a small notebook and laying it on the table between them. "You've seen the eyes, haven't you? In every creature, in every shadow?"

Darren nodded, feeling a strange sense of relief at the shared experience, but also a deep, unsettling dread. "How do I stop it? How do I make it end?"

The man leaned forward, his gaze intense. "You can't stop it. But you can disrupt it—temporarily, at least. The network is fragile in certain ways, reliant on signals, on pathways that link every living creature. Disrupt those signals, and you create blind spots, gaps in their observation."

Darren's mind raced. "How? How do I create these... gaps?"

The man reached into his pocket, pulling out a small device—a metal box with a switch and a single blinking light. "This emits a signal they can't track, can't record. It scrambles the connections between their eyes, creates a kind of static that interrupts their surveillance. But it only works within a limited range, and it only lasts as long as the battery."

Darren took the device, feeling its weight in his hands, his heart racing with hope. "And then what? Do I just... use it, and they'll leave me alone?"

The man's smile faded, his gaze darkening. "They'll know you're trying to escape. They'll be angry. They'll come after you, harder, more intensely. Once you've disrupted their network, they'll see you as a threat, a variable they need to control. And they'll do whatever it takes to make sure you can't run, that you stay in line."

A chill ran down Darren's spine, the weight of the man's words pressing down on him, filling him with a dread he couldn't escape. "Then... why did you do it?"

The man's eyes were distant, haunted. "Because living under their gaze, knowing that my every thought, my every moment, was being observed—it was worse than anything they could do to me. I'd rather be hunted than live as their puppet."

Darren clenched the device in his hands, feeling the weight of his decision, the choice that lay before him. He could live under their watchful eyes, surrender to their observation, or he could fight back, disrupt their network, knowing it would make him a target.

The man rose, his face obscured by shadow. "Choose carefully, Darren. Once you disrupt their gaze, there's no going back."

And with that, he turned, disappearing into the shadows, leaving Darren alone in the empty warehouse, the device clutched in his hand, his mind racing with questions, fears, and a strange, unyielding resolve.

Back in his apartment, Darren sat in silence, the device resting on the table in front of him. Outside, he could feel them—the creatures watching, the eyes of insects and birds and people all turned toward him, a network of invisible gazes pressing down on him, filling him with a suffocating sense of helplessness.

He knew the risks. He knew that using the device would make him a target, that it would disrupt their network, turn their attention on him in ways he couldn't imagine. But the thought of living under their surveillance, of surrendering to their control, was unbearable.

He reached for the device, his hands trembling as he flicked the switch. A faint hum filled the room, a low, vibrating sound that sent a shockwave through his mind, a sense of freedom that felt almost foreign.

For the first time in weeks, he felt alone.

The silence was thick, a void where the static of their surveillance had once been, a freedom that filled him with a mixture of relief and terror. He glanced around, his eyes scanning the room, his mind filled with a strange, exhilarating sense of freedom, of possibility.

But then, in the silence, he heard it—a faint scratching at the window, a soft tapping that filled the air, growing louder, more insistent, as though something were pressing against the glass, desperate to break through.

He froze, his heart pounding, his mind racing as he realized the truth: they knew.

The network had been disrupted, their gaze broken, and now they were coming for him.

The scratching grew louder, filling the room, a cacophony of sound that seemed to press in from all sides, filling the air with a sense of impending doom.

And as he backed away, his mind reeling, he knew that he had made his choice, that he had defied the surveillance, that he was no longer a passive subject.

He was the hunted.

The tapping at Darren's window grew louder, a relentless beat that echoed through the stillness of his apartment, filling him with a creeping dread. He stumbled back, his eyes fixed on the shadowy figures just beyond the glass. Through the faint glow of his kitchen light, he could see them—birds, insects, and even stray cats perched outside, their eyes glinting with an unnatural intensity, their gaze cold and unyielding.

He knew he had only minutes before they would break through, before the network would close in on him with a force he could barely comprehend. He couldn't stay here. Grabbing a few essentials, he threw on a jacket and shoved the scrambling device into his pocket, flicking the switch off to conserve its limited battery life. Taking a deep breath, he darted out the back door, his footsteps echoing in the quiet of the night.

As he stepped into the alley, the silence of the city felt wrong, oppressive. It was as if the entire world were holding its breath, waiting, watching.

Darren's only thought was to get as far from the city as possible. He remembered reading that the network was more concentrated in urban areas, where dense populations and endless surveillance made for easy targets. His best chance was to get out, to find a place where the network's reach might be weaker.

The streets stretched out like a maze before him, every corner shadowed, every lamppost a potential hiding place for those prying eyes. The city itself seemed darker, the streetlights casting eerie pools of light that felt more like traps than beacons.

He broke into a run, his breath coming in short gasps as he made his way down an abandoned side street. A low rustling sound filled the air behind him, like the quiet stirring of leaves, and he knew without looking that they were following him—drawn to him, to his defiance, to the brief disruption he had caused in their meticulously woven web.

As he neared the city's edge, he stopped under the flickering light of an old gas station to catch his breath. The silence around him felt heavy, charged, as though he were standing on the edge of something vast and terrifying.

In the distance, he could see a line of headlights approaching, illuminating the street in long, sweeping beams. Instinctively, he ducked into a narrow alleyway, his heart pounding as he watched the headlights draw closer, the car slowing as it neared the gas station.

A figure stepped out of the car—a man in a dark suit, his expression unreadable, his gaze fixed on the gas station as though searching, scanning. Darren's pulse quickened as he realized what was happening. They had sent human agents, proxies of the network, individuals who had surrendered their autonomy to the alien intelligence and become part of the surveillance.

The man lingered for a moment, his head turning slowly as he scanned the area, his movements almost mechanical, precise. Darren held his breath, pressing himself against the cold brick wall, his body tense as he waited for the man to pass.

After a few agonizing seconds, the figure returned to the car, the headlights sweeping past as he drove off, disappearing into the night.

Darren let out a shaky breath, his mind racing. The network wasn't just using animals and insects—they were using people. His paranoia deepened as he wondered how many others in his life had been mere extensions of the network, watching him, recording him, silently ensuring he stayed under control.

As dawn began to break, Darren found himself on the outskirts of the city, the skyscrapers and bright lights fading into the background as he walked along a dirt road that led into a dense forest. He felt a strange sense of relief in the natural darkness of the trees, the quiet hum of nature filling the air, a stark contrast to the artificial silence of the city.

He paused by a narrow stream, cupping his hands to drink, the cold water grounding him, refreshing him. But as he looked up, he saw it—another set of eyes watching him from the underbrush, a fox, its gaze intense, unblinking.

He clenched his jaw, feeling the familiar pulse of fear rise in him. Even here, miles from civilization, he was still being watched, the network stretching beyond the boundaries of the city, reaching into the depths of the forest, an invisible, unbreakable web.

He flicked on the scrambling device, hoping to create a small shield, a space of silence where the network couldn't reach him, where he could breathe without the suffocating weight of surveillance pressing down on him. For a moment, he felt a reprieve, a quiet that he hadn't experienced in days. The fox's eyes grew distant, unfocused, as though its connection to the network had been severed.

But the device wouldn't last long. He could feel the battery draining, the hum growing weaker, and he knew it was only a matter of time before the network reestablished its grip on him.

He had to keep moving.

As he ventured deeper into the forest, Darren felt the oppressive presence of the network lessen, though he knew it was still watching, lurking at the edges of his awareness. The creatures became fewer, the surveillance scattered, as though the forest itself was resisting their intrusion, its ancient roots offering a small sanctuary against the technological web that had ensnared him.

But then, in a small clearing, he saw it—an old, decaying cabin, its windows dark, its roof partially caved in. He approached cautiously, feeling a strange sense of recognition, as though he had been drawn here by an invisible force.

Inside, the air was thick with dust, the floorboards creaking under his weight as he moved through the narrow, shadowed rooms. On a table in the corner, he found a collection of strange devices, wires, and monitors covered in dust, as though someone had abandoned them years ago. Among the items, he noticed a notebook, its pages yellowed and fragile, filled with cramped handwriting that seemed to mirror his own desperation.

The entries detailed a man's descent into paranoia, his discovery of the network, his attempts to escape. It was eerily familiar, the words reflecting his own fears, his own experiences, as though the writer had lived through the same nightmare.

"They cannot be escaped," one entry read. *"The network stretches beyond cities, beyond nature. Every creature, every mind is part of them. To be unseen is to cease to exist."*

Darren felt a chill settle over him as he flipped through the pages, the final entry a scrawled warning: *"If you are reading this, you have been marked. The only freedom lies beyond their gaze. Don't let them find you."*

He felt a strange, sinking realization as he read the words. The network's reach extended beyond any physical space; it was a force embedded in life itself, woven into the very fabric of existence. To escape, he would need to become invisible, to erase his presence from their surveillance.

As he left the cabin, the sun was setting, casting long shadows across the forest floor. He knew he couldn't keep running forever, that eventually, they would catch up, reclaiming him as a subject in their vast study.

But something had shifted within him. He was no longer willing to live as their puppet, their specimen. He would rather disappear completely, remove himself from the network, than live as a pawn under their constant, watchful gaze.

He took out the scrambling device, its battery nearly drained, and walked to the edge of a cliff that overlooked the forest, the distant lights of the city barely visible in the fading light. The air was thick with silence, the world around him holding its breath, as though waiting for his decision.

In a final act of defiance, he raised the device high above his head and threw it over the edge, watching as it disappeared into the darkness, severing the last connection, the final link between him and the network.

For a moment, he felt a sense of peace, a freedom that was as terrifying as it was exhilarating. He was no longer a subject, no longer a piece of data in their web.

But as he stood there, alone in the gathering darkness, he knew that the network would never truly let him go. They would find him, eventually. They would reclaim their lost piece, bringing him back into the fold of their surveillance, their study.

And in that final moment, he understood the truth: there was no escape, no place beyond their reach. He was part of the network, part of the world they controlled, and he would remain under their gaze until the end.

For in a world of watchers, to be unseen was to cease to exist.

The End

28
THE SEWER PEOPLE

New York City's underground was a labyrinth—a vast, sprawling network of tunnels and pipes that stretched for miles beneath the bustling streets above. Few people thought about what lay beneath their feet as they hurried across sidewalks, caught up in the fast-paced rhythm of the city. But there were stories. Stories of strange sounds echoing from sewer grates, of shadows moving just out of sight, of people who went missing, leaving behind only a vague sense of unease.

Most people brushed off these tales as urban legends, just part of the city's gritty charm. But those who ventured too close to the edge, who walked alone at night near certain dark alleys, learned a terrifying truth: the sewers were not empty.

Far below, hidden in the damp, putrid depths, a small, twisted society lurked. They were grotesque creatures—once human, perhaps, though barely recognizable now. The Sewer People had adapted to their dark, forsaken home, and over time, they had developed a terrible hunger.

The creatures had lived in the sewers for decades, forgotten remnants of society. Driven underground by desperation, neglect, or crime, they had adapted to the darkness, their skin pale and sallow, their eyes large and hungry. At first, they scavenged what they could—scraps of food that washed down the drains, the occasional rat that wandered too close. But over the years, as their numbers grew, their needs grew too, and they began to crave something more.

They started by dragging animals down into the depths, stray dogs and cats snatched from alleys above. But even that was not enough. Soon, their hunger turned darker, their appetites shifting toward something that offered both sustenance and the thrill of the hunt. And so, the Sewer People began to turn their eyes toward the surface.

They moved quietly, emerging from manholes under the cover of night, lurking in the shadows, waiting for those who wandered too close to the grates or strayed from the crowds. They had become adept at reading the rhythms of the streets, studying the city's pulse, learning when and where to strike.

One damp October evening, a young woman named Leah was making her way home after a long shift at a nearby bar. Her feet ached, her head pounded, and all she wanted was to collapse into bed. The streets were nearly empty, a thin mist clinging to the ground as she walked, the city's usual hum muffled by the fog.

She passed by an alley near the corner of 12th and Cedar, her steps quickening as a strange feeling of unease washed over her. The streetlights cast long, eerie shadows, illuminating only part of the alley while the rest was swallowed in darkness. She told herself it was nothing, just a trick of the mind brought on by exhaustion.

But as she passed, she heard it—a soft, shuffling sound, like something wet being dragged across the ground. She froze, straining her ears, trying to place the noise. It was faint, almost imperceptible, but it sent chills down her spine.

"Hello?" she called out, her voice trembling slightly.

Silence.

She took a step forward, curiosity tugging at her despite her fear. And then she saw it—a pair of glistening eyes peering out from the shadows, watching her, unblinking, filled with a kind of dark, primal hunger that made her skin crawl.

Leah took a step back, her heart pounding, but it was too late. A pair of pale, bony hands shot out from the darkness, grabbing her ankle, pulling her off balance. She screamed, her voice echoing through the empty streets as she clawed at the ground, trying to pull herself free. But the hands were relentless, their grip cold and unyielding, dragging her toward the open manhole at the end of the alley.

Her scream faded into the night as she disappeared below, swallowed by the darkness, her fate sealed by the unseen horrors lurking beneath the city.

The Sewer People dragged Leah's limp form through the filthy tunnels, their hunched bodies scuttling through the darkness like rats, their eyes wide and wild, their breath coming in low, raspy gasps. Their bodies were twisted, deformed by years of living underground, their skin pale and rubbery, stretched thin over jutting bones.

They moved quickly, their excitement palpable, their voices low, guttural, each one chittering to the others in a language that had become their own, a garbled mix of growls and half-formed words. They dragged her to a small chamber deep within the sewers, a space they had claimed as their own—a dark, damp hollow lined with makeshift nests of discarded rags and garbage.

The Sewer People surrounded Leah, their eyes gleaming as they leaned in, their noses twitching as they caught the scent of fresh blood, their fingers twitching with anticipation. This was their ritual, their twisted communion, a grim ceremony that bound them together in a macabre feast.

As they leaned over her, their faces close, their mouths twisted into grotesque smiles, they began to feed, their low, raspy breaths filling the chamber, their voices rising in a dark, haunting chant, a song that echoed through the tunnels, a song of hunger, of darkness, of the terrible bond that held them together.

The next day, Leah's absence was noticed by her coworkers, who reported her missing when she failed to show up for her shift. Her friends plastered posters around the neighborhood, and the police conducted a half-hearted search, but no one could explain where she'd gone. There was no evidence, no witnesses—just a faint, unsettling rumor that began to spread, whispers about people vanishing near certain alleys, about strange sounds coming from the sewers at night.

Most people dismissed the stories as nonsense, urban legends concocted by paranoid minds. But those who had heard the stories before, those who remembered the old tales of the Sewer People, knew there was a terrible truth buried beneath the city.

The Sewer People watched from below, their twisted faces pressed against the grates, their hollow eyes scanning the streets, waiting for the next unfortunate soul to wander too close. Their hunger was insatiable, and as the city above moved on, oblivious to the horrors lurking beneath its feet, the Sewer People continued to wait, their bodies hidden in the darkness, their hands reaching up, always ready to drag another victim into their forgotten world.

As weeks passed, more people disappeared—first a homeless man, then a pair of late-night revelers, and even a police officer who had been investigating the reports. Each disappearance was chalked up to coincidence, to the chaos of the city, but those who lived near the affected areas began to grow uneasy, noticing strange smells, odd sounds, a sense of something watching from below.

One night, a maintenance worker named Ray, assigned to inspect a clogged sewer line near Cedar Street, found himself face-to-face with the truth. Descending into the damp, foul-smelling tunnels, he noticed strange markings on the walls, handprints smeared in dirt, and a lingering smell that made his stomach turn.

As he turned a corner, his flashlight caught a glimpse of something—a figure hunched in the shadows, watching him with gleaming eyes, its mouth stretched into a grotesque smile. Ray staggered back, his heart pounding as he realized what he was looking at.

The creature lunged, its body a blur of pale skin and bony limbs, its fingers curled into claws as it reached for him. Ray screamed, scrambling back, but his voice was swallowed by the darkness as the creature's hand closed around his throat, dragging him down, down into the depths, into the world of the Sewer People.

By morning, Ray's disappearance was all over the news, another mysterious vanishing in a growing list. The people of New York began to talk, their whispers growing louder, fear creeping into their voices as they traded stories, each one more horrific than the last. Some spoke of pale figures lurking in the sewers, of hands reaching up from the grates, of eyes watching from the darkness.

But the city moved on, as it always did, the people pushing the fear aside, telling themselves it was just stories, just rumors, just the city's gritty charm.

But deep below, in the twisted, foul-smelling tunnels, the Sewer People waited, their eyes gleaming, their fingers twitching, their hunger growing with each passing day. They had tasted the thrill of the hunt, the satisfaction of the kill, and they knew there would be more.

Because New York was a city that never slept—a city with endless prey, a city that would feed their hunger forever.

And the Sewer People would be waiting, always watching, always hungry, their dark kingdom hidden beneath the streets, their hands reaching up, ready to claim the next unwitting soul who wandered too close.

Detective Lisa Morales had seen her share of strange cases in New York, but the recent string of disappearances around Cedar Street was different. Homeless people vanishing wasn't uncommon, but lately, it wasn't just vagrants who were disappearing. The cases had begun with a few drifters, but now regular citizens—bartenders, joggers, even a fellow officer—were vanishing, with no leads and no evidence. It was as if the earth itself had swallowed them.

Lisa was assigned to investigate Ray's disappearance, the maintenance worker who had last been seen near a sewer access point on Cedar Street. His tools had been found near the open manhole, but the worker was nowhere to be found. Lisa's team hadn't turned up anything useful, so she'd decided to take matters into her own hands. Tonight, she would investigate the sewers herself.

As she prepared to descend, she felt a chill, a creeping unease that whispered she was walking into something far worse than a simple missing persons case. But she pushed it aside, determined to uncover the truth.

With a flashlight in one hand and her gun strapped to her side, Lisa climbed down the rickety metal ladder into the darkness. The smell was worse than she'd imagined, thick and oppressive, the air humid with rot and decay. Her flashlight illuminated the slick walls of the sewer, casting long shadows that seemed to shift as she moved.

The deeper she went, the more oppressive the silence became. Her footsteps echoed, bouncing off the walls, the only sound in an otherwise dead quiet. Every now and then, she thought she heard something—a faint, shuffling sound, almost too soft to notice. But whenever she stopped to listen, it vanished, swallowed by the darkness.

"Ray?" she called out, her voice trembling slightly as it echoed through the tunnels. "Anyone down here?"

Her voice was met with silence, and she felt a wave of unease settle over her. But she pushed on, her flashlight slicing through the gloom, determined to find something, anything that might explain what was happening.

After a few minutes, she reached a junction, a larger chamber where several tunnels intersected. Her flashlight swept over the walls, and she froze, her breath catching as she noticed something strange: handprints smeared across the concrete, dark stains that looked almost like dried blood, leading deeper into one of the tunnels.

A chill ran down her spine, but she forced herself to move closer, her heart pounding as she examined the prints. They were unmistakably human, but there was something wrong about them—long, bony fingers with nails that had left deep scratches in the concrete.

Her stomach twisted, a sick feeling settling over her as she realized these weren't the marks of a struggling victim. They were deliberate, as if someone—or something—had left them as a warning.

Lisa took a deep breath, steadying herself as she turned down the tunnel. She moved cautiously, her senses on high alert, every nerve in her body screaming for her to turn back. But she ignored the fear, focusing on the task at hand, determined to find answers.

The tunnel led to another chamber, larger this time, with pipes snaking across the walls, leaking water that dripped into shallow pools scattered across the floor. Her flashlight caught a glimpse of something ahead—a pile of rags, or so she thought at first. But as she moved closer, she saw it was a body.

Her heart dropped. The man's face was frozen in terror, his mouth twisted open in a silent scream, his eyes wide and empty. His skin was pale, his body emaciated, as if something had drained the very life from him.

Lisa took a shaky breath, her mind racing as she tried to process the horror in front of her. She knelt beside the body, examining the wounds on his arms and neck—deep, jagged bites, like those of a wild animal.

She was about to radio for backup when she heard it—a faint, shuffling sound echoing through the chamber, growing louder, closer. She spun around, her flashlight slicing through the darkness, and for a brief moment, she caught a glimpse of something moving in the shadows.

A figure crouched at the edge of the light, its body hunched and twisted, its skin pale and rubbery, stretched tight over bony limbs. Its eyes glinted in the light, wide and unblinking, filled with a primal hunger that sent a wave of terror through her.

It stared at her for a moment, its mouth twisted into a grotesque smile, revealing rows of broken, jagged teeth.

And then, it lunged.

Lisa stumbled back, raising her gun and firing, the shots echoing through the tunnel as she struggled to keep her aim steady. The creature shrieked, a sound that seemed to reverberate through the tunnels, chilling her to the bone. She fired again, but it was fast, ducking out of the beam of her flashlight, disappearing into the shadows.

Breathing heavily, Lisa turned and ran, her footsteps splashing through the shallow pools of water, the creature's shrieks echoing behind her. She could hear more sounds now—other footsteps, low, raspy breaths, the faint whisper of movement all around her.

Panic clawed at her as she realized the truth. There was more than one of them.

She sprinted through the tunnels, her flashlight flickering as she tried to navigate the maze of corridors, her mind racing as she searched for the way back. The air grew colder, the darkness pressing in around her, and she felt the creatures closing in, their presence like a dark, suffocating cloud that filled the air with the stench of rot.

At last, she saw the ladder, the faint glimmer of streetlight filtering down from above, and she scrambled up, her hands slick with sweat, her heart pounding as she climbed out of the darkness and into the light.

Lisa stumbled onto the street, gasping for air, her clothes soaked, her mind reeling from the horror of what she had seen. She barely noticed the few pedestrians who stared at her, their faces filled with confusion and alarm as she hurried back to her car, her hands shaking as she gripped the steering wheel.

She drove straight to the station, her mind racing as she tried to make sense of it all. Who were those creatures? How had they ended up in the sewers? And what kind of hunger drove them to hunt in the darkness?

When she filed her report, her fellow officers looked at her with skepticism, disbelief etched into their faces. Sewer creatures? Cannibalistic figures lurking beneath the city? It sounded like something out of a horror movie, and even as she spoke, she could see the doubt in their eyes.

But Lisa knew what she had seen. She had faced the darkness below, felt its cold, unyielding gaze, heard the hunger in their voices. And she knew one thing for certain:

The Sewer People were real, and they were hunting.

In the days that followed, more bodies turned up—pale, emaciated, marked with deep, jagged wounds. The city tried to hide it, chalking up the deaths to gang violence or animal attacks, but Lisa knew the truth. The creatures were becoming bolder, emerging from the darkness more frequently, taking more victims, their hunger growing with each passing day.

Lisa became obsessed, spending hours poring over maps of the city's sewer system, tracing the patterns of the disappearances, trying to find the creatures' lair. She worked alone, her colleagues having dismissed her warnings, treating her as though she were unraveling, haunted by shadows.

But she knew she was close. She could feel it, a sense of dread building as she prepared to return to the depths, to confront the darkness once more, to uncover the truth about the Sewer People and the terrible, insatiable hunger that drove them.

And as she descended into the sewers once again, her flashlight cutting through the gloom, she knew that this time, she might not make it back.

Because in the darkness below, the Sewer People were waiting.

Detective Lisa Morales couldn't let go of the case. Even after the city's officials ignored her report, dismissing her warnings as paranoia, she found herself returning again and again to the sewers, driven by an insatiable need to understand the creatures lurking beneath New York's streets. She spent days piecing together missing persons reports, odd disappearances that had gone uninvestigated, scraps of information that no one had connected before. And as her investigation deepened, she began to suspect that the history of the Sewer People went back much further than she'd realized.

After weeks of combing through forgotten records, she uncovered something that chilled her to the core: whispers of an "underground community" dating back to the 1800s, a group of people who had vanished from society and retreated to the sewers for survival. They were rumored to have formed a strange society of their own, bound by a set of dark, twisted rules. But the most disturbing part was yet to come—a story of starvation, madness, and the transformation of human beings into something monstrous.

In the late 1800s, New York City was rapidly expanding, but the prosperity hadn't reached everyone. The poorest residents, including many who had arrived on Ellis Island with nowhere else to go, were left struggling to survive in overcrowded tenements, eking out a miserable existence in the narrow alleyways and squalid backstreets. Some of these unfortunates began to vanish, slipping into the underground tunnels and sewers in hopes of finding shelter, food, or even a place to hide from the law.

By 1892, this hidden colony of outcasts had taken root in the sewers. They were known only as "The Forgotten"—a group of castaways who had banded together to survive, living off scraps that washed down from the city above, keeping warm around burning barrels, adapting to the darkness. But over time, as food grew scarce, they faced starvation. Many tried to return to the surface but found themselves rejected, or worse, hunted down by officials eager to rid the city of its "vermin."

Desperation twisted their minds. And soon, they turned to the unthinkable.

The first reported incident was documented in a yellowed police file from 1893, labeled "Classified" and sealed away in the NYPD archives. It told of a pair of officers who had ventured into the sewers to investigate a missing woman's report. They found her clothes neatly folded beside a drain, but no body. All they could hear in the tunnels was a faint, haunting chant—a string of guttural sounds they couldn't understand.

The officers reported seeing a figure hunched in the shadows, a figure that appeared more beast than human. But when they approached, it vanished, melting back into the darkness.

From then on, the disappearances became more frequent, and the legend of "The Forgotten" grew. Whispers of cannibalism and ritualistic practices emerged, rumors that the colony had devolved into something monstrous. Those who dared to venture into the depths told tales of eyes watching from the shadows, of bones picked clean and scattered like offerings.

The Forgotten, in their desperation, had turned on one another. Cannibalism had become not just a means of survival but a dark ritual, a rite that transformed the colony, warping them into creatures with twisted bodies and minds, beings that fed on flesh and sustained themselves through a brutal, ancient pact: eat, survive, and grow stronger.

As the years passed, The Forgotten developed their own twisted hierarchy. They were no longer just outcasts; they had become something else, something driven by hunger and hatred for the world above that had cast them aside. At the center of their society was a leader they called "The Father of the Depths"—a gaunt, skeletal figure who had once been a respected member of society, a doctor, perhaps, though no one knew for sure. He was said to be the first to take part in the cannibalistic rituals, the first to embrace the transformation.

The Father preached a grim doctrine, one that justified their dark acts as necessary sacrifices. "The flesh is the key to survival," he'd told them, his words whispered through the sewers, spreading his doctrine of survival and vengeance. "To consume is to thrive, to feed on the life of others is to rise above."

Under his twisted teachings, The Forgotten came to believe they were no longer human but creatures of the dark, bound by an ancient hunger, a hunger that tied them to the sewers, to the endless hunt.

Their bodies changed with time, adapting to the cold, the damp, their skin paling, their eyes growing larger to see in the dark, their limbs elongated and bony. And as they grew accustomed to their new forms, they found they could move faster, slip into shadows, vanish without a trace.

And all the while, they waited, watching from below, bound by a pact they could never escape—a pact of hunger, of blood, and of a hatred that ran so deep it had seeped into the very bones of the city.

Lisa's hands shook as she read through the files, her heart pounding as she absorbed the horror of what she had uncovered. The creatures she had encountered were no urban legend. They were the twisted descendants of *The Forgotten,* creatures bound by a pact that had been made more than a century ago, a pact that could only be sustained through a constant supply of human flesh.

And she realized that the recent increase in disappearances wasn't random. The Sewer People were multiplying, growing bolder, their hunger stronger, their population swelling. They needed more bodies, more flesh, to sustain their dark society.

But the question that haunted her was why now? What had changed?

After hours of combing through old records, she stumbled upon an unsettling theory. With the increase in construction projects around the city, some of the sewer lines had been expanded and extended, inadvertently opening up parts of the underground network that had been closed off for decades. It was possible that new tunnels had connected previously isolated sections of the city's underground, giving the Sewer People easier access to neighborhoods that had once been safe.

The creatures were no longer bound to the deepest, darkest parts of the city. They were moving through newly opened routes, expanding their hunting grounds, and they would stop at nothing to feed the insatiable hunger that bound them.

The grim knowledge weighed on her, and Lisa knew she couldn't keep this to herself. She gathered her closest allies on the force, those who believed her, and laid out her findings. They knew the city wouldn't sanction an operation based on folklore and old reports, so they devised their own plan—a series of raids on the most vulnerable sewer access points, using high-powered lights and specialized weapons to drive the creatures back, to force them to retreat into the deeper tunnels.

They would attempt to cut off the creatures' newly gained access to the surface, blocking entrances, sealing off tunnels. It wouldn't end the threat, but it might buy them time, keep the people of the city safe for a little longer.

As they prepared for the operation, Lisa felt a gnawing fear settle over her, a dark certainty that the Sewer People wouldn't go quietly. She knew they were cunning, driven by a desperation that could rival anything she'd ever faced. And as she stood at the entrance to the first tunnel, flashlight in hand, she thought of the whisper she'd heard that night in the sewer, the haunting chant of The Forgotten, their voices rising from the depths.

With her team by her side, Lisa descended into the darkness once more, knowing that she was walking into the heart of the creatures' territory. The silence was thick, oppressive, broken only by the echo of their footsteps and the faint, almost imperceptible sound of something moving just out of sight.

She took a deep breath, her flashlight steady, her resolve firm. She would confront the darkness, face the ancient hunger, and if she had to, she would make a sacrifice of her own to put an end to the horrors that lurked beneath the city.

Because the Sewer People were coming, and they wouldn't stop until the city was theirs.

Detective Lisa Morales had always been courageous, but descending deeper into the sewers with only a handful of her most trusted colleagues pushed her courage to its limit. The flickering beams of their flashlights were the only light in the endless maze of darkness, illuminating the slimy, damp walls that seemed to close in tighter as they moved forward. Each step felt heavier than the last, as though the very air grew denser, charged with an unseen force, an ancient, primal energy that lurked just out of sight.

Lisa knew they were close to something. She could feel it—the heavy, suffocating dread that settled over them like a dark cloud. Somewhere deep in these tunnels, hidden from the light for over a century, waited the leader of the Sewer People, the being that all the others followed. She had read enough about him in the old records to know he went by a single name: *The Father of the Depths.*

The deeper they went, the more disturbing signs they found. The walls were smeared with strange symbols, painted in dark, dried blood and dirt, marking the territory of the Sewer People. Bones littered the ground, scattered across the floor in grotesque arrangements, some piled high in mounds that looked almost ceremonial. Broken skulls, cracked ribs, and brittle femurs were organized as if placed with purpose, their hollow eyes watching as the intruders passed by.

They reached a wide, open chamber deep in the sewer system. It was different from the others—a larger, domed room where multiple tunnels intersected. The air was thick and stale, with a faint metallic tang that clung to the back of their throats. In the center of the chamber stood an altar fashioned from stone, dark and slick with something viscous that reflected their flashlights. Around the altar lay more bones, organized in a twisted mockery of reverence.

And standing beside the altar, bathed in the eerie glow of their flashlights, was a figure. He was tall, gaunt, with pale, rubbery skin stretched tightly over bones that jutted out at sharp angles. His eyes were wide and dark, too large for his face, and his mouth stretched into a grotesque, almost welcoming smile, revealing rows of crooked, yellowed teeth. He wore the remnants of old clothing—tattered, filthy, the fabric long faded but once fine. He might have once been a man of dignity, a man of science or law. But now, he was something else entirely.

The Father of the Depths raised his head, meeting Lisa's gaze, and when he spoke, his voice was a rasping whisper, barely more than a breath but filled with a terrible, commanding power.

"Welcome, strangers," he said, his voice echoing off the walls. "You have come far... farther than most."

Lisa held her ground, her gun trained on him, her voice steady. "You're the one they call the Father. The one who leads... *them*."

He smiled, a slow, twisted expression that spread across his face like a crack splitting the earth. "The Father," he echoed, his gaze drifting over her with a cold, unblinking curiosity. "I am the guide, the shepherd of the lost. I am the beginning and the end, the hunger that never dies."

His eyes fixed on Lisa, filled with a dark intensity that made her skin crawl. "And you... are you here to feed the hunger? Or to stop it?"

"We're here to put an end to this," Lisa replied, her voice firm. "You and your people have been taking innocent lives. It ends tonight."

The Father let out a low, raspy laugh, his eyes gleaming with a terrible amusement. "Innocent lives?" he repeated, as though tasting the words. "There are no innocents, not in this city. They live above us, feeding on each other, using each other... and yet you call us the monsters."

He took a step closer, his movements slow, deliberate, his gaze never leaving hers. "Do you think they care for you, Detective? Do you think they will remember you when you are gone?"

Lisa's jaw tightened, her grip on the gun steady, but she felt the weight of his words, the darkness that clung to them like a shroud. "It doesn't matter. This ends tonight."

The Father's smile widened, his eyes narrowing. "You think you can stop us? We are bound to this place, woven into the very stone beneath their feet. We are the forgotten, the abandoned, those they left to rot. And in return, we feed on them, just as they fed on us. We are the hunger that never dies."

He raised his arms, his bony fingers splayed, and from the shadows, a dozen figures emerged—pale, twisted forms, their eyes wide, empty, their mouths stretched into silent screams. They moved closer, surrounding her team, their bodies hunched and broken, their movements jerky, unnatural, as though driven by a force they could not resist.

Lisa's team raised their weapons, their flashlights casting frantic beams of light across the chamber, illuminating the grotesque faces of the Sewer People as they closed in. The Father watched with dark satisfaction, his eyes gleaming, his voice a whisper that filled the chamber, thick with malice.

"Will you join us, Detective?" he murmured. "Or will you become the next feast?"

Lisa took a step forward, her flashlight trained on him, her voice filled with a fierce determination. "You may have survived down here, but your reign is over. Your people, your so-called 'hunger'—it ends now."

The Father chuckled, a low, hollow sound. "I am eternal, Detective. You cannot kill what was already forgotten." He gestured to his followers, his smile widening. "We are bound by hunger, by the pact made in blood. You cannot break it."

Without hesitation, Lisa shouted to her team, "Lights—on them! Full blast!"

Her team switched on their high-powered lights, flooding the chamber with a blinding glare. The Sewer People shrieked, stumbling back, their pale, bulging eyes unable to bear the light, their skin smoking as though the brightness itself burned them. But the Father stood firm, his gaze fixed on Lisa, his eyes dark, unblinking.

"Light will not stop me," he hissed, his voice filled with a venomous fury. "I have survived a hundred years in darkness. I *am* the darkness."

Lisa raised her gun, aiming directly at him. "Then maybe you've lived long enough."

She fired, the shot echoing through the chamber, and the bullet hit the Father square in the chest. He staggered, his smile faltering, but he did not fall. His expression twisted into something darker, angrier, as he reached up, touching the blood seeping from the wound.

"You think... a bullet will stop me?" he rasped, his voice filled with disbelief and fury. "I am eternal. I am the hunger that—"

But Lisa wasn't finished. She stepped forward, her eyes cold, determined. "It may not be enough to kill you. But it'll be enough to bury you."

She signaled to her team, who began throwing canisters into the chamber—powerful explosives designed to collapse tunnels, to seal off entire sections of the sewers. The Father's eyes widened as he realized what she intended, his voice rising in a furious scream.

"No! You cannot trap us! We are *the forgotten!* We will rise again!"

But Lisa ignored his words, her heart pounding as the countdown began, the seconds ticking down as she and her team retreated, their footsteps echoing through the tunnels as they ran, the Father's screams fading into the darkness behind them.

They barely made it out of the tunnels before the explosives detonated, the ground shaking beneath their feet as the sewers collapsed, the entrance caving in, sealing the creatures below. Dust and debris filled the air, and as the rumbling subsided, Lisa turned back, her face streaked with dirt and sweat, her expression grim.

The Father and his followers were buried, entombed in the darkness they had claimed as their own, their voices silenced, their hunger sealed away.

Days later, Lisa stood at the site of the collapsed tunnel, the city still buzzing with rumors, whispers of strange creatures, of monsters lurking below. The authorities had dismissed the incident as a "structural failure," refusing to acknowledge what had truly happened.

But Lisa knew the truth. She could still hear the Father's voice in her mind, his final words echoing in the silence.

"We are the forgotten... we will rise again..."

She knew the darkness was never truly gone, that some horrors could never be fully buried. But for now, the city was safe, the creatures bound once more to the depths where they belonged.

And as she walked away, she felt a chill run down her spine, a faint, lingering whisper in the air—a reminder that some hungers, once awakened, can never truly be satisfied.

The End

29
THE ARTIST

The studio was shrouded in quiet shadows, its only light coming from a single lamp casting a warm, steady glow across a nearly finished canvas. Julian Mercer leaned in close, his fingers dancing over the oil paint, adding the final, delicate strokes to the image before him. The woman's face on the canvas looked back at him, her eyes haunting, a mixture of beauty and pain. Julian felt a thrill as he painted, the brush gliding with precision, his movements precise, intimate, as though he were capturing more than just her likeness.

Julian was fresh from the Rhode Island School of Design, a recent graduate whose talent had caught the eye of New York's most discerning art critics. His work was different—hypnotic, unsettling, his portraits possessed a depth that seemed to pull the viewer in, to touch something beyond the skin, something uncomfortably close to the soul. Within weeks of arriving in New York, he had been picked up by one of the city's most prestigious galleries, Kessler & Associates, with a promise of exhibitions, representation, and a growing list of clients who couldn't wait to own a piece of his work.

But there was a darkness in Julian's process, a secret that lay beneath the surface of his canvases. What the gallery owners, his patrons, and even his closest friends didn't know was that Julian didn't just paint his models—he consumed them, quite literally. Each of his portraits was a macabre masterpiece, created not just with paint, but with pieces of the women themselves—strands of hair, droplets of blood, fragments of bone—woven into the layers of oil paint, bound into the very essence of his work.

This was his signature, the final step in his process: to immortalize his subjects by making them part of the canvas, an offering that captured not just their beauty, but their very being.

Julian's career had exploded almost overnight. His first exhibition had been a sold-out success, and his clients were clamoring for more, drawn to the dark allure of his work. They couldn't explain it, but there was something visceral about his portraits, something that seemed to reach out from the canvas, whispering secrets, holding their gaze with an intensity that was almost hypnotic.

As he walked into the Kessler Gallery that afternoon, he could see the heads turning, the hushed whispers of admiration from patrons and staff alike. Julian was greeted by Miriam Kessler herself, the gallery's owner, a shrewd woman who had built an empire around spotting raw, unsettling talent.

"Julian," she said, her voice warm, her eyes glinting with excitement. "You're becoming quite the sensation. We already have clients eager to commission their own portraits. Tell me, are you ready to take on a few?"

Julian forced a smile, though the words were music to his ears. "Of course, Miriam. I'm always ready to create."

She led him into her office, where a small group of patrons awaited him—wealthy art collectors, high-profile socialites, each eager to introduce themselves, to be in the presence of the gallery's newest star. As he shook hands and exchanged pleasantries, Julian couldn't help but feel a thrill at the prospect. His next muse was likely standing right in front of him.

After the meeting, Miriam handed him a list of names, each one accompanied by a promise of payment far beyond what he'd been making as a student. Julian scanned the list, his eyes lingering on one name in particular: Lila Montgomery.

Lila was a well-known figure in the art world, a woman of impeccable taste and a beauty that had enchanted artists and photographers for years. She was also one of the gallery's wealthiest clients, and she'd requested a portrait done by Julian herself. The thought of capturing her, of making her part of his next work, sent a dark excitement coursing through him.

Days later, Lila arrived at Julian's studio, her presence filling the room with an almost ethereal beauty. She was elegant, poised, with striking eyes that seemed to see right through him. Julian studied her as she took her place on the small platform he'd set up, her movements graceful, her features illuminated by the soft glow of his studio lights.

He began with the basics, sketching her outline, filling in the delicate details of her face, her eyes, her lips. As he worked, they spoke, Lila asking questions about his inspirations, his process, and the things that drove him to create. Julian was careful with his answers, steering the conversation away from anything that might give her pause. He painted her with focus, his mind already thinking of the final step, the ritual that would complete the portrait and make it uniquely his.

By the time he finished the first session, he had captured Lila's likeness, the beginnings of her portrait emerging from the canvas like a haunting reflection of her beauty. But it wasn't enough. For Julian, a painting wasn't complete until he had imbued it with the essence of his subject, a practice he had perfected over the years, first with small animals, then with anonymous models he'd hired during his time in school.

But Lila was different. She was famous, wealthy, and people would notice if she simply vanished. He needed to be cautious, to draw her in slowly, ensuring she trusted him, that she would return for session after session, until he had enough of her essence to complete the work.

Julian waited until the third session to initiate the next step. As Lila sat on the platform, holding a glass of water he'd prepared for her, Julian noticed the faintest twinge of drowsiness in her eyes. She blinked, fighting off the effects of the sedative he'd slipped into her drink, her eyelids growing heavy as she began to drift into a light sleep.

Once she was unconscious, Julian moved quickly. He took a sterilized scalpel from his toolkit, carefully snipping a few strands of her hair, wrapping them around his fingers before mixing them with the oils on his palette. He added the hair to the canvas, blending it into the background, each stroke filled with a dark satisfaction.

The process had begun. Each time she returned, he would take a little more—a few drops of blood drawn under the guise of a finger prick for color mixing, a nail clipping tucked discreetly into the shadows of the painting. Over time, the canvas began to change, Lila's face becoming more lifelike, her eyes glinting with a light that seemed almost real. Julian could feel the thrill of creation, the sense of power that came with knowing he was binding her essence to the work, making her part of it forever.

Weeks passed, and the gallery hung Lila's portrait in the main showroom, an unveiling that drew attention from critics and collectors alike. The painting was exquisite, haunting, Lila's eyes staring out from the canvas with an intensity that left viewers mesmerized. It sold within hours of its unveiling, purchased by an anonymous buyer with instructions for immediate delivery.

But then the questions started.

"Who was the model?" one patron asked him at a gallery event, his eyes lingering on the fine details of another portrait, this one of a young woman with dark hair and a soft smile.

Julian offered a vague smile, brushing off the question. "An acquaintance. She agreed to model for me but preferred to remain anonymous."

But the questions continued. One of the gallery's patrons recognized the woman in his previous portrait as a model who had vanished several months earlier, her disappearance unsolved, the investigation turning cold. Another client, studying one of Julian's smaller works, claimed to know the young woman on the canvas, a server at a bar downtown who hadn't been seen in weeks.

Rumors began to circulate—whispers that his models had vanished, that they had somehow become part of the paintings themselves. Clients asked the gallery staff, hinting at the eerie lifelikeness of the portraits, the sense that each subject was somehow frozen in time, staring out from the canvas with eyes that seemed almost real.

As Julian worked on his latest portrait, he could feel the net closing in, the questions growing louder, the whispers following him wherever he went. But he couldn't stop—not when he was so close. His obsession had taken hold, driving him to finish the final portrait, a piece that he knew would capture Lila's beauty in a way that no other work had before.

On the night of the last session, he lured her into the studio, offering her wine, soft music, his charm as he prepared her for the final sitting. This time, he would take more than just a few strands of hair or drops of blood. He would take enough to bind her fully to the canvas, to make her essence part of the painting itself.

But as he moved toward her, scalpel in hand, he felt a shift in the air—a presence, a pressure that seemed to emanate from the walls themselves. The portraits hanging in the studio seemed to watch him, their eyes fixed on him, accusing, silent, as though the women within them were somehow aware of his actions, their spirits trapped, bound to the canvases, bearing witness to the darkness he had woven into his art.

For the first time, Julian felt a chill of fear, a whisper of something dark and powerful, as though the souls of his models were reaching out to him, calling for justice.

And as he lifted the scalpel, his hands trembling, he felt it—a presence behind him, cold fingers pressing into his shoulder, a low, whispering voice in his ear, filled with fury and pain.

"Let us go..."

The studio fell silent, the shadows deepening, and Julian realized, with a bone-deep terror, that his art had claimed him too.

The studio was silent, thick with an atmosphere that seemed to pulse with something dark and unseen. Julian stood alone, surrounded by his own creations, the eyes of his painted muses watching him from every corner. The air was colder than usual, a chill that had nothing to do with the season, but he tried to ignore it, forcing himself to focus on his work.

He thought he could silence the doubts, push away the feeling that something was wrong. But every time he looked at his canvases, the faces of his models seemed to change, their expressions twisting, their eyes staring at him with a mixture of sorrow and anger. It was subtle, barely perceptible, but he could feel it—the sense that they were watching, waiting, and that they knew what he had done.

Julian wiped his hands, his eyes moving over the canvases that lined the walls. Lila's portrait hung in the center, her eyes glinting with a depth that went beyond mere paint. There was something alive in her gaze, a flicker of accusation that he could feel whenever he met her eyes.

He shook his head, muttering to himself, willing away the unease that had settled over him. But as he turned away from the painting, he heard it—a faint, almost imperceptible whisper, barely more than a breath.

"Why did you take us?"

Julian froze, his pulse quickening. He looked around the studio, but he was alone. He could feel a cold sweat trickling down his spine, the whisper echoing in his mind, filling him with a dread that he couldn't ignore. He forced himself to breathe, to calm down, but the whisper returned, louder this time, filled with a sorrow that seemed to seep into the walls.

"Let us go..."

He stepped back, his gaze darting to the paintings, his mind racing. He tried to convince himself that it was his imagination, a trick of the mind. But the feeling only grew stronger, an oppressive weight that pressed down on him, filling the studio with an energy that felt almost alive.

Days passed, but Julian's sense of unease only deepened. He barely left his studio, driven by an obsession to finish his latest piece—a self-portrait, one that would capture his own genius, his intensity, the raw talent that had propelled him to fame. But every time he tried to paint, he felt a resistance, a heaviness that made it impossible to focus. The brush would shake in his hand, the paint would smear, and his reflection in the mirror would seem to change, taking on a hollow, haunted look.

He became increasingly paranoid, convinced that he could hear whispers in the dead of night, faint voices calling his name, accusing, pleading. The voices grew louder, filling the silence, until they became impossible to ignore. He saw shadows moving in the corners of his studio, figures flickering just beyond his vision, and he could feel their eyes on him, watching, waiting.

One night, as he sat alone in his studio, he caught sight of something that made his blood run cold. In Lila's portrait, her face seemed to have changed—the delicate lines of her features twisted, her eyes filled with a rage he hadn't painted, her mouth open as though frozen mid-scream. It was subtle, barely noticeable, but he could feel it, a shift in the energy of the room, a presence that was as real as his own.

He stumbled back, his heart pounding, the faces in his paintings seeming to loom over him, their expressions shifting, each one filled with a silent fury. He could feel their eyes on him, and in that moment, he knew—he had bound their spirits to the canvases, but they weren't as silent as he had thought. They were there, trapped, aware, and they wanted vengeance.

That night, Julian barely slept. He lay awake, staring at the ceiling, his mind racing with the knowledge that his muses were watching him, that their spirits lingered, bound to the canvases, waiting for their moment. He tried to convince himself it was all in his head, the result of too many late nights and too much time alone. But the feeling persisted, a gnawing dread that settled into his bones, filling him with a fear he couldn't shake.

As dawn approached, he slipped into a restless sleep, his mind drifting in and out of nightmares. He dreamed of his studio, but it was dark, silent, filled with shadows. The faces in his paintings stared at him, their eyes hollow, accusing, their mouths twisted in silent screams.

And then he saw her—Lila, standing at the edge of the room, her body thin, almost skeletal, her face a mask of sorrow and fury. She reached out to him, her fingers long, bony, her eyes fixed on him with a gaze that pierced his soul.

"Let us go," she whispered, her voice soft, filled with an anguish that chilled him to the core. "Why did you take us? Why did you bind us here?"

Julian tried to speak, to explain, but his words caught in his throat, his voice a strangled gasp. He could feel her presence pressing down on him, her spirit heavy, oppressive, filling the room with an energy that seemed to sap the very air from his lungs.

And then she lunged at him, her hands reaching for his throat, her fingers cold as ice, closing around his neck, her voice a scream that echoed through his mind.

"Release us!"

Julian woke with a start, gasping for breath, his body drenched in sweat. The studio was silent, but he could feel her presence lingering, a weight that pressed down on him, filling him with a fear that he couldn't shake. He knew, in that moment, that he was no longer alone.

Over the next few days, Julian became consumed by his guilt, haunted by the faces of his victims, the knowledge that he had taken their lives, bound them to his art, trapping their souls within his canvases. He could feel their presence, the energy in his studio growing darker, heavier, as though the walls themselves were closing in on him.

He stopped painting, abandoning his brushes, his palette, his self-portrait half-finished, the colors dull and lifeless. The whispers had grown louder, filling his mind with a constant, unrelenting chorus of voices, each one calling his name, accusing, pleading.

Driven to the edge of madness, he searched for a way to free them, desperate to release the souls he had bound, to silence the voices that haunted him. He poured over old texts, books on the occult, rituals that promised to release spirits, to sever the ties that bound them to the physical world. But no matter what he tried, the spirits remained, their presence growing stronger, their whispers filling his mind with a darkness that seemed to seep into his very soul.

One night, as he stood before Lila's portrait, his mind fractured, his body weak, he raised a knife, his hand trembling as he prepared to cut through the canvas, hoping that it might release her, free her from the prison he had created.

But as the blade touched the surface, a cold wind swept through the studio, extinguishing the lights, plunging him into darkness. The shadows closed in, thick and suffocating, and he could feel them, the spirits of his muses, pressing against him, their hands reaching for him, their voices a low, haunting whisper.

"You cannot free us, Julian," they said, their voices blending into a single, chilling harmony. "You bound us here, and now... you will join us."

He tried to scream, to run, but their hands closed around him, pulling him into the darkness, their fingers cold and unyielding. He felt his body growing heavy, his vision blurring, his soul slipping away, bound to the very canvases that had claimed his victims.

And as the darkness consumed him, he saw his reflection in Lila's eyes, his face twisted in terror, frozen forever within the canvas, a final masterpiece, a haunting reminder of the price of his obsession.

It was nearly a month after Julian Mercer's sudden disappearance that Miriam Kessler, the owner of Kessler Gallery, began to grow concerned. His clients, growing impatient, had demanded answers about their unfinished commissions, but Julian hadn't returned any calls, emails, or messages. She tried reaching out to his friends and family, but no one had seen him. His reputation was too valuable to let go, so she decided to investigate herself.

On a cold, gray afternoon, Miriam arrived at Julian's studio, a narrow, dimly lit space in the East Village. The building manager unlocked the door, pushing it open with a shrug before quickly excusing himself, leaving Miriam to step inside alone.

The air was stale, thick with the scent of oil paint and something darker, metallic, that lingered beneath it. Shadows pooled in the corners of the room, as though the light itself dared not intrude. Miriam shivered as she looked around, her eyes adjusting to the dim light, taking in the canvases that lined the walls. They were Julian's works, each one an exquisite portrait, a masterpiece, but as she stepped closer, something about them unsettled her.

The first canvas she approached was of a woman she recognized—a young model who had gone missing several months earlier. The woman's eyes seemed to follow her, their gaze intense, almost pleading, and Miriam felt a chill crawl down her spine as she reached out, her fingers grazing the surface. The paint felt strange, rough, as though something were woven into it, something that made her pull her hand back instinctively.

Moving further into the studio, Miriam stopped in front of Lila Montgomery's portrait. She'd heard rumors of Lila's disappearance, the whispered suspicions that surrounded Julian, but she had never believed them. Now, standing face to face with Lila's image, she couldn't ignore the feeling of dread that seeped into her, chilling her to the core.

Lila's eyes were different from the others, filled with a rage that seemed barely contained, as though she were trying to reach out, to break free from the canvas. Her mouth, painted with haunting precision, seemed frozen mid-scream, her expression one of desperation and fury.

Miriam took a step back, her mind racing, the horrifying realization dawning on her. She remembered the whispers, the unsettling rumors about Julian's process, the clients who had asked where his models had gone, and now, looking at these portraits, she understood the truth.

The models weren't missing—they were here, their spirits bound to the canvases, trapped within the layers of paint, woven into the fibers of the canvas, victims of Julian's twisted artistry.

Her eyes moved to Julian's final work, a half-finished self-portrait propped on an easel near the center of the room. She approached it slowly, her breath catching as she took in the details. Julian's face stared back at her, but it wasn't the confident, smirking expression she remembered. His eyes were hollow, wide with terror, his mouth twisted in a silent scream, his hand reaching out, as though he were trying to escape.

The painting had an unnatural depth, an almost lifelike quality that made her skin crawl. She took a step closer, squinting, and for a fleeting moment, she thought she saw his hand move, his fingers pressing against the canvas, his face twisting in agony.

A faint, almost imperceptible whisper echoed in the room, a single word that sent a chill down her spine.

"Help..."

Miriam stumbled back, her heart racing, the portraits seeming to close in around her, their eyes filled with anger, pain, desperation. She could feel them watching, could hear the faintest murmur of voices, their whispers blending into a low, haunting chorus, filling the air with a sense of longing, a plea for freedom.

Unable to bear it any longer, Miriam turned and fled, slamming the door behind her. She could still feel their eyes on her as she hurried down the hall, their silent screams echoing in her mind, haunting her with the knowledge that their souls remained trapped, bound to the canvases, held captive by Julian's dark legacy.

The gallery would remain empty, Julian's work untouched, his final collection hidden from the world, a testament to his twisted genius, a prison for the souls he had taken.

And in the quiet, shadowed corners of the abandoned studio, the portraits waited, their eyes watching, their whispers growing louder, their rage building, waiting for the moment when someone else would dare to step inside, to gaze upon the haunted faces, and hear their desperate plea:

Release us.

Months passed, and rumors about Julian Mercer's disappearance continued to circulate through New York's art scene, his absence leaving a lingering mystery. His studio remained sealed, abandoned, the whispers about his final works growing darker, the chilling reality of his creations an unspoken truth among those who had known him. But not everyone was content to leave the mystery unsolved.

A few weeks after Miriam's fateful visit to the studio, an art restoration specialist named Dr. Harold Thompson was approached by a collector who had privately purchased one of Julian's early works. The painting—a haunting portrait of a young woman with deep, piercing eyes—had a strange quality that was wearing at the collector, a feeling that something dark and unseen was embedded within it. The client insisted that Harold examine the piece, to uncover whatever secrets might lie beneath its surface.

Curious, Harold took on the project, unaware of what lay in store. He set up the painting in his lab, scrutinizing it with a restorer's trained eye. The portrait was beautiful, disturbingly so, but as he moved closer, he noticed something strange about the texture. There were inconsistencies in the layers, odd fibers embedded within the paint, giving it an almost organic feel.

Setting up a microscope, Harold took a small sample from a discreet area of the canvas, a fragment of the dark paint that made up the background. He placed it under the lens, adjusting the magnification, and his heart skipped a beat when he saw it—hair. Human hair, embedded into the layers of paint, woven into the very fabric of the piece. Shocked, he moved to another area of the painting, scraping a small fleck from the edge, and found more—this time, a sliver of what looked like fingernail.

A sense of horror washed over him as he realized the implications. Julian's paintings weren't just art—they were physical pieces of his models, their essence bound to the canvas in a literal, macabre form.

Unable to contain his curiosity, Harold conducted further analysis, taking samples from various parts of the painting. What he uncovered was more unsettling than he could have imagined: bloodstains, traces of bone, and other organic materials, all blended seamlessly into the oil, each stroke a fusion of pigment and human remains. It was as if

Julian had painted not just his subjects' images, but their very beings.

Driven by a morbid fascination, Harold reached out to other collectors known to own Julian's work, securing permission to examine additional pieces. One by one, he confirmed his suspicion. Each painting contained organic material—hair, blood, even minuscule fragments of bone. The paintings were not just likenesses; they were vessels, each one containing a part of the model's very essence, bound forever within the strokes of Julian's brush.

As Harold examined the paintings, he began to feel an almost tangible presence emanating from them. Alone in his lab, he would hear faint whispers, soft murmurs that seemed to come from the shadows, voices echoing in the silent room. The portraits themselves seemed to shift, their expressions twisting in subtle, unsettling ways, as though aware of his intrusion, resentful of the scrutiny.

But the more he uncovered, the deeper his horror grew. Julian hadn't just painted these women—he had trapped their souls, binding their life force to the canvases. Each painting wasn't merely an image; it was a prison, a cursed artifact housing the trapped spirit of a once-living person.

Haunted by his discoveries, Harold dove into the murky depths of Julian's life, searching for any clues that might explain how such a horrific practice had begun. He scoured old interviews, personal letters, and any record he could find of Julian's time at the Rhode Island School of Design. Finally, buried in the university's archives, he came across a thesis Julian had written during his final year. The document was titled *"The Bound Form: Capturing Essence Through*

Art"—a strange, academic-sounding title, but one that hinted at a disturbing obsession.

The thesis was a mixture of art theory, psychological musings, and occult references. Julian wrote about the "power of art to transcend the physical," the idea that a portrait could capture more than just a likeness; it could capture a person's very soul. He cited historical accounts of ancient civilizations, tribes that believed portraits could imprison spirits, keeping them bound to a specific place or object. There were references to dark rituals, alchemical processes, and spells used by early artists to imbue their work with a form of life.

But the most disturbing part was Julian's description of his own experiments, practices he had undertaken in secret. He described his process in chilling detail—how he would mix his subjects' hair, blood, and fragments of bone into his paint, a "final binding" that would capture their essence, making the painting more than just an image, but a "living vessel." He wrote about the thrill he felt, the satisfaction of knowing that his subjects would live forever through his art, each one becoming an eternal part of his legacy.

The thesis ended abruptly, as though Julian had cut himself off, aware that his theories might be seen as nothing short of monstrous. Harold felt a sickening realization wash over him: Julian hadn't seen his actions as murder, but as a form of immortality, a way of elevating his art to something divine. The models he had killed weren't victims to him—they were offerings, sacrifices to his own twisted vision of art.

Harold knew he had stumbled upon something far darker than he could have imagined, and the more he uncovered, the more the whispers grew, filling his mind, invading his dreams. The paintings haunted him, the faces of Julian's victims seeming to watch him wherever he went, their eyes filled with silent pleas. He felt their presence, a tangible weight that lingered in the air, and he realized with a bone-deep dread that their spirits weren't at rest. They were trapped, bound to the canvases, screaming for release.

Determined to put an end to Julian's legacy, Harold began a process he had never attempted before. Working carefully, he stripped the paintings, meticulously scraping away the layers, hoping to separate the organic material from the paint, to sever the connection that bound the spirits within. But each attempt was met with resistance—the air around him growing colder, the whispers louder, the lights flickering as though the spirits were fighting against his efforts.

Then, one night, as he worked on the final portrait—a half-finished image of Julian himself—the painting began to change. The eyes in the portrait seemed to narrow, the face twisting into a look of pure malice. Harold felt a cold hand press against his back, heard a voice whisper in his ear, low and filled with rage.

"You think you can undo what I've created?" the voice hissed, unmistakably Julian's. "They are mine. Forever."

The room grew dark, the shadows thickening around him, pressing down on him, filling his lungs with a cold that felt like death. The faces of the models appeared around him, their eyes filled with sorrow, with fear, reaching out, desperate, pleading. And as the darkness closed in, Harold understood, with a sickening certainty, that the souls were beyond saving, bound to Julian's cursed art by a power far darker than he could break.

The next morning, Harold's assistant found the lab in disarray, the paintings scattered, the canvases torn, but Harold was nowhere to be found. The portraits remained untouched, their eyes filled with the same haunting expressions, as though aware of the attempts to destroy them, bound now by not only Julian's sinister art but the souls of those who had dared to reveal his secrets.

And in the shadows, in the quiet halls of the Kessler Gallery where the paintings would eventually return, the whispers grew louder, waiting for the next unlucky soul to look into the haunted eyes, to feel the weight of the souls trapped within, to hear the silent, endless chorus of voices calling out in desperation:

"Help us..."

The End

30

SLAP SHOT

Friday nights in Port Credit had a rhythm all their own, especially during hockey season. The town's heartbeat pulsed in sync with the slap of sticks on ice, the scrape of skates, and the roar of the crowd. Tonight was no exception. The Dixie Beehives were on home ice, locked in a battle with the Oakville Blades, and the rink was packed. The smell of popcorn and sweat mixed in the cold air as fans in thick coats and bright Beehives scarves crammed into the narrow bleachers, shouting encouragement and slews of insults at the rival team.

In the second period, the game took a fierce, gritty turn. Skaters crashed into the boards, fists were thrown, and penalties piled up, but the home crowd loved every minute of it. Among the noise, one name was chanted again and again: *"Rapid Robert!"* Robert Montgomery was Port Credit's golden boy, known for his blazing speed and his wicked slap shot. He was a stalky, wiry center with golden blond hair and stone-cold blue eyes that burned with a competitive edge. When he hit the ice, fans leaned forward, waiting for him to make magic.

About halfway through the second, the Beehives were down by one. Tension built as Montgomery skated up center ice, weaving through two defensemen and winding up for one of his legendary slap shots. The crowd held its breath as he drew back, the muscles in his arms tensing, and then *wham* — he struck the ice with a blazing fast release. The puck rocketed towards the Blades' goalie, who barely had time to raise his glove. The puck slammed off the top edge of his stick, redirecting at a lethal angle. It hurtled over the boards, toward the stands, slicing through the air with a deadly precision.

The crowd gasped as the puck struck an older man in the third row. The sickening sound of impact was followed by silence, and then the man slumped forward, blood pooling from his head onto the plastic seat. People scrambled, some reaching out to help, others backing away in horror. Paramedics rushed to the man's side, but it was clear he was gone. The crowd watched, stunned, as the announcer called a brief pause in the game. By the time the paramedics wheeled the stretcher out of the rink, his face covered with a sheet, the game was officially postponed.

The town was rocked. A freak accident, the papers called it, though many struggled to shake off the eerie chill that had swept through the rink. Over the next few games, the Beehives resumed their season, cautiously, respectfully honoring the tragedy with a moment of silence before each game. But the season rolled on, and hockey being hockey, things gradually began to return to normal.

Then, one night a few weeks later, it happened again.

This time, it was a defenseman from the visiting team, winding up for a slap shot. The puck ricocheted, this time off a Beehives' player's skate, and hurtled into the stands, striking a young woman in the neck. She collapsed instantly, her body sprawled across the seats, her face frozen in shock. People screamed, rushing for exits, and again, the rink fell silent as paramedics pronounced her dead on the scene.

The news spread fast, both deaths creating a shadow over Port Credit's cherished hockey season. As the weeks went on, the town's once-beloved sport turned into something sinister, drawing a morbid curiosity from neighboring cities. People spoke in hushed tones of the "curse," whispering about how, after each slap shot, the puck seemed to defy all logic, seeking out a new victim.

The local papers fed off the tragedies, dubbing it "The Port Credit Curse." Reporters came from Toronto, and soon television news trucks lined up outside the small arena, their lights casting an eerie glow on the frost-rimmed glass doors. But the Beehives kept playing, and people, however afraid, kept showing up. The townspeople whispered about it in cafes and in the aisles of the grocery store. The arena became a place of morbid fascination, drawing people who wanted to witness the unexplainable events for themselves.

The players, though, were unnerved. In the locker room, Rapid Robert Montgomery and his teammates grew anxious. No one wanted to talk about it openly, but they felt the weight of something wrong hanging over the ice. Between periods and practices, Montgomery often caught his teammates glancing at each other, their eyes full of questions they couldn't answer.

Then came the night of the third death.

It was a Friday night, and the stands were packed again, despite the chilling stories. Fans couldn't stay away, some for the love of the game, others simply driven by that dark curiosity. The Beehives were up against the Kingston Voyageurs, and the tension on the ice was thick, every player's movements laced with caution.

As the third period neared its end, the score was tied, and Rapid Robert, feeling the pressure, took control of the puck. The crowd, as if under a spell, went silent, eyes fixed on him as he darted down the ice. He wound up, his slap shot a furious blur of muscle and momentum. The puck shot off his stick, flying toward the goal. But as if gripped by an invisible hand, it veered off course at the last second, glancing off the goalie's helmet and into the audience.

The gasps began, but they were cut short by a collective scream. The puck had struck a man square in the chest, and he fell back, clutching his chest. He was dead before his body hit the ground.

The team was devastated. The Beehives' coach called an emergency meeting after the game, his face pale as he looked at his players. "I don't know what's going on here," he said, voice trembling. "But we can't pretend this isn't real. It's like the damn puck is possessed."

Montgomery shifted in his seat, jaw clenched. He wanted to believe it was all coincidence, but three deaths? There was no explaining it.

Over the next week, the league threatened to shut down Port Credit's games, but the town's council, along with the arena's owner, pushed back, citing tradition and the financial impact of canceling their season. Yet whispers of the curse spread, and attendance began to drop. Parents kept their children home, and even the most die-hard fans seemed skittish, looking over their shoulders as if something unseen were lurking in the shadows of the stands.

Montgomery couldn't shake the feeling that he was at the center of it all. It was always his slap shots that seemed to trigger the deadly chain of events. After another gruesome game, he decided to investigate. He approached Lou, the arena's timekeeper, a strange and solitary figure who had worked in that booth above the rink for as long as anyone could remember. Lou was an older man with an icy demeanor, his eyes shadowed and distant, and he'd been the one to handle all the pucks since before Montgomery even started playing.

Montgomery waited until the rink was empty, shadows stretching across the ice, and climbed up the narrow staircase to the timekeeper's booth. Lou was there, as usual, sitting in the dim light, his gaze fixed on the darkened rink below.

"Lou," Montgomery said, his voice tense, "we need to talk."

Lou turned slowly, his eyes blank, almost as if he'd been expecting him. "About what, kid?" he asked in a low, gravelly tone.

"You've been here a long time," Montgomery said, trying to steady his voice. "You've seen what's been happening, right? The accidents."

Lou gave a slow, chilling smile. "Accidents," he murmured, "is that what you think they are?"

Montgomery's pulse quickened. "What else would they be?"

Lou leaned forward, resting his gnarled hands on the edge of the table. "There's power in things, Robert. Power people don't understand. They think a puck's just a piece of rubber, just like they think a game's just a game. But everything leaves a mark, and sometimes things don't want to be forgotten." He lifted a worn black puck, holding it up for Montgomery to see. "These pucks...they're more than they seem."

Montgomery's gaze locked onto the puck, his stomach churning. "What did you do, Lou?"

Lou's smile widened, showing yellowed teeth. "I didn't do anything but give people what they wanted. A game they'd never forget."

A cold realization settled over Montgomery. He felt his blood run cold as he stared at the puck in Lou's hand, the way it seemed to gleam unnaturally in the dim light. "These pucks...are they cursed?"

Lou shrugged, his voice barely a whisper. "You could call it that. But I'd say they're just doing what they're meant to do. They're here to remind people of what they've forgotten, the blood and sweat that went into making this place."

Montgomery backed away, the horror rising in his chest as Lou's words sank in. The deaths weren't random. They were part of something dark, something ancient and twisted that had taken root in the very heart of Port Credit's cherished rink. And now, he knew, there was no going back.

As he descended the stairs, Lou's final words echoed in his mind, chilling him to the bone.

"You keep taking those slap shots, Robert. Let's see just how many people remember."

Montgomery barely slept that night. Lou's words played over and over in his head, mingling with the images of each death he had witnessed from the ice. Every time he closed his eyes, he saw their faces—the elderly man, the young woman, the fan struck down just last week. All casualties of his own slap shots, as if he were pulling the trigger himself.

The next morning, Montgomery called a team meeting, inviting only his closest teammates: Matt "Sticks" Larson, their sharp-eyed winger, and Henry "The Tank" Miller, their tough-as-nails defenseman who had been his best friend since they were kids.

As they huddled in the empty locker room, Montgomery shared everything he'd learned from Lou. Sticks and Tank listened in horrified silence, the color draining from their faces as he spoke.

"You're telling me," Tank said, his voice barely above a whisper, "that the pucks...are cursed? That Lou's somehow...possessed them?"

"Not just that," Montgomery replied. "He's using them. He knew what would happen, and he *wanted* it to happen. He called it 'giving people a game they'd never forget.'"

"Forget?" Sticks shook his head in disbelief. "People are dead, Rob! This is sick. Why would he do something like that?"

Montgomery leaned forward, eyes haunted. "I don't know. He talked about blood and sweat, about history. Maybe...maybe he thinks the rink is owed something."

Silence fell over the three of them, broken only by the distant hum of the arena's cooling system. Finally, Tank spoke up, his voice steady with determination. "We can't let him keep doing this. There's gotta be a way to break it."

They spent hours brainstorming, sifting through half-formed ideas and superstition. None of them knew anything about curses, let alone how to break one. Finally, Sticks spoke up, his voice tentative.

"My uncle," he said, glancing around, "he...he's into weird stuff. Old stories and legends, that kind of thing. He always talked about how curses get attached to places and objects. He said if something's cursed, it can sometimes be broken by...destroying the thing it's attached to."

Montgomery's eyes narrowed. "The pucks."

Sticks nodded. "Yeah. If Lou's using these cursed pucks, maybe destroying them will break whatever hold they have over the rink."

They waited until night fell and the arena was closed, the only sounds in the rink the creaks of old metal beams and the muffled drip of melting ice. They slipped into the rink's storage room, a cluttered, chilly space crammed with old equipment and spare pucks.

Montgomery opened a drawer near the back, where Lou had always kept the game pucks. Inside were rows of jet-black pucks, identical but somehow menacing in the dim light. Each one seemed to hold a strange weight, as if it radiated a cold malice. Montgomery picked one up, feeling a strange pulse in his palm, as if the puck were alive.

They gathered the pucks in a worn equipment bag and made their way to the empty parking lot. Montgomery, Sticks, and Tank stood in a rough circle around the bag, the cold night air biting at their faces as they stared down at the collection of pucks.

"Let's do this," Tank said, grabbing the first puck and hurling it to the ground, his foot coming down hard to crush it into the pavement.

The puck cracked, splintering into chunks, and for a split second, Montgomery thought he heard something—a faint, echoing scream that seemed to come from inside the shattered puck. He shivered, his fingers trembling as he grabbed the next one. They went through the bag one by one, each puck crushed to pieces. With each one, the air around them felt heavier, colder, as if something angry and unseen were being torn apart.

By the time they finished, the pavement was littered with rubber fragments, and the three men were breathing heavily, as if the destruction of each puck had drained them. Tank wiped a shaky hand across his brow, his eyes darting around the empty lot.

"Think...think that did it?" he asked, his voice barely above a whisper.

Montgomery felt a strange lightness, as if a dark cloud had lifted. He nodded, forcing himself to believe. "It has to. Lou can't curse what doesn't exist anymore."

But in the back of his mind, Montgomery wasn't so sure. The memory of Lou's chilling smile lingered, and he knew the twisted timekeeper wasn't someone who would simply give up.

The following Friday, the Beehives returned to the ice. The crowd, subdued but steady, had trickled back into the stands, the morbid whispers fading as people let themselves believe that the accidents were over. The atmosphere was tense but hopeful; they were here to reclaim their game.

Lou sat in his booth above, staring down at the ice, his eyes fixed on Montgomery. The young player felt that icy gaze prickling the back of his neck as he skated warm-up laps. Lou's expression was unreadable, but there was something in his eyes that sent a shiver down Montgomery's spine.

The game started, and the Beehives played hard, finally finding their rhythm after the shadowed weeks behind them. Montgomery was in the zone, his movements sharp and fluid, a renewed energy fueling every shift. The third period came, and the Beehives were up by one goal.

Montgomery felt a familiar, almost electric sensation as he sped down the ice, the puck under his control. He wound up for his signature slap shot, feeling the exhilarating power surge through him as his stick struck the ice. The puck shot forward, a clean, powerful drive toward the goal.

But halfway through its trajectory, the puck twisted, as if caught by an invisible force. It veered, arcing unnaturally toward the stands.

The arena erupted in screams as the puck zeroed in on a section of fans, its deadly course unaltered. But at the last second, it struck the glass, splintering into a spiderweb of cracks. Montgomery's heart thundered, his breaths shallow as he stared up at the timekeeper's booth, where Lou was grinning, a cold, triumphant gleam in his eyes.

Lou lifted a hand, gesturing as if he were holding something. And that's when Montgomery saw it—the puck in Lou's hand, pitch black, identical to the cursed ones they had destroyed.

A new dread settled over him. They hadn't stopped it. Lou had more—an endless supply, it seemed, of cursed pucks bound to claim lives and draw blood, all for reasons only Lou seemed to understand.

Montgomery clenched his fists, a fierce resolve settling in. This wasn't over, but now he knew what he had to do. Lou wasn't just cursing pucks; he was feeding something darker, and until they stopped him, the deaths would continue.

As the final buzzer sounded, the Beehives victorious but shaken, Montgomery skated off the ice, his jaw set. He was ready for whatever came next.

After the game, Montgomery didn't head to the locker room. Instead, he waited near the stairwell that led up to Lou's booth, his pulse quickening as he glanced up at the small, dimly lit room above. The arena had mostly cleared out, with only a few workers lingering to clean up, and the muffled sounds of their conversation echoed through the empty space.

Sticks and Tank appeared at his side, looking at him with worry etched on their faces.

"You're not going up there alone, Rob," Sticks said, his voice firm. "This guy's dangerous, and who knows what else he's hiding up there."

Montgomery nodded, grateful for their loyalty. Together, the three of them climbed the narrow staircase leading up to the booth. Each step felt heavier than the last, and as they approached, they could hear the soft murmur of Lou's voice, though no one else was in the booth with him.

Tank shot Montgomery a look, mouthing, *"Who's he talking to?"*

Montgomery shook his head, unsure. His hand reached for the door, pausing just a moment before he pushed it open.

Inside, Lou sat at his small, cluttered desk, his back to them. In front of him lay another black puck, identical to the ones they had smashed to pieces. But this one seemed different, darker somehow, as if it absorbed the dim light instead of reflecting it. Lou murmured something unintelligible under his breath, his hands hovering above the puck, almost reverent.

"Lou," Montgomery called, his voice harsher than he intended.

Lou stiffened, his hand pausing mid-gesture, before he slowly turned his head to look at them. His face was blank, eyes void of warmth, but a slight, eerie smile pulled at the corners of his mouth.

"Couldn't leave it alone, could you, boys?" Lou said, his voice soft and mocking. "Always have to meddle where you don't belong."

"What are you doing?" Montgomery demanded, stepping forward. "What's with the pucks? Why are people dying?"

Lou's expression didn't change. Instead, he sighed, picking up the puck and cradling it in his hands as if it were something precious. "You kids...you play this game and think it's all fun and glory. But there's a cost to everything, and this arena—this rink—was built on a lot more than ice and boards. You have no idea how many sacrifices it took to build this place."

Montgomery's brow furrowed, trying to make sense of Lou's words. "Sacrifices?"

Lou nodded slowly, his voice taking on an almost wistful tone. "Back when they built this arena, the land...let's just say it didn't want to be disturbed. They had to *appease* it, so to speak. There were accidents, workers who went missing. Rumors that the ground itself was cursed. But they ignored the warnings, buried the bodies, and built over them anyway."

Tank's face twisted in horror. "So you're saying...this place is haunted? And you're using these cursed pucks to—what? Avenge them?"

Lou let out a dark chuckle. "Something like that. It's not about revenge. It's about respect. The land was disturbed, and now it wants something back. A reminder, a...balance. These pucks are a way to settle the debt, to honor those who were forgotten. Blood for blood."

Montgomery felt a chill run through him. "So you're just going to keep killing people? Because of something that happened decades ago?"

Lou shrugged, his gaze cold. "It's not me doing the killing, Robert. It's the land, the spirits that live here. I'm just...facilitating it. Giving them a way to reach through, to remind people of their place. And the best part is—" his grin widened—"there's nothing you can do to stop it."

Montgomery's eyes narrowed. He lunged forward, grabbing for the puck in Lou's hand, but Lou jerked back with surprising speed, clutching the puck to his chest.

"Careful, now," Lou hissed, his eyes wild. "You break it here, and you might just unleash more than you're ready for."

But Montgomery didn't care anymore. Fueled by anger and fear, he reached forward, wrestling with Lou. Sticks and Tank jumped in, and together, they struggled with Lou, each trying to pry the puck from his grasp. Lou fought with unnatural strength, his nails digging into Montgomery's arm, his face contorted in a grotesque rage.

Finally, with a powerful shove, Montgomery wrenched the puck free and hurled it to the ground. It shattered, the pieces scattering across the booth floor. For a moment, everything went silent.

Then, a cold gust of air swept through the booth, chilling them to the bone. The lights flickered, and shadows seemed to grow and shift around them. A low, guttural sound filled the room, like a rumble from beneath the earth itself, vibrating through their bodies.

Lou's face twisted with horror, his eyes wide as he backed away from the shattered pieces of the puck. "What...what have you done?" he whispered, his voice laced with genuine fear.

The floor beneath them began to tremble, as if something deep below was waking up. Montgomery, Sticks, and Tank looked at each other, their faces pale, as the entire arena seemed to groan and shake, the shadows deepening into shapes, figures that loomed in the corners of the room.

Lou stumbled back, his hands clawing at his face. "No...no, this wasn't supposed to happen!" he screamed, but it was too late. The shadows closed in around him, pulling him down as he thrashed and screamed. His voice grew fainter, swallowed by the darkness that seemed to consume him.

Then, as quickly as it began, the tremors stopped, and the shadows receded, leaving nothing but silence and the cold, empty booth.

Montgomery, breathing hard, looked around, trying to steady his racing heart. Lou was gone, vanished into whatever darkness he had unleashed.

"Is it...is it over?" Sticks asked, his voice barely above a whisper.

Montgomery nodded, though he wasn't entirely sure. "I think...whatever curse he unleashed, whatever he was using to keep this going, it's gone now. The land wanted him, and it took him."

They left the booth in silence, descending the stairs as the arena lights flickered back to life, casting a faint glow over the ice below. The rink was eerily quiet, the usual buzz of the arena replaced by a heavy stillness. It felt, somehow, like the place was finally at rest.

The next game, a few days later, went on without incident. The crowd was thinner than usual, and the lingering chill of recent events kept the energy subdued, but there were no accidents, no rogue pucks careening into the stands, no shadowed whispers in the corners.

In time, the town began to heal, the horror of the past few months fading into uneasy memories. Montgomery and his teammates returned to their routine, though they never quite felt the same about the rink. They played hard, but each slap shot, each ricochet off the boards, brought a flicker of dread, a reminder of the curse they had nearly been consumed by.

And sometimes, after the last game of the night, Montgomery would glance up at the timekeeper's booth, half-expecting to see Lou's twisted grin staring down at him from the shadows.

But the booth stayed empty, a dark reminder of the secret that lay buried beneath the ice, a story that Port Credit would never forget.

Months passed, and the dark days of the "Port Credit Curse" became something of a ghost story around town, whispered about in hushed voices. Hockey resumed its place as a proud, beloved pastime, and for a while, it seemed like everything had gone back to normal. The Beehives even made it to the playoffs, the fans cheering with a new intensity, as if to drive away the lingering memories of death that had haunted the arena.

But for Montgomery, things were far from normal. Though Lou was gone, though he'd seen the man swallowed up by the very darkness he had unleashed, something lingered—something that made Montgomery wake up in cold sweats, heart pounding, certain he'd heard faint voices calling his name. He tried to shrug it off, to convince himself it was just trauma from a dark time, but the feeling only grew stronger.

One night, after a hard-fought game that ended in a victory, Montgomery stayed behind to grab some sticks he'd left by the benches. The rest of the team had already cleared out, and the arena was quiet, the rows of seats casting long, empty shadows over the ice.

As he walked down the aisle toward the benches, his steps echoing off the concrete walls, a faint sound caught his ear. It was soft, almost like a whisper, drifting through the empty arena. He stopped, straining to listen.

"Robert..."

He froze, the hairs on the back of his neck standing on end. The voice was familiar. It was low, scratchy—Lou's voice. But Lou was gone. He had seen it happen, seen Lou dragged down by whatever vengeful spirits he had been meddling with.

He took a shaky step forward, his eyes scanning the empty seats, looking for any sign of movement. Nothing. Just row after row of dark, vacant seats stretching into the shadows. He forced himself to move again, willing his legs to ignore the chilling fear settling in his bones.

But the whisper came again, clearer this time. *"Robert...you can't leave them."*

The air in the rink felt colder, and his breaths came out in misty clouds. The whisper grew, as if several voices joined in, a low chorus that echoed off the rafters and reverberated through his skull.

"They're still here... They're still waiting..."

Panicked, Montgomery turned, ready to bolt out of the arena, but stopped dead in his tracks. Standing at the far end of the ice, just visible in the dim light, was a figure. It was shadowy, indistinct, but he could see the outline of a man, his posture familiar—the crooked shoulders, the slouching, twisted frame. Lou.

Montgomery's mind raced, his feet frozen in place. This was impossible. He had seen Lou disappear, consumed by whatever dark forces had finally claimed him. But here he was, or at least, *something* that looked like him.

"Lou?" he called, his voice barely above a whisper.

The figure didn't answer. It just stood there, unmoving, but somehow, its gaze felt heavy, pressing down on him. Then, slowly, it raised one hand and pointed toward the far side of the rink.

Montgomery followed the gesture, his eyes tracing over the rows of seats and settling on something small and dark lying at the edge of the boards. His stomach dropped. It was a puck—a black, cracked puck that looked almost identical to the ones Lou had used, the ones he and his friends had destroyed. But this one was different. It was wrapped in shadows, as if darkness clung to it like smoke.

The whispers grew louder, almost deafening, filling his head with an unholy chorus that seemed to come from the very walls around him. The voices chanted words he couldn't understand, an ancient, guttural language that seemed to claw at his mind, each syllable sharp and painful.

"The debt is not paid... The debt must be honored..."

Montgomery stumbled forward, driven by a compulsion he couldn't resist, his eyes locked on the puck. He reached out, his fingers trembling as he touched its cold, cracked surface. A shock shot through him, freezing his breath in his lungs.

The rink around him seemed to fade, the lights dimming, until he stood alone in darkness, the ice beneath him feeling brittle and wrong. He looked up, his surroundings shifting, and found himself in a version of the arena he'd never seen before. The walls were old, crumbling, lined with shadows that seemed to pulse with life. Rows of spectral figures filled the seats, ghostly forms with hollow eyes watching him in silence.

A low, growling voice echoed from somewhere above him, deep and terrible. "You took them from their rest," it said. "You disturbed the ground, and now you must give it back."

Montgomery's heart pounded as he looked up to see the ghostly figures begin to rise, the shadows peeling off their faces to reveal hollow, twisted visages of men and women from ages past. They seemed to reach out, their hands claw-like, their expressions frozen in grief and anger.

"No!" he shouted, backing away. "I didn't do this! It was Lou! He's the one who cursed this place!"

The shadows seemed to ignore his pleas, drifting toward him with agonizing slowness, their hollow eyes burning with a strange, accusatory light. He tried to move, to run, but his legs felt like lead, his body paralyzed by a bone-deep terror.

Then, from the darkness, he heard Lou's voice once more, but this time it sounded...different. Desperate.

"They're taking me too, Robert. They're taking us all. There's no escape."

Montgomery's mind reeled, his thoughts scrambling for an answer, a way out. And then, through the fog of fear, he remembered something Sticks had said that night in the parking lot: *"Sometimes, the only way to end a curse is to break its hold on the place."*

He looked down at the puck in his hand, feeling the weight of it, the icy pulse that seemed to carry every ounce of darkness that had settled over the rink. Maybe, just maybe, destroying it here, in this twisted version of the arena, would break the curse once and for all.

With every ounce of strength he had left, Montgomery raised the puck above his head and slammed it down onto the ice. It shattered, shards of black scattering across the frozen surface.

For a moment, silence fell. The spectral figures paused, their faces flickering, as if uncertain. Then, one by one, they began to dissipate, the shadows peeling away like smoke caught in a breeze. The arena around him faded, the crumbling walls returning to their familiar solid form, the ghostly spectators disappearing into the ether.

Montgomery found himself alone on the ice, the lights bright and steady overhead. The whispering voices were gone, the oppressive cold lifted. He let out a shaky breath, dropping to his knees, exhaustion and relief washing over him.

As he glanced around, his eyes caught a faint shimmer on the ice where he had shattered the puck. It was faint, barely visible, but as he stared, he thought he saw the shadowy outline of Lou's face, twisted in agony, before it melted into the ice and vanished.

The next morning, Montgomery sat with Sticks and Tank, explaining everything, his friends listening in stunned silence.

"So...it's over?" Sticks asked, his voice tinged with disbelief.

Montgomery nodded. "I think so. Whatever hold that place had...whatever Lou stirred up, it's gone now. For good."

They looked at each other, silent for a long moment, then lifted their coffees in a quiet toast, a tribute to the end of a nightmare.

As the weeks passed, the rink felt different, lighter. The games resumed without incident, and the ghost stories began to fade, slipping into memory, like all dark things that eventually pass.

But every so often, as Montgomery skated down the ice, he felt a cold shiver, a faint whisper of the past brushing against him like a shadow, a reminder of the darkness he'd confronted—and the debt that had, at last, been paid.

The End

ABOUT THE AUTHOR

Blair Edward Russell (B.E. Russell) was born in 1979 in Etobicoke, Ontario, just outside of Toronto. Summers were a blur of outdoor activities—roaming forests, wading through creeks in search of fish, and skateboarding around the neighborhood. After finishing high school, Blair pursued his education at York University in Toronto, graduating in 2007. Not long after, he embarked on a new adventure, relocating to Miami, Florida, with his wife, Ginna, to build their life together in the Sunshine State.

Blair's creativity doesn't stop at writing. He's also an avid oil painter, a domain name investor, and an accomplished internet entrepreneur. Most of all, he's a passionate angler, especially when it comes to fly fishing. He writes many types of novels—including Epic Fantasy Adventures, Light Horror, Mysterious Tales, and novels about the Outdoors—drawing heavily on his love of fishing to craft stories that hook readers and take them on thrilling, unforgettable journeys.

Today, Blair lives in South Florida with his wife Ginna. Whether he's crafting a new original tale, painting in his studio, or casting a line into tranquil waters, Blair finds inspiration in life's simple yet extraordinary moments.

ACKNOWLEDGEMENTS

I would like to thank the following people who have helped inspire me and supported me throughout my life in all the various projects and endeavors I have been through.

My wife Ginna, My father and mother Bob and Marie, My brother and sister Bobby and Stacey, all of my friends and extended family as well as you my passionate reader.

You are all the ones who inspire me to share my dreams and ideas with the world.

FURTHER READING

Please be sure to check out the other fine books from **B.E. Russell** including:

- *Trial by Fire*
- *Emberheart*
- *The Quest for Eternal Light*

If you enjoyed reading this novel be sure to join my mailing list at www.BlairEdwardRussell.com. And check in on my website often to find information on my latest novels.

www.ingramcontent.com/pod-product-compliance
Lightning Source LLC
Chambersburg PA
CBHW020259030826
48979CB00026B/1499/J

9781966245148